SIRIUS

SEVER YOUR SPINE

THE GENTLEMEN
DEMON SERIES

Curious Corvid
PUBLISHING

For Janus

You always believed in me.

For Ellis

You continue to inspire to me.

For Irene

These worlds are always ours.

For Amy

I hope your life is still a grand adventure.

For Kit

There is only one Violet.

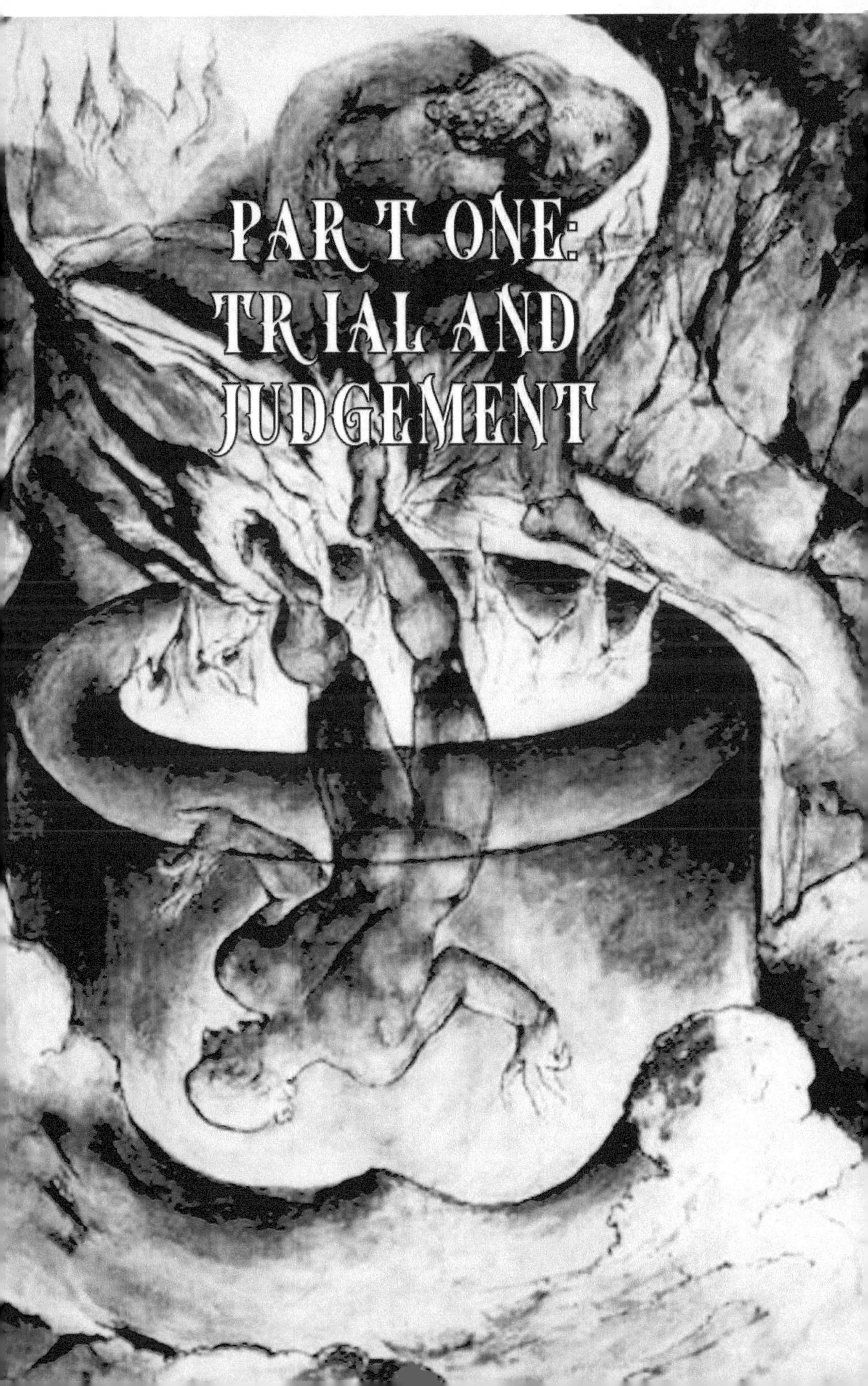

PART ONE:
TRIAL AND
JUDGEMENT

CHAPTER I

J asmine and myrrh mingled together, smothering the cramped room in a decadent perfume reminiscent of death. It was sweet like decay, and over time it had started to seep into the walls.

There was not much by way of furniture. There was a makeshift altar—little more than a shaky table with an embroidered silk cloth thrown over the top. It could easily be dismantled and disposed of within minutes. On top of the cloth, a few burning purple candle stubs were arranged in a distinct pattern around a dish of smoldering resin. White jasmine flowers had been scattered across the floor, a few even resting on the edges of the altar.

Set beside the resin was a miniature salver, made of pure silver with the de Voclain crest forever stamped into the intricate design. It was older than the house – old as the family name. It was worth more than anything they had lost to the destruction of radicals or raids, and they kept it here—buried in a humid vault. Six teeth, solid molars almost entirely free of rot, convened in the center and huddled closely together.

As much of a mausoleum as the space underneath the house had become, it was a haven from the slaughter and terror that reigned with brutal despotism right above their heads.

"Jean," Suzanne had a voice made for scandalous whispers behind painted fans. Her brother had told her before that he felt it was wasted on such dismal surroundings. "There must be something missing."

Jean-François tilted his head, loose copper curls tumbling out of place. "A blood sacrifice, perhaps?"

She gave him a scathing look, letting him know that his jests — as usual — were not amusing.

Jean-François spread his hands helplessly. "I know little more of summoning demons than you."

It was a superfluous statement, considering they were both very knowledgeable of the subject.

There was a jarring pop, like a joint being wrenched out of place. The short conversation ceased as brother and sister both threw their gazes back at the altar.

Teeth were rattling in their salver as the altar trembled. The popping noise was followed by heinous crackling; something like cartilage being torn or broken. Suzanne lifted a handkerchief to cover her mouth and nose — the harsh incense had been working its way into every breath, irritating her throat which had swollen to the point where she felt like she was attempting to swallow a hot needle.

Her black skirt rustled as it brushed against the sinking, mildewing floor. Spaces between the floorboards gaped wide open like stretched, tortured mouths—groaning in agony and splintering with the tension. Dark mud and brackish water squeezed between the cracks, welling up and oozing like pus from a sore.

In the room above their heads, Marquis Ghyslain de Voclain was just starting to retire. The empty glass on his bedside table still had a thin spread of cognac gathering at the bottom, barely enough to have a color.

The marquis reached up and tugged on his cravat, loosening it up just enough to get the knot undone. It was a relief to feel the rough fabric slip away. His throat was also feeling a bit tight—it was like he had a hair caught in the back of it, and he couldn't cough enough to get it out. He had given himself a headache trying.

Ghyslain coughed one last time, hacking into his sleeve as he pulled his shirt from the band of his pants. He walked over to a mirror that was hanging over a vanity—a relic from his late wife set in heavy brass. He opened his mouth as wide as he could and leaned forward, flattening his tongue to try and get a clear look down his throat. The dim candlelight was making it difficult. He kept turning his head and finally the light caught something. He hooked his fingers around the corners of his mouth, pulling them down and leaning even closer, until his breath fogged the glass. There was something white — and large — resting at the very back of his throat.

And then it moved. Ghyslain's eyes widened, and he gagged, clutching at his neck, watching as the fingers unfurled and long, almond-shaped nails started scratching at the surface of this tongue.

He reeled back, nearly falling flat on his backside as he tried to pull away from the mirror. His whole body jerked painfully, and he shivered in his skin. It suddenly felt very loose, as if someone was scrambling his insides and his skin was just the wrinkled bag holding it all together.

Ghyslain felt the hand sliding up the back of his throat. His nose burned as blood and bile was pushed up into his nasal cavities, running down his face and chin in ugly dark red and sickly yellow streams. He couldn't breathe anymore, his mouth was being forced wider and wider apart — until the hinges of his jaw felt like they were on fire, and he could feel the corners of his mouth breaking apart, splitting and ripping open his cheeks. Once they got going, they tore open like paper.

His jaw cracked, then snapped and suddenly he couldn't feel much of anything anymore. An entire arm emerged from the ruins of his mouth — squeezing out a shoulder, and then stretching. A grimy hand flailed, searching for something to grab onto and finish the process.

Even though Ghyslain was quickly losing sensation in all of his limbs, he could still feel his insides swirling — getting pushed down towards his stomach like someone was using them as steppingstones.

And inside of his head, just before the top of it tipped so far back that he could see his own spine, he could hear nothing but a merry humming.

Manifesting had never been easy, but the demon felt like he was getting more creative. The hardest part was learning how to walk again. Human beings had such soft, fleshy feet…it was rather like walking on a sponge cake.

The old man's boots had been too small, but the rest of his clothes hung off the demon's frame in bloodstained tatters making him look as ragged as a scarecrow. He shuffled down the cold basement stairs, bare feet landing and turning awkwardly, the weak ankles straining, coming dangerously close to breaking. Human bones were so fragile, he had to remember not to put so much pressure on them.

He was an old hat to this trick, but the ankles almost ruined him every time.

"Can you not walk?" a woman's voice tore a gash in the silence.

He looked up, his hand resting on the wall as he leaned heavily for support. "Is that a problem?" he shot a challenging look her way. She met his gaze, eyes the color of aventurine boring straight into his skull. He had never been on the receiving end of such a potent glare…it was markedly refreshing.

"You are wearing father's cravat." A far more grating, decidedly masculine voice felt the need to point out. The demon rolled his eyes in the other direction, glancing briefly at the mop of copper curls and obtrusive freckles that had been smacked onto a rather unremarkable face and stuffed into an aristocratic costume.

"I don't think he has need of it any longer." The demon responded smoothly. "And it is absolutely filthy." He loosened it up around his throat, the thoroughly soaked cloth resisting his fingers.

He let go of the wall, confident now in his ability to stand on his own two feet. Standing straight, he was an impressive height.

The demon held out his grubby, blood-encrusted hand. He looked straight at the woman once more, bending his fingers slightly in a bidding gesture.

She moved as if breaking from a trance. She turned quickly to the little altar they had set up behind them and swept up a miniature salver. He heard the teeth rattle on the dish and was instantly captivated; his reaction similar to that of a dog when its bowl is filled.

The small room smelled overwhelmingly of myrrh, and it had been a long time since anyone had burned the resin for him. He was aware that she had gone through great pains to obtain it. The teeth had probably been easier to come by. Summoning an Elder Demon was no simple task, and she had performed the rite without a hitch. The teeth, the incense — it was the work of an authentic cultist.

She held out the dish in front of her. It hovered an inch out of his reach. "I am Suzanne de Voclain. This is my brother, Jean-Francois."

He ground his own teeth, able to hear the calcium creaking as he stared at the offering, barely refraining from reaching out and ripping it from her hands. "Charlie Banks."

She did not seem overly impressed. "A rather underwhelming name for a demon."

"It serves as well as any other. And it's easy to remember."

Something touched Suzanne's face—what seemed to be a realization of his enthrallment with the offering. She smiled; an expression that did not suit her face well, suggesting she did not do it very often. She proffered the salver, getting it close enough to him so that the edge bumped his fingertips. He snatched it instantly from her hands, pulling it close. His eyes were riveted to the white molars that rolled around and clacked against one another, teasing him.

The soft fingers of his recently attained flesh were having a hard time picking up the teeth. It was a task he was going to have to work on.

"Do you believe in the Almighty, cultist?" he asked while pinching determinedly at the pieces.

Narrow lips wound their way into a shrewd moue. "I believe in reason."

Charlie scoffed. "Is apathy the latest fashion? I thought times of terror always rebirthed religion."

"Not when the leader is a philosopher, surrounded by rabble-rousers desperate to prove their autonomy." Suzanne responded.

Jean-François dragged his tongue over his visibly dry lips, seeming to hesitate before he spoke. "So, is he dead?"

Charlie flicked another annoyed glance his way. "Who?"

"Father." Jean-François plucked at his cuffs, making eye contact with the demon and regretting it almost instantly. Charlie's cobalt eyes drilled into his skull as if the demon was wondering just how much effort it would take to crack it open.

Charlie sucked on his teeth, his eyes rolling up a little in an exaggerated motion.

"That would depend," his tongue *tsked,* "entirely on your definition of deceased."

"Was his heart still beating?" Jean-François asked a little more brazenly.

Charlie grinned. "It was when I left it on the floor."

Jean-François turned green in the face, a color that did not suit his coppery curls in the least. He swayed a bit on his feet and reached out as if seeking support that was not there. Suzanne could have reached out to aid him, but she did not. Instead, she let the moment pass. Once he had regained himself, Jean-Francois gave Suzanne a sour look. She shook her head at him. There was nothing further between them that was worth expressing aloud.

They were in too deep. There was no turning back. Ghyslain was already dead. They would be, too, if they angered this creature any further.

Hesitation. It was his greatest weakness. Hers was that she never thought things through; she knew that about herself. And it was a quality that Jean-Francois had always said he enjoyed about her. With doubt clouding his eyes, she wondered silently if that had changed.

The demon was growing impatient with the teeth in the salver. He tipped the dish over and slipped the teeth into his palm, letting them drop one by one into the soft bed of pale, pink flesh. "If I eat these, your bones are mine."

"And the bones of so many more." Suzanne's eyes gleamed. "I knew I was summoning a gluttonous demon."

"Oh," Charlie said softly. "I doubt you knew what you were summoning, dear. I doubt very much." He scrunched up his hand and set one of the teeth on the tip of his tongue, treating it like an after-dinner mint.

"I think I will prove far more capable than you suspect, my lord."

Charlie snorted, sending the tooth into the back of his mouth. It cracked easily and his head was filled with that satisfying, gritty sound as he ground it between his back molars. "Do not address me as *my lord*, it is just Charlie. Charles if you absolutely *must*." He popped another tooth into his mouth. "Formalities fuck up the business."

Suzanne's lips quirked in amusement. "Are we business partners, then?"

"It is always only business." Charlie shoved the rest of the teeth into his mouth. Jean-François visibly paled, and as the demon advanced, he stepped back several spaces.

"You have to sign the contract," Charlie said. "In blood or ink, I don't think it matters these days. When I was young, it was blood. But it has been many eons since then."

"I have an appreciation for the classics," Suzanne said. "And blood is binding."

"Have it your way." Charlie reached into his vest and pulled out a slip of paper, flashing a smile at the coppery redhead who regarded him with curiosity. Charlie unfolded the paper and set it down on top of the altar, his tongue searching the crevices of his mouth for any further remnants of the offering he had just devoured. "Both of you will sign."

"Both?" Jean-François echoed.

"*Both,*" Charlie emphasized, drawing out the word as if Jean-François was incapable of comprehending. "Your skeleton is on the table here too, I hope that is clear."

"Well," Jean-François said tersely. "It is now."

Satan supposed he shouldn't be surprised that the Director of Hell's third ring was something of a minimalist.

He liked everything tall, straight, and thin. He wanted his cigarettes slim and unfiltered. He ordered his suits tailored so closely to his body that they were almost a second skin, coming in so tightly at his waspy waistline that it looked like one good pull on either end could separate him down the middle. Were it not for his thick blonde hair, pulled back away from his face and slipped into a fashionable knot, he could have easily been mistaken for a dead man. He was practically a skeleton shrink-wrapped with olive, freckled skin. His oxblood colored eyes were set deep beneath pencil-thin, carefully tweezed eyebrows. The tails had trailed off almost into nothing, making him appear very skeptical most of the time.

He didn't seem to believe in chairs, either. There were only two compact pieces of furniture to distract from the maddening combination of blank white walls and stark white carpeting that made up the expansive living room. Near dead center of the room was a glass top coffee table, disturbingly flawless in as it was entirely free of fingerprint smudges. Aside from that, there was only a short black leather loveseat covered in a thick layer of clear plastic.

The director was already seated, rigid legs crossed with one arm thrown possessively over his wife's powder-white shoulders. She was slouched in her seat, long legs thrown over the loveseat's thick arm. Her silky skirt was riding up far enough to flash the white lace garter that had become her trademark. The fabric was stretched to its limit around her firm thigh, and Satan developed an instant irrational fear that it would snap and take out one of his eyes. She had her vaudeville-red lips wrapped around the white, unfiltered end of one of her husband's favored cigarettes. Her ash blue eyes, the color of a washed-out starlet, were regarding Satan intently from behind a wispy stream of curling smoke. She had her other free hand buried elbow-deep in a pink box of powdered cookies, the stiff cardboard shoved between her legs in a very unprofessional position.

They were Famine and Gluttony—Hell's most controversial pairing. The tabloids were always hungry for them.

Satan shifted his weight. He was already starting to wish that he had worn more comfortable shoes for this encounter. He had nowhere to sit, and all of the empty space was starting to make him feel uneasy.

"I think it sounds like an awful lot of trouble," Famine was saying, "for two fairly young demons."

"Well," Satan responded immediately, "I don't do anything halfway. Besides, according to your reports, you and your wife have exhausted a good portion of your own resources seeking out a demon who broke free from your circle's prison not too long ago."

Famine set his jaw and exchanged a look with his wife. Gluttony shrugged her shoulders, pulling her hand free from the box and licking the sweet powder away from her fingers.

"That is different." She said. "Rahman-Reza is dangerous."

"Any who defies Hell is dangerous." Satan reminded her, his voice laced with warning.

"But he has violated almost every contract he seals." She sat up and set the box down on the table, brushing her hands together to dust off the remnants of powder. "He has murdered other demons. They refer to him as the Executioner because he has made so many disappear. And now he is on the lam."

"He tried to break the seal that bound him to his prison by clawing it off his throat." Famine added. "In the end, he just bore the excruciating pain all the way past limbo. When he broke the crust, the seal lost its power, and we lost our only method of tracking him down."

Satan felt a familiar headache reach its boiling point at the base of his skull. The pain was starting to radiate out, driving into his brain like a nail.

"I will grant you access to ample amounts of materials in order to continue your pursuit of Rahman-Reza, if you add Jahangir and Mojgan to your list." Satan said.

"That is all well and generous of you." Gluttony said. "But there doesn't seem to be any real gain on my end. Stray demons are my husband's problem…I have more domestic concerns."

Of course. Satan was trying to swallow his rising temper like a bitter pill. It just wouldn't stay down.

"I am also willing to offer an expansion on your ring. I've made arrangements to slice a little off the fourth circle, a deal which will increase your holdings by a third."

"A third?" Gluttony grinned. "How is Greed handling that news?"

"Let's just say she is fortunate to still be clinging to her rung on the corporate ladder. I was not at all pleased with her performance last quarter."

"So we heard." Gluttony looked up at Famine, her smile spreading like a smear of bright red jam. "I wonder what is next. A promotion, maybe?"

"Drive these demons back to Hell, and I will be open to discussing anything you like." Satan was having a hard time focusing on the business at hand. The only thing he could think about was how hungry he was even though he had eaten right before his arrival. Famine had that effect. Gluttony only made it worse.

If the Horseman could tell that his boss was struggling, he didn't seem bothered by it. He split his lips with another skinny cigarette and flipped open a lean silver lighter with the other hand. He caught the end of the cigarette with the narrow, flickering flame and held it there until weak wisps of smoke started spilling from the glowing paper edges.

"You're the boss." Famine said, smoke pouring from his lips like long, writhing tentacles. "Whatever you say goes."

Satan huffed. If only *all* his employees had that mentality.

The demon was struggling to keep his entrails from spilling out, a sight that Claire observed without a shred of pity. It must not have been as bad as his howling made it seem, or he would not have still been trying to run.

He ran with his hand pressed against his bulging intestinal wall, which seemed to be doing its best to eject hot, spongey bowels all over the ground. Blood gushed from the vicious wound, soaking through his expensive waistcoat and turning the berry red a gruesome shade of dark purple. With every step, it looked like the pain was increasing to the point where it had to be crippling—if the way he was limping and dragging along the sides of his feet was anything to go by. Claire followed him steadily, keeping a sure pace as the echoes of her heels bounced off the narrow alley walls with ominous intention.

They had taken him by surprise. There was no way he could have seen the blade that split open his skin like ripe fruit in time to scurry away. She and Edward had worked to pin the creature down by his shoulders in order to make the work more efficient. The demon had slipped out of their hands only because he was covered in so much blood and fled through the kitchen door, trailing an unseemly mess.

"It ends here." She saw his head snap around with the hard words as she took back control of the situation. "You have nowhere further to go."

The demon lifted his head, blue eyes piercing through sweaty locks of pitch black hair. She had spoken correctly. A solid brick wall was interrupting his path. To go any further, he would either have to scale it or turn around and run back into the street. Neither of those options were feasible when his insides were threatening to become his outsides, and blood was streaming through his fingers with such vigor that it spurted like a small fountain.

"Do you know who I am?" his voice shook even as he tried to speak with confidence. "I am Calixte Labelle! Butler to…"

"…To the Marquis de Michaud." She finished for him. His attention was visibly split between her and the bloody mess that he was about to have on his hands, which was precisely what she needed. "Yes, he was very clear on the role you selected to play. I would elaborate but we are on a tight schedule."

"He said you would be very difficult to bring down." Edward's voice joined hers. "Imagine our disappointment."

The demon's mouth opened, and his cheeks puffed out. He looked like he was going to throw up. He braced himself against the dirty wall, presumably to keep himself upright from how badly his knees were trembling.

"Who are you?" Calixte whispered. Each breath looked as though it cost him precious amounts of energy from how he was wilting, his shoulders stooped and his injured stomach squelching around his fingers while his free hand dragged across the brick wall.

Claire raised her head to look up at the dark sky. Light, fine raindrops had started to fall—but she would rather not be caught outside when it started to pick up. There were many ways a hunt could drag on, and sometimes Edward had a knack for slowing things down, but there was no reason for this to go any further.

Even with his stomach almost hanging out, it was still possible for the demon to heal if he escaped. It would take days, maybe weeks, but they could mend from a mortal wound if they were not executed properly.

Claire was close enough to the demon, now, that she did not need to lunge to reach him. Edward was behind her and would be able to spear Calixte if he bolted. She grasped the hilt of her weapon and swung, bludgeoning the demon on the side of the head. She heard his teeth clack together and then he fell, collapsing against the cobblestone in a pool of fallen rain and his own blood.

Claire crouched and tapped the tip of her blade against the soft, still very human underside of the demon's chin. She tilted his head back until she could stare him in the eyes. They exchanged a passionless look.

"You can't kill me," the demon said. "You can kill the flesh form I inhabit, but you can't kill *me*. And you know why."

"On the contrary," she leaned in just a little bit closer. "I can."

Her last words were so soft they were little more than a hiss of scalding breath slipping between the edges of her teeth. She tapped the blade underneath his chin, drawing it back a little so that the sharp edge created a thin red line, but it did not cut deep enough to bleed.

"Obsidian," she said. "That is all it takes."

Whatever blood remained in the demon's body drained from his face. Calixte swallowed hard and it made his larynx bob, although the blade stopped it from making a full descent.

"Do you want to hear me beg?" he asked, his voice tight with anxiety. She shrugged, uninterested either way, and twisted the blade to drive it a little closer to his throat.

"Please!" The rain was coming down a little faster, now, and it splashed against his cheeks. The fat droplets spilled into the creases of the demon's eyes and swirled around them, creating long red streaks like trails of tears down his face. "Please, don't do this…"

"You made a contract with the Marquis for his soul." She tilted her head. It was hard to have sympathy for such a pathetic display. "You are a no good grubby little vulture. You are a filthy scavenger who wears the colors of a fierce predator—yet it is obvious what you are. You lack finesse. And dignity." She drove the obsidian blade deep into his throat, jerking it free before jamming it underneath his chin and driving it deep into his skull. The demon made a horrible gurgling sound, jerking violently on the end of her knife as dark blood poured from his lips thicker than syrup. She jiggled the blade, twisting it around a little bit as she watched the light fade from the demon's eyes. She watched as Calixte's pupils dilated then contracted, becoming nothing more than little pinpricks of black ink in a sea of sky blue. She saw the blue break up, giving way to patches of bright orange that consumed the irises like flames. She watched the orange quickly turn to dark, muddy brown before the irises broke apart, the pupils sinking down to fill the empty spaces.

She gave the knife one more satisfying thrust before pulling it free for the final time.

Claire Clifton sighed and readjusted herself on the wet ground, sliding her legs out from the uncomfortable crouch they had been bent into and setting the gory weapon down beside her.

"Do you need help?" Edward asked as he approached her, one gloved hand already extended. She waved him away.

"I need a moment," she told him. "My leg is full of pins and needles."

"Ah," he looked down at the demon's corpse and nudged it with the toe of his boot, his mouth set into a thin, severe line of distaste. "I despise it when they beg."

"It was a final act of desperation with no real witnesses." Claire responded. Even to her own ears, her tone sounded flat. "It did not matter."

"The fall, when that is all there is, matters." Edward tossed her another look. "Are you going to mark it down, or shall I?"

"You mark it. Do some work for a change." She was massaging her calf, trying to get some feeling to return. "I had to spend an hour logging the Marquis' repentance earlier. Have you ever been trapped in a room with a man who is sweating so profusely that he might very well drown himself… listening to him blubber about needing the grace of Heaven while having to politely nod and act sympathetic?"

They both had. It was half their job description. The other half consisted of far more enjoyable, if bloodier work.

"I must ask you not to be rhetorical with me. It gets tiresome." Edward picked her knife up off the ground and began the process of cleaning it, pulling a stained linen rag from a leather case on his belt. "After we complete the report, where do we meet the Winged Man?"

Claire shrugged, finally pulling her legs back underneath her so that she could rise to her feet. Her right leg was still tingling, but not so badly that she couldn't find her balance. "I have not heard from him these past few days. So, unless you have information I do not, I suggest we return to the hotel and wait for our next assignment."

"It is as good a plan as any." Edward returned his sister's knife to her while giving the corpse one last look. "Do you think they will have duck again?"

"They might," she said, "if you hurry with that report."

Edward reached back into the leather case, stashing the crumpled-up rag and lifting out a small notebook no bigger than his hand bound in moleskin. A fountain pen was already wedged between the middle pages, snuggled up close to the spine. He flipped the notebook open and found the page where the Marquis' case had been jotted down, the space for 'confirmed extermination' still empty.

"Go ahead," Edward urged her. "I can walk and write at the same time."

Claire adjusted her skirts, taking her leave of the alley without a single look behind her. Edward followed closely; his nose pressed closely to the journal's softened parchment pages. Neither of them was overly worried about the body. They knew it would be gone long before it had a chance to be discovered.

Say what one would about demons, but they were quite efficient in disposing of their own.

CHAPTER II

Everything was red; blood was the favored shade. The spray from the guillotine seemed all-encompassing as nothing appeared untouched by the fine mist of gore. It settled on top of the uneven cobblestone streets, already streaked with grime. It swirled on the surface of putrid puddles, mysterious groundwater that always collected in deep holes worn into the streets by carriages.

The city had been likened to a morgue before, but in James' opinion it was more of a corpse itself. Already rotten it was now decaying, the bleak abandoned buildings piling up like so many discarded bones.

"This place smells like blood," Henry whispered, crinkling his nose and holding a handkerchief up to it. The handkerchief had been pretty once, but now it was wrinkled beyond all recognition and stained to the point where even James had forgotten that it was once white. But it still held its scent, a very faint trace of violets that perfumed the air whenever he waved it around. "And shit." Henry added.

"It reeks of fear, worst of all." James amended, shoving his hands deeper into the pockets of his heavy wool coat. It was wearing thin in several places, and the brisk night air was like a knife penetrating the vulnerable spots. He shivered and glanced at his companion. "There are so many voices, so many cries and pleas we could be answering. If there was ever a soul desperate for a demon, we could find it here."

"I know," Henry said. "I know. I wish…" He trailed off.

Hunger pains were making James' stomach gurgle wretchedly. He knew that they both wished a lot of things. James wished that once, just once, they could answer a call for a demon. It had been so long since either of them had tasted a soul. They had been doing everything they could to avoid being noticed. All it would take was one slip, one glimpse of their names on a sheet of paper, and all Hell would be hot on their heels once more. As it stood, they had *just* reached the point where they were comfortable walking without looking over their shoulders every few seconds.

"Me too." James finished the sentiment. He would have given anything for a meal. A thousand years chained to the floor of Hell was starting to sound like a pittance.

"We could always turn ourselves in." Henry suggested it at least once a day.

"As I've told you about eight times already; you first."

"Like Hell." Henry's smile was a weary one. "You would let me take the plunge and then you would take off. Like a coward."

"You act as though I could abandon you so easily" James snorted softly. "I have not been able to shake you off *yet*. And I have tried."

"You have not!" Henry crowed.

"I tried to leave you in that one coffee shop." James reminded him.

"I would not consider that a true attempt, when you barely made an effort."

They were beginning to disregard their volume. James caught the slip and motioned that they both needed to quiet down. The streets were abandoned on account of it being well past midnight yet probably not past three in the morning. Henry pressed his lips together pettishly until they turned white. He always resented being told to shut his mouth, even with by a non-verbal order.

James rolled his eyes and slipped his hands up the lapels of his coat, adjusting his high collar and listening as Henry resumed the conversation in an unnecessarily forced whisper. He was only half-listening this time. Something else had caught his attention.

It was a harsh, grinding sound. Something like bones breaking, snapping.

James stopped in his tracks. He held out his arm and thudded it against Henry's chest, forcing him to come to a halt as well.

"Henry," James hissed. "Do you hear that?"

Henry paused. He tilted his head a little and leaned in the direction of the sound. There was another grisly crack, and then a loud wet *pop* that made James' skin crawl in revulsion.

"I heard *that.*" Henry said. "Although I wish I hadn't."

James was already headed for the source, morbid curiosity taking over. Henry followed him closely, and James was glad that he was taking care not to separate them.

"Are you mad?" Henry prodded. "You are going to get us killed."

"I doubt that." James said dismissively. "Besides, you cannot tell me that you are not the least bit curious."

"Not in the slightest." Henry made a grab for his sleeve.

"What better do we have to do?" James pulled away and continue to advance, now maintaining a pace of one step swifter than the other demon.

They passed through the main square. It was a large, open area dominated by a man-made titan of justice. The guillotine loomed a full thirteen feet in height, and that was without the tall platform. The sides of the blade were dull and bloodstained, yet the moonlight teased its razor edge enough to give it a wicked gleam. Constructed as simply as it was, there was still no competition for magnificence in its surroundings. Not even the matching stone buildings, dazzling in their ancient composition, could hold a candle to this beauty. They simply faded into the background.

Fear without a source dragged its nails over James' skin as they passed, yet he could not tear his eyes away from the sight. He watched Henry crane his neck to keep the monstrosity in his line of vision until he could strain no more, and then he whipped his head back around.

"I do not think we should be here." Henry said, sounding apprehensive.

"Do not let it get to you." James replied. "It is not meant for us."

The sound was getting louder. They walked until they could see the other side of the platform where a cart was waiting. It looked like it had been pulled around and then just abandoned; four coffins were stacked in its wide bed, three on the bottom and one resting on top. They were crudely cobbled together—cheap, splintery wood held together with nothing more than bent nails and determination. The lid had been ripped away from the coffin on the very top, and the headless corpse inside had been lifted out. It was now splayed over the mouth of the coffin, legs and arms kept it from falling back in. The neck had been savaged—no longer looking like it had been severed with the clean stroke of a blade. There was a line of torn flesh where the spine had been grabbed and ripped out. Shreds of clothing littered the floor of the cart, enough to leave the corpse's back exposed.

The entire length of the spine had been torn out. Henry and James balked just a few feet away from the cart. For James, it was his morbid curiosity overriding common sense.

A white hand stained with blood appeared, smacking into the side of the topmost coffin and sending it skidding. It sailed for a few inches, crashing against the ground and breaking apart on impact. The body rolled over the pieces, flopping as uselessly as a rag doll. James' eyes darted back towards the cart, catching movement in his peripherals.

There was a man standing on top of the remaining coffins. In the dim moonlight, you couldn't see the blood against his bright crimson vest. There was some splattered over his crème-colored shirt and his fingertips were stained beyond redemption, but he didn't seem bothered by any of this.

The man braced himself and grasped the edges of another coffin lid. It squeaked and groaned awfully as he started to pull it up—and it quickly gave way with the sound of splitting wood. He tossed it aside like it was made of cardboard and reached down to grab hold of his prize. The body was that of a delicate woman, or at least that was what it appeared to be. He wrapped her headless corpse up in his arms like a lover and started trailing his fingers down the back of her filthy dress, fingers working deftly to unlatch each hook that held her bodice together as he dug for the bones that were lying just underneath her meat.

"It can't be." Henry whispered.

"I thought we would have been able to at least sense another demon." Was James' response, his fingers trembling a bit as he went to adjust his glasses. "But he doesn't have a scent."

"The Elder ones don't smell like anything." Henry's voice was barely able to be heard. "But give it to me straight. If he is here…how fucked are we?"

"I don't know," James admitted, "I don't think he has seen us."

"So that's something." Henry was already backing away. "Let's go."

James nodded his agreement, his worn shoes scuffling against the cobblestones as he set himself in reverse. He ground his heel against the stones, ready to spin around and start bolting in the other direction.

But then the Elder demon spoke, and his voice was curiously soothing.

"They still have their souls." He said, peeling the dress down over the corpse's shoulders and then touching the bloodied neck stump, feeling for the bone. "No one has been by to collect them yet."

James licked his lips, the mere mention of souls already whetting his ferocious appetite.

"No one? So there are more demons in the city?" There was no use putting on a ruse. They were all very well aware of what the other was. To play dumb would have been both insulting and juvenile.

"Not that I am aware." The Elder demon dug his fingers down into the neck until he could grab hold of the spine. "Mostly grim reapers, but they tend to stay away until I have finished my work." He jerked his arm back, and the entire spine came out in one clean motion. For a brief moment, the whole of the square echoed with the sound of wet flesh tearing and more bones snapping as the ribs broke away, still embedded deep in the body.

James took a hesitant step forward and gave Henry a conflicted look. The blonde demon shrugged helplessly, his hungry gaze already devouring the corpse that rested on the ground.

That was more than enough answer to his question. James felt like he had lost control of his entire body as he fell on the corpse in front of him, his hands plunging straight into the opening that had already been made. The body that the Elder had been harvesting from fell like mana from the sky, crashing against the grubby street with a sound like rotten fruit. Henry grabbed it, claws already ripping his human nails from their beds as he dug for the luscious soul.

James found the soul easily. At this point, he cared nothing about color, and nothing about taste. All he cared about was the frenzy of feeding. The soul had been, at some point, dislodged and was speared against a splinter of broken bone. He slipped the little pocket of muscle out and removed the bone carefully, his finger puncturing the hole that it had left behind. The soul inside was dark forest green, and when he opened his mouth, he nearly salivated all over his prize.

James pressed the muscle against his mouth and sucked the soul out in the way that humans consume oysters. The succulent beads burst as soon as they hit his tongue, and his mouth was filled with juices of bitter, bitter anguish. He could taste shame, humiliation, and rage. He rolled fear around on his tongue, sucking all of the flavor that he could out of them before swallowing.

He paused, gasping for breath as he rocked back on his heels. He was in danger of falling backwards, but he managed to regain some of his balance. James closed his eyes and took a deep breath. His stomach moaned and garbled a protest, demanding more, but he had to force himself to stay calm. It was difficult to frenzy-feed when there were limited resources. And from the sounds Henry was making behind him, he could tell his companion was similarly suffering.

"What is your name?" James asked, slipping his tongue up the side of his hand to catch the last of any lingering juices. He rolled his eyes up to regard the Elder demon, who looked down on him with the cold dispassion of a faineant god as he peeled away undesirable remnants of flesh and tangles of nerves from the spine in his hands.

"Rahman-Reza." Was the response. Henry and James exchanged sideways glances, and the Elder made a petulant sound as he twisted one of the vertebrae free.

"Oh, we're not doing that? Fine. It's Charlie, then. And you are?"

"Henry,"

"James." He gave his simultaneous reply.

"Charmed. Where do you come from?" he nibbled on the edge of a vertebrae before hooking his tongue underneath a ridge and pulling the entire thing into his mouth.

"With all due respect," Henry said, "you are the first demon we have encountered in a long time. You will forgive us if we are skeptical of your presence."

"It does seem like a coincidence, does it not? But I promise you; it is exactly that." Charlie crouched close to the edge of the cart, his stained fingers dangling as he moved fragments of bone around in his mouth, sucking on them and using his tongue to shove them into his cheek. "What are you running from?"

James adjusted his glasses indignantly. "Nothing more than our own mistakes."

Charlie furrowed his brow as if he didn't quite understand. "Mistakes? We don't make mistakes. We feed. That is the entirety of our existence."

"Well, things got a little more complicated than that while we were in-between courses." Henry supplied. "I suppose you could say that Hell has turned this into a rather, ah, *heated* situation."

Charlie's brow cleared. "So, you have both gone rogue?"

James shrugged, already unwilling to divulge even that much information. Charlie's scrupulous gaze was unsettling.

James had never before met someone whose eyes could stay fixed in one place for so long.

"Is that why you are both wandering around dressed entirely out of century?" Charlie stood up, straightening his back. "You look a sorry pair, like two ragged drowned kittens."

"These *rags* were all the rage." Henry lifted his arm; his limp, soiled cuff slumping over the back of his hand. "Once."

"I'm sure." Charlie scoffed. "Yet there is never an excuse for sticking out like a broken bone. I have as much reason to avoid Hell as you do." He slipped his fingers down the side of his cravat, tugging on the fine linen until it began to unravel. The lace slithered out of its knot, its coils slacking until his white throat was bared. His milky skin was marred by an ugly red brand that looked like it had been pressed so deep it was a marvel that it had not pierced through the skin altogether.

James had only ever seen drawings of such a brand before. They had covered an entire section of his training manuals that exhaustively detailed Hell's system for imprisonment. That beastly symbol should have been enough to kill the Elder demon at his first thought of breaking free.

And yet here he was, a capricious smile creeping across his face—contorting innocent, swollen lips that were the same soft pink as a Hedgerow rose.

"How bold of you," Henry said quietly after a moment had passed. "How can you be sure we are not agents of Hell?"

Charlie cocked an eyebrow, his tongue flickering out over his lips. "It wouldn't matter. I could destroy you regardless."

That was hardly reassuring. When neither responded, Charlie started tugging on the loose ends of his cravat, pulling the fabric tight around his throat once more and concealing the damning mark.

"I have one more coffin to go. Once I have finished here I am going to return to the house of my current contract. You can stick around, eat…then follow me back, and I'm sure they will see you outfitted in something suitable." He was already turning his attention back to the corpse he had temporarily dropped. "If you choose not to do so, well—I would wish you luck, but we all know you won't have any after this."

James wished Henry could read his mind, but he also knew that in this instance they were thinking the exact same thing. Neither trusted the demon in front of them, but their options were slim. He was right after all—they *did* stick out badly. They needed somewhere to recoup and figure out their next move.

Neither Henry nor James were sure about how to operate without a contract to cushion their social conduct. They had grappled for their independence blindly.

"Well," Henry said, glancing at James from the corner of his eye. "I don't know about you, but I happen to be starving."

That answered it, then.

Charlie set the sole of his fine shoe against the headless corpse he had been feeding on, using his foot to push it off the cart and onto the street. It landed with a ghastly crunch, the spine torn out so savagely that they could already see the soul glittering inside with some of the bright blue beads spilling from the torn pocket.

"There you have it, younglings." He said. "Tuck in."

Jean-François placed one of the delicate forks down on the table, setting his fingers on top of its fragile stem and adjusting it *just so* next to the gold charger.

All of the servants had left long ago. Jean-François' father had watched them walk away peacefully on the bloodiest day of the revolution's outset. Jean-François watched them leave as well, his fingers itching to wrap around the trigger of his pistol for the pleasure of seeing each one of them fall with a spark of gunpowder.

Ghyslain had discouraged it. "They will be dead in the streets by tomorrow afternoon. There is no use in wasting your shot."

It would have been worth it just to put a hole through one of their hearts. Jean-François had never seen such a disgusting display of entitlement. The sheer *ingratitude* had galled him; the way they had puckered their lips and spat directly into the faces of the people who had kept them off the streets by way of honest employment for years. Some of those servants had been with the family for decades, bound as closely to the de Voclain name as one could be without a blood tether.

They had dropped their aprons to the floor and trampled them as they left. Jean-François had never seen such a ghastly display of undeserved arrogance. He knew his outrage was warranted, but he had failed to lash out.

That was right before the nobility started dropping like flies.

In part he blamed himself, but he wasn't the only one at fault. There were hundreds of others who had done the same—they let the lower class get out of hand. They had watched them rally in the streets and made no move to put an end to it. Now so many were dead, and more were falling every day. Entire houses had been wiped out within hours. The few who remained alive did so by either the whim of fate or by their own clever device. The de Voclain family had survived this long by adopting and maintaining a muted presence. Pride would not let them be invisible, even though there had been many attempts to humble them. The more recent attacks and lootings of both their country and city properties were examples of such, though they had failed to bring the family to their knees.

For now, it seemed that the ever feared and venerated Committee had turned a disinterested eye to de Voclain affairs. Ghyslain was dead, and the fact that he had failed to prepare either of his children to take on his mantle was undisputed. Jean-François himself was barely twenty and a known lush with a penchant for gambling. Suzanne had turned nineteen just a few weeks prior and it was common knowledge that she lead her brother by the nose on a chain of his vices.

"Switch those two."

Jean-François felt the rush of breath skitter over his ear before he even registered that someone was speaking to him.

His shoulders shuddered and he tried to move away, but he failed to take into account that there was a chair right in front of him, blocking an advance. He glanced over his shoulder, his aristocratic nose nearly colliding with a sharp, noble chin.

"What?" Jean-François whispered, feeling unable to raise his voice as the space between them was as intimate as if they were lovers. Charlie reached over Jean-François' shoulder, twitching his fingers so that they briefly crossed.

"Those two," he said, indicating a pair of forks. "Switch them. You look like you don't know the difference between a cake and a salad fork."

They looked the same to Jean, but he wasn't going to put up an argument. He went to make the exchange, unhappy with the fact that Charlie had yet to pull away.

"Does it matter?" Jean-François asked. "It is just the three of us for dinner."

"Yes." Charlie said bluntly. "And it is more than the three. You will need to set two extra places."

Jean-François looked at the demon again like he had lost his mind. "Who else is coming?" he demanded.

"I met two foreign gentlemen in the square while I was out this evening." Charlie said, straightening. He did not pull away, so there was still absolutely no space between their bodies. "They are aristocracy such as yourself, but you would not know it from the state of their clothes. I invited them for dinner, as well as a change of linens."

Jean-François pressed his lips together crossly. "We are not given to charity."

"Happy news. It isn't charity." Charlie finally started to step back.

Jean-François nearly choked on a sharp intake of breath, as if the demon's hand had been wrapped around his throat the entire time.

"I will see to them once I have finished here." He said, his voice sounding a little thick.

"They are not in any particular hurry." Charlie responded, already moving across the room and headed for the opposite entrance. "Although I expect things to be taken care of by the time I have finished my conversation with Suzanne."

"How long will that take?" Jean-François glared after him, trying not to sound like he was whining.

"No longer than it needs to. If I were you, I would just err on the side of caution." With that, Charlie vanished through the painted doors, nearly catching the tails of his crimson coat between them as they closed at his heels.

CHAPTER III

Michael pinched the band of his sunglasses and lifted them away from his eyes, pushing them up into his closely cropped blonde hair as he let out a long sigh he didn't know he had been holding. There was really no reason for him to still be wearing sunglasses. It was past eight o' clock and the sun had already set. He hadn't even realized until he reached up to scratch his eyelid that he still had them on. Now there was a thumb print on the lens, and that was going to annoy him.

The hotel where his charges were currently residing was shoddier than usual. He didn't know how many times he had to encourage them to find nicer places to stay. They were starting to make Heaven, and its budget, look bad.

No one greeted him at the door. He was able to waltz in without a problem. There didn't appear to be anyone at the front desk, either. He was beginning to suspect that the entire building had been abandoned and that he was going to find them huddled together around a small fire, heating up cans of beans or whatever this century's equivalent of terrible poverty food was.

Michael drifted through the lobby, casually taking in the elegant décor that looked like it had been ransacked and defiled at least once or twice. Shortly thereafter he started up the stairs, his sleek black business shoes reflecting dim lamplight and the cuff of his dress shirt sleeve collecting a thin streak of dust as he slid it over the banister.

He reached the top of the stairs and peeked down at the little notecard he was clenching in the same hand as his briefcase. *No. 27.* There was a key attached, but he wouldn't need it.

All of the doors had the numbers painted on with cheap gold paint. When he found Room 27, so much of the numbers had flaked off that they were barely identifiable as numerals. He touched the knob—it was locked. He gave it an extra insistent twist and heard the lock pop angrily as he pushed the door open and entered the room, not even bothering to tap on it and announce his presence.

The room was far cleaner than he expected. That fact was easy to overlook at first, as there were clothes strewn all over the place along with an assortment of pens, journals, and sewing needles. The only well-kept items seemed to be the weapons, which were all set out next to a cleaning kit on top of the one desk that had been placed in there. Michael swept his displeased gaze over the scene before finally settling on the two he had come to see.

This was why he was determined to never have children. Young people, even those with ties to divine blood, seemed to be incapable of employing the full functionality of their brains.

Claire was seated at the desk, halfway through the process of dismantling and cleaning a pistol. She stood up as soon as she saw Michael walk through the door, wiping her hands on her thin white blouse and leaving streaks of dark grime.

"Edward!" she hissed through her teeth. Her brother stirred, having fallen asleep in a half-upright position on the only bed.

"Good evening," Michael said. "You two look as though you have been doing well."

"Exceedingly. Edward!" Claire reached down to pick up one of her slippers, hurling it across the room with deadly accuracy. The slipper beamed her brother in the head and Edward sat bolt upright, his arms flying up belatedly to protect him.

"What?" he asked, lowering his hands to rub his face. His voice was thick with sleep, a peek of his accent coming through with the grogginess. Michael had done well in training them out of their accents—it was better if they could speak with a neutral tongue, sharp and commanding yet absolutely unremarkable—not memorable in the least. Yet sleep and sickness always brought it out of them, especially in Edward's case.

"The ledger." Claire wiggled her fingers in his direction.

Edward's eyes rolled nearly into the back of his head as he turned onto his side, shoving his hand beneath the depressed mattress and searching for the journal he kept shoved underneath it.

"Good to see you," Edward said, looking up enough to give Michael a small nod.

"Likewise." Michael was ready to be out and on his way home. He didn't know why information could not be exchanged by way of a lesser messenger. But the Almighty had delivered unto him a dirty glower at the mere suggestion of sending down anyone else.

"Your pets, your project—your problem." There had not been very much room for argument.

Edward managed to slip off the bed, bare feet closing the short distance between him and the angel as he handed over the battered journal. Michael took it from him, holding it carefully so that none of the loose pages had a chance to fly out.

"My," he said. "You have been busy."

"You have another job for us?" There was a hopeful lilt in Claire's voice.

Michael nodded, sitting down at the desk she had abandoned and opening up the ledger, finding the last report he had recorded in his own small notebook and working forward from that point. "The boss says that you are ready for larger game. The end that we have been trying to reach is close at hand."

Claire's breath caught in her throat and her hand shot out to grasp her brother's—wrapping his warm fingers up in her icy ones.

"The demon named Henry." Michael spoke as nonchalantly as if he were discussing the weather. "You knew him, once."

The silence that followed could have made a dead man's ears ring. Michael finished transcribing all of the new records before shutting the journal and turning around in his seat, clicking his expensive pen and tucking it into his blazer pocket.

"Did you not hear me?" he asked, beginning to question whether he had actually spoken at all.

"We heard you." Claire said. "But I wish I hadn't."

"Why?" Michael cocked a tired eyebrow. "You knew it was coming."

"No. You said that your boss had an end game, and a big one, but you never bothered to explain what it was."

It had gone from *our boss* to *your boss* in under twenty seconds flat. That was not a good sign.

"Henry Wickes, the demon *Jahangir*, killed your mother." He reminded them, as if it was possible that they had forgotten.

"We remember quite clearly," Edward said quietly. "As well I remember when agonizing hunger twisted my stomach and I consumed my baby sister to sate the beast that clawed at my insides. We are all monsters in this room, sir."

Michael had half a mind to be insulted, but the statement wasn't far from the truth either. For all these children knew, he *was* a monster, just a different type. They had referred to him as nothing other than 'the winged man' ever since their mother had turned their souls over to him. He had never given them his name, nor the identity of the Almighty — though they would have guessed the latter.

In the event that they were captured by Hell and interrogated, Michael did not want his name to come up. Any ambiguity would muddle Hell's paperwork, and the Almighty did not want a single divine fingerprint all over a matter so… unclean.

"It is not negotiable." The angel finally said. "You owe a great debt. Your assignments are your payment, and you execute them without complaint."

"We have executed dozens without question — but none were our own flesh!" Claire's eyes blazed. Humans never had any real color to their eyes, but Michael always saw the purest shade of blue in hers. He found that unsettling.

"There is a rather romantic connotation to the term '*flesh of my flesh*', and your father has no business being attached to it. Think of him more like a wart, and you're having him removed." Michael stood, letting his height and broad frame fill the room. "It is not," he repeated, "negotiable."

Claire wasn't going to back down. "Why do we hate demons?"

Michael furrowed his brow. It was a simple question, but he had a feeling she was searching for a complicated answer. "Because they go against the will of the Almighty."

"What drives them to do so?"

"Base sins. Greed, gluttony, wrath."

"They are no better than humans, then."

"No." Michael agreed. "Are you about to ask why humans get cut a break?" he didn't even wait for her to answer. "It is because humans are created in the image of the Almighty, and demons are formed in their own. Yet they take on the visage of humanity from time to time and make mockery of it."

"But is it a mockery, or just too painful a reflection?" Claire shot back.

Michael realized, briefly, how easy it would be to keep her quiet by crushing her windpipe.

"You know, according to this," he tapped the hard cover of his small notebook. "You did not have a problem murdering them at the beginning of the night."

"And what gives me the capacity to kill them is an inherited trait. The irony must delight you, but I do not kill demons because I hate them. I kill them because that is what I am employed to do, and I do not value their lives over any others. I could just as easily hunt down other humans. Or angels."

Michael straightened, clutching his notebook so tightly that his knuckles paled. He wanted to bring the full wrath of God down on her head. He wanted to rip out her brother's guts and shove her face in them like an untrained dog who soiled the floor.

"It is the will of Heaven." It was the last argument he had.

She leaned forward, her mouth pulling itself into a harsh shape to form the terribly predictable words, *"Fuck Heaven."*

Michael's fingers twitched.

Your pets.

He could rip her head off if he wanted to.

Your project.

But he would never hear the end of it if he did.

Your problem.

He could almost see that smirk, as well as the reflection of his own infuriated face in the mirrored lenses of designer aviator sunglasses. If he killed her now, the next round of golf was going to be painful. He dreaded the conversation that would come up.

The archangel sucked in a deep breath, turning the full dark fury of his gaze onto Edward.

"Do you share your sister's sentiment?" he asked.

Edward didn't even flinch. "Like any other, we are entitled to free will."

Michael slammed his notebook down on the surface of the shitty wooden table. The damn thing almost cracked, but instead it shuddered terribly. He saw them cringe, which made him feel a little better.

"No matter where you take your business, they will ask you for the same thing. Jahangir is a wanted demon, and Satan will not be as forgiving. That is, if Satan even bothers to entertain such a pair of abominations. You would be a poor addition even to his filthy Hell."

Claire took Edward's hand again.

"Any who want our services can pay us for them." She said. "But we will work for none exclusively, sir, and we reserve the right to turn down any unsavory business."

Eden had not seen a pair of brats so ungrateful. Michael shifted his bottom jaw and started towards the door, too angry to even remember that he could have just vanished. He did not even need to go through the trouble of walking out.

"I will find you again in a few days," was all he managed to sputter out. "If you have changed your minds by then..." he didn't even finish his sentence. He slammed the door before he could, a crack starting at the base and splitting the wood open as far as halfway up.

Ungrateful fucking brats.

A graceful foot, small like a dancer's, dipped into the toe of a silken stocking and filled it out, heel and all, before Suzanne started rolling it up the length of her calf. After the stockings came her shoes with their fashionably pointed toes and slender wedged heels. They were barely visible behind the hem of her voluminous pale pink skirts, peeking out only occasionally when she walked—a subtle wink of color.

She had not seen a glimpse of pink in months, even though it had always been her favorite color. Revolution had painted the world red, while her own small piece of it had remained black as if she were in mourning. It had all been part of keeping a low profile. Mute colors were vital to the ruse, according to her father, but she hated them all the same. She knew that brown did nothing for her skin except make it look dusty, and black only served to make her look as grim as a corpse. She needed *color*—she needed pastel blue and faint white stripes with flowers embroidered on her skirts and lace dripping from her sleeves.

But most of all she needed pink. She needed soft, friendly pink like the blush on a virgin's cheeks.

The first thing Suzanne had done the night Charlie appeared was return to her room and sweep her favorite dress out of the closet. Jean-François had cleared away the shreds of their father's body with nothing but his hands and a large picnic basket while she pulled a new ribbon through the eyelets of her corset. Her brother would never understand her need. He could not fathom the joy that she felt upon realizing that her dresses still smelled faintly of orange flower perfume, and nothing like the butcher's shop odor that poisoned the atmosphere outside.

He was a man, and as a result his instincts were too base to appreciate anything refined. Men were brutal beasts — which is why their fashion consistently remained a poorly hacked and hemmed version of feminine splendor.

Sharp knuckles struck the doorframe twice and shattered the quiet. Suzanne pinched the glass stopper of a cranberry-colored perfume bottle between her fingertips and lifted it.

"You have guests, *demoiselle.*" Charlie announced urbanely. Suzanne puckered her lips and turned to face him, artificial red sausage curls brushing her long neck indignantly.

"Is it not tawdry enough that you refuse to address me properly — you will insult me with a diminutive as well?" she dabbed scent onto her wrists; acerbic orange flower complimented by dulcet undertones of vanilla.

She caught sight of his eyes in the mirror. He looked impervious to say the least.

"You have guests, *Suzanne.*" He repeated, taking on a tone far more taciturn.

She set the perfume bottle down with a deliberate *clunk,* maintaining eye contact with him in the mirror. "I do not recall inviting anyone to dinner."

"I did not think it necessary to ask mother if my friends could come over and play."

Her whole body tensed, the tendons in her neck tightening and standing out with anger only visible otherwise in her flushed face.

"You are seeking to expose us." Her voice was a white-hot whisper.

"Not at all." His own words were like a splatter of boiling oil. "And I don't like having my motives questioned."

"Why are they here?"

"They did not raise an eyebrow at the idea of seemingly reasonable people dining at such an absurd hour. Men who don't ask too many questions deserve to be rewarded. Besides," Charlie reached into his frock coat pocket, withdrawing his gold-and-ivory snuff box. "I told them that you are friendly."

She snatched the perfume bottle off her vanity, twisting in her chair and hurling it behind her. The expensive glass smashed against her closed bedroom door, teardrops of priceless perfume racing down the deep grooves in the wood. And yet Charlie was nowhere to be seen.

Suzanne paused, her heart slammed into her chest as she stared at the spot where she could have sworn he had been standing. A half second later a spot of color grabbed the corner of her eye, pulling her head around until she was facing the mirror again.

His reflection was still there. He had closed the top of his snuff box, his nostrils twitching a bit as he sniffed.

"So are we to expect you?" he asked. "Or are you in bed with a headache?"

"I have a headache." The response sprang off her tongue, which suddenly felt heavy. "But I will be there presently."

"Good of you." He turned and made his exit. Suzanne sighed and turned around in her chair once more, her fingertips resting against her forehead where she could feel painful pressure start creep in from the back of her skull.

The door, she couldn't help but notice, was wide open.

An excess of gold stucco bedecked the otherwise plain powder blue walls. It was almost as distracting as the array of mirrors, also painted gold, that were spread across the entire dining area like a pox. James, for one, did not see the appeal in having so many. He disliked being forced to watch people eat and it was unfathomable that one might wish to observe such a thing from a variety of different angles.

Of course, none of the mirrors were in a position that would have made it easy to look at one's own reflection, much less unintentionally glimpse at someone else's. They were set in odd places higher up on the wall and well out of the way, seeming only to only reflect each other and giving the unsettling appearance of passageways to alternate planes trapped inside ornate frames.

Their host, the name of whom James still did not know, was lingering by the only exit as if his intentions were to bolt as soon as he was given the opportunity. He was on his second glass of colorful Malbec wine, the alcoholic flush on his cheeks well-hidden by the thick blanket of freckles that mottled his complexion beyond all repair. It was an unfortunate condition, and James could not help but liken it to leprosy in his mind. Without the freckles, the man might have had a redeemable face. His cheekbones were high and his jaw was strong, but his firm, swollen lips were also discolored and his long, unruly copper curls flopped around his face while simultaneously sticking out in all directions. To a degree, James sympathized. Curly hair was difficult to tame, but he doubted an honest attempt had been made here.

Henry was less interested in waiting politely and more intrigued by things he wasn't supposed to touch. It was all James could do not to grab his companion and severely cripple him—if nothing else, bend his fingers so far backwards that they couldn't touch another expensive porcelain figurine.

"This one is quite sweet." Henry commented, slipping his fingers down the long white legs of a graceful dancer. "I must commend your taste."

Their host cleared his throat and took another long sip of wine, stalling on the need for a response. "My mother's." he said, apparently refusing to speak in complete sentences.

Henry broke out a delighted grin. It was like he had discovered a new game, and the entire goal was to see how uncomfortable he could make this person.

Before things could get worse, the dining room door opened. Charlie stepped through, their host skittering back a pace like a startled deer.

"She will be here 'presently'," Charlie said, "even though she has a headache."

"How good of her." Their host replied, sounding oddly skeptical. "That took a while."

"No, it didn't." Charlie swept his eyes over both Henry and James, quickly appraising their appearance. "The clothes are a bit roomy, but I knew they would be. It will do for now."

James reached up self-consciously and adjusted the waterfall of white lace that was wrapped around his throat.

Their host nodded, swirling the last of his wine around the bottom of his glass. "I did what I could."

Charlie was already moving on, crossing the room quickly until he was standing beside Henry. James watched as his golden-haired companion spared the elder demon a glance, never once moving his fingers from the top of the porcelain dancer's head.

"I was just complementing our host on his exquisite taste." Henry said. "I have never seen such garish décor."

"It is appalling, isn't it?" Charlie was close enough that when he lifted his arm, he brushed sleeves with the other demon. James' spine stiffened and he swallowed hard when he saw the soft folds bend with the contact. He did not care, at all, for someone he did not trust being so close to Henry.

"You will find that excess is something of the theme, here." Charlie continued. "Excess. Indulgence. Pastels." He cast a short, disdainful look at the wall in front of him. "There is nothing I hate more than a dusty pastel, particularly pink. Like watered down blood—Suzanne wears a good deal of it."

"Who is this Suzanne?" Henry kept his voice low. Charlie's fingers moved back and forth as he stroked the figurine's slender shoulders.

"She is my latest contract." Charlie responded. "I do not know the color of her soul. Her eyes are green. Doesn't it have something to do with the eyes?"

"Green eyes are a promising start." Henry said.

"I will never understand the palate of your brand of Eater." Charlie scoffed, a disdainful little rush of air. "Souls have no substance. They are slippery, gritty…it's like swallowing a handful of wet sand. And you can never tell what color they are…which I am told affects the taste."

"And what of bones?" Henry lifted a blonde eyebrow. There was an intrigued edge to his voice—curiosity that James knew well and always dreaded, because it too often ended in disaster. "They must all taste the same."

"Not remotely." Charlie glanced at him. "Each skeleton has a signature."

An amused smile tugged at Henry's lips. "A signature? What, is it affected by what they eat?"

Charlie rolled his eyes. "No, nothing like that."

"You can't even explain it." Henry teased.

"Oh, prithee. How does the color of the eyes affect the flavor of the soul?"

Henry opened his mouth. There was a moment when it appeared as though he was straining to articulate, but he seemed to give up when he clamped it shut again and shrugged. "It just does."

"That is what I thought. You can tell me that it does but you cannot tell me *why*." Charlie moved so that if there had existed an inch of space between them, it was immediately quashed. He was several inches taller than Henry, his chin almost coming to rest on the bridge of the younger demon's nose. "Although we often waste time seeking out the 'why'. I find it much easier to accept things as they are. Are you of a similar sentiment?"

Henry's eyes rolled upward. It was getting difficult for James to make out the snatches of their conversation, but he could still recognize most of Henry's words. "Are you suggesting that I not ask questions?"

"We hardly know each other. Yet you already seem to be less…academic than your friend."

That rankled. The corners of James' mouth turned down, but he still did not interject to comment.

"Dumber, you mean." Henry's lip curled.

"Not remotely. I only mean to imply that you see the type to make a fast decision rather than dwell on the potential pitfalls."

Henry scrunched up his brow. "I am not sure I follow."

Charlie lifted one shoulder in a casual half-shrug. "I think you and I will work well together."

An incisive smile spread across Henry's lips. "Am I to understand that you and James would not?"

"Call it a hunch. I can feel his disdain from here."

James looked away from the pair, just in case either looked over to catch him listening in. He did not see the expression on Henry's face, but he heard him say, "Well, that's just because you're standing close to me."

The Elder let out a short, disapproving hiss. "Well, the evening for us is still young. It is still anyone's game."

The sound of movement pulled James' head back around. He noticed Charlie stepping away and Henry reaching up to grip his own arm. Henry gripped his arm self-consciously. James did not approve of Charlie's lack of concern for personal space and Henry's discomfort with the entire situation was nearly palpable.

The entire exchange only furthered his opinion that they should find an excuse to leave as soon as possible.

"I hope you were not waiting on me." A voice like nettles, stinging and abrupt, interrupted the series of strained social interactions. "I'm sure our guests must be famished."

The voice came from a woman who stood in the doorway. Her fingers were curled around the edge of the frame, and she was leaning forward, all but hanging from it like a child. James' eyebrows went up as he reached to adjust his glasses. The way she spoke made her sound older than she probably was. It was not possible for this girl to be a day over nineteen.

"We *were* waiting for you," their host spoke before anyone else could, visibly relieved to see his sister. He held his hand out for her as if reaching for a lifeline, and she slid her own slender fingers across his.

"You needn't have." She glanced briefly at her brother. "Will you introduce me to our guests?"

"I—ah." Even the abundance of freckles could not smother the blush quickly spreading over his cheeks. "I'm afraid I don't..."

"James Highmore," James saw that the man was struggling and dove in to save him any further embarrassment. "*Doctor* James Highmore. And this is my friend, Lord Henry Wickes."

Henry nodded. "It is a pleasure."

"It is good to meet you both. I am Suzanne de Voclain, and I see that Jean-François has already introduced himself."

Henry looked like he was having a hard time swallowing a snicker.

"Indeed. We are very thankful for your help." James remained unfailingly polite as always. "My companion and I were in somewhat sordid condition when we entered the city."

"It was absolutely pitiful." Charlie added, making the first steps towards the dinner table.

"Are you not from around here?" Suzanne asked, waiting for Jean-François to pull out her chair before settling down.

"No," Henry said. "We are practically a world away."

Charlie put his fingertips together, resting his elbows on the table as he looked very intently at Suzanne, who was seated opposite of him. He looked like he was holding something on the tip of his tongue, just waiting for the right moment to unleash it.

James could not keep down the dreaded feeling that the cat was about to be let out of the bag. On one hand he could think of no reason why it shouldn't be — if the woman was in a contract with a demon, why maintain the illusion? On the other hand…

James really, *really* did not want this woman to know anything about him. And he could not place why.

Charlie sucked on his teeth. "We have a very similar background. In fact, I found that we have many things in common. Aside from the fact that souls are their preferred fare."

Henry didn't miss a beat. "Not even a dash of embellishment—I see you have little flair for theatrics."

Charlie's smile seemed forced. "I try to remain direct."

"A master of tact, complimented beautifully by elderly wisdom. I covet every weapon in your arsenal."

James was quick to cut in. "Henry, you're being…"

He was interrupted.

"I would not be so quick," Charlie countered. "You have not seen everything there is."

"Oh, I greatly anticipate that which has yet to be unveiled." Henry smiled over the rim of his cup.

Jean-François held up a hand. "I do not understand what is being said here." He stated, looking between the two of them for an explanation.

Henry's cup made a slow descent as he lowered it back to the table. He pressed his lips together in what read as a poor attempt to maintain his composure. "Speaking of things that are *quick*."

James dug the toe of his shoe into Henry's shin.

Suzanne set her hand on top of her brother's to force it back down. She was fighting to keep a placid expression on her face and ended up doing little to conceal her rising agitation.

"I hope you will stay." She said, turning to address Henry. "You and your companion."

"I don't think we can." James spoke up before anyone had the chance to contradict him. "We appreciate the offer, of course, but we cannot afford to linger." Something about this place did not settle well with him at all. But he could see that it had already enraptured Henry.

Or maybe it was the beautiful redhead who had done that. James had not looked twice at her until now, but she was by most standards *exceedingly* pretty.

If Henry's senses completely abandoned him by the end of this, James was going to hold her personally responsible.

"We will discuss it." Henry said, unfailingly infuriating. "I hardly think taking advantage of your generous offer would prove detrimental for one night."

James stiffly pushed his glasses back up the bridge of his nose. Charlie said nothing, he just ran his tongue over the rim of his cup, flashing Suzanne that Cheshire cat grin.

68

CHAPTER IV

A file as thick as Satan's wrist came crashing down on his desk. Papers slid and a set of busy hands fluttered to try and contain them, patting the edges and pushing them back into their respective confinement.

Satan looked at the file and then up at the Unchaste who presented them before letting his fork swing downward like a pendulum and spear a cherry tomato from the middle of his salad.

"Boss!" Preston, the over-eager files investigator from the eighth circle, was trying to both catch his breath and speak at the same time. He was a strange little man who liked to run everywhere – even though every major structure in Hell had perfectly functioning elevators.

He was also the sort of person who paired white running shoes with formal business attire. Satan never once questioned what this man had done to deserve eternal flames.

"What is that?" Satan asked, popping the tomato into his mouth.

Preston tapped the folder, thoroughly pleased with himself. "A whole lot of good news for us, boss."

"I'm all ears." Satan let his fork swing down again, this time grazing a piece of hard-boiled egg.

Preston huffed, as if a gust of wind had been let out of his sails. He quickly recovered. "You know the Clifton children?"

"The two eldest?"

"Yes. They went missing after the end of Violet Clifton's contract?"

"Mhm." Satan picked up a few leaves with his egg.

"Well! There was a long-standing rumor that they were being harbored by the archangel Michael. And our sources recently confirmed this to be true." Preston waved his hand frantically in front of Satan's face, not aware of how perilously close he was to losing it. "But that isn't why I am here! I came all the way down to your office today, sir, because Claire and Edward Clifton have broken their contract with Heaven. It has been *confirmed!*" a little bit of spittle flew with his final word, and he stood there, red-faced, waiting for the outstanding reaction he had been anticipating for an entire morning.

Satan paused, and then crunched a crouton purposefully.

"Do you mean to tell me you jogged down a flight of stairs and interrupted my lunch to tell me *that?*"

Preston stared at him for a moment, then furrowed his brow with confusion, tapping the folder rapidly. "Do you know what this means? They are mercenaries now. They are guns-for-hire."

"They are obsidian blades for hire." Satan said. "I'm not sending any sort of demon up to contact them, not when we're so short-staffed."

Preston was all but waving his arms up and down in frustration. The poor man looked like he was about to explode. He bounced on his heels and flapped his hands, as if somehow that could pull the whole conversation together. "They are top-notch slayers. Look, I know it would hardly be seemly to bring them up here and allow them to parade around the office. But I thought if we could, at the very least, forward their contact information to Famine and Gluttony…"

Satan picked up his head. He stared so intently at Preston that the man became visibly uncomfortable.

"You think that those children could take down Rahman-Reza?"

"Well they could *find* him, for sure…"

"I need a bit more of a guarantee than that, Preston."

"Well I…I have no guarantees." The Unchaste was sweating bullets. "But I have a *very* good guess."

"You're a nitwit, Preston." Satan broke the eye contact, looking back down at the remains of his salad.

"Thank you, sir." Preston reached up to wipe the sweat away from his shiny forehead with a handkerchief.

"I want you to do exactly as you suggested. Forward the hunters' contact information to Gluttony, *but-!*" he held up his fork, waving it threateningly. "Remind her to use *extreme* caution. Emphasize that there must be *extra* care taken or she will never listen."

"Do you honestly think they could kill one as powerful as her?" Preston asked, genuinely concerned.

Satan shrugged powerful shoulders. "We've never dealt with anything like this before." He said. "And I would rather not take the chance."

Preston nodded, his head bobbing up and down on his scrawny neck like a bird.

"I will forward the documents right away, sir." He picked the file back up and spun on his heels, the rubber soles of his running shoes squeaking as he walked out of the room.

Satan cringed at the sound, stabbing his salad vindictively when the office door finally shut.

"**W**as that entirely necessary?"

Dinner had played out its melodrama and ended with Charlie inviting both guests into the parlor for brandy and a game of Hazard. Suzanne and Jean-François had both retired for the evening, declaring exhaustion on both their parts.

James had asked for a moment and adjourned to the hallway, dragging Henry behind him like a misbehaving child.

"What are you talking about?" Henry reclaimed his arm, tearing it out of James' grip.

"Undermining me like that," James glared up at him over the gleaming rims of his round glasses. "You said that we might consider taking advantage of their 'generosity' for a night—are you absolutely *mad?*"

"Oh, forgive me." Henry set a hand on his chest, feigning contrition. "I thought you might enjoy a feather bed for a change."

"Do not insult me by acting like this is for my sake." James derided. "It is not *my* bed you have an interest in."

"My dear doctor, do not tell me that you think I am besotted with desire for a woman I barely know."

"I would not put it past you. I saw the way you were eyeing her."

"Yes, you were ogling her as well." Henry snipped. "Do not deny that you were also searching for the color of her soul."

"I was," James admitted. "And I found it to be brown — not only unremarkable, but also lacking in true bitterness. She has a soul that harbors resentment, the same as any young, spoiled child who is born into privilege and has most of it taken away. It is certainly not risking our necks over."

"Do you honestly think we are in danger, here?" Henry sounded skeptical. "If she is so much a child — and her brother so absolutely clueless — what have we to fear?"

"How about," James lowered his voice to a murmur, "the demon in the other room?"

Henry furrowed his brow. "You don't like Charlie?"

"He makes my skin crawl. I don't know why." James felt uncomfortable even admitting it. "But the way he looks at me is vastly different from the way he does you. Believe me Henry, I have seen it. If I don't step out of the way, he will push me."

"You know what I think?" Henry tried to turn the conversation around, granting his voice a teasing lilt, "I think that you are a bit jealous."

"And I think that *you* are being obnoxious." James set his teeth. "You have dragged me into your madness before, Henry, but this is something different. It does not settle well with me, and I refuse to sleep with a sour stomach. I am not staying here tonight. You can either leave with me, or catch up later if you are still in one piece."

"I don't know where you think you are going to go." Henry said, any traces of mirth dissipating in the face of James' unrelenting dour mood. "So long after dark and so far from dawn."

"Almost anywhere is preferable to here." James felt another shiver crawling up the length his spine. "The walls are brighter, but it is just as ugly as its surrounding. It is terror and tyranny in small. Can you not see that?"

"I never thought I would hear you complain about the smell of death."

"It isn't the smell that bothers me. It is the lack of it." James leaned in. "Charlie is so old, so powerful. I don't know what he is capable of. Neither do you. And neither does Suzanne."

"I think you are overreacting, which should not surprise me. You have always been an anxious little creature."

That struck a hurtful chord. James stepped back, already turning on his heel to leave.

"If you have need of me, I will be in town. Although I will try my best to be difficult to find."

"If I need you," Henry assured him, "I will find you."

James nodded, pausing to give Henry one last, meaningful look.

"I know." James said. "Just make sure that Charlie doesn't do the same."

With that, James left, making sure to grab a coat on his way out.

Charlie rattled the pair of dice in his hand. The way their smooth sides knocked together created such an appealing sound—almost good enough to consider eating. They *were* made of bone, but it was whalebone. Nothing he was interested in.

Henry stepped into the parlor, closing the double doors behind him. Charlie stopped shaking the dice long enough to look up at him and gesture towards the bottle of brandy.

"Help yourself," he said.

"Thank you," was Henry's reply. He walked towards the bottle and grabbed it by the neck, lifting it and holding it up long enough to examine the contents before tipping it over and filling up a small glass.

"Your companion has gone?" Charlie shook the dice again and released them onto the little painted table.

"He is none too happy with me." Henry collapsed into a chair across from the Elder and sipped his brandy. Charlie eyed him surreptitiously.

"That is a shame." Charlie said. "But nothing less than what I expected."

Henry shrugged. "He will come around. James doesn't like to walk into anything he doesn't feel like he has complete control over. And he doesn't trust you."

"Do *you* trust me?" Charlie leaned back in his seat, bringing up one ankle to rest across the opposite knee.

Henry hesitated, narrowing his eyes. "No, not especially. But I am intrigued by you."

"Intrigue is twice as dangerous as trust." Charlie replied. "We would risk all to satisfy our curiosity."

"I have a feeling that you are going to tempt me with an offer." Henry said. "Even if I do not accept it, I can still take notes on the method. There is much to be *learned* from you.

I am not as young as James, but I've never encountered a true Elder, either."

Charlie drummed his fingers against the side of his glass. "You don't even know if I *have* an offer."

"Don't you?"

"Perhaps." Charlie slipped one finger along the rim of the glass, gathering up the traces of brandy left behind by his lips. "I could go on to make a pious speech about the opprobrium of waste. But the fact of it is that this city has already drawn a lot of attention from the higher-ups." Charlie placed his fingertip against his bottom lip, making it shiny with a smear of alcohol. "And I don't just mean Heaven and Hell. This place was crawling with grim reapers when I arrived. I haven't seen as many recently, but I do not need those vultures flocking and pillaging corpses. The Upside-Down may be a neutral institution, but I would rather not risk being seen and pursued. Crimson and I are not on the best of terms."

"Crimson Death, the head of their Ministry? I feel like there is a decent story behind that." Henry interjected.

Charlie waved his hand dismissively. "What I am insinuating is that with another demon following behind me to clean up the souls of the bodies I dismantle, the reapers will have less to gather and their numbers will dwindle. The angels will disappear altogether—though I haven't sensed many around here to begin with."

Henry nodded. "The Almighty has no interest in the fall of the corrupt. Now if this were a religious inquisition, we would be beating angels off with sticks."

Charlie scowled. "I prefer not to ruminate. I dread the next period of reform."

"I think it an interesting proposal." Henry said, turning his nearly-empty glass in his hand. "Though it does come with its own set of risks. For instance, the gathering of souls without a contract…"

"Henry," Charlie said derisively, "neither of us are here because we are good at following procedure."

Henry conceded with a wry smile. "I don't consider myself rebellious. All I care about is eating."

"Well then," Charlie smiled, fingering his glass coyly. "If Hell will not give us bread, then let us eat pastry."

Dawn was spewing sickly yellow smears across a pale blue sky, the color trickling like bile down the chin of a cholera victim. James regarded it through the thin speckled layer of grime that was collecting on the lens of his glasses, adjusting his position so that every sore muscle in his body screamed. At least his leg, which had spent almost an hour numb, finally felt like it was coming back to life.

He had spent the tail end of the night on the stoop of a small shop. There was no sign over the door, nothing propped up in the window to give even a slight indication of what sort of business was conducted here. He had only stopped because he had grown tired of walking, and he was grousing over the idea that he would eventually have to return to Henry.

He would move on eventually. Right now, his leg was asleep.

James took off his glasses and whipped a handkerchief out of his pocket. He swept the cloth over his lenses, rubbing away the stubborn flecks of dirt and water spots that had accumulated on the expensive glass. While he was occupied, something brushed over the back of his neck.

He thought it was a bug until he felt a sharp tug on one his curls. James lurched forward, staggering to his feet. He turned around, dragging the leg that was still tingling, and slipped his glasses back up his nose; as if he needed them for anything more than style.

A scrawny boy was perched on the top step, his narrow shoulder practically married to the door. His thick, unruly white hair had been pulled back into a loose knot with several rebellious strands escaping to curl near the nape of his neck. His dusty blue coat looked too small, as if it had fit not too long ago but he had since grown out of it. He stared at James, unblinking, from behind round frames large enough to cover the better part of his face.

"It is good quality," the boy said. "And very soft."

James furrowed his brow. *"What?"*

"Your hair." The boy cocked his head, eyes widening like a particularly exasperated owl. "I use that kind for my sweethearts."

Clearly, the urchin was deranged.

"How nice." James responded, disgruntled.

"You look tired." The boy stood. "You could use a spot of tea."

As soon as he stretched to his full height the word *'boy'* fled from James' head entirely. This person was well over six feet tall by five inches or more. He eclipsed the doorway where he stood, but he still had the face of a youth. He didn't look like he could have been older than seventeen.

He wasn't human. There was no way in Hell, even though he did look more like Heaven's type.

"Come on inside." The man opened the door to the little shop—even though it had been locked and he did not bother to pull out a key. "Sorry the place is a bit of a mess."

James shook his head ardently. "No, thank you. I have to be somewhere."

"Mhm." The man gave him a wintry artificial smile and then stooped to step through the doorway. James watched him disappear, suddenly feeling compelled to follow.

Incognizant of the fact that he had even moved, James found himself back on the steps. The empty black doorway gaped open like a mouth, the very act of going forward too much like being swallowed by a snake.

It didn't feel like he had much of a choice between this creature's will and his own damning curiosity. James held his breath, taking his first step across the threshold. He stretched out his right hand and held it in front of him cautiously as he took another step.

Light spilled onto his fingers—the ugly yellow kind emitted by a gas flame. The world was suddenly much brighter as James entered the cramped and cluttered shop where every corner and empty shelf was stuffed with blinding, colorful lamps.

The man hummed, stripping off his coat almost immediately and throwing it over the back of an overstuffed chair. James shut the door behind him, his head twisting every which way it could as he tried to take in his surroundings. The ceiling looked much higher than it should have been, and he could not actually see it, despite the lights keeping everything else so well-lit. The walls were filled with shelves which held nothing but attractive lamps and rows upon rows of dolls. They were all different sizes, some as large as children while others were small enough to fit in his hand. Their long, delicate limbs were jointed; even the fingers on some of the larger models had joints, which amazed him. Their bodies were all skillfully painted and hyper-realistic—with glass eyes and what looked like genuine hair. With the way the shadows played off their faces, they looked very much alive.

James realized his mouth was hanging open. He looked over at the man now sitting in the big chair, who smirked as he reached behind his head to gather up his loose hair and re-wrap it into a tighter knot.

All James could think to say was, "A *bit* of a mess?"

"I know." The man tied off his hair and his hands fell into his lap. "It is actually awful."

The man set his worn boots up on a desk, his soles facing an oriel window. The street was clearly visible from within, but James remembered trying to look inside the window earlier and being greeted by nothing but darkness. There had not even been a hint of the wooden desk that was pushed so far up against it now.

"And these are your 'sweethearts'?" James swept a hand over his head to indicate the surrounding dolls.

The man nodded. "Every one. I know all of their names." He tilted his head back, the light reflecting off his large glasses and turning them into beams. "I have a new one coming along—Cassandra. Except she's being a bit stubborn." He slid his boots off the desk and sat up straight, leaning over to touch the bald head of a doll that James hadn't noticed beforehand.

"It's her hair." The man sighed. "The wig I made for her was not *right*." He turned opaline eyes towards James again. "That is why I was enamored with yours. I think it is *perfect*."

That was the line, right there. James was not going to negotiate his release with a pair of shears held up to his hair. As much as he hated his curls, he hated the idea of being without them even more.

The man must have noticed the look on his face. "That isn't why I brought you in here."

"Right," James said tersely. "I believe you mentioned tea."

"Yes," the man sprang out of the chair, sliding his hand over the back of it as he pivoted and vanished behind a bookcase—a space where James had assumed there was nothing but wall. "Tea brightens the soul. But you wouldn't know about that, would you?"

James paused. "Is it so obvious?"

The man re-emerged, pushing a small tea tray. "You smell like offal and considering you look rather well-kempt, I chalked the stink up to Sulphur. Did I miss the mark?"

"No," James said. "But it does seem to put me at a disadvantage, considering I have no idea what you are or what division you are from."

The wheels on the cart squealed as they came to a halt. Impossibly long fingers wrapped around the teapot handle, lifting it from the very center of the tray.

"Life is full of annoying little disadvantages. And as they say, the Devil is in the details." the dollmaker tipped the teapot just enough to start filling up the little China cups he had set out. "I am not the Devil." He punctuated. "But you probably knew that."

"You are from Heaven, aren't you?" James looked him up and down.

"That would be correct." That earned him a grin, a flash of unnaturally pointed teeth.

"I thought so." James said. "Your type never quite learned how to blend in."

"My type?" white eyebrows shot up, and the smile quickly slipped into a sneer. "You don't even know what 'my type' is. Yours was easy — *demon.*"

"Yes, well." James sniffed imperiously. "Only two things fall from Heaven: mana and angels. And you don't look edible."

"I take personal offense to that." The Heavenly creature pouted. "You haven't even tried to taste."

James shot him a dry look, and the angel lifted up a lemon wedge, giving it a playful squeeze.

"Lemon?" he asked.

"Thank you." James nodded.

"My name is Virgil." The angel swept an annoying strand of hair back from his eyes as he lifted the teacup by its saucer and offered it to James. "Virgil Abney. Or Yehiel. Whichever — they're equally pretentious."

"James Highmore. Or Mojgan. I prefer James."

"Really? I wouldn't have pegged you for a 'James'." Virgil sat back down in his chair, blowing on his tea. "Have a seat."

James shrugged. "It was assigned by my department." He looked around for a chair, uncovering a stool by pushing a haphazard stack of newspapers onto the floor. He sat down on top of it, hooking an ankle around one of the legs.

"Hell continues to impress." Virgil sipped his tea, the fingers of his free hand busily dancing over the shoulders his latest project still sitting on his desk. "I thought red would go nicely with her eyes. They are such a nice shade of green but she didn't seem to agree. Black would go better I suppose. But those curls. How do you manage them?"

"I don't," James admitted. "They just act out on their own."

"I am afraid she would not be able to keep up with them. But who am I to say... I am weak in the face of their desires."

James just kept nodding.

"Did Heaven grant you an assignment?" he tried to change the subject and ended up veering onto the unasked question that made his guts quiver.

"Not exactly." Virgil picked up Cassandra and started playing with her small fingers, his tea forgotten. Her hand was a third of his. "I've been told I am a disgrace."

"So..." James took another sip of his tea, even though he had already decided that he didn't care for this kind. "You are Fallen?"

"No," Virgil answered firmly. "I am on unpaid leave."

"The difference being...?"

"To be officially categorized as Unchaste, Hell would have to process my papers." The angel said. "And they can't do that, considering I lost them. I could obtain copies from Heaven, but I would rather not. I like where I am. My sweethearts give me joy, and I am a creature of joy."

"I thought angels were creatures of vengeance?" James seemed amused.

Virgil pouted his lips again. "Little more than a sword." His words faded out as he started picking at a small flaw on Cassandra's face. "Little more than a sword…must you remind me?"

James barely heard the final words. The angel, now engrossed with his project, had forgotten his tea altogether and did not seem interested in carrying on further conversation.

James sighed internally and resigned himself to watching. There were far worse ways to pass an afternoon.

CHAPTER V

It was nearly impossible to breathe. The small dining room was so hot that the air had become thick and uncomfortable, scorching the nasal passages and tickling the throat with a thorny burn. Every window was shut, every curtain was drawn, and every door was pulled closed and locked. There was no light except for the orange glow of the fire, where the 'former' Duchess Babette de Bellerose was kneeling, tending to the hearth and drenched in so much sweat that her thin nightgown was soaked through, clinging to her full figure. Claire did not envy their hostess at all. Even sitting across the room as close to the exit as possible, her eyes were watering to the point where she could barely see and her throat felt like it was going to swell shut. It was a necessary wickedness, the use of heat. And all that mattered was that the duke and duchess were sweating far more than she was.

Not only were they all suffering immensely, but the persimmon pudding was beginning to soften.

Their host, Duke Cosme de Bellerose, had not touched it. His own piece still sat snugly in a chipped teacup, as Claire and Edward had been particularly insistent against the use of plates. Claire had watched the stiff point droop over the course of the incredibly intense meal, during which nothing had been said and the only sounds were the crackling of the fireplace and gold spoons tapping against China cups.

Finally, Claire rested her spoon across the mouth of her teacup. Her quick fingers snatched up a linen napkin and twisted up one of the corners so she could dab at the corner of her mouth. A smear of dark red lipstick transferred onto the cloth.

Across the table, her brother belched. It went magnanimously ignored.

"Tell me about your problem, Duke de Bellerose." Claire used his title without a qualm, hoping that it would gratify Cosme enough to speak. The duke puffed up his chest a little bit and leaned forward, one finger idly stroking the curved lip of his teacup.

"You have to understand, we are not entirely sure how the creature found us." He squinted, as if he was having a hard time seeing through the haze of firelight. "It sort of just..."

"Appeared?" Edward prompted. Claire kicked him so hard underneath the table that he spilt wine all over his chin.

"*Infested.*" The duke dabbed his sweaty forehead with a defeated handkerchief. "It began with the house...the way it groaned and creaked more than usual. There were water spots where none had existed before, and over time they grew bigger and bigger, growing black with mold and then bulging, peeling. We found a lot of insects, they would gather around the area of breed there it seemed. Then there was this sound which, at first, we thought we might have rats. It was like someone was scratching the walls from the other side of the plaster. Then it got worse—" he mopped his forehead again, his handkerchief traveling down to swipe underneath his jowls and blot the back of his neck. "At night, we thought we could hear voices."

"Whispers?" Claire leaned forward.

The duke shook his head. "It was always when we were sleeping. One of us would wake up because we heard someone screaming in our ear. It was always a nasty insult and a very loud, abrupt sound. It did not continue once we opened our eyes and managed to sit up. But then it would happen again the next night. Whatever is *in this house,* it is trying to drive us all mad."

"It drove your son mad," Claire added. "Christophe?"

Babette made a sound like she was choking back a sob. She put her hand over her mouth, a hot tear escaping to stream down her flushed pink cheek.

"He…" Cosme clenched the arm of his chair. "He killed himself."

"He put his hands on his head and crushed his own skull like an eggshell." Babette said, her voice strained. "And there was nothing inside. It was like someone had scooped out his brain."

"Or eaten it." Claire kept her eyes riveted on the duke across from her. "Your grace, I believe your son was responsible for the presence of the demon."

"He claimed he couldn't hear the voices." The duchess continued in her overwhelming grief. "But he saw things we couldn't."

"We only saw the bugs." The duke added. "He saw people. He said they were 'peeking shadows' and that he would catch them peering around corners and staring at him with 'round white eyes bigger than teacup saucers'. He said their eyes were so bright that they kept him awake at night. He said they never spoke, and every time he tried to look at them directly, they would vanish."

"The itching…" Babette added.

The duke nodded. "He scratched at his arms, he chewed on his nails and picked at the edges of the nail beds until they bled. Towards the end, he had started acting like he was trying to turn himself inside out."

Edward sucked another dollop of persimmon pudding loudly off his spoon, casting his sister a look from the corner of his eye. He popped it out his mouth and waved it almost accusingly in the direction of his host.

"If your son *was* responsible, and the demon claimed its prize, then it should be gone by now. There is no reason for it to linger."

"Unless," Claire interjected, "he signed away the duke and duchess as well." They may as well have been alone.

All the blood drained from Cosme's face. "I—"

"That does *not* make it your fault." Edward assured him. "The policy is a bit unclear on this one, but because you had no knowledge of your son's actions, I do not think you should have to recant before we take action."

"He might sign an official statement." Claire drummed her fingernails on the table. "Just to be on the safe side."

"Sure," Edward agreed. "He may do so while we start looking. I had a *feeling* you know—as soon as we walked through the door. Do you think it might be in the walls?"

"It might be." Claire mused. "Or it might already be in his blood."

Edward nodded, already standing up. "Thank you for the pudding," he said. "It was delightful."

"Where are you going?" the duke stood as well, feeling queasy all the sudden. "What do you mean, in my blood?"

"Do not trouble yourself with it." Claire stood and pushed her chair back underneath the table, throwing down her napkin on top of the abandoned place setting. "You have the cheque?"

The duke paused, as if he was taking a moment to process what she was saying. He then nodded vigorously, reaching into his jacket and withdrawing a folded piece of paper. "It is what you asked for," he said, "and more, as thanks…"

"Greatly appreciated." She plucked it out of his hand, cramming it inside her immodestly low bodice and glancing over her shoulder at her brother. "Are you ready?"

"As I will ever be." Edward bowed to their host. "Kindly remember not to open the windows or any other doors until we have gone. If you do so, the consequences will be dire." He flashed a smile and made his exit, following closely at Claire's heels.

"All right," Edward said, closing the door behind them once they had entered the hallway. "That room was unnecessarily hot."

"They argue less the more they sweat." Claire pushed back a panel of her skirt, pulling the obsidian blade free from the sheath that was strapped to her upper thigh. "And I prefer to keep the meetings brief."

"You make a fair point." Edward shrugged, sliding his own blade out from its place within his sleeve. "I thought the pudding was mediocre."

"Yes, they could have done better with that." She agreed.

The walls groaned. Claire held out her hand, motioning for her brother to halt as she glanced around, tightening her hold on the blade. Her stomach fluttered as she glanced up at the roof, expecting to see the tell-tale signs that the duke had described to them earlier: the dark water-spots, the nest of insects...

Instead, they were met with sudden silence. The groaning stopped, and all Claire could hear was the sound of her own blood roaring in her ears.

Then there was a sudden, sickly thump sounding like a dozen hands thudding against the wall at once. It was followed by a cacophony of scratches—nails raking against wood and plaster, harsh and grating while getting louder and louder. The roar was deafening and Claire almost dropped her knife in an attempt to reach up and cover her ears, cringing at the horrible sound.

At the end of the hall, she saw blinking white lights. She could barely make out a vaguely humanoid shadow peering around the corner, and it vanished as soon as she looked twice.

"Edward!" she took off down the hall, yelling for her brother to follow her. He bolted in the same direction, following her lead even though she wasn't altogether sure whether they had seen the same thing. The hallway ended unexpectedly, with the shadows cast by the low lighting giving it the illusion of being longer than it was. The hunters came to a grinding halt, the rug bunching up underneath their feet as they narrowly avoided crashing into a wall.

Claire leaned heavily against the wall, suddenly finding it very difficult to breathe. It bothered her, because she was not easily winded.

"Claire," Edward whispered. "I think it's…"

A loud, distorted moan swallowed up the rest of his sentence. Claire swallowed hard and lifted her head, her eyes fighting to adjust enough to the darkness to see what was right in front of her.

It was a swarm of large, black flies. Their buzzing made a sound like a human groan, warped like it was coming from the end of a long tunnel. They came together, forming a tight ball, then expanded once more into a cloud that hovered in the middle of the hallway. There was no getting past them, and there was barely a foot of space in-between them and the two hunters. Claire kept her back against the wall, her fingers still wrapped around the slim handle of her obsidian blade. She refused to tear her eyes away, unsure as to how she was going to kill something with no real form.

The cloud shrank again, the unbearable moaning getting loud as the flies started crowding against each other. They writhed in the air, dense bodies clicking like marbles as they bumped into one another. They parted slightly down the middle, their shape now resembling a yawning, open mouth.

The moaning died down and what looked like a human form was starting to bleed into being, eking out from the surrounding darkness. The flies disbanded, or perhaps they simply melded into the demon that was forming in their midst. Claire saw mottled grey hands reach up to adjust the wide brim of a tall back hat, luminous red eyes rolling upwards to regard her with a sneer that closely followed.

Suddenly it was easier to breathe; but her chest ached and her head felt light.

"*Clifton,*" the demon wheezed, its voice sounding like it was being played off a wax cylinder. "*Vio-let Clif-ton.*"

"Violet Clifton was my mother." Claire said, gritting her teeth. "My name is Claire."

"Violet Clifton was swallowed whole, a demon dug the silver right out of her." The sneer turned into a grin that flaunted sharp, jagged teeth. *"But left the parts, the tasty parts. Brains and bladder and lungs and guts…"*

"Claire!" there was a streak of panic in Edward's voice, he brandished his knife, the blade practically invisible in the shadows. "Make it stop!"

"…Kidneys and liver and a thrashing tongue, hot and writhing and screaming…"

Claire stuck the demon with her knife, but her hand went right through its chest as if it were composed of nothing more than vapor. The demon didn't even seemed fazed.

"Demon blood is bitter blood. Your blood is poison, your guts are black…"

It grabbed her wrists, pulling her up and flinging her back. She hit the wall, her head colliding with white stucco. Stars burst across her vision as she fell to the ground, only vaguely aware once she hit the floor that she was no longer holding her knife.

Edward gripped his own blade, slicing it through the air. The demon turned towards him, snarling, and before it could move again the blade collided with its throat, the edge burying itself deep into uncomfortably soft flesh.

The demon gurgled, red eyes flickering like a sputtering candle flame. Its death-colored hands reached up to claw at the blade stuck in its throat, but Edward pulled the knife out and watched as blood, black and thick as tar, seeped sluggishly from the opening. Red eyes flashed white, turning back to their original color before the demon's form completely dissipated, the walls wet and black with mold after the fact.

Edward immediately moved to be by his sister's side, but Claire was already pushing herself up off the floor. The blow to her head had knocked most of her hair out of its careful arrangement, but otherwise she did not seem harmed.

She pushed her loose curls out of her face, annoyed. "Where is my knife?" she asked.

Edward looked around, finally spotting it close by her foot. He picked it up and handed it back to her. There was a pause as she inspected it, taking a moment before deciding she was satisfied and slipping it back into its sheath.

"I don't think the demon is gone." She looked up at her brother, holding out a hand for his help. "I think it has already found its way into the duke's blood. You can't kill a demon of infestation with a blade, not when it has a host."

"So what do we do?" Edward assisted in pulling her up to her feet.

"Burn it all down." She said. "Duke, duchess, and ancestral home. We've no other choice."

"Won't they be able to get out?"

"How, Edward? They are penned in the dining room."

He fretted a moment, worrying his bottom lip as he looked around. The walls were in grim condition, and he knew they had only witnessed a fraction of the demon's capabilities.

"They have already paid us, correct?" he queried.

"Yes." She responded.

"All right," he said, already eyeing one of the few burning lamps. "Let's do it and have this be over."

"Where do you want to go after this?" she was moving as quickly as her sore limbs would allow, favoring her right foot slightly.

"I don't know." He admitted. "Somewhere with a bed."

"It looks as though you have done it at last, Jean."

Jean-François looked up in surprise, his morning tea paused halfway to his lips. His ginger curls nearly obscured his light red eyebrows when they shot upward in a quizzical expression. "What have I done?"

"Well, *you* did nothing I suppose. Which is for the better." Suzanne sat down next to him, grabbing the ruffled edge of her robe and pulling it around to cover her legs as she crossed them. She set a letter down on top of his breakfast plate, the butter from his roll seeping into the paper from the middle and blurring the ink.

Jean-François set his tea down quickly, picking the letter before it became indecipherable.

"The Committee had this brought to us just now." Suzanne told him. "It is a letter announcing your promotion. A seat above yours just opened up and they want your ass to fill it. And this is only the beginning." She picked up his roll, pulling apart the soft middle and placing it on her tongue.

He gave her an annoyed look. "So in other words, everything is going as it should?"

"So far." She answered with a nod. "And things will continue to go this well, if the demon delivers."

"He ought to, for his price." Jean-François set the letter back down beside his plate and picked up his tea once more.

"I know our plan was only one seat every few months to keep suspicion from arising." She said. "But I believe that we have the room to move faster. And I think we *should*. The sooner you topple the Head of the Committee, the sooner we can turn things around bring everything back to…"

She paused, stopping herself short of uttering the words 'back to normal'. A state of normality was not one that either of them craved. Yet they did want things to be *different.*

As de Voclains, they were perfectionists. The utopia of their minds was best formed by their own hands.

"I will make my way to them anon. May I finish my breakfast?"

"Eat quickly." She scoffed, setting the remnant of his roll back down on his plate and standing up. "We don't wish for them to realize their mistake."

"You have an inspiring amount of faith in me." He said dryly, reaching for new roll.

"Brother," Suzanne sucked sweet butter off her fingertips. "If I thought you could accomplish this on your own, I would not have summoned a demon to do it instead."

"**D**o you think this era has phones?"

Famine slammed on his brakes. Not because his wife was still talking forty minutes after their departure from the apartment; but because traffic was backed up both ways with no end in sight. They had not even reached the gates of Hell. Apparently, everyone was in as much of a hurry to get in as they were leave.

"Doubtful, baby cakes." He started fiddling with the knob of the radio. As usual for this region, it was only playing NPR no matter what station it landed on. He sighed inwardly and leaned back in his seat, fingers like steel coils around the steering wheel, making the leather whimper with maltreatment. "Phones are fairly recent for them down there."

"But Daddy-O, how are Vanity and I supposed to keep up?"

"You and I both know that Vanity is perfectly capable of holding a conversation with herself for at least a millennium. If not longer."

"Don't be rude. That only happened once, and it was *only* half a century."

"You set down the phone right before we launched the campaign for a new world war. She was still talking when you picked it back up."

"She knew I was busy!"

"She could have kept going." Famine slammed on his brakes again, grinding his palm into the center of the wheel to blare his horn. "…Bless it!"

"What if she has to call me? What if I have to call *her*?"

He ground his teeth. His cheeks were so gaunt his shifting jawbone was visible in the rearview mirror, the motion only emphasized by the spread of blonde hair that made up his trimmed goatee.

"The old-fashioned way. Draw a sigil on the floor and start chanting."

"That's *so* impractical. Besides, I thought the boss said that we weren't allowed to make any new summons without approval?"

"And our company motto is to always question authority." He replied shortly.

Gluttony leaned back in her seat. She looked like she was going to put her feet up on the dashboard — even though he had told her countless times how much he hated that. "And look at how well that worked out for Rahman-Reza."

His lip curled into a barely restrained snarl, flashing pointed canines. Rahman-Reza, the splinter in his ass for over a century, was not his favorite topic. But the demon was *her* wayward child, not his. She had every right to speak about him and process her grief how she pleased.

"He was worth more than all the others, Famine."

"So you say. And then he proved himself to be just like all of them…gluttonous, savage, and relentless."

"I was so proud." She sniffed.

"It is disgusting. All of Hell lacks control."

"With the exception of you and yours." She reached down into the floorboard and grabbed the handles of her beaded clutch purse, pulling it up into her lap and popping it open. Her hand dove inside, digging around the satin-lined depths in search of her stash of sweets. "Mister 'if any slack is given, I pick it up and pull too tight'."

"Only the weak are ever broken by hunger."

"You say as I stuff my face!" she murmured through a mouthful of dark chocolate.

"I never said that I approved of your incessant binging."

"Mm, you only tolerate it because you like thick thighs."

He scoffed audibly. "I never said that either." The traffic was beginning to pick up—and thank the Netherlord for it. He was nearly ready to be on the surface where the sounds of chewing and crinkling candy wrappers would not drive him absolutely out of his mind.

She could have any figure she wanted—yet she deliberately chose thick thighs and rounded hips *knowing* how much he hated anything broader than a stickpin. She kept her bosom voluptuous as well, but she forewent a broad middle — opting instead to keep her waist trim. Despite this, her stomach was not flat. There was still enough flesh for him to grab whenever he reached around to hold her.

He told her, the night before their union, that she should at least *try* to look like a woman he would marry. Her response was to make him feed her ceremonial cake the next day.

"If I am so vile then why do you still sleep with me?" she asked him snidely, running her tongue viciously over the white inside of her candy wrapper.

A ridiculous question — and one he was not sure how to answer. Rather than spew out something he would regret, he just kept silent. At this stage of the argument nothing would have satisfied her, anyway.

Gluttony was never satisfied.

She hit the radio button with a solitary unsullied finger. They were out of NPR range at this point, but now they had to suffer through a multitude of stations dedicated entirely to amateur sludge metal.

Outstanding. Damnation had been far kinder in the era of synth pop.

"Just turn it off," he said, "I can't stand it. I would rather the silence."

"I could sing." She threatened.

The argument ended there.

It was going to be a long drive to the mortal coil.

CHAPTER VI

He knew there was going to be an issue because no one called him Meriwether anymore. Not even Francis—even when he was angry.

And yet the letter sprawling so gracelessly across the painted surface of his sitting room table had it splayed brashly across the headline in bold typeface. *Meriwether Lou Hayward.*

They didn't even bother to abbreviate the middle name. Something was *definitely* up.

Lady laced his fingers together and glanced up at his husband. Francis was the one who had brought the letter in. He had apparently found it crammed into their letterbox which Lady *thought* he had glued shut.

"Don't look at me," the dark-haired man said, lifting his thick eyebrows and shrugging to indicate helplessness. "I haven't read past the first line either."

"I am very disappointed in you." Lady squinted, trying to make out the smaller, narrower words underneath his name without having to actually pick it up and read it. "If I don't get my fingerprints on it, they have no proof that I ever received it, right? I cannot be held responsible for what I never read."

"The seal is broken. And you are wearing gloves." Francis reminded him, lifting the dark mug off the table and extending it towards his partner. "Here is your coffee."

Lady spared his husband a disdainful glance before extending his aforementioned finely gloved hand and wrapping his fingers around the mug's middle. It warmed the satin and might have burned him if Francis didn't release enough of the handle for Lady to take hold of the rigid curve.

"I did not think that anyone in Hell knew where we were." Lady muttered, dragging his lips over the blistering rim and letting the steam cloud his glasses. He was past caring. "And it so unlike them to be courteous enough to send a note before exacting *doom*."

Francis only nodded, half-listening as he picked up the letter and turned it around in his hands. The paper was thick and old, devoid of any official letterhead or bold signature. The body of it had been typed with some of the ink fading or rubbing off in places.

"It doesn't make a lot of sense." Francis finally said, ready to crumple it up in his hands out of frustration. "It's talking about—what is this word, *droids?*"

Lady's eyes widened. He hopped onto his feet and set down his mug, snatching the letter out of his husband's hands. "You're useless." He said, making a shooing motion with his free hand as his own tawny-colored eyes scanned the page. "This isn't from Hell."

Francis acknowledged this statement with a soft *'mm'* as he went back to his own coffee, settling down onto the opposite side of the divan and taking a sip.

"This is from Raziel." Lady flicked the middle of the paper, nearly punching a hole right through. "And it does not have Heaven's letterhead so it's personal—only *he* knows where we are. Why he would bother to write me I don't know…"

"To tell you about his droids. Presumably."

"Other than that." Lady flipped the letter over. There was a single orphan sentence on the back, sitting right on top of a small signature so insignificant and cramped that it was no wonder Francis had missed it the first time.

Lady fell silent. Francis sipped loudly again from his rim, although that was not enough to distract Lady from noticing how he was still being watched.

Lady glanced back up. His fingers gripped the paper so tightly that it was a wonder the whole letter did not disintegrate in his hands.

"Let me guess," the former intern tried to lift some of the tension away, "he asked for your hand in marriage?"

Lady shook his head, tossing the paper down onto the table and spinning on his heel until he had flopped gracelessly down onto the divan, one hand flying up dramatically to rest on his brow bone as his eyelids sank to a close, his breath escaping from between his full lips with a curious whimper.

"Screw the coffee," he said. "I need whiskey."

Francis didn't say a word, but Lady heard the heavy bottom of his mug clatter as it came to rest against the table.

"He said that there is a rumor going around. It's nothing official yet. But he said he heard the latest from Michael, so it might as well be." Even as he spoke the words, Lady groaned. He had not experienced tension headaches in a while, but he could feel one charging towards the back of his skull with startling velocity. "Heaven is going to extend an offer to—take me back."

"*What?*" Francis nearly dropped the glass decanter he was holding. "After all this time? How many years since you were processed, sir?"

"It's been five hundred years. And Heaven wants to wipe all of that from the record, apparently." Lady leaned forward, resting his elbows on his knees as he pushed his face into his hands. His auburn hair tumbled forward, loose waves curling around his wrists. "If the Almighty gives approval—and I don't know why he *would*—I'm done for…I am absolutely done for, Francis, and so are you."

"I would not go that far." Francis said quickly. "If Heaven accepts you back into the fold, so to speak, then the Almighty can grant amnesty over whatever charges Hell might think to drudge up—"

"Right. Do you think I *care* about that right now, Frank? Do you *know* how hard it is to slack off in Heaven? If I get pulled back up there, I am going to be tethered to a desk and they are going to expect every slip of paper to be turned in on time without fail. Hand me that goddamn whiskey."

His hands were still trembling, but not quite as badly as they had been. Francis picked up the decanter and turned back around, passing the entire thing off to his partner as there was no way a stubby glass was going to be sufficient. "Do you not get a choice…?"

"If Heaven decides to pick me up and Hell agrees to the transfer? No. I don't get a choice. Granted, it seems only Raziel knows where we are and that doesn't necessarily mean that we are easy to find. But we *will* be found, if Heaven tries to claim me, and then…" Lady trailed off, taking a long drink from the decanter.

"And then?" Francis prompted when his partner lowered the bottle.

Lady extended a hand, wagging his finger as he took a moment more to swallow, his nostrils burning and tears pricking the backs of his eyes. "And then you get assigned a new mentor and you have fifty more years of labor to complete your internship. That is *after* your punishment for aiding me in avoiding Hell's 'justice', and *before* you get assigned your own desk. Is that what you want Frank? To push papers for all eternity?"

"Well, to be fair I…did not realize I could have higher aspirations…before I met you." Francis paused as a prominent red blush rose quickly over his collar.

For a moment, Lady was taken aback, batting his gingery lashes in surprise. A smirk jumped onto his lips, a pretty twist of his nicely shaped mouth. "That's very sweet of you, Frank. It is nice to know that after all this time I have finally managed to cultivate a successful case of capture bonding within you."

Francis laughed, rubbing the back of his neck and looking up shyly over the rims of his glasses. "You make it sound as though you have been holding a gun to my head this entire time."

"It has no doubt been the equivalent." Lady took one last sip before setting his coffee cup down.

"What are we going to do about this letter?" Francis slid a coaster tactfully underneath the descending mug just in time.

"Take it for what it is: a warning, not a welcome. We are going to have to keep moving with Heaven on our trail now as much as Hell." Lady made an irate noise, unable to relax his rigid posture enough to even slump into his seat. "You know, sometimes I wish I had never left my office."

Henry did not know when he would cease to be dazzled by the trappings of mortal wealth, but he couldn't foresee it being anytime soon.

The de Voclain's world was a dream. He had never thought himself fond of pastels until he saw them bedecked with golden stucco. He never thought he could tolerate ruffles on his shoes or floral print on the lining of his brocade coats. And Charlie…

Charlie was an artist. It seemed as though he had been as methodical in piecing his own skeleton together as he was in pulling apart others. His graceful neck led into a square jaw, edges cut like diamonds that came together towards a pointed chin. His straight nose had a prominent ridge, sweeping upwards towards his heavy brow bone which shaded cobalt blue eyes, large and round with a watery pink line. His fingers were those of a pianist; cold, white, and unforgiving. They were impossible to follow, flashing so quickly as they worked that they were dazzling even in the gruesome process of peeling flesh away from bones.

There was something more about him too. He devoured his meals with such panache. It was difficult to watch him eat and not be mesmerized by his method, the way he pulled bones free from the red flesh that clung so stubbornly to them. If he was dining in the home, he would crack the bones between the vicious teeth of an engraved metal clamp and use his tongue to scoop out the gritty marrow from the dark centers.

He particularly liked phalanges; Henry was quickly coming to realize. He devoured them so effortlessly.

"You would enjoy your meals as well if you stopped to savor them." Charlie remarked, glancing at his companion while cracking another bone between his brutal clamps. His fingers were braced by a pair of small lions on either side of the graceful handles.

Henry picked his gaze up, forcing his eyes to meet the restless blue stare seated just a foot away. "I do," he sounded offended, his voice too loud for the small amount of distance that rested between them. "Were you under the impression that I...?"

"You eat like a starving dog at its bowl." Charlie's lips curled upward, and his long tongue slithered out betwixt his teeth. He set a sharp bone shard on the end and pulled it back into his mouth, crunching it purposefully between his back molars.

If he noticed that Henry was staring at his legs, then he was magnanimous enough not to bring it up. The long, well-toned limbs of a mercurial prince where the silken flesh and muscular calves were barely concealed by the thin white stockings of fashion's decree.

"So I have heard before," Henry muttered, shifting in embarrassment underneath the judgmental stare. "Instinct works against me in this case."

"True refinement is learning how to straddle the line that runs between our most barbaric instincts and the repression of our natures." Charlie slid the length of one leg across his other knee, pulling it back so that his thighs were spread further apart and he leaned forward, resting a hand on top of his sinful ankle. "It is lazy to place the blame on instinct when you are the master of your own flesh, are you not?"

Henry pursed his lips. "Verily."

"You have a better hold over your body than any mortal man. You choose and craft your own corporeal form." Charlie squeezed the metal clamp in his hands, flexing it open and closed as if he could not stand to keep his fingers still. "I can see you for what you truly are, *Jahangir*, and I know you are a far more capable fool than you would allow Hell to believe."

Henry snorted, trying to hide his obvious pleasure at having made even a miniscule impression. "One of my best kept secrets. You can't give them too much to work with or they will work you to death."

Charlie laughed. It was a sharp, sudden sound like a bone breaking in half. Henry's heart leapt, slamming into his ribcage with no indication as to whether fear or another, heavier emotion propelled it forward.

"You know I would love to break your skull apart." The elder demon teased. "If I ripped it off your neck and shook it up, I wonder what coquettish thoughts I could lick up from the fragments?"

Henry's lips gave way to a nervous smile. "I'm afraid there isn't much up there to scramble. You would be wasting your time."

"There you go once more, never quite giving yourself enough credit." Charlie's lashes were a lazy lace canopy draped over sharp cobalt eyes; barely dulling them enough to deflect their ability to completely etiolate the will. "I will decide how my time is best spent. Would you care to accompany me?"

Without missing a beat, Charlie was already standing. It appeared that the expectation was that Henry would follow his lead and Henry, within the whirling confines of his own skull, could not think of a reason to resist.

"As long as your intention is not to lead me to some dark alley and start extracting the ossicles from my ears."

Charlie scoffed, his hands traveling to flick life back into his limp coattails. "I am dining out, dearest, but not on you."

"It is just as well." Henry spoke before he could stop himself. "I have far more pleasing extremities for you to gorge to your satisfaction."

Silence dropped between them. Charlie rotated on a golden heel and drew darkness around his shoulders like a cloak, the very motion seemingly sapping all of the light from the room. He took a step towards his companion, his white hand ghostly as it settled against Henry's cheek, chilling him down to the core, forming a ball of ice in his throat.

"Oh," his voice was as smooth as the surface of a still lake, "if I were to make a feast of you, dearest, I would be kind enough to snap your neck first."

Henry swallowed, his guts liquidating as each of Charlie's words dug in. "See," he tried to turn around the uncomfortable moment with a laugh, "that does not sound as pleasurable as my suggestion."

Charlie grinned, his teeth the very portrait of a demon. "See, it was not meant to."

Hunger pulled Edward from his sleep with all the viciousness of a wild animal attempting to rip his stomach out with its teeth. It had compelled him to roll out of bed and grope blindly in the dark for something more to wear than just his thin nightshirt. He had grabbed a pair of pants—never mind that they were Claire's—and pulled them on. He was barely able to get them to rest properly around his hips, but he didn't care about that. He had to get out of his room. At the very least, he needed some fresh air so that every breath did not feel like shards of glass being cycled through his lungs.

His feet fumbled with his shoes. His toes were too cold to slip the hard leather on properly, and he found himself giving up without much fuss. He would go barefoot. The hunger was too painful. It was all he could do to keep himself from doubling over, every pang a vicious, crippling cramp. His thighs were shaking, and he knew—he *knew*—that if he stayed here a minute longer he was going to eat Claire.

Claire. His sister. She was all he had. She understood. She distracted him.

He was going to claw his way through her back and shove his greedy maw into the soul that rested just behind her heart.

It felt too much like Nellie. Poor Nellie...the night she died he had felt the same pangs. He had picked his baby sister up out of her crib and pulled her apart like an oyster. He had sucked out her succulent soul and then Claire had sutured the terrible wound. Everything had been erased within minutes, yet here he was...still dreaming about it after all this time.

It still kept him up at night. But this was different. This time it was not the result of a nightmare.

Edward stumbled out the door, picking his way through the darkness with only moderate success. The dented metal doorknob turned with some halting protest, and the door was momentarily jammed, the warped wood unyielding this time of night. The young hunter's bare feet shuffled, calloused heels rasping across the wooden boards of the hotel floor.

The closer he got to the door, the more desperate he felt himself becoming. He felt himself doubling over mid-stride, close to crawling as he finally reached the front entrance. His hand was trembling as he grasped the handle, and he threw all that remained of his weak weight against the wood.

It felt like the hotel spat him out as the door opened easily and dumped him unceremoniously onto the stairs. Edward swore under his breath and rose, gripping the iron banister that wound its way up the side of the stairs, shaped with beaten gold leaves to resembling climbing ivy.

A casual glance around reminded him that he was not alone. Nearby a woman stood — at least, *woman* was his best and nearest guess. It could have been anything at all. And over the length of his career, he had come to learn that he should never assume *anything* to be human.

Yet she did not smell like Sulphur, and she did not seem to be in possession of the tell-tale bright blue eyes that seemed to mark every demon possessing a form.

He was moving closer, but he didn't realize it until he caught a sliver of yellow gaslight from the grim streetlamps highlighting the backs of his bruised knuckles.

The ugly red and purple blotches that marred his fair, lordly hands complimented her eyeshadow perfectly. It was smeared across her lids like a bruise and climbed up too close to her drawn-on arching black eyebrow. She puckered her lips in what looked like a pout as she waited on him, one hip bobbing up and down to a jazzy tune that only she could hear.

His stopped only a few feet away from her, enough to see that the unflattering yellow light illuminated only half her face, casting the rest in ominous shadow. He caught the scent of, rather than saw, the curl of smoke that seemed to make up the polluted trail of every demon he had ever encountered.

Except again, she still didn't feel like a demon. The only thing she made him feel was hungry.

When she spoke, she had the lilting voice of a long-dead starlet. It sounded slightly grainy, like the needle of a record player was scratching at her throat.

"I know it hurts, boy-o, but it won't for long."

He saw a glimmer—a flash of something metallic as it flipped through the air and landed at his feet. Edward skittered back before he realized what it was. It looked like it had been slightly quashed, chocolate oozing out of the bulging breaks in the packaging.

He furrowed his brow. Glancing up, he was aware that his mouth was gaping open, and he was unable to snap it closed. His tongue slapped gracelessly against his teeth like a dried-up kipper.

"I...I..." he attempted to stammer out. "I can't..."

Whatever words remaining that he might have managed to choke out were plucked from his mouth and stolen by a pair of burning red eyes that appeared not too far behind her. They were the color of old blood. And while her bright violet eyes were glossy, these were dull. The burning end of her companion's cigarette was brighter as grey ash fell away like an unsightly scab and the glowing tip was left raw and exposed like a wound.

The crackling of burning paper. The heavy scent of tobacco.

At this point, Edward could taste breakfast.

"They removed your horns." The one with the red eyes remarked, stepping forward so that the ugly light splashed over hair so blonde it blended in near seamlessly with ashen skin. "Or did you have that done yourself?"

"It was cosmetic." That was Edward's automatic reply. He never wanted to talk about it, never had the occasion to bring it up. The memory of acute pain was enough to white out the more reasonable response: *how did they know he ever had horns?*

"No one would ever do that to themselves." She sounded offended, as if she had guessed he was lying and saw no reason why he should hide anything from her. "The angels cut them, didn't they? Awful things. The Almighty's supreme creation happens to be His most colossal fuck-up."

"No pity. No mercy." The man with red eyes held out his half-finished cigarette. It was still burning when she took it, slipping it between her fingers so that now she was holding two.

"What do you want from me?" Edward just wanted to leave. He would have crawled away, if he could have managed. Any amount of distance sounded like a good thing, anything to ease the pain…

"We have a proposal for you. For you and your sister." They exchanged looks, these two dark entities who he had no name for. The woman continued to speak. "If you would be kind enough to lead us her way, that is."

The last thing Edward wanted to do was to take them anywhere near Claire. Yet he didn't feel as though he had a choice. The pain was so great that he felt like he was being dragged by a lead of his own intestines.

"If I take you there," he gasped, "does the pain stop?"

"How quickly you cave," the woman said. "This simple pain could be considered no more than a mere prick to the gut. You have never known true hunger. How strange it is to me that even your unusual heritage has never provided you with so much as a glimpse of insight into a demon's crippling, maddening appetite." She shook her head. "Do not worry, child. It will all go away. Neither of us are here to hurt you. Like I said, me and this tall drink of water over here just want a chat."

Edward nodded. His mouth was so parched that the insides felt sticky.

"All right," he said, considering himself to have no options as far as rejecting their advances, "follow me then, please."

The woman cast a look at the sinister man, who gestured that she should lead the way as he pulled another cigarette from its case.

CHAPTER VII

Charlie's world was often grey.

Of the three eyelids he possessed, he rarely ever lifted the second. Mortal earth was overly saturated with color. Even the soft pastels gave him a headache. The ghastly dyes, the cheap paints and sickly oils were such poor imitations of the true colors that were born in the spiral of eternity.

He wondered what demon had brought the colors to humans first, or if that was closer to the work of a misguided angel. If they could peek into the future and see what wretched injustice humans had done to one of eternity's greatest gifts, would they do it again?

Henry stood out, as all demons did. Being supernatural, Henry could not hide his colors from the Elder demon's sight. Charlie was always vividly aware of the blonde that capered by his side, feet clad in daintily pointed boots that skipped over the patches of thin ice forming on the uneven streets. His vivacious nature made it impossible for him to stay morose for long which was a trait Charlie found equal parts endearing and annoying.

They were a garish pair in plum and scarlet, ambling down the glacial streets while dark clouds that threatened snow swirled above their heads resembling the lazy strokes of a careless painter.

"No stars out tonight." Henry said as his hands sank deeper into his coat pockets. "Pity, although I suppose the snowflakes will make up for their loss."

Charlie reigned in the urge to scoff, drawing the disdainful sound in with his tongue and running it over his lips instead. Stars and snowflakes never mattered. However, Henry's legs were long and tantalizingly straight. Charlie had to force himself to pull his gaze away, allowing it to crawl up this well-crafted skeleton that moved with such eager finesse.

Henry flickered a glance at the Elder demon and his grin widened as he pulled the lapels of his coat tighter across his chest. "I like the way you eye me, sir. You make me feel as desirable as a colorful piece of candy in a shop window."

"And am I the orphan with his nose pressed against the glass?" Charlie remarked, not flattered by the comparison.

"Forsooth, you are the wretched urchin of the story." Henry confirmed with a coy tilt of his head. "How long will it take for you to devour your prize?"

"If you are offering, I have already plotted your dissection. I know exactly where I will begin..." Charlie's eyes dropped back down to Henry's kneecaps before his starved gaze found those flitting fingers. They trailed through the air with wisps of blond hair clinging to the tips, the faint strands slipping away only seconds later and spiraling off into the darkness. "I don't think you are going to miss *all* of your fingers."

Henry drew his fingers to his mouth, as if he knew exactly what the Elder demon was eyeing. He placed the tip of one almond-shaped fingernail between his teeth, tugging on it as if he intended to rip it straight from the nail bed.

Charlie's breath quickened. He closed the distance between them — reaching out and taking hold of that flighty hand. He pulled it to his mouth, gripping the nail between his own teeth as his cobalt eyes bore into Henry's cornflower blue ones.

"Stop," Henry hissed between his teeth, his fingers going rigid with the sudden contact. "You are going to lose yourself."

"I have perfect control. Thank you." Charlie slipped his tongue around Henry's middle finger, sucking on the tip. He could feel the stalwart bone tempting him beneath ductile flesh. "Age grants it to me."

"How fortunate," a soft gasp was pulled from Henry's lips as he curled his fingers inward and away from Charlie's mouth. Charlie's long tongue snaked out and slid down the side of Henry's retreating finger, capturing the tip and stopping only once it hit the webbing at the base.

"I met a boy once," Charlie meandered off-topic, retracting his tongue but keeping hold of Henry's hand, thumbs working to massage the palm—seeking out the tendons to stroke them dotingly. "A part of his jaw had to be removed early on in life. It was necessary, not cosmetic. There was a lump of scar tissue where the incision had been made, right along here." He allowed one hand to briefly swipe across his own sharp jawline. "He was allergic to anesthetic and felt every jagged tooth of the bone saw."

"Holy shit." The expletive slipped through teeth, bringing out a wince when Charlie's fingers dug deeper into his palm. "That poor child—"

"Don't be deceived. He recalled it with such fondness. And it made him much more than a decadent feast. I dare say, the way his body trembled every time I bit through a finger was as close to a religious experience as creatures like us can have."

Revulsion played across Henry's face. Whether he meant to allow it to show or not, Charlie delighted that the other demon could not hide such disgust from him. Charlie understood that the mantra of most demons was that it was one thing to play around with food. Those who devoured souls believed that bitterness was best cultivated through pain, after all, and absinthial souls—according to the gourmets among them—were the most satisfying. Yet, they would flinch at suffering that had nothing to do with the taste. It was hypocrisy, in his opinion, but what demon did not thrive off a double-standard?

"I've lost you." The corners of Charlie's mouth curved upwards, lips stretching like gashes cut into a Glasgow smile. "You are turned off."

"I was never turned on." Henry's faltering voice was so convincing as he tried, again, to pull his hand away. Charlie's grip kept it firmly in place, that gaze never wavering. "I will admit I am a touch unsettled."

"It is good for you to feel that way. Unsettled, exposed...*raw*. How often is a demon left at a disadvantage? If you have never felt powerless, you can't know real strength."

"I would rather the illusion of strength than to struggle in the jaws of a predator." Henry pulled his hand free at last, Charlie's grip slackening to allow the motion.

A sigh rattled past Charlie's lips, like the longsuffering sound of an aging father as he turned away from the younger demon. "I am hungry. You are not helping."

"I'm sorry," Henry sucked in a breath. "What should we…?"

"Just quiet." Charlie snipped. Whatever parts of him that had warmed to Henry had gone cold again in a matter of seconds. "Follow me."

Henry nodded and picked up his pace as his boots splashed in the shallow puddles on the street, breaking thin layers of ice underneath his heel.

Sunlight always made Cassandra's eyes the wrong color, taking them from emerald green to a faded, more complex mixture of blue and grey. Virgil had not even taken notice of the encroaching dawn, content to ignore it while he plugged stands of black curly hair into the bare patches on her scalp. But the moment weak morning beams fell onto his beloved's face, he hissed and reached up to grab the worn, tasseled pull that drew the moth-eaten curtains closed.

Natural lighting, in this case, was not a woman's best friend. He hated what it did to her eyes as much as he hated how it brought out the harsh lines in his paint. She didn't look *real* in the sunlight.

Virgil reached out, grabbing one of his lamps by the thick glass base and dragging it closer to his workspace. He wasn't quite done touching up the paint on her lips, and he refused to give either of them rest until he had made a half-decent amount of progress. The problem was that they were too full, and the corners curled up too far, and no amount of paint could cover up a botched job like that. It was his fault. He should have taken more care before casting such a travesty in resin…

Three sharp knocks startled the angel out of his reverie. Virgil cradled Cassandra in his hands, absent-mindedly stroking her white shoulders as he stared at the door. If he had thought about it, the human heart he was wearing would have started racing. But he couldn't be bothered with the internal organs half the time. It was enough work to make certain everything external was in functioning order.

Three more knocks. He set Cassandra down, propping her up on the small divan he had crafted just for her. She slumped to the side, her arm dangling over the edge as her glass eyes regarded him with nothing less than impatience.

She was tired. It had been a long night for both of them. He clucked his tongue and stood up, brushing stray black hair off the front of his robe.

"I'm sorry," he whispered, reaching out to touch her cheek, being careful not to smear the pink blush that may or may not have completely dried. "It will only be a moment. Then I will take you to bed."

He picked his way to the door, long legs unable to avoid the mess that was strewn across his path. He muttered something unsavory underneath his breath before his hands finally reached the knob, giving it a resentful twist as he pulled the door open.

"God, you look tired."

Virgil lifted a long hand to shield himself from the vengeful knives of sunlight that were intent on driving out his eyes. He squinted, bumping his glasses with his wrist to adjust them.

"What are you talking about?" he asked. "I have been working all night."

"I could stash my scythe in those bags underneath your eyes." A steel blade glimmered as the deadly tip of a switchblade prodded his thigh with interest. "That is, if I could reach."

Virgil drew back, retreating further into the darkness of his small shop. His hand gripped the door, struggling not to slam it shut in the face of the grim reaper that had placed themselves so curtly on his doorstep.

"Don't point that thing at me!" he hissed.

"Relax, I don't want your fitful spirit." The switchblade vanished briefly from his sight as the reaper clinked it against the lid of a mason jar that was holstered at their side. "Besides, I'm full up. Now can I come in?"

"No," Virgil shook his head too quickly. "Cassandra hasn't slept and I…" He didn't want to let slip about his guest. As long as he had known Butterfly, he did not think they would take too kindly to the sight of a haggard demon snoring in his chair. "I haven't made any tea."

Butterfly shrugged, willing to accept the excuse without argument. "I didn't come here to push boundaries. I just came here to give you something I found." They rolled pixie-like shoulders, pulling a black backpack around and swinging it towards the ground as they knelt swiftly. The reaper flipped open the top, plunging their hand inside and digging around until their fingers found a much smaller mason jar. They pulled it out, glancing at it to make sure it was the right one before tossing it up at the angel.

Virgil stepped forward again, feeling a bit friendlier with the promise of presents over vicious prods. He caught the jar in his hands, bringing it close to his face to examine the contents.

Locks of curly hair gleaming with oil, the ends ragged from being cut filled nearly every inch of empty space. At first glance it was black, but the awful sunlight brought out the dark brown streaks that prevented it from being exactly what he needed.

Still, he smiled.

"Thank you," he gushed sincerely, drawing the jar closer to his chest. Butterfly stood up again, slipping their backpack strap up over one shoulder and letting it thud against their small back.

"I saw those curls on a baron's head and couldn't resist. I know you have been looking to finish Cassandra for some time."

Virgil forced his smile a little wider, hoping it didn't appear too feigned though he was well aware that almost any expression came across as artificial on his not-quite human face. He did not know how to tell her, however, that while he was grateful for the trouble she had gone through, he already procured the perfect color to finish his Cassandra.

The demon had needed a trim anyway.

"You are far too thoughtful. If my shop was in any sort of order...I do mean...if I had made tea...I would be happy to receive you for an hour or so. As it stands..."

"Yeah," Butterfly waved their hand, shooting Virgil the barest of smiles. "No problem, really. I just wanted you to have that. I should get to work anyway."

"Thank you again. I am certain Cassandra will be very happy."

Butterfly nodded, turning their back on Virgil as a single step allowed them to vanish back into the foggy streets. Virgil retreated once more, closing the door and allowing himself to draw in a deep breath that hurt his lungs, which seldom worked as it was.

It took his eyes a moment to re-adjust to the darkness as he set the jar down on his desk. His fingers traveled back over to Cassandra and landed on her swan-like neck as he stroked it with the tip of his index. He took another deep breath that made his chest burn, considering he hadn't entirely released the first one yet. He looked over at James, who was still sprawled out over the chair like a drunken patron at a bar. The demon's head was thrown back so far that his shorn curls fell away from his face, round glasses riding up the bridge of his nose and threatening to fall off.

Reluctant to pull away from Cassandra, the angel lifted his foot and prodded the chair, shoving it across the floor with strength that did not match his wiry frame. It slammed against a solid bookcase and evicted its unwanted tenant, sending James toppling to the floor, nearly landing on his face.

The demon's hands flew out, bracing against the floor and absorbing the majority of the impact. He groaned, rubbing his face and pushing his fingers into the corners of his eyes.

"Can I help you?" he snarled. "There are far more polite ways to rouse a person…"

"Yes, but they would have involved touching you."

"Are we touch-averse now? Is that all angels, fallen or not?" James spared him a glance and managed to draw his knees up enough to pull himself into a sitting position. He leaned against the chair, reaching up to fix the limp cravat that had come unraveled around his throat. "Was I disturbing your great work?"

Virgil was just relieved to be making progress in their conversation. He turned back to the desk, pulling his chair back out so he could settle into the sunken seat.

"You were snoring. It was very distracting. Also, a friend stopped by and nearly spotted you."

"Ah. I would hate to put a crimp on your social life."

"Shush. They're a grim reaper. Which, if I am not mistaken, are your kind's notorious eternal rivals." Virgil slouched in his chair, his long white ponytail bunching up behind his head as he slid down the back.

"Well," James scoffed, "maybe they should stop stealing all of our food."

"Your kind has no business devouring souls that have a chance at being cycled into another life." Virgil plucked at a loose thread in the chair's brocade. It was an argument as old as the ages. He himself had repeated it at least a dozen times.

"Some souls have no business being recycled." James pulled himself up off the floor, collapsing back into the chair behind him. He reached up to run his hand through his curls, his fingers stopping short midway down his scalp.

Virgil's eyes widened at the hesitation, and he sat up, reaching behind his head to cinch his ponytail tighter. "So, so. You can't stay here all day. You need to get out. You should get some exercise."

James did not seem to be processing any new information. His mouth was partially open, and he kept rubbing the back of his neck, plucking at some stray, choppy curls until his brow finally furrowed and a new vein popped out on his forehead. "Did you cut my—?"

Virgil cut the accusation off in its infancy. "And I have work to do! I can't have you loafing about. You may return tonight but I demand you make yourself scarce for a few hours *at least.* Take a stroll down to the public square. Watch an execution. Stretch your legs. Eat."

James stared emptily for a moment at the loose hairs covering his fingertips before he finally spoke again.

"…Executions, you say?"

Virgil grinned. "Absolutely. Come now, demon, doesn't that sound delicious?"

CHAPTER VIII

An elegant rapier blade hummed as it sliced through the air meeting its opponent midway for a quick, violent kiss. Jean-François' ginger brow twitched anxiously as Charlie's straight edge batted his away like a feather. The demon did not believe in treating fencing as a *sport,* at least not in the way that a simple lace-clad human might wish to perceive it.

Suzanne sat nearby, peeling tissue-thin pieces of paper away from the edges of short cupcakes heaped with pink frosting. She ran her tongue over the edge of one to lick away some of the thick icing before biting down and lifting her hand to catch some of the crumbs. She looked at Charlie, smiling despite her blunder, and started to suck her fingers clean.

The action did nothing at all for him. He continued pacing in a tight circle, his blade making impatient circles in the air with every flick of his wrist. Jean-François' movements were more reluctant, stilted, as he appeared to be trying to predict what move the demon might make next.

One more step, and then Charlie lunged. Jean-François barely managed a parry, bringing up his blade in time to save his jugular. Charlie's sword clacked against his and the demon bore down on him. For the span of a heartbeat, Charlie's face was close enough that a puff of his breath made Jean-Francois' eyes blink, and then the demon pulled back only to resume his pacing.

"You are bad at this," Charlie sneered with a short, haughty pant. "I expected someone with breeding to be well-versed in handling a sword. You wield it little better than a cleaver."

"Father taught Jean how to fight," Suzanne commented as she took another bite of cupcake.

"Good thing that he is dead then and does not have to bear witness to this sad display." Charlie lunged again, and Jean-François side-stepped him, avoiding the blade altogether this time.

"Father never put much emphasis on combat," Jean-François said defensively. "He thought our gifts were better spent on academics."

"In other words, he recognized you were a shit swordsman from the get-go and decided not to waste his time." Charlie's blade swiped across Jean-François' shoulder, a thin red line quickly bleeding through the dark white shirt. "At least try to keep up. I will end up having you dismembered piecemeal before supper."

"You would like that!" Jean-François' breath came out in a ragged gasp as he tried to gain the advantage; but his footwork was just not up to par. Charlie moved as an extension of the blade, and Jean-François looked like he was stumbling in the dark by comparison.

"Don't be cruel to poor Jean when he is so clearly having a hard time keeping up." Suzanne picked up another cupcake. "And when you two are quite done taking off bits of each other, I want to talk to you."

"You wish a word? Regarding?" Charlie swiped his blade at Jean-François' other shoulder. He missed this time, but it was deliberate. Now he was just toying with the man.

"Jean-François got called into town to oversee executions this afternoon. It is a good sign for his upward mobility. And I would like for you to accompany him."

Jean-François stumbled, shooting his sister a stunned look. "I am in no need of a baby minder!" he insisted, sounding deeply offended.

"Are you sure?" Charlie clicked his tongue tartly. "You may find yourself in need of a nurse if you let your hamstrings get sliced."

"Charlie is not going to act as a nursemaid, Jean. I am sending him for the express purpose of marking his next target. If you are to move up the committee there must be a seat for you to occupy."

"I should be the one marking the next target," Jean-François insisted. "I know the committee best!"

"You need to be able to concentrate on doing your job." Suzanne glanced at Charlie, as if hoping for his approval. The demon just shrugged gallantly.

"Are we finished, here?" Charlie asked. "Because if so, I should dress in something more suitable for a public appearance."

"*No,* we are not finished!" Jean-François spun around, brandishing his sword. He gripped it in both hands as he brought it gracelessly down towards Charlie's head. The demon did not hesitate as he lifted his rapier, parrying the blow and slicing his blade across Jean-François' face, opening the noble's cheek. The freckled skin split, and blood flew off the blade's tip, splattering across the pink frosted cupcake sitting on Suzanne's plate.

Suzanne picked the cupcake up again, turning it around in her hands before looking at Charlie.

"I think you two are finished." She said, taking her index finger and scooping up a generous heap of bloody frosting. She sucked it away with one swipe of her lips and a loud, wet pop.

This time, Charlie paid attention.

Considering how the streets had been gutted by revolutionaries, James was glad to see that at least one coffee shop had been spared. He had been staring at the door for almost twenty minutes, debating on whether or not it would be worth it to walk inside and indulge in a cup or two before proceeding to the main square to enjoy the executions.

"Come on, James," a familiar, if not all-too-welcome voice spoke close to his ear. "There is always time for coffee."

James scowled, bringing the collar of his coat up higher as if that could discourage Henry from getting too close. "It is good to see you are still alive."

"Alive, my friend. And well fed. Charlie treated me to the best the city had to offer last night. And it seems as though you are starving."

James reached up to bat his companion away like an annoying fly. "Must you hover so?"

"Your forgiveness." Henry rocked back on his heels, shoving his hands deep in his pockets as if to show he was capable of behaving. "Are you going inside? I should like to accompany you."

"I'm considering it." James reached out, taking hold of the shop's door handle. "Although answer me this, Henry… why did you come back for me?"

"It is pure coincidence, I assure you. I was going to let you rot."

James rolled his eyes. "Right." He opened the door and stepped aside to let Henry in first. Henry placed a hand on his chest as if he was flattered, ducking his head to step inside the short doorway. James followed him, already unbuttoning the front of his coat.

"A perfect host or not, I still don't trust Charlie." James grabbed the seat that was closest to the window and farthest from the other patrons, pulling it out from the small table and sitting down.

"You don't trust him, and he doesn't like you. What is a poor boy to do?" Henry settled down in his own chair, leaning back and stretching his legs out in front of him underneath the table. "I feel like the protagonist of a romantic novel."

"Right. Except neither of us are interested in you." James slipped his coat off altogether and let it drape over the back of his chair. "Well, he might be. You know I have a terrible radar for that sort of thing."

"Don't get me started on Elliot when *the rest of us* saw that coming from a mile away…"

"'The rest of us' being…?"

"Violet and I had a bet. If she hadn't died, I would have won."

"Somehow, I don't believe that." James paused as the server approached their table. He ordered a pot of black coffee and requested milk be brought with it before turning back to Henry. "To tell you the truth, I would much prefer a proper cup of tea. But I don't think tea is fashionable here."

"Tea is as out of style as the aristocracy, I'm afraid. Coffee is the drink of the common man here although I could never hazard a guess as to *why*." Henry pulled at his gloves as he looked around, drinking in the atmosphere of the humble café. It smelled like freshly ground coffee and warm bread; large windows allowed sunlight to brighten up the dark wood floors and the hodge-podge selection of furniture.

A young man sat at the table closest to theirs. He looked vaguely familiar, although Henry could not place where he had seen him before. His hair was an unruly black mop and his stern, rectangular glasses obscured murky green eyes.

He was lean like a grasshopper and had counted out the tip three times already, as if he was afraid the math in his head was wrong. Or perhaps he was just second-guessing whether or not people of this era even left tips.

Henry pursed his lips and glanced at James, nudging his companion's ankle with his foot. "Darling, look at that man. Does he seem a bit off to you?"

James glanced over, adjusting his glasses prudishly. "No."

"Do you think he is human?"

"He reeks. You can smell him from here…and you have the nerve to ask me a question like that?"

Henry leaned forward, stroking his chin and the wispy blonde hairs that were starting to form. He was badly in need of a shave. "I don't think he is the kind to devour souls. But he doesn't seem like he fits Charlie's mold either. I wonder…"

"His name is Francis. He is my husband, so you can quit ogling."

Henry jumped. James' head jerked up at the same time and his cerulean eyes almost popped out of his head.

"Lady…?" Henry sat up straight in his chair as the Unchaste stepped into full view, hovering closer in proximity to the demon than he ever had before.

"I did not dare suspect I would run into either of you in a place like this." Lady scoffed. "Much less did I believe I would find you *together*. But I suppose true love outlasts the ages."

"We are not together." James interjected. "It was just easier than traveling alone."

"He is in denial," Henry whispered, cupping his hand at the side of his mouth and delivering a boyish wink. "He doesn't know it is our honeymoon."

"Mm, Frank is still in denial about our marriage." Lady looked over his shoulder, beckoning his spouse forward. "Don't be shy, come say hello. I won't let these scoundrels bite you."

"Nothing much to bite, I always thought you would have higher standards." Henry smirked.

"He buys me shoes." Lady made a three-quarters turn, allowing the slightly taller demon to join the awkward company.

Neither of them were dressed properly for the era. They both looked as though they had stepped right out of Hell's main offices. Lady's suit was sleek and feminine, far more so than anything Henry had ever seen him in. His collared shirt and tie had been replaced by a ruffled white satin blouse. And his practical square-toed dress shoes had been ditched for a pair of short black heels that only granted him an extra inch or two in height.

"How do you do?" Francis muttered, nodding towards Henry and James in turn. "Francis Hislop."

"I think I have heard of you before." Henry said. "As in your name was dropped somewhere within earshot when I was dicking around Hell. Maybe I was dropping off papers at Lady's office or something."

"He was my intern for half a century. Way to be observant." Lady rested a hand on his hip, shooting Henry an unimpressed look.

"Intern? Now there's a scandal. Sleeping with the boss — or rather, I suppose occupying the same twelve foot radius as the boss on a regular basis *which*, in Lady's case, is the same thing." Henry relaxed in his chair again, granting Francis his most charming smile. "You are made of tougher stuff than I."

"You are both plenty thick. I cannot tolerate masculine-presenting demons and I don't know why I try." Lady looked over at James. "You haven't said much, sir."

"I haven't had my coffee yet." James indicated the empty table. "Where are you two staying? In town?"

"Well, we haven't found a place to settle down yet." Francis exchanged looks with Lady. "We more or less just arrived."

"You're not on the run, are you?" Henry asked, pretending to be scandalized by the very thought.

"From Hell? Always. But now…" Lady paused, as if considering how much information he should drop at once. Whatever he decided internally, he kept going. "Well, let's just say I'm in a bind which is largely your fault, and in fact I might go out on a limb and pin the blame on you entirely."

"If you know somewhere we can stay, any intel is greatly appreciated." Francis added with the air of someone well-accustomed to soothing over their partner's indiscriminate hostility.

"I will say that there is not much room where either of us are staying." James glanced at Henry. "I don't know if you have any suggestions…"

"I passed a hotel last night." Henry offered, craning his neck a bit to look at Francis. "I can give you the address. I don't know what sort of state it is in or anything of that nature…"

"It is better than nothing." Francis pulled a leather-bound pad of paper and an expensive pen from his blazer, handing it over to Henry. "And certainly better than trying to figure it out for ourselves. I appreciate it."

"We are going into town to watch some heads roll. Care to join?" James asked as Henry took the offered pad and started scribbling down an address and some concise directions.

"No thank you. I have seen my fair share of executions and they are, quite honestly, boring." Lady answered before Francis could even bother. "Enjoy your coffee. Stay out of trouble."

"Shouldn't that be my line to you?" Henry winked and slid the pad back towards Francis, who pressed his lips together to keep from laughing out loud.

"As if you had any cause to worry over *me*." Lady turned his back to them all, kitten heels clicking disdainfully across the wooden floor as he walked back to his table. Francis nodded again to the two demons before following his spouse, tucking Henry's directions back into his blazer.

"Odd pairing," James muttered.

"I think they're perfect for each other. Francis seems pretty compliant." Henry settled back in his chair just in time for coffee to be brought, served on a battered tea tray by a ruddy-faced girl. "Curious though, is it not? Angels, I know, are capable of affection—even if it seems to manifest largely as unhealthy attachments. Even obsessions. But I have never seen a demon express even a modicum of romantic interest. It makes you wonder, does it not?"

"Wonder what?" James picked up the creamer and tilted it over his coffee, watching the color go from black to sickeningly light brown. In fact, he did wonder. He wondered every time he saw Charlie get a little too close to Henry for his liking. He wondered every time he caught the light in Henry's eyes, or whenever the sunlight touched that golden hair and made him glow like one of the saints on the roof of the Basilica. Yet, he would never admit that. Not to Henry, not to anyone.

"If we're capable." Henry rested his chin on his hand, his gaze long and unwavering as he looked at James. "Don't tell me you've never wondered."

"Of course I have wondered." James said impatiently, picking up a spoon to stir his coffee. "I have wondered every day since…well. Since Elliot." It sounded like a lie, to him, but he hoped that Henry bought it anyway. James did not spare nearly as much thought towards Elliot as he liked to play off. "However, I have never read a single piece of literature that would ever suggest that demons are capable of developing feelings outside of hunger or companionship.

I have no reason to believe we are, either. I certainly do not intend to find out." He clipped his words with finality.

"How sad that we should be condemned to such apathetic existences." Henry's hand left his chin, pointed fingernails descending to drum against the tabletop. "I am of a different opinion, of course."

"Of course." James expected nothing less. Henry was allowed to be a rogue, to be romantic, to stray away from everything that had ever been established about their kind. Henry never liked rules and never fancied having to live by them. James *needed* rules. He needed consistency. Henry was many things; beautiful, mercurial, and hideously *in*consistent.

"I don't think we are capable of feeling love towards *humans*. But that makes sense, doesn't it? They are good for a meal and little else." Henry said. "When it comes to each other, however, I believe we are absolutely capable of something deeper. We may be solitary creatures by nature, whatever our nature — but we crave companionship just like everything else. All things created have a ruling passion for not being alone."

"All things *created*." James shot his companion a glance over the metallic rims of his glasses. "By that you mean all things formed by the hand of Elohim."

Henry scowled.

"Demons are born from sounds." James reminded him, finally sipping from the rim of his cup. "No semblance of affection or fleshly desire is part of our making. So why would you assume we share natural desires with any other living thing? We are unlike any other creature, living or dead."

Henry waved his hand dismissively. "Stop dismantling my argument."

"If you wish to form a better one, I could recommend some excellent reading." James offered.

"No, thank you. I will stick to my delusions and fancies." Henry folded his arms. "As well as my apparently *un*natural desires."

"I just think you are a little bit confused, that's all. You have been on mortal earth too long."

"And we will be here a while yet, so it is only going to get worse. Finish your coffee, I'm ready to go." Henry turned his head back towards the window and lapsed into sulky silence.

James almost opened his mouth again, but he did not want to upset Henry further. For their whole argument, James did not want the outcome to be the capricious light dimming in Henry's eyes. If his companion was correct, and there was something *more* – he was not sure that it was worth dwelling on. Why start something that could potentially end in so much disaster?

Besides, Henry did not want *him*. James knew that. He was not beautiful, elegant, or vicious in the ways that Henry seemed to favor in lovers. He was bookish, quiet, sour.

Yet, if even some small part of what Henry said was possible, then James knew that he would give anything to be the type that Henry might be inclined to crave. The realization made his stomach twist. James liked to think that he never needed anyone but the idea of losing Henry to someone else tore an empty hole inside his chest where no wound had even yet been made.

He finished his coffee, but it had lost its appeal. Henry was silent, and so the whole world had become deadwood.

CHAPTER IX

Michael hated stepping into God's office building. It was over one hundred thousand floors, and it was impossible to see past the tenth. Its glass curtain walls reflected the open blue sky around it so well that the building itself was nearly invisible to the naked eye; making it both obnoxious and a hazard.

Michael suspected that something about his response was entirely Pavlonian. Being summoned to God's desk was never a good thing—as the Lord Himself only ever set foot behind the damn thing about once a quarter (if that)—and made it clear how much He hated every moment. He rarely stayed clocked in for longer than fifteen minutes at a time—just long enough to appear and let His omnipotence sink in. Once His absolute authority had been established yet again He was back out on the golfing green, always leaving behind a heap of unanswered prayers for His secretary to deal with.

The poor woman had not had a holiday since the seventh day of Creation.

Michael stopped in front of the secretary's desk, greeting her with a cursory sympathetic nod. She didn't respond at first beyond tapping her headset and rolling her eyes. She leaned back in her cushioned chair, the leather creaking and the accordion spine scrunching up behind her as it threatened to tilt back on its rollers.

"Once again, the Almighty isn't in. He's very busy — yes, yes. Mhm. Yes, I understand you have been waiting for a quarter of a century. There is nothing I can…" before she could even finish her sentence, she was met with the smug click of an ended call. She made an annoyed sound in the back of her throat and pulled the mouthpiece of her headset down, turning her baleful silver gaze on the archangel.

"Sorry about that." She said, even though she wasn't really. "What can I do for you, hon?"

"I have an appointment…" Michael pointed at the calendar on her desk. Her eyes dropped briefly down to it.

"So does everyone else. You're probably one He wants to keep, though." She lifted the corner of a page and turned it, glancing at the other side before letting it fall back into place. "You can probably just head into His office. I doubt He is busy."

Michael nodded again. "Just avoiding the calls?"

"I swear to all that is Holy, it is as bad as trying to get ahold of you some days." She grumbled.

He opened his mouth to argue, but he couldn't hardly. "Well, at least I'm not in heavy demand. I mean, who is trying to call upon an archangel these days? Even Gabriel got picked for the last big announcement over me."

"Yes." She clipped. "But don't chalk that up due to lack of popularity on your part. The Almighty kept you here because the both of you had a tournament that week."

"I remember." Michael said, and added almost defensively, "which is why I will be pulling double duty when it comes to Judgment Day."

"Will you, now?" She sounded like she didn't believe him. The office phone rang again and she picked it up, only to slam it back down on its cradle with a hideous clang. "You better go in. This is just going to continue. Also, He's been waiting for an hour."

"Shit," Michael said under his breath as he moved past the desk. "You might have mentioned that before."

The Archangel grabbed hold of the door handle, taking a deep breath and putting on his professional white smile before entering the room. God was sitting at His cherry wood desk, the surface of which was wiped completely clean with the exception of a can of diet soda resting on a neat, circular coaster. His soft manicured hands darted over the thin silver keyboard of His expensive computer. He had not pulled His eyes away from the screen yet, but Michael knew that He knew he was there—because of course, the Almighty knew everything.

Michael stood there, knowing it would be futile to try and pull the Almighty's attention away from whatever He was doing. God's brow was furrowed as if He was in the middle of something difficult, a broad description which could have applied to something as simple as forwarding a chain email.

"You wanted to see me?" after nearly ten minutes, Michael's desperation to fill the silence overcame his patience. He regretted speaking at all when the Almighty's gaze swiveled away from the screen and landed on him.

"I wanted to talk about your charges. We had an agreement. Take a seat."

Michael felt a chair hit the back of his knees. He sat down immediately, hands going down to clench the fabric-padded arms. He tried not to seem as nervous as he was. It was easy to forget the man he played golf with every afternoon was not a man at all, but the father of an entire universe that He had created more or less by accident.

"I know." Michael leapt to his own defense. "I remember the agreement."

"We have no idea how half-breeds should be treated." The Almighty spat out *'half-breed'* as if the word itself left a disgusting taste in his mouth. "And now they are without a leash. They have broken their contract with you, is that correct?"

"Something to that affect."

"Why did you not slaughter them the moment they turned their backs?"

Michael didn't know. He hadn't even considered it. He shifted in his chair, bringing up one leg to rest across his other one, trying to appear as collected as he had been a minute ago.

"I didn't think about it." It was a lazy excuse. He decided to focus his gaze on the sweating soda can that was resting on the Almighty's desk. It was beginning to form a small puddle on the coaster where it sat. Michael had never before related so whole-heartedly with an inanimate object.

"*Mikha'el,*" like a stern parent chastising a child, God dragged out the archangel's full archaic name. "You have always been one of my best."

Michael's throat tightened past the point of swallowing. He nodded, flashing the Almighty his most winning smile in spite of himself.

"You have often mentioned as much, Lord."

God's Midwest blue eyes clouded, darkening faster than a sudden storm. Michael instantly regretted his cheekiness, but it was too late to take it back. This was what happened when angels exhibited too much personality.

"Do you remember the Metatron?" It was less of a question and more of a thinly concealed threat. Michael nodded faster than he could process the recollection. All of Heaven remembered what happened with the Metatron. The entire first three rows of witnesses to that particular scourging had been splattered with blood.

The most terrifying thing about that incident was not the Almighty's fury. Rather it had been that the Metatron had never once screamed. God's fiery whip had reduced their back to ruins. Michael was among those who could claim that they had seen ribs peeking out from shredded flesh. But that wretched, beautiful angel had never once let out as much as a sob.

Michael knew for a fact that the first lash would have done him in. The Metatron never once asked for undeserved mercy. They bent their knee. They submitted. They were the perfect servant. And God had ruined them anyway.

"I do not want pride to be your downfall." God said when Michael could not manage a proper response. "Pride. Vanity. I have sent angels hurling into the pit for less."

"I know." Michael's voice croaked a bit. He touched his throat and cleared it before trying that sentence again. "I know. I will not be one of the Fallen."

"I have always had faith in you." God picked up His soda can and took a loud sip from the rim. Michael felt his knees weaken.

"I want you to find your half-breeds. Take care of them one way or another. If they will not submit, then they will be destroyed. Such is the way things have always been."

Michael nodded. "Always." He had seen it play out often enough. He watched as the emptied can crumpled up like paper in God's hand. The Almighty tossed the can towards the wastebin, not even looking to see if He made the shot. He did.

"**F**rank. We are not staying here."

"Why not?" Francis asked, his voice a little too cheerful for Lady's liking, given their surroundings. It was not exactly an up-to-date place. The roof was leaking, and the water damage on the walls was so horrendous that it managed to stand out even against the ugly rippling flower pattern that was already there. It was a whole lot better than

Francis had been expecting, no doubt, when he made the arrangements, but Lady's standards were much higher. "I'm sure it is much better upstairs." Francis continued. "You know the lobby is always the least impressive area."

"No, dear, the *upstairs* always hides what the lobby is too afraid to show you. And if the lobby looks like this then the upstairs must be where they are stashing all of the doomed aristocracy." Lady snorted.

Francis hefted the suitcase at his side, acting like it was heavy. Which, in Lady's opinion, was a touch dramatic.

"Can we at least approach the desk?" Francis was already stepping towards that direction. "Please?"

"You are out of your mind." Lady followed his husband, the usual two steps worth of distance between them narrowed down to one.

Francis came to a stop at the front desk, setting the suitcase down and flexing his gloved hand. The desk was an impressively solid structure that wrapped around where a clerk should have been standing. And yet, to no one's surprise; there was not a soul to be seen.

"Even the person they pay to work here knows better than to linger." Lady glanced around the room as if the offender could be spotted crouched behind the molding couch. "There are other places we can try."

"I did not see them." Francis answered, sounding weary. "We have already circled this block twice —"

Somewhere off to the side, a shotgun was cocked. Lady did not have a chance to react before Francis' head spun around and his hand lashed out. Francis' hand wrapped around his upper arm and the entire world went sideways as Lady was pulled down out of the way. Lady let out an indignant squawk of protest — but Francis did not release him. He moved to fill the empty space and stashed the Unchaste behind him.

It wasn't as if a shotgun could kill either of them on its own. But it could certainly blow a few holes.

"You are best off trying somewhere else." The hostile greeting was punctuated by the shotgun being lifted higher.

"My sentiment exactly." Lady muttered from behind his husband, reaching up to shove his glasses as far up the bridge of his pert nose as they would go. "Are you going to listen to reason now that it is staring at you down the barrel of a shotgun, *darling?*"

Francis only glanced over at him. Lady peeked out from behind his husband, brown sugar eyes narrowed as he struggled to recognize the woman who was so brashly threatening them. "I know you." The Unchaste said, perhaps a bit too loudly. "You look —"

Who did she look like? He felt like he ought to know. But he had seen so many faces over the centuries that they all sort of blended together. Her eyes were darker than his; her hair was thick and close to black. Yet she was as pale and grey as a corpse. She bore an uncanny resemblance to…

Someone.

His stomach lurched. A hand flew to his mouth and Lady pinched his nose between gloved fingers, afraid he otherwise might vomit. He turned his gaze away from the woman and closed his eyes, fighting the stabbing pain in his gut that threatened to bring him to his knees. He could feel Francis wavering in front of him, knees trembling as the young demon fought to remain upright as well.

"I know it hurts." the sick feeling doubled in the pit of Lady's stomach at the familiar voice. A husky Blues-y voice made for speakeasies and garbled radio broadcasts. "It never lasts for long."

Broken glass popped underneath a firm heel.

"It has been a long time since you have eaten. Hunger is so easy to find." Water blurred Lady's vision as he caught sight of a face he had never been important enough to meet up close. But Famine's portrait had been hanging in the hallway that Lady passed through every morning to get to work. Lady could have easily picked out the entire board of directors on that basis alone.

"Wait!" The girl stepped tentatively forward, clinging to her shotgun as if it was the only thing that still made sense. "I don't...I know this person."

"She knows you, Meriwether." Famine's hand shot out, grasping Lady by the chin and tilting the Unchaste's head up until it hurt to breathe.

"So do you," Lady said faintly, his stomach turning again at the unwanted sudden contact. "Apparently."

"We did not come down here for you." Famine released his hold on Lady's chin. "So do not force yourself into a nasty situation where you have no business prodding your nose. Or I will pull it off."

"There is no need to threaten me." Lady pressed his fingers against the soft, spreading bruise under the underside of his chin. "It isn't as though it is very difficult."

"I do not like creatures who cannot seem to refrain from gorging themselves at every turn." Famine turned his attention towards Francis. "Unchaste are bad about it. Humans are even worse. But there is no out-matching a demon when it comes to gluttony."

"Are you not...master of —?" Francis seemed unable to push the words out of his mouth fast enough.

"Some seven thousand? Yes. I have a handful of demons I can call my own. Not many are willing to give up what they think they need." Famine pressed disapproving fingers into Francis' soft cheek, grinding into his jawbone. The demon winced. "Do you not hate your own soft, disgusting flesh? Do you not find it abhorrent, the way it hangs like a used sponge? What is your vice, demon? What sort of indulgence do you cram into your mouth until you can't swallow another gritty, greasy bite?"

Francis made a face. "Brains."

"Brains. Of course. Another odd demon out who was born from tragedy rather than sound." Famine grabbed both sides of Francis' face, using the hold to lift him over an inch off the ground. Francis gasped in pain, grasping the Horseman's thick wrist. "You should hate your own impure nature. You are little more than a buzzing poltergeist stuffed into a meat suit."

A few more harrowing seconds passed before the Horseman dropped him, and Francis staggered. His shoulders lurched forward as he held his jaw, tears springing to his eyes. He glanced up over the rims of his glasses just in time for Famine to move away, fingers clamping down on the woman's shoulder.

"Don't touch me," she said quietly. She still had not let go of her shotgun.

He shrugged and dropped his hand. "There will be time for you, Meriwether Hayward." The Horseman said, turning his head to face Lady once again. "Hide as well as you can. My wife will want to find you next."

Lady felt his mouth go bone dry. He wasn't sure what hit him harder—the threat, or the fact that he finally recognized the woman in front of him.

She was Claire—Claire Clifton. She bore an uncanny resemblance to her mother—although she had a good deal more taste. He remembered, vaguely, hearing a rumor that she and one of her brothers had been taken under the wing of an archangel.

Saints in their graves. That had to be only the reason she was still *alive*.

Her gaze lingered on him for only a minute longer—as if she too was struggling to recognize him. She seemingly gave up, turning away to fall into step beside Famine as he started walking up the wide, questionable staircase that vanished into the upper levels.

Lady was so consumed by what had just occurred that he didn't even bother to ask himself how Famine and Claire might have ended up on the same side in the first place.

Famine made it halfway up the stairs before he turned his head again. He extended his hand and snapped his fingers—it was a crisp, resonant sound like Styrofoam squealing. Claire appeared hesitant, but she passed the shotgun to him, and Famine hoisted it up. Against his thin body, it looked almost comically oversized.

"Hayward," he said. "You do not have all day."

The shotgun smoked, and the booming sound that followed seemed delayed. Lady's ears rang, and he could not hear anything—but he saw Francis drop. Lady opened his mouth, although no sound came out.

Everything was moving at half speed. Everything was unraveling faster than he could keep track.

Francis raised his head. He was alive, but there was black blood oozing sluggishly from a massive hole in his leg.

"Frank?" Lady's voice sounded tinny to his own ears. "For the love of Hell—!"

Claire started to descend the staircase, as if she wanted to help, but she stopped herself. Lady felt like his heart was sitting underneath his tongue. Famine cocked the shotgun again.

"I hate," the Horseman said, "having to repeat myself."

CHAPTER X

Too many people were packed into the public square like cocks in a cage readying for a fight. There were not as many as James feared, but there were certainly more than was comfortable. He found himself stepping over muddy boots and filthy hems as he elbowed his way through, tugging Henry behind him like a child in danger of wandering. The younger demon kept ducking his head, pushing his glasses up his nose and murmuring every time he nearly ran into another body. Barely a head turned as they made their way towards the front, yet it felt as though every eye was on them.

It was less crowded up front. One man warned them that it was in the way of 'splatter', whatever that meant. The few who were standing even closer to the platform than the two demons were, James hoped, exceptionally near-sighted. Because he could think of no other reason for wanting to stand practically on top of the carnage.

A cart rumbled noisily as the crowd split down the middle to allow it through. The cobblestones made the tumbrel jerk and sway from side to side dangerously, already weighed down unevenly by the number of people that were piled in its hold.

The cart rolled to a halt at the foot of the guillotine, one of its wooden wheels bumping against the bottom step. James' eyes wandered back up to the platform where two soldiers were now standing, one with his hand out to assist an ascending official with a mop of copper curls and a face freckled beyond redemption. Jean-François was dressed in such a fashion that James nearly did not recognize him, having become accustomed to seeing the man lounge around the house in loose-fitting shirts and no shoes. Of course, his hair still looked like it had not been combed in a year — which was somehow oddly satisfying.

Jean-François ripped his hand away from the soldier as soon as he set both feet solidly against the platform, angrily grabbing his lapels to adjust them and sweeping both hands through his hair as if he had some form of dignity to preserve. He did not turn around to acknowledge Charlie, who stepped agilely up onto the platform with no assistance. As tense as the Elder demon's body language was, if Charlie felt any irritation, it did not show on his face. If anything, he appeared a little too pleased with himself, though his back was too rigid, and his shoulders were tight as he paced around to the other side of the guillotine. James had to wonder if any terse words had passed between him and Jean-François moments before. He could only imagine what they might have been.

The crowd was starting to get antsy, the tension too much for their frantic common hearts to bear. Objects were being thrown at the aristocrats in the cart, most of them missing and landing somewhere along the wheels or buried in the mud. James slid a little closer to Henry.

"I did not know Charlie would be here." Henry said defensively.

"Neither did I." James hissed through his teeth. "But he is. Do you think he has seen us?"

"If he has not seen us, then he can smell us. So, there is no point in attempting to fade into the back." Henry glanced over his shoulder as he spoke.

The outskirts were the thickest part of the crowd, but that was also where old women were sitting on platforms, crocheting with oily strands of hair that looked it had been tugged or cut from the scalps of the deceased. James was not about to jeopardize either of them by brushing elbows with a few cackling hags who might find his companion's golden curls desirable, deceased or not.

"What do you think our chances of getting splattered are? Good?" Henry asked.

"I think our chances of getting eaten are better." James said dryly, glancing again at the guillotine as its blade rose towards the watery grey sky. He could barely hear Henry over the din of drums as thin wooden sticks battered their tops. "It is never too late to leave."

Henry ignored him and stepped back only an inch. The blade did not look as sharp as it should have been, and it was so different in the sleepy afternoon light. He had barely caught a glimpse of it in the dark but seeing it in broad daylight was like staring into the spinning rings of a Throne.

James' eyes fell back down to the soldiers, who were pulling a young woman up the steps. She struggled in their grip, but her hands were bound in front of her, and she did not look like she had the strength to fight very hard. She was clearly exhausted, but not resigned like some of the older women who bore their final moments with a bit more dignity.

When they got her to the guillotine, they pushed her down onto her knees. She made a despairing choking sound as they doubled her over, forcing her head down onto the worn indentation in the wood with an edge that dug into her soft throat. She swallowed hard and rolled her eyes up until the whites flashed, trying to catch a glimpse of the blade. She couldn't manage it, and her head dropped as she finally gave up, her shoulders sagging as they locked another piece of wood in place around her neck and stepped back. Neither of those bold soldiers wanted to be within inches of the deadly instrument.

Jean-François stepped forward, making a show of seeming very self-important as he gave the final word to the soldiers. Charlie hung around the edges of the platform, shifting his weight so that his heels made the weakening places in the wooden boards creak. He looked like a bored child.

The blade was silent as it came down, easy to miss if one was not paying attention. It gleamed, its grim edge glowing faintly red as it bit into the neck of its waiting victim.

The crowd fell silent. Charlie stopped rocking; his interest piqued as the corpse gave a violent twitch in the guillotine's merciless grip. The blade was stuck, somehow only half-buried in the young woman's neck. It had been enough to kill her, but not enough to sever the head.

The soldiers glanced at Jean-François, unsure of what they should do. The young noble was so pale his face was almost green, his own revulsion clear as he lifted a hand to his face, covering his mouth and nose.

The soldiers took a tentative step forward. They could pull the blade free, but were they expected to let it fall, again, and finish the job? There was no guarantee, either, that the blade would not get stuck again. The next victim might not be so fortunate as to die right away.

Charlie seemed exasperated by the lack of a prompt decision. He crossed the platform in five succinct steps and stopped right where the victim's head was dangling, half-cut, barely bleeding because of the blade. He pursed his lips and lifted his hands into the air, shaking them so that his long lace cuffs were out of the way. He pushed the sleeves up to his elbow, his forearms white as bone in grisly contrast to the crimson of his velvet coat. He plunged his hand downward and tangled his fingers into the corpse's dirty, knotted hair. He gripped it as close to the skull as he could, lifting his foot and pressing his sole flat against the wood for leverage. There was a gory pop as he wrenched the head around and blood sprayed from the wound, fanning in the air and spattering all over his fine clothes. Another twist, and he jerked his arm back. The head came free altogether and he hoisted it into the air, blood streaming down his hand and forearm, soaking the lace around his elbows.

The crowd had recalibrated. Shocked as they were by the display of strength and brutality, they drowned the moment in their bloodthirsty approval and cries of 'long live the Republic'.

James' ears buzzed from all of the noise. He glanced over at Henry and shoved his hands even deeper into his large coat, leaning forward as he strained to be heard.

"We need to leave," he said.

"I know." Even though Henry agreed with him aloud, his eyes were still locked on Charlie. James followed the line of Henry's gaze and nearly locked eyes with the Elder demon, himself. Charlie glanced down from the platform, a smug expression sliding over his handsome face as he pulled the head down closer to his mouth. His long tongue snaked out, dragging over the ragged piece of bone that was sticking out from the severed head's torn neck.

James watched Henry's throat convulse with a swallow and then he could not take it anymore. He grabbed Henry's arm, squeezing it and pulling his companion closer to try and break the trance.

"Let's go," he whispered, not caring if he was heard as he pulled Henry backwards into the riotous crowd. Somehow, it felt a lot a safer than standing within a foot of Charlie.

The doors to his sister's bedroom flung open without any resistance. And they slammed closed just as promptly as Jean-Francois strode into the inner chamber, ripping the suffocating cravat away from his throat. He threw himself down onto her divan, tossing the cravat into a corner and falling back with a sigh.

"Everything went well, I presume?" Suzanne asked serenely. From the corner of his eye, he saw her turning away from her vanity to face him.

"That demon cannot be controlled!" The words bubbled up from Jean-Francois' throat in a snarl. "He is dangerous, Suzanne. He made a public spectacle of me in the square. He stopped that blade somehow — I don't know how, but he did — and then made a show of wrenching off the head. I'm telling you, he is undermining me on purpose in front of my peers. I will not tolerate this!" His rant was slowing as his anger tapered off into a quiet rage, his chest heaving with the labor of his anger while his cheeks burned hot.

"Charlie is under control." Suzanne assured him in that soothing, patronizing tone of hers. "Deep breaths."

"I don't know how you can say that." He set his teeth. "We did not know what we were getting into when we summoned him from the void, I wish you could just *admit* that..."

"We knew *exactly* what we wanted, and we reached out and called it forth!" She shot back, gripping the back of her chair angrily. "Father would have been proud!"

"But he cannot be proud, can he? Because he is dead. And that *is* our fault." Jean-François sat up, slapping his hands against his knees and arresting her gaze with his. "You cannot look me in the eye and deny that."

She drew herself up, straightening her back and drilling her glare back at him. "I will not let the blame for everything rest on our shoulders. Or *my* shoulders, rather, considering you refuse to take responsibility for anything."

"Don't you dare!" He stood, his flashy red anger reignited as he clenched his fists and stomped over to where she was sitting. He loomed over her where she was sitting, but Suzanne did so much as shrink back. "I have done everything you have asked of me!"

"A good little lapdog." She shot back the smug jibe. "You always do as you are told."

"It is not the same thing. It is not close to the same thing!" He turned away from her, forcing himself to take a deep breath. He was dizzy. The details of the room were starting to run together as water welled up in his eyes, heat and frustration becoming too much to hold in. "He did not come home with me. The demon, I mean. I don't know where he is."

"Eating, no doubt. A happy reprieve for you." She turned back to her mirror, reaching out to take hold of the puff sitting on top of its little silver dish of powder. "Speaking of meals, are you going to prepare ours?"

"We need some servants again in this place." He murmured, already boiling at the idea of having to make dinner for his sister when a spoonful of arsenic would have been preferable.

"Soon." She reassured him. "Until then, you will do."

"Why don't you make Charlie do it sometime?" Jean-François sneered. "Since he is so well-trained."

"I will consider it." She did not seem to think he was joking. Suzanne pressed the powder puff against her cheek and left behind a streak of white. "For now, keep doing as you are told. You are doing so well."

She missed the horrible glower her brother gave her before he left, slamming the door again just for the satisfaction.

"Where are you staying?" Henry asked. "I will walk you back."

James shook his head. He did not want Henry to know that he was currently sleeping under the same roof as an angel. The older demon would have pitched a royal fit. "I can go by myself. I'm not as shaken as I probably look."

It was a blatant lie. He did not know how long Charlie had lingered at the scene after that display, but if he was to run into him—James certainly did not want to do it *alone*. Then again, if Charlie was going to come after either of them, it would be Henry. James' chances of surviving that encounter were probably better if he managed to remove himself from Henry as quickly as possible.

"I am not letting you walk alone." Henry insisted. "Besides, I…"

"You had no problem letting me out on my own the other night." James snapped back impatiently. "I will be fine. I don't need you to take me home, I am not a damsel in distress. You should get back before you are missed. He will probably be looking for you."

"No doubt." Henry folded his arms. "You are uncharacteristically hostile—I sort of like it. Will I win if I keep fighting this?"

"No," James groused. "What do you mean, 'uncharacteristically'? My entire manner is hostile."

"Not as of late. I thought you had softened up on me."

"I am the one who is soft? And you were in the coffee shop talking about our ability to love!" James shook his head, shoving his glasses up his nose. "If you love him so much, I suggest you go find him. Before he finds *you* first and tears you to pieces."

"I—I beg your pardon!" Henry's jaw slackened and his cheeks flushed. "I never said that I was in love with *him!*"

"You did not need to. You know, quite frankly, I think it is disgusting." James started advancing in the opposite direction, keeping his long stride too fast for Henry to catch up without running. "If you have need of me, I am sure we will find each other again. You somehow manage to always appear!"

With that, he left Henry behind. Regret for their quarrel came almost immediately, but he pushed it down as he continued to walk away.

It was not possible for two half-human terrors to just disappear.

At least, that was what Michael clung to in order to reassure himself that he had not lost two of Heaven's most volatile wild cards. He had already checked the hotel where they had last met but they were gone; everything had been packed away and they were no doubt squirreled away in another flea-infested rat-hole on the other side of the city.

Of course, they could have been *anywhere*, in theory. They may have left the city altogether. There was no way for him to tell anymore.

He used to be able to sense when they were near, but even now that tenuous connection between them had been cut off. He did not know if they had found a way to block his intrusive, searching thoughts or if another entity was doing it for them. He silently prayed that it was not the latter. This did not need to be more complicated than it already was.

There was only one other creature of any significant power that Michael was aware of within the city walls. And while Virgil had been living on the mortal plane for quite some time, he was still the only thing that Michael could think of powerful enough to break the connection between an angel and his marked.

The little shop where Virgil spent most of his days hiding seemed to recoil as Michael approached it. Every wooden board and beam in that house was bound together with Virgil's energy, so much so that the building itself seemed alive. The doorknob trembled underneath his touch as Michael wrapped his hand around the brass. He ground his perfect teeth impatiently and did not wait to knock and see if someone would answer. He twisted the knob until the brass screeched and the lock broke. He ripped the knob free altogether and it fell to the ground with a heavy clank. He slammed his palm against the door and forced it open, stepping in and nearly gagging on the heavy odor of Sulphur and paint.

"Have you been harboring demons?" He demanded. Virgil stood, towering in the corner like a thin shadowy monster from a children's story. The disgraced angel winced, lifting a hand to shield himself from the sunlight that poured in through the violated doorway.

"*Harboring* is a poor choice of words." Virgil said. "Hosting, more like, and it is only one demon. He was in a bad way and he needed some tea…"

"You don't give demons *tea*. You banish them back to Hell. You are not dense, Virgil, so why can't you think straight?"

Virgil gave a helpless shrug. Michael quickly closed the distance between them. In his gut, he knew that Claire and

Edward were not going to be found here. But that was not about to stop him from taking his anger out on the nearest, most convenient victim.

"The half-breeds, the hunters. You know of them. Where are they?" Michael growled, slamming his hand against the wall so that Virgil was pinned into the corner where he was already standing. Virgil looked down at the archangel, reaching up to fumble with his glasses nervously.

"I don't know!" Virgil said breathily. His soft, genteel voice was particularly annoying under the circumstances. "I have never set eyes on them, Michael, I only know *of* them like everyone else."

"You did not know they were in the city?" Michael demanded, his fingers curling inward, nails dragging down the wall and peeling up the cheap paint.

"I—perhaps I knew, but I have never seen them. Like I said, I only knew of them and you know I largely keep to myself. I stay in here with my dolls!"

"When you are not harboring demons."

"This is a very strict violation of regulations—!" Virgil's words were cut off when Michael's hand came down across his face, jamming his glasses and skewing them over the bridge of his nose. The tall angel whimpered, and Michael pulled back, his fist clenched in righteous fury.

"This is not an official inquisition. I'm asking questions and I expect better answers." Michael looked around the room, as if searching for inspiration. "It would be easy to stuff them into the corners of this place, wouldn't it? You have so much crap piled up they could be under any pile of your fabric scraps."

"I assure you, they are not." Virgil slid his glasses away from his face, inspecting the bent frame. "I don't want anything to do with your half-breeds. I heard a rumor that you did not want anything more to do with them, either…"

"You shouldn't entertain gossip. Nor spread it. A fool's mouth invites a beating, and all." Michael picked up one of the dolls from its place on the shelf. It was heavier than he expected and he nearly dropped it onto the floor. "You keep dolls? These are so human in their likeness it is disgusting. How can you stand to sleep with all of these surrounding you?"

He closed his fist around the doll's head, wrenching it around until it popped off its neck. Virgil's breath caught in his chest, but he remained silent.

Michael let the doll and its head fall to the floor. He reached out again, grabbing the next doll on the shelf, and used it to sweep the others off. They tumbled down, resin and porcelain cracking as they landed on top of one another.

Michael threw the one he as holding over his shoulder and turned on his heel, glancing at the bay window that looked out onto the street.

And then his eyes settled on the doll. She looked very satisfied with her existence as she sat in a quaint model chair, her hands folded over her knee.

"She is nearly finished," Virgil whispered, unable to help himself. "Don't touch her, please."

"She isn't the best one." Michael picked her up, his thumb pressed up into her chin so that her head was tilted as far back as it could go without breaking. "And frail by comparison."

"Yes, yes, she is very dear. Please...!" Virgil reached out, taking a careful step closer. He wanted to snatch his beloved out of the cruel archangel's hands, but he was afraid to make a sudden move and trigger a hot-tempered reaction. "Just set her down."

Michael looked at Virgil, the expression on his catalog-model face twisting it into something inhuman, something utterly reviled.

"What sort of perverse sentiment have you attached to this?" He shook the doll in his hands. "Do you have carnal desire towards resin and human hair? Do you have to apply fresh paint on her lips after you wipe off her face every night?"

Virgil cringed, his own anger making his words hot. "Don't be disgusting!"

"*You* are disgusting! Disgraceful, perverted fool!" Michael gripped Cassandra in both of her hands, ripping down the middle as if she was made of nothing more than paper.

Virgil let out an agonized, inhuman sound and caught the pieces before they could hit the ground, sinking to his knees and pulling his ruined sweetheart close to his chest. His trembling lips parted for a sob, but it was bile that gushed out. He vomited onto the floor, on top of the corpses of his other beauties. But he did not get a drop on *her*.

"You will be grateful that I do not tell the Almighty about what I have seen!" Michael snarled. "He doesn't have the time to correct a fallen angel. He would just smite you where you wallowed in your bilge!" Furious, the archangel stomped back towards the door, grabbing hold of it to slam behind him. Without its handle, the door just sprang back, leaving Virgil's pain on humiliating public display.

CHAPTER XI

"And here, I thought I had lost you." In the silent alleyway, Charlie's voice broke through like a crack of lightning. Henry's heart jumped up into his throat at the sound. He knew Charlie would find him, but he did not really expect to be found quite so quickly.

"You ran fast enough, to be sure." Charlie continued to speak when Henry did not respond. "One would think you had never seen a head being ripped off a corpse."

"It was not that." Henry said dismissively, brushing away the matter that had obviously perturbed him. "I suppose it was the…"

"Ease? Do you fear I could rip you into pieces the same way?"

Yes. Henry shook his head. "No," he said aloud. "I suppose it was that you did it so casually. As if you were tugging on a stubborn weed. And then you dragged your tongue across the broken spine and quite frankly, I thought you had exposed our entire existence in that very moment."

"It would take a fair bit more than that to convince the entire population that demons exist." Charlie snorted. "Few noticed. Of those who did; no one cared. I can assure you that your pitiful, small existence is safe." He set both of his hands on Henry's shoulders, squeezing them. "Does that comfort you?"

"Not particularly." Henry shivered under the demon's touch. "Aren't you afraid of anything?"

"Do you believe I have a reason to be?" Charlie's hands slid over the curves of Henry's shoulders, traveling down his arms and then back up. One hand came up further, reaching up to brush cold fingers against the demon's brown cheek. "I do not believe in fear for the sake of humility. Fear is a device. Use it or have it used against you. Are you not tired, Henry? So tired of being afraid?"

Henry felt suddenly like he was trying to breathe with water in his lungs.

"I never knew fear," Henry began, "before entering the mortal coil."

"Demons are creatures born in fear. Sounds tremble when they are made." Charlie's grin spread from one ear to the other and his fingers traveled over the shell of Henry's ear. "It is deeper than your marrow."

"And do you propose a cure?" Henry asked quietly. "Will you drive yourself deeper than my fears, sir?"

"Do you deserve to be devoured?" Charlie retaliated flippantly. "Or is your own desperate hunger overriding your sense of self?"

"I am more aware of myself than I have ever been." Henry said.

"Therein lies the tragedy." Charlie's fingers skated over Henry's cheek once more, diving down to press underneath his chin and lift it up enough so that their noses nearly touched. Charlie was so close that Henry could almost feel the Elder's soft petal pink bottom lip brush against his own. "A demon who has starved himself to the brink of madness — and his madness comes in the form of believe himself to be human."

"I don't…"

Before Henry could even finish his sentence, Charlie's fingers gripped his chin, squeezing it callously. "Your desire for me now is the most disgusting human impulse. Can you deny that it exists?" His free hand dove down, grabbing between Henry's legs and squeezing his half-erect cock through the cloth of his trousers. Henry narrowed his eyes, grabbing Charlie's hand and pushing it up harder against him.

"If so, would you spend the evening in denial with me?" Henry set his narrow lips together, feeling them being overtaken by a smirk he could not help.

Something in Charlie's voice trembled; a strange quiver that betrayed his anger. "I do not respond well at all," he warned, "to propositions."

"It seems to me as though you have never been made a tempting enough offer." Henry pressed himself closer until the hips were touching, his hand and Charlie's now trapped between their melding bodies. "Or are you afraid of losing yourself, as well?"

"There is nothing of me to lose." Charlie responded imperiously. "Do not be fooled by my borrowed face."

"A demon is more than a husk sewn together to house rotting meat. We are energy. We are the stuff from which flesh is *made*." Henry insisted. "I am not implying that we exist on the same level as most of humanity…"

"Yet, you are. And it is incredible how you can be so blind as to your own ludicrous shortcomings. But then, your ability to soak up humanity's worst traits like a sponge comes as no surprise. It comes from being on the run, and from spending too much time cavorting in their beds."

"And you never considered, not *once*, pulling Suzanne into yours?" Henry demanded, his face hot from his rising anger and humiliation at Charlie's mocking, candid tone.

"Never." Charlie said, blue eyes glimmering in the falling late afternoon sun. "Although I am sure you have considered it."

"Suzanne? I've thought of her before." Henry confessed, unsure of how bold he was feeling. Charlie's scrupulous gaze was bearing down on him, and he could not bear its pressure much longer. "It is nearly impossible to avoid. After all, she is so beautiful, if not usually my type. I think of you far more often."

Charlie did not bat an eyelash. Henry pressed the matter before the Elder changed the subject yet again.

"Have you ever been with another demon?"

Charlie reached into his jacket, withdrawing his snuffbox and tapping on the lid before flipping it open.

"I have never had a reason." He responded prudishly.

"The opportunity, you mean. You don't ever need a *reason*."

"Are you about to give me one?" He pinched from the box and sprinkled ivory powder onto the side of his clenched hand, lifting it to his nose and inhaling sharply. He flipped the lid down in the process and the box clinked shut.

"All I am suggesting," Henry said coyly as his eyes followed every gesture, "is that you take me home."

It was dark in the de Voclain house when Charlie returned home with his prize. Suzanne and Jean-François may not have been asleep, but they had very clearly retired if the doused lights and dead quiet were anything to go by. Charlie was not in the mood to rouse them; besides that, there was no point.

Fingers tapped his shoulder before he was barely two feet inside of the door. Charlie turned his head, feeling long fingers slide over his cheek as Henry's lips rose to greet his. Their mouths collided, Henry's parting to allow his hot, thrashing tongue to brazenly shove its way past Charlie's pink lips. Charlie opened obligingly and allowed Henry to explore; his experienced red tongue searching every crevice. He was not sure what to do with his own hands, so he kept them at his side, nails dragging along the invisible seams of his satin breeches. The younger demon was stubborn, and Charlie had a feeling that if he did not acquiesce, the remainder of his existence was going to be one long continuation of their previous conversation with this panting, starving youngling nipping at his heels.

Best to let the younger have what he wanted and be done with it all. Charlie awkwardly lifted one hand, touching Henry's shoulder in order to pull him a bit closer. Henry responded enthusiastically, hips rolling as he lifted his hand to run through Charlie's platinum blonde locks. The Elder demon fought not to recoil at the touch, snatching Henry's hand and growling. He dug his fingernails into the soft palm, sliding his tongue over gifted fingers in a gesture that most would have considered threatening.

Henry pulled his hand free and trailed it down Charlie's embroidered lapels. The path of his retreating fingers pulled Charlie's jacket down from his shoulders before finding the soft cravat around his throat. It was soon bared, exposed, and Henry's hot mouth came to rest against his jugular. The younger demon lingered there for a moment, stroking the heartline curiously with the tip of his tongue.

"You barely feel alive," Henry whispered.

"I'm not." Charlie grabbed Henry's face with both of his hands, taking advantage of the intimacy to scrutinize the younger demon's bone structure. Exquisite cheekbones and a masculine brow bone that led into an aristocratic nose that fell in line with a pointed chin. A strong, square jawline partially obscured by fine strands of long blonde hair.

Charlie grabbed Henry's cravat, pulling on it so that the fabric dug into the younger demon's soft neck. Henry choked, but Charlie did not alleviate his grip even as the fabric began to tear. Charlie pulled again, even harder, and the expensive fabric ripped. He brushed the shreds away from Henry's neck, starting in on his vest. Threads snapped and buttons popped, scattering in all directions. The shirt underneath the vest was buttoned as well and Charlie growled in frustration. So many ridiculous impediments.

"Here," Henry responded coolly, lifting his hands to start on the shirt. "Let me…"

"*No.*" Charlie smacked Henry's hands away, grabbing the shirt again and curling his fingers in-between the spaces where the buttons were. With another forceful tug, the shirt buttons sprang free from their bonds and launched into the air – winking out of existence somewhere in the corners of the room. Charlie barely noticed. He was far too focused on what he had been seeking this entire time.

Henry's sunken clavicle was just as beautiful as he had hoped. It took a great deal of restraint for Charlie not to grab it between his teeth and rip it free from the disgusting flesh that was keeping it bound in place. It arched gracefully into Henry's narrow shoulders, which Charlie gripped as he drew himself closer and pressed his nose against the hollow of Henry's throat. He could hear the younger demon gasp with the sudden contact. Charlie licked the bone, his whole body shivering with equal amounts of ecstasy and revulsion. On one hand he could taste nothing but the oil and sweat on Henry's skin— that greasy, disgusting human mixture. On the other hand, that beautiful clavicle teased him so…

His mouth was dripping. Charlie reached up to wipe the corners and seized Henry by the hair. Henry yelped, pressing his hands up against Charlie's chest in surprise as their mouths found each other once more. Charlie grabbed Henry by the throat, shoving him up against the wall, his tongue leaving a wet trail along Henry's jawline.

"Charlie!" Henry could not flush his words out quickly enough. "For a man who claims to know nothing…!"

Charlie watched the Adam's apple in Henry's throat bob as he spoke, but he did not hear a word. He slammed his hand against Henry's cheek, shoving his face up against the wall so that he could focus on the neck and bit of chest that the torn shirt left exposed. Charlie licked his lips, shoving his face against Henry's chest again and dragging his teeth and tongue over the sternum. Henry moaned, hips bucking and conforming to Charlie's forceful frame.

Charlie snarled in frustration. Short of killing him, there did not seem to be a way to keep Henry still. He shoved his hands down the band of the younger demon's breeches where there was a trimmed trail of downy blonde hair leading towards the mass of skin and cartilage that Charlie had no interest in. Henry was already half-erect and gasped when Charlie's icy fingers touched his swollen cock. Charlie rolled his eyes, wrapping his fingers around the member and giving it a good squeeze. He felt Henry grow in his hand until that hot, throbbing cock was resting against Charlie's forearm, no longer able to fit in his palm. He moved his hand down to stroke the base, paying scarce attention to the scrotum which he could not really bring himself to touch. Charlie's fingers traveled up the length, skating over the racing vein and teasing the head before moving back down. How cartilage was so like bone, and yet how it fell so short. He grabbed Henry's cock again, stroking it, the satin foreskin moving easily with the motion of his hands. Charlie focused on his due, the attractive clavicle that would be his reward at the end of all of this. Perhaps not when they were finished, but soon…

Henry moaned, his fingers curling against Charlie's back until the edges of his nails dragged over the stiff fabric of his shirt. Charlie heard the fabric squeal as it resisted, only the barest of distractions from the demon that was pumping desperately in his hands. Henry's chest rose and up and down with short, shallow breaths—each one more frantic than the last. There was sweat on his skin already, sliding down in gossamer beads. He was completely pliant and willing in Charlie's hands, and the Elder demon was barely humoring him as it was.

"Fuck me," Henry growled into Charlie's shoulder. "What are you waiting for?"

"Your gratitude is inspiring." Charlie slid his thumb over the head of Henry's cock, strings of shimmering pre-cum clinging to his skin.

"I'm..." Henry groaned again, hips spasming out of his control when Charlie started stroking him from base to head. "S-so, so close..."

Charlie clenched his teeth impatiently. His wrist was starting to ache as Henry's hips slowed, pressing hard into Charlie's hand as his orgasm reached its climax. Henry nearly sliced open Charlie's skin, clawing at his back and swallowing an inhuman sound as his orgasm erupted and spilled over the sides of his cock, thick and hot. Charlie pulled his hand out quickly, flicking it as if to fling off any offensive substances he might have touched. He flexed his fingers, frowning a bit.

"That is more work than it should be."

"What did you expect?" Henry panted, closing his eyes and resting his forehead against Charlie's stone wall of a chest. "I am not some pubescent boy, one stroke and done."

Charlie snorted, pulling back. "Go to bed."

"Come with me." Henry replied cheekily.

"No." If he joined Henry in bed, the man would wake up missing an arm. And Charlie had no intention of caving into his desires and tearing the younger demon apart at the joints.

Not yet, anyhow.

Wind caught the broken door and jerked it callously to the side, slamming it against the small shop's wooden frame. James knew something was amiss as soon as he saw it, reaching out to catch it with his hand and stop the infernal banging. He glanced inside, his eyes taking a moment to adjust. He thought he caught a glimpse of Virgil doubled over on the floor, arms wrapped around his middle, glasses pushed away from his face and resting on top of his head in a nest of white hair.

"What happened?" Glass popped underneath James' shoes as he stepped further inside. Bits of resin and splinters from the door dug into his soles in a desperate attempt to pierce through.

For a few brief seconds, he did not think that Virgil would be able to speak. The angel kept opening and closing his mouth looking for the world like a gasping fish.

"M-Michael." He finally managed to stammer out. James' mouth fell open before he could stop himself.

"The Archangel? Why?"

"*Mikhail!* The warrior saint! There is none other in Heaven." Blood and spittle bubbled up between Virgil's clenched teeth as he raked his fingernails across the floor. "He has always been a jealous, prideful shit. And now he has come through and destroyed… everything." The angel cast a woeful look at the doll he was cradling in his lap. James recognized the pieces as having belonged to the once-beautiful Cassandra.

Had Virgil even had a chance to finish her before this happened?

"I'm truly sorry." James was trying to discern how best to comfort the angel and the only thing he could think to do was to kneel down and start picking up the pieces of resin and glass.

Virgil let out a heartbroken sound, his anger evaporating on the sad little mewl. The angel began to crawl across the floor still dragging the broken Cassandra underneath his hand as he reached out with trembling fingers and began to pluck up the sharp, delicate shards.

"It is all ruined, now." An agonized moan shook the angel's entire body. "Everything is ruined and in pieces."

James swept up another handful of glass that had been ground to powder. The pieces sank into his skin. He watched them disappear. They made it too painful to even flex his hand.

"Yes," he could only think of Henry. "Yes, it is."

CHAPTER XII

"**Y**our guardian angel is looking for you again."

Claire paused, processing the statement for a minute before setting down the pieces of the pistol she had been cleaning and arranging them between her legs in an innocuous pattern.

"It has been three months." She muttered, sniffing and lifting her hand to dash it across her nose. "Don't angels give up?"

"I don't think they know how." Famine stepped further into the room, and she felt that deep, painful hunger shove itself down further into her gut. She winced, wiping her nose again, as if she rubbed it hard enough she could distract herself from the pain.

"I think he is just waiting," she said, "for you to get bored with us."

"He will be waiting for a long time, then." Famine's eyes burned like hot coals buried under a pile of ashes, a flicker of life trying desperately to feed. "Are you ready to hear our offer?"

Claire was quiet. She and Edward had been waiting for three full months to be told why two of Hell's most highly regarded names had even bothered to wipe their feet at the door of the moldering hotel.

"There is a demon named Rahman-Reza. Have you ever heard his name?"

Claire shrugged. "Once." She said. "Do you want us to kill him?"

"No. We want him found. We want him detained. But we don't want him dead. There is more." Famine cut her off before she could respond. "There are others."

Claire swallowed. A single demon she and her brother could handle. But multiple? They had never been set on a trail that was blackened by more than one entity.

"Rahman-Reza is dangerous. He is known for brutalizing his contracts as well as other demons. He is an eater of bones, and he has no scruples. That means he will tear you apart if he gets the chance. Don't give him one."

Claire felt her heart pounding in her throat, and she knew there was still more to be said. She only nodded, accepting the information and waiting for the rest.

"Mojgan and Jahangir are names you should recognize." Famine continued, moving so that he could stand by the window. The paint had long ago peeled up and flaked away. Now it was just a bare, gouged wooden frame that looked out onto a grey rain-drenched street. "Unless you were too young to remember the faces behind them."

So that was what this was about. She should not have been the least bit surprised. Claire pursed her lips.

"Mojgan is a little fuzzy in my mind." She said. "His name has been thrown in my face more times than I can count. But when I try to remember, all I get are the faintest details. Edward is the same way. But…" She tilted her head back to meet his eyes, a flicker of rising anger enough to grant her a modicum of bravery. "I remember Jahangir very plainly. And Edward and I have already had this discussion before. We are not going to hunt him down for anyone. We are entitled to our free will, and to that choice."

Famine drummed his clipped fingernails against the wooden pane. "Except when you aren't. Do you wonder why your angel hasn't been able to find you yet?"

She said nothing. She just looked at him.

"He has been cut off from the ability to read your thoughts. That is *almost* the whole of it. If he is given access again, he will find you. Now, I understand your free will — or free will as you understand it — is very important to you. I will remind you that everything is your decision. But we are here to be mutually beneficial to one another and in this case, if you will not provide me with the service I require, I will have no reason to continue providing for you either."

Claire's eyes dropped. She stared at the dismantled pistol that was resting just within reach. Even if she could put it together fast enough to blast an obsidian bullet through his skull, she doubted it would actually kill him. He had no reason to be afraid of her.

She, on the other hand, had every reason to be afraid of him. She would have to go along with this for Edward's sake if nothing else.

"Tell me more about the marks." She said, trying to make her voice sound as cold as possible.

Famine's expression did not change to give any indication of victory. He just continued down his line of thought. "They are not as dangerous, but they are wanted by hell. If they are in league with Rahman-Reza for any reason, they will have *become* dangerous. You will need to use more caution than you usually exercise."

"What is it about Rahman-Reza that makes him so dangerous?"

"He is an Eater of Bones. They are already a mean breed. He is gluttonous beyond his nature and ruthless in acquiring his meals. He never forms attachments. He never caves to temptation; he never settles down for very long. We are working with a limited window, because I feel that he is getting ready to move on again. It will be harder to chase him down, because he does not *usually* get locked into contracts. This time was a fluke."

"Ah."

"He has broken free of the bonds Hell. That alone should be of concern to you."

"Mmm," Claire mulled over it, sliding her finger down the barrel of the pistol resting on the empty space between her thighs. "And what is the price of failure?"

Famine's mouth became a thin line, vanishing into his blonde goatee. "Failure is not on the table."

"Are you going to deliver us into the hands of our old guardian?" Claire gave a voice to the thoughts that had been haunting her since he arrived.

"I very well might. Or I might do worse. Do as you are told, so that you don't find out."

"**W**hat is this?" Suzanne's eyes followed the teacup as it made its long descent. Charlie's lips curved into an unsettling grin, and he balanced the teacup, saucer and all on the curved arm of the divan where she was seated.

"Tea." He responded, dropping down into an adjoining chair. "I'd like to think you know what it looks like by now."

She gave him a look but picked up the cup regardless, if for no other reason than to keep it from tipping over and toppling to the floor. There was still steam rising off the surface, but she took her first sip anyway. She did not recognize the type, but it had an overwhelming hibiscus flavor.

She crinkled her pert nose. "I prefer coffee." She said.

"So does the rest of the country." Charlie made a suffering sound. "Tea is the mark of the elite, is it not? Or is that elsewhere? I don't pay attention."

"It comes and goes. Our noble palettes can only handle so much." Suzanne took another sip.

"Your brother is doing well." Charlie said conversationally. "Are you satisfied with his progress?"

Suzanne scoffed softly. "It is my curse that I will never be satisfied." She said, lowering the teacup. "Jean-François is making progress, yes, but not as much as I would like. It has been months and I fear he is showing signs of stagnating. At this rate, it could take him years. And we don't have years. We could both be dead by then. People are still being arrested and executed, and I cannot host a lavish dinner party or make an extensive public appearance without fear of having eyes fall on me. It is exhausting, living in terror. It is especially so when I have a powerful weapon in play, and I still can't seem to get anywhere."

Charlie's eyes sparked, but he didn't reply.

"I need more. And I need it quickly." She turned her head towards Charlie. "I am going to make a contract with Henry."

"You are already in a contract." Charlie idly pointed out.

"For my bones. My soul has not been spoken for."

"Do you really think you can hold the leashes of two demons, when you barely have control of one?" Charlie was openly scornful now, adjusting himself so that he was sitting upright in the chair. "Henry is younger than I and not nearly as powerful. There is nothing he can do for you that I can't."

"Maybe so," she shot back temperamentally. "But you are not doing well on your own, are you? Perhaps you need competition to motivate you. Or perhaps you just need someone of near-equal power to hold you accountable."

Charlie's grin sliced his face open once again, this time baring way too many savage teeth.

"It will be your mistake. Although I suppose it doesn't matter. You are going to be dead in the end, regardless. How many stomachs your corpse fills up is your prerogative." He pushed himself up to his feet in a single fluid motion. "I could stop you, but I won't. Henry happens to like women. He might even fancy you. I'm sure you can use that to your advantage somehow."

Her bright pink lip curled as she snarled at him. "You are out of line."

"Truly? Put me back in my place." He fixed his eyes on her, his grin widening to the point where it looked like his skull was going to split in half. "How will you do it, madame? How do you correct a demon?"

Her fingers curled, nails dragging against the expensive fabric of the divan as she stared him down but did not move.

She couldn't move to correct him. They both knew it. Charlie leaned forward over the arm of the divan, not breaking eye contact as he whispered, his breath tickling the shell of her ear: "I am impatient as well. And I am never satisfied. We are far more alike than you think. The only difference is that I am stronger, and I will pry every bone away from your greasy, fatty flesh with no more effort than it takes to eat a crab. You and your loathsome brother are succulent treats at a stop I did not intend to make, but I have met many women who have made me fight harder for my food. I'm sure that by now I am the only one who even gives them an occasional thought. So you are going to have to do better, if you want anyone to remember you existed at all."

Her pulse hammered in her throat as he dragged his fingernail up to scrape underneath her chin. She felt something warm trickle down to the collarbone—blood, perhaps. The sting implied that he had broken skin.

"Henry likes women." Charlie remarked flippantly as he turned away, making long strides towards the door. "He isn't very picky either, so I am certain his taste extends to you. Although I don't think you will have much luck imprinting yourself on *his* memory, either."

"Go to hell," Suzanne choked.

He tossed a glance over his shoulder, all smiles and white hot anger.

"Enjoy your tea." He slammed the door shut.

"I am not going to break." Francis reassured his partner for what felt like the twelfth time in an hour.

"You are already broken." Lady scolded him sharply. "Let me help."

Francis sighed and acquiesced to allowing himself to be helped out of the chair. The damage done to his body had been fairly devastating, though not nearly as bad as it could have been. He had not lost the ability to walk, but he was still having a good deal of trouble and still favored his left leg heavily over his right. Lady had gone into town on the third day of his recovery and had a walking stick commissioned—an elegant black piece with an ivory handle shaped like a swan. He was considerate in every detail.

And in all of the time they had been together, Francis never imagined that Lady would be a hands-on caretaker. But here they were, and he was still amazed every time his husband held out a hand to assist in any way.

Lady pushed the cane into Francis' hand once the demon was standing. Francis clenched the handle, leaning onto it so that he could let go of Lady's arm. Nodding his thanks, he began his short journey down the hallway. Lady followed at his side, relentlessly attentive.

"I am getting better." Francis said, hoping that his husband might agree.

"A little bit each day." Lady barely let him have that much, pushing the bedroom door open for him. "Don't let your progress get to your head. Or one day you are going to let go of that walking stick and break your hip on a fall."

"I wouldn't make you carry me, if I did." Francis teased.

"I wouldn't try. I would just wait for you to expire and then make the coroner handle you." A strand of loose ginger hair fell out of place, falling into Lady's eyes as he bent over the narrow bed to turn down the sheets. "I am going into town again, so don't do something stupid like try to get out of bed until I get back."

"I can manage." Francis said again, sitting down on the edge of the bed. He swallowed an exasperated sigh underneath a withering brown glare and handed over his cane, half-expecting to be beaten with it.

Lady took the walking stick away and propped it up in a corner, motioning for Francis to lay down. "Do you want the covers up?"

Francis shook his head. "I would like the window open, please."

Lady crossed the room and went over to the small window, gripping the bottom and yanking it upwards. Something cracked above his head, but he didn't pay it any mind. "I am going to pick up coffee and some more bread. I know you want tobacco, and you're not getting it. So is there anything else?"

"Brandy." Francis said dryly. Lady nodded.

"That goes without saying." He stepped away from the window. "Behave. Don't summon anyone, don't set anything on fire."

"You spoil all my best plans." Francis put his arms behind his head, closing his eyes. He felt his glasses being lifted off his nose and heard Lady set them on the dresser beside his bed.

"I know." The Unchaste said. "How do you ever manage to stay married to me?"

"I hear I have no choice." Francis said. "In fact, I have been threatened several times."

"I should be canonized for putting up with you." Lady was already on his way out. Francis could hear his voice fading as his footsteps made their way down the hall.

Lady pulled his coat down from the rack, threading his arms through it before grasping the door handle and letting himself out. There was not much to be said for the small apartment they rented. With Francis in such a bad way, Lady wanted something more stable than a hotel to see them through the long nights, but also something small and nondescript enough to allow them to slip through the cracks.

Francis was getting better, but not fast enough. Every day they had to stay in the apartment, Lady worried that they might be found. He knew it was only a matter of time before Famine came after them once again. And they would not survive a second encounter.

Besides this, Henry needed to know. A man deserved to be told when his children were after his blood — especially when they were backed by the bourgeoisie of Hell. It wasn't just out of courtesy, either. Once they killed Henry, and whoever else was in their path, they were going to hunt down Lady. And he could not have that. Not at all. It wouldn't do.

The idea had haunted him for weeks, but he had only recently convinced himself that it was safe to leave Francis alone. Even so, Lady wasn't planning on being gone for long. He had to make this quick.

He did not know exactly where to find Henry, but he doubted it could be that hard. He had, after all, managed to do it at least once.

276

CHAPTER XIII

Suzanne's bedchamber was a nightmare. Henry had no idea how the woman even slept at night. His head hurt just from looking at the nauseating pink and white stripes that bled into the baseboards, every few inches studded with gold stucco. The covers on her bed were pink as well, and the pillows were piled so high that he wondered how she managed to sit down without rolling off.

He closed the doors behind him, as he had been instructed to do. She had told him an hour ago to meet him here, but to wait until the clock struck past noon. He ventured a few steps further, his peripherals catching unexpected movement on the bed.

There was a flash of bare white leg, and Suzanne sat up, her long red hair streaming around her shoulders like strands of exotic silk. Her frilled dressing gown served to help her blend in with the sumptuous comforter, which was no doubt why he had not seen her beforehand. The front of the gown was completely open, and she was wearing nothing underneath. Her naked white breasts were small enough to fit into his hand; her nipples had been rouged to make them appear red and perfectly round, like cinnamon candy.

"How good of you to keep our appointment." She tilted her head and smiled at him, lifting her hand and bending graceful fingers to beckon him forward. Beneath the white face paint, he could still see the faintest trace of freckles. Not quite as heavy as her brother's, but certainly present. "I was hoping we could talk."

"Well, you have my attention." Henry moved closer to the bed, watching her closely as his leg brushed against the comforter. She reached out and touched his arm, fingers pinching and tugging on the expensive fabric of his jacket.

"Sit with me." She said. "Allow yourself to unwind."

"Madame," he did not pull his arm away, his eyes briefly traveling down the length of her body, her figure like a ribbon of pale silk. His gaze made the leisurely journey back up to meet hers. She had eyes like sea glass, the diaphanous green ruined by the faint orange ring that encircled them.

She pursed artificially pink lips. "Do not call me 'madame'."

"A dreadful habit. Forgive me, I implore you."

She tugged on his sleeve again, but when he did not himself up onto the bed, she moved into what she had brought him here to say. "Has Charlie spoken to you at all?"

"Charlie hardly speaks to me." Henry said. "And I would hazard that we have not yet crossed paths today."

"As close as you two are? Always beside each other. You scrambling after his heels like a faithful page in the service of a prince." She smirked. "I suppose it is hard not to, after all. When he holds so much more power."

Henry's eye twitched. "He would not want me for a valet. I rarely do as I am told."

"And I suppose, then, that means you are not interested in a contract?" She leaned back against her pillows, adjusting the skirt of her robe so that is draped over her thigh, allowing only a sliver of flesh leading down to her shapely foot.

Her question was framed innocently enough, but Henry understood the game now.

"You are already in a contract," he spoke as if she needed reminding. He set his hand on top of her small ankle, his hand tracing over the curve of her calf and gliding up towards the promising warmth of her thigh.

"For my bones." She said, her breath hitching at his touch. "Not my soul. Don't you want to taste my soul, Henry?"

He did not respond immediately. His let his hand linger on her thigh, his fingers making little circles over her damp, heated skin. He was fascinated by the delightful reddish gold hairs that curled over his fingers as he went up further and touched her entrance, stroking delicately until he stirred up wetness.

Suzanne moaned, rolling her hips and trying to push herself down onto his fingers. Henry kept his hand where it was, not pushing it any deeper. He just continued to tease.

"Orange," he said finally. "So much about you is orange. Especially your soul. It is such a vile, temperamental color. And yours has not seen enough to cultivate a fine bitter taste."

"My soul has seen—!" she gasped indignantly, her thighs clenching around his hand.

"Plenty? Nineteen years, I have that right? Your soul does not know what bitterness is. But if you were to live another thousand, no amount of pain can turn an orange soul black. So if you were searching for a younger, more pliant demon that you could control, who could possibly save you from the egregious mistake you made in summoning an eater of bones…" Henry pushed his fingers in deeper. "You missed your mark. I don't want your sour little soul."

Suzanne sucked in a breath so quickly that it turned into a cough. Henry felt her already tight entrance clench around his fingers and he pulled them out, startled. He looked up at her, waiting patiently for her to regain herself, but she only coughed harder.

Suzanne sat up, blood trickling down from her pointed nose and dripping down her chin. She held up her hand to catch it as it fell in bright red splatters against her porcelain fingers. She regarded him with horror, her eyes bright with panic.

"What did you do to me?" She demanded. All of her previous temper had been erased, and now she just sounded frightened. She coughed again, speckles of blood marring the garish color on her lips.

"Nothing!" Henry insisted, frozen in his place. He had not done anything that would trigger *that*. If she was coughing up blood, then there was blood in her lungs. And since she had not been shot or stabbed, what was there to suspect but...

A hand landed on his shoulder. Henry jumped, that chilling touch more familiar to him than the voice that followed.

"Thank you, Henry." Charlie was so close that Henry could feel every word brush against his neck. "I will take over from here."

"Poison is tawdry, you know." Henry whispered back. "And it spoils your food."

"It is not all poison." Charlie said almost defensively. He pushed Henry firmly to the side, stepping forward to fill his place. "Run along, little boy. This meal was not made for you."

Henry looked at Suzanne one last time, her eyes only granting him a partial window into the full of her terror. She coughed again, and darker blood sprayed from her lips into her hand. It was time for him to go.

Henry left as quickly as he was able. He thought that Suzanne might have tried to say something to him, but he ignored her. Charlie was right. This was not his food. And he was not going to be the one to stand between a starved demon and his meal.

Of course, once Suzanne was dead, there would only be her brother…what was going to happen when Charlie was free of the contract that bound him?

Maybe it was time find James and apologize.

R aziel stuffed his hands underneath his armpits, huddling in the oversized brown trench coat that swallowed his broad frame. It had not been drizzling when he arrived on this plane, but now it was just starting to pick up. Of course, he had not thought to bring an umbrella. He already looked out of place as it was. But there was no point in taking pains to dress for an era that he was going to be leaving behind in less than an hour anyway.

He could only hope that his flip-flops went unnoticed. They didn't even belong to him. They were too big and kept slipping off, but Uriel had left them behind during his last visit. They had since been conveniently repossessed, being the only shoes Raziel had seen around the house in almost thirty years. The trench coat wasn't his either, although he couldn't remember exactly who had left it behind.

He shuffled down the street, doing his best to try and innocuously grab Lady's attention. The Unchaste stood by the window of a tired old coffee shop and stared somewhat dismally at the gaping hole that had been left behind by a brick or something similar. He kept peering inside as if he expected someone might be in there regardless of the fact that it looked like the front door hadn't opened in a week.

Raziel tried to stand close enough to hover at the edge of Lady's peripherals, but he was still being profoundly ignored. He huffed, not sure what to do, and shuffled a little bit closer, lifting his hand and wriggling his fingers in not-quite-a-wave. Lady just turned on his heel and started walking in the opposite direction of where Raziel was standing.

The angel picked up speed trying to catch up. His toes were already soaked, and his wet flip-flops had no traction against the slick cobblestoned street. A single slip could send him careening into his target…

Lady wasn't turning around. What kind of person didn't even look over their shoulder? Raziel could feel heat sweeping up to his cheeks as he caught up, moving again into Lady's peripherals, inching closer and closer as he tried to make himself more obvious.

He didn't realize exactly how close he was getting until he nearly collided with the Unchaste, who caught sight of him just in time to maneuver out of the way, dainty heeled boot skipping disdainfully over the top of Raziel's foot.

"What is wrong with you?" Lady snarled, whipping around like a feral cat bristling with anger.

"It was more difficult than I thought!" Raziel gasped, simultaneously relieved to have finally caught Lady's attention and mortified at having nearly run him over.

Lady paused, mouth half open, brow furrowed as he looked the angel up and down. He didn't seem to recognize

Raziel at first, and the angel was too flustered and focused on backtracking his half-formed sentence to explain.

"Finding you!" Raziel waved his arms in mild distress, fighting to form his thought. "It was harder than I thought! I got the era wrong twice and had to keep changing lanes — there!" He bit his lip, looking at Lady in hopes the Unchaste understood. Lady's brow cleared and he folded his arms, pursing his lips shrewdly as those warm brown eyes flickered up and down again. So judgmental.

"What are you doing here, Raziel?" Lady demanded.

"Did you get my letter?" Raziel tilted his head, his voice making an upward inquiring lilt.

"I did. But Francis has been indisposed and we have been in no position to make a move towards Heaven. Or anywhere else." Lady uncrossed his arms, fidgeting with the hem of his short, pristinely cut jacket. "Did you come all the way down here just to ask me that?"

"No!" Raziel said defensively, his cheeks flushing as he shifted on his feet, trying not to seem like he was squirming underneath the Unchaste's scrutinizing gaze. "It was just that…well, I wanted to see if you needed help. Getting back to Heaven and all. If you were going to come up though I can't imagine why you would want to go back down to Hell."

"We have had this discussion, Raziel. It's quieter. The whiskey is cheaper. No one bothers you in Hell and if they do, you're expected to ignore them. I can't deal with Heaven and its constant expectations."

"And I get that!" Raziel nodded emphatically to show that he did, indeed, understand. "My plants, you know, they need quiet. You could come stay with me and it wouldn't be so bad. I mean, it's a bit messy. And dark. But you've met my robots and they are all very nice."

"Yes, I have met your robots. And they are grand." Lady sighed. "In truth, I am more focused on Francis at the moment. As I said, he's in no condition to go anywhere. Even if you were kind enough to help us up to Heaven, I think the trip would do a number on him. And I'm not willing to risk it."

"I understand." Raziel responded quietly. "It is very important. I hope he feels better soon. But when he does feel better, do you promise to think about it some more?"

"I promise to at least visit." Lady said. "But I don't think you should talk about it too loudly anymore, dear, because someone up in Heaven is going to hear. And I've already got Hell on my ass. I really don't want this coming at me from two fronts. Hiding is hard enough."

"Yes, it is." Raziel said solemnly, straightening up a bit. Droplets of rain rolled off his wide shoulders as he looked around. "It is wet. Where are you going?"

"I need to find Henry Wickes. One if not both of his children are after his blood, and I will be lucky if he isn't already dead. You haven't seen him, by chance?"

Raziel shook his head.

"But you remember them, yes? You've heard of the Clifton..."

"Oh, I know who you are talking about." Raziel reassured him. "We all know. But I don't know where Jahangir is. If I knew...I suspect it would end badly for him."

"I have no doubt." Lady shook his head. "Thank you for checking in at any rate. It was ah — good to see you."

"It was good to see you!" Raziel beamed. "Come up any time. You sure you don't need me to follow you?"

Lady hesitated.

"I'll be fine." He finally replied before flashing Raziel the bare minimum requirement for a smile. "You go on home. I'm sure your plants need you. And err... your droids."

"Yes, they do. I will see you later, then..." Raziel gave Lady another tiny wave, flashing him a quick smile before shoving his hands down into his pockets and turning to walk off.

The attic was packed with what Virgil referred to as his 'human clutter'. It was mostly odds and ends of things usually left to antique shops. James had tripped over three dolls already—*'but not pretty ones'*, the angel had assured him, *'so it's all right'*. Henry sat cross-legged on the attic floor, his finger making patterns in the thick layer of grey dust that blanketed the wooden boards. His blonde hair swept over his cheeks, obscuring most of his face as he seemed to be concentrating very hard on the whimsical shapes.

"Repeat back what I just said." James used the toe of his shoe to shove another box out of the way.

Cluttered or not, it was the only place where James felt safe discussing anything. Virgil had been so mired in depression over Cassandra's ruin that he hadn't even bothered to fix the damn front door.

"You said you are sorry that you're a wanker. Or, wait – was that my line?" Henry looked up, flashing a smile.

"No. I asked you what we are going to do about Charlie." James shoved another box out of the way and sat down next to his companion.

"Oh," Henry dropped his head back down, returning the large part of his concentration to his shapes. "I don't know. I don't think there is anything we *can* do about Charlie. We can run, I suppose. Again."

"And draw attention to ourselves." James muttered, rubbing his face, pushing up his glasses so that he could grind his fingers into the wet corners of his eyes. "Which seems counter-productive."

"Only a little. I don't much like this era anyway." Henry sighed, leaning back on his palms and stretching his long legs out in front of him, tilting his head back so he could look at James. "So much for finding somewhere to wait for the dust to settle. Something tells me that we are going to be kicking it up for the remainder of our existence."

"Maybe we will have better luck not being trailed by a complete lunatic in the next era." James said even though he doubted, very strongly, that they were going to be that lucky.

CHAPTER XIV

"**S**uzanne?"

Jean-François did not usually feel the need to call out for his sister. He wouldn't have, except that he felt his heart hit the pit of his stomach like a stone as soon as he walked through the door. The silence stretched on even after he shut the front door behind him, feeling anxiety claw at his throat and hold back his shallow breath.

Every lamp had been doused so that Jean-François could barely see his hands out in front of him as he tried to pick his way towards the staircase. He kept jamming his knuckles into walls and bumping into door frames. He never realized exactly how helpless he was in the dark.

His feet found the staircase before he did. He hissed when he felt his toes crunch up against the bottom step and he looked up, reaching out to grip the banister that he knew was there. He could see yellow light dancing at the top of the stairs flickering just barely out of sight. He swallowed hard, not daring to call for his sister again as trepidation settled into his bones. He started a slow ascent, his reluctant legs dragging out each step. He did not want to know what waited for him at the top of the stairs. He didn't know if he could outrun it, at this rate.

He closed his eyes right before the last step, making another attempt at a deep breath as he brought his foot down firmly at the top. He opened only one eye, craning his head to glance down the hall as he tried to catch sight of what was there. Nothing, of course…nothing but an open doorway and a low, flickering yellow light. Suzanne was just burning candles. Of course…she rather liked candles. Born in the wrong decade, that woman.

Jean-François opened both eyes again and started down the hallway, apprehension still weighing heavily on his chest. Even if it *was* just Suzanne, she was no doubt going to have a few choice words for him because he was so late coming home. That was not, of course, his fault. His meeting had run late. But he would rather have her berate him, at this point—anything to know that she was well and robust as usual.

He stopped at the doorway to his sister's bedroom. Her door was cracked, and he wrapped his hand around the knob. Squeezing the brass, he thrust the door open, and the ugly yellow light assaulted his vision, blinding him temporarily. He could already smell blood.

"Nice of you to knock." That evil demon spoke, and Jean-François' head spun. His vision started to clear and the first thing he saw was his sister's favorite petal pink robe. It was ripped scandalously down the back and thrown carelessly over the foot of her bed. It was drenched with blood, brown in the places where it was starting to dry.

"What have you done?" Jean-François felt the words die on his tongue. His throat contracted as he could not bring himself to pull his eyes further up the bed. He did not want to see what wanton position the demon had laid her out in. He did not want to see all the parts of her that were missing.

"You are a coward." Charlie laughed. Jean-François flinched as he heard a bone snap and the demon paused to suck out the marrow, not even masking the loud slurping sound. "Look up."

Jean-François cringed. Feeling he had no choice, he lifted his head just a little bit, raising his eyes to confront the carnage. Suzanne was sprawled across her bed, her legs flat like jelly smeared across bread. There was not much left of them. The demon had pulled out every bone up to her waist. She was not conscious but judging from the way her eyelids would still twitch every now and again she had to still be alive.

"Dear God…" Jean-François felt his voice climb until it squeaked. He reached up, clenching the cravat that was suddenly too tight around his throat. The demon was sitting on the edge of the bed, perched with one leg tucked underneath him. His hose were soaked with blood. His mouth and chin were vibrant red and more blood bubbled up between his vicious teeth when he grinned. He opened his mouth, running a cherry tongue over his lips and lifting his fingers to suck the blood off their tips.

"The contract..." Jean-François continued, sweat beading on his brow as he started to back out of the room. "It wasn't...it is not complete..."

"It is over." Charlie's merciless cold blue eyes sent an icy pang straight into Jean-François' heart. "Don't think for a minute that I'm going to forget you, either."

Jean-François froze. He held the demon's gaze for as long as he could. It lasted all of a minute, maybe less, until Charlie moved – sliding off the side of the bed and pulling himself up on his feet. The eater of bones bared his teeth again and a feral, hungry growl rumbled in his chest.

Jean-François broke. He turned on his heel and ran, nearly colliding with the door as he tore out of the room. His thoughts were racing. There was nowhere in this city where he could seek asylum. No one was going to understand. He had to escape. Escape before he was devoured...

The hall rug bunched up underneath his feet, twisting around the toe of his shoe. His hands went numb with impact when he fell, pain shooting up his legs, his knees cracking as they hit the hard floor. Jean-François groaned, clawing at the floor as he tried to crawl away, chest heaving with each ragged breath.

A pointed shoe slammed into the back of his head. Jean-François cried out in agony, spit and blood flying from his gaping mouth and sliding down his chin. He choked, trying to push himself upright, and the shoe drove into the back of his skull again. A merciless heel came crashing down on the small of his back, grinding down into his kidneys. He was barely able to swallow a scream of agony as he struggled to pull away, unable to writhe or buck his way free like an insect pinned to a board.

"P-Please…!" Jean-François could barely speak, straining to push every word through his chattering teeth. The demon growled, grinding his heel down harder until Jean-François felt like his insides were going to burst underneath the pressure.

"There is no mercy for a man trying to squirm his way out from underneath the heel of a demon." Charlie sneered, leaning over Jean-François' prostrate form with blood-stained white hands resting on his narrow hips. "Although these things are usually so much less of a veritable punch to the face."

"It was my sister…it was Suzanne who summoned you!" Jean-François spat a glob of blood onto the floor; his nose and throat still burning like he was drowning.

"You cringe so unattractively." Charlie crouched down, putting all of his weight on those damn heels and wrenching another loud moan from Jean-François' throat. Lithe fingers crawled across Jean-François' face, prying open his mouth and slipping inside like a spider. Jean-François tried to bite down in defense, but he could not even make the intrusive fingers so much as bend underneath the pressure.

"Here, now." Charlie cooed, his fingers reaching towards the back of Jean-François' mouth. Jean-François gagged, feeling his stomach spasm with the threat of vomit. Charlie pinched one of Jean-François' molars between his fingertips, cooing again as he wrenched the tooth and pulled it free, root and all. Jean-François' mouth filled with more blood and he was forced to swallow some of it, his mouth still gaping open around Charlie's invasive fingers. "I am going to pull out every single one, Jean. I hope you stay awake for the entire process. Because then I am going to work my way down and devour you slowly. So very slowly. So that you hardly realize it is happening until you can no longer feel your fingers or your toes."

Jean-François heard bone shatter between the demon's ferocious incisors. He managed to pull his arm free, clawing the ground above his head. His weak nails split down to the quick with the pressure. He whimpered again. Before he could pull his other arm free, he felt the weight of the heel being lifted from his back. Expensive shoes struck the floor, one landing on his hand, finger bones crunching painfully. Jean-François saw speckles, fighting not to pass out with the pain.

"You are going to have to try harder than that." Charlie's voice was almost a whisper. "Are you going to make me fight for this? There is something so exhilarating about chasing one's meal." He lifted his foot off Jean-François' hand, his sharp, unsettling laugh cracking like a whip. "All right then. Go! Play the hunted rabbit for me. I want your heart pounding when I pin you down again."

Jean-François pulled his hand back, cradling it against his chest as he scrambled to his feet. His knees trembled as he swayed, unable to stay steady. Green eyes brimming with pain glanced up from behind red curls that hung around his face like rusted coils. He thought Charlie would hit him again, pull him down to the floor, but the demon didn't move. In the darkness, the only parts of him that were visible were his stony blue eyes and illuminated sections of his white hair, shining like an obscured Christ-figure.

"Run." The demon ushered impatiently. Jean-François did not wait to be told a third time. He clenched his hand tighter, blood streaming from his broken skin as he darted down the hall his mind and heart racing out of sync as he racked his scattered brain for somewhere — anywhere — to hide.

He waited for the sounds of pursuit. So far, there were none. And somehow that was not comforting.

His foot landed awkwardly on the stairs, nearly causing him to fall forward. Jean-François grabbed hold of the railing, his grip lubricated by his own blood as he slid, dragging his feet down the steps.

The door was just ahead. If he could make it, he could leave. Charlie was finally starting to follow him. The bone eater hummed to himself as he made his leisurely descent, building the apprehension as he moved.

Jean-François did not linger. He bolted for the door, his good hand out to grasp the handle. He never found it, but the door still flew open when he slammed his whole body against the wood. His left side was tingling as he staggered out into the street, losing one shoe in the process and abandoning the other for the sake of speed.

Clouds were breaking apart above his head, giving way to the canopy of stars that pocked the night sky. The moon was still obscured, and so the light was minimal. The streets were still slick with rain, making it that much harder for him to keep his footing. Everything was so quiet. He did not realize how many people would already be abed…

Something dashed across the street. At first he thought it was a dog, but a second look revealed it to be very human. The figure was at least tall as he was in platform boots with jutting spikes running down the spine of the heel. Crimson-and-black dreadlocks were swept over one shoulder to avoid interfering with the fearsome weapon that was strapped to their back. Exactly what it was, he couldn't tell. But he felt a glimmer of hope at the sight. It was enough to propel him forward, almost sprinting the last few inches, waving his good hand in hopes of catching this person's attention.

"Help me!" Jean-François screamed at the top of his lungs, not caring if the demon behind him heard or not. "Please! Somebody!"

The figure looked up. He caught a flash of glowing yellow eyes but he was sure it had to be a trick of the light.

They reached up and touched the weapon that rested against their back, pulling it free of its leather holster. He heard the straps thudding against their heavy jacket, and by the time they had pulled it around completely, he was close enough to see what it was.

The T-shaped handle was black, a gloved finger resting on top of a red switch. It looked big and heavy enough to require two hands. Attached was a slim, twisted metal cylinder that was as long as Jean-François' arm and the very end flattened into the shape of a spade.

The stranger said nothing. Jean-François was close enough that if he fell, he would certainly land on top of them. He drew in a deep breath and gasped, glancing down at the weapon and back up at them, his eyes watering.

"Help me," he whispered again. He could hear Charlie's footsteps closing in on him from behind. His knees were trembling again, in danger of giving out underneath him. "Please, he is going to kill me…"

The metal cylinder whirred, letting out an awful, shrill sound as it swung around. He saw it flash in the corner of his eye, and then he felt searing pain rip through his chest as the metal pierced him, the spade end spinning and shredding his heart. Jean-François' whole body went numb. He couldn't even feel himself hit the ground. He could barely hear the dull thud of his head cracking against the cobblestones.

The footsteps stopped. Charlie slid his hands into his pockets and glanced up at the reaper who stared back at him with cold, pale yellow eyes. A final mashing of the trigger, and the drill shrieked again as they set a boot on Jean-François' shoulder to give themselves some leverage to yank the drill bit free from his chest.

Charlie did not say a word. He only nodded, puffing in exasperation as he watched the reaper step away from the corpse. They turned around, resting the drill on their shoulder and continued on their way in the opposite direction. He was surprised that this one did not stop to collect the soul. Then again, they probably had no interest in this weak, corrupt specimen.

CHAPTER XV

"I don't think you should go," the angel said to James. Virgil clearly felt strongly enough about the situation to protest, but not strongly enough to get out of his chair. He had been sitting in that same old, sunken chair for several weeks. His long hair was falling free of its tie, greasy tendrils slipping down his long neck and resting on his shoulders. His glasses were dull, having not been cleaned in a while. Rubbing the hem of his shirt over the lenses did little more than spread the grime around.

"We have to." James slipped his coat up over his shoulders. "We are in danger the longer we stay here. And consequently so are you."

"It is late." Virgil sounded like he himself was only half-convinced of his own argument as he glanced dismally outside. "There will be traffic. Reapers and angels and who knows what else."

"Sins." Henry muttered. "You can smell it all in the air. That is why we have to go."

"And your boyfriend." Virgil looked away. "Don't forget about that."

James had done his best to stay mindful of the angel's fragile state of being. However, he was also doing his very best not to reach out and snap the creature's neck at the same time.

"Charlie is not my boyfriend." Henry protested, sounding wistful at the fact.

"I am going to kill both of you." James announced, straightening his collar irately before stomping towards the door. "Stay here and keep each other company. Wait for Charlie to get back so he can smash the rest of your dolls and *your* fool skull." He turned his glare on Henry. "I am not going to wait around to become a meal."

"I don't think he would eat *you*." Henry hissed, moving quickly to join him. "I think your bones would be sour."

"My bones are hollow." James said dryly. "Like my existence."

"Come off it." Henry's fingers twitched as if he were fighting the impulse to smack his companion upside the head. "We are going. See? This is me. Walking."

"Walk faster." James pushed his hand against the small of Henry's back, only glancing at Virgil over his shoulder. "Thank you, I suppose, for allowing me to stay."

"Don't mention it." Virgil groused. "Maybe when you come back, I will have fixed that door."

"I doubt it." James pushed Henry out the doorway, propelling him into the streets. Henry huffed and moved himself out of James' reach, pulling his own coat tighter around his shoulders. "All right, so where do we…?"

"Oh, for the love of Hell," James interrupted him, pointing across the street. "Something wicked this way comes."

Henry followed the line of James' vision. Momentary terror flashed across his face but was quickly replaced by a vague annoyance.

Lady did not look happy to see them either. But he did look uncharacteristically relieved, giving the impression that he may have been seeking them out on purpose.

"You!" Lady wagged his finger in their direction, hopping across the narrow street that separated them. Henry lifted an inquisitive brow.

"Me. Us?" Henry glanced at James. "Who are you looking for, exactly?"

"I am here for *you*." Lady rested a hand on his hip, leaning a bit heavily as if he had been running and needed to catch his breath. "How is it that you are always around exactly when I don't want you but the minute I decide I actually need you, you are nowhere to be found?"

"I am a walking inconvenience." Henry said wryly. "You should not put yourself out over me."

"I came to give you a warning, you stupid ass." Lady snipped. "I don't think you will believe who I happened to run into recently."

"Whom?" Henry glanced at James again, although James ignored him completely.

"Your daughter." Lady said, his hand dropping away from his hip as he straightened. "I don't know if you remember Claire. She was one of the unseemly brood that you spawned during your days with Violet Clifton."

"Of course I remember her." Henry sounded more than slightly offended. "What about her, in particular?"

"She has had a run-in with Hell, and they have attached a Sin and a Horseman to her. Gluttony and Famine, to be precise. I am sure you know those two well."

"Not my ring," Henry admitted, "but damn close. I've met them both before. I don't think either like me very much."

"No one likes you." Lady assured him. "Least of all anyone whose hierarchy you have tried to throw a wrench into. But that's only half the point. Do you understand what I am saying? Your daughter is going to come after you and she is going to have Hell backing her up. That should be enough incentive for you to pack yourself up tonight and haul yourself into another dimension altogether."

Henry burst out laughing. "I am afraid you have wasted your precious time, Mx. Hayward. We are already on our way out. In fact, the longer we linger here, the more I worry about Rahman-Reza catching up to us. And that appears to be a thousand times worse than Hell."

Lady held up his hands. "That is all I wanted to say." He pursed his lips, adjusting his glasses sharply. "I am going back now. Francis needs me. We are not lingering very long, ourselves. I would say that I hope to see you in the next era but all you seem to do is attract attention. So I am going to settle for a simple 'no thank you' and 'kindly sod off'." The Unchaste turned around at that, starting down the street in the opposite direction from which he came. A breeze tousled his auburn hair, whipping the gelled strands around despite their best efforts at resistance.

"I don't like him." James said. "Have I ever mentioned that?"

"Once. Twice. A dozen times." Henry rolled his eyes. "I don't like him either, I don't think."

Claire had come out here alone, something Edward made her swear she would never do. But Edward was nowhere to be found, and she was not going to make any progress waiting around for him.

The thought of her brother caused Claire's heart to skip with worry. She pushed the feeling down. She could not afford to dwell on it right now. She had to focus on what was ahead.

She was lightly armed, as the chances of her running into trouble seemed low. It was just going to be a walk around the city. She would be well-prepared for any demons who might try to cross her path, but she took comfort in the fact that she knew there were reapers out gathering souls tonight. Not many demons were willing to cross paths with them.

Claire's head felt light, but she could chalk that up to the fact that she could not remember the last full meal she had eaten. Her thick jacket still did not feel like enough to keep out the merciless cold that gnawed on her nose and made her ears ache.

Footsteps echoed behind her. Claire did not break her stride, but she could feel the muscles tensing in her shoulders. She lifted her hand, reaching down and gripping the large rubber handle of her favorite knife. The way the steps had suddenly picked up, rather than falling naturally into place coming from the opposite direction, told her that the presence was preternatural. She could not smell Sulphur, but that did not necessarily mean much…

She stopped at the street curb, breathing lightly as she strained to hear any change in the approaching steps. It was just one, long, continuous gait that did not stop, shuffle, or otherwise change at any point. It sounded like the sound was being played on a reel. She was certain they should have caught up to her by now.

Claire furrowed her brow, feeling frozen in place. She was not sure whether it was time to dart across the street and try to shake them off, or whether she should continue as if she did not know she was being followed. Either way, she had to shake them…

"I don't think you have enough weapons." The voice came from right beside her. Claire jumped, springing to the side as she pulled her knife free, brandishing it as a warning.

"That is not going to do much against demons." The person who spoke was shorter than her and slight; a woman of indeterminate age with ghoulish blue hair cut in a disastrous style. When she spoke, metal piercings glittered in the street lighting.

"Do you know from experience?" Claire snipped, eyes scanning the woman up and down for any sight of vulnerability. She did not seem to be carrying a weapon of her own. Even more peculiar was the strand of bubble-shaped glass jars strung across her hips.

"I've taken down a demon or two in my time, yes." The woman flashed a smile and flicked her wrist. Claire saw the flash of a narrow blade, but the woman's actions were not so much of a threat as they were showing off. "But I know a bad one is out tonight."

"I am looking for a bad one." Claire forced herself to meet the woman's eyes, which were as dark as ink. "Do you know where I could find him?"

"Hard to say. He is probably still eating. My superior took down his meal not too far back down that way." The knife flicked again, and she used it to gesture over her shoulder. "Is he someone you're related to?"

Claire's lip curled.

"No," she said. "Not this one."

"Cambion don't crop up too often. It's always nice to see one of nature's great mysteries." The woman sneered and hooked her thumbs onto her shallow front pockets, turning her head away. "Her name is Crimson, my superior. That bit will be helpful when you are asking her nicely not to kill you. She doesn't really like your kind."

"*My kind,*" Claire muttered under her breath before speaking up again. "And what name should I give her in case I need a character reference to make my case?"

The woman laughed. "Butterfly." She said. "Although that won't help you any."

There was blood on the street. It was so thick and pungent that James caught scent of it on the breeze well before they even stumbled onto the scene. Jean-François, whom he barely recognized, lay face-down in a dark pool. His rust-colored curls were soaked, as were his fine clothes. He did not look like he had been dead for very long.

"There are pieces of him missing," James said, reaching up to cover his mouth and nose with one gloved hand.

"Yes, I'm guessing Charlie got to him first. Poor lad." Henry crinkled his nose, waving his hand in front of his face. "His corpse reeks of fear."

"Do you blame him?" James shook his head, crouching down a little bit closer to the body as he reached out hesitantly to make an inspection. "Everfather's eyes…half of his face is missing."

"I find cheekbones irresistible." Charlie's voice oozed like oil onto the sidewalk. "I could not risk his going to waste."

If Henry heard the Elder demon approach, he reacted too late. Charlie gripped Henry's upper arm, pulling him close and sliding his fingers down the strong line of his jaw.

James snarled, his body tensing, ready to lunge at the older demon. His gums were throbbing, but feeling threatened was not enough to allow his true form to break the surface of his skin. As young as he was, he could not change form on a dime. He sprang to his feet and lunged for the older demon.

Charlie's hand pulled away from Henry's face. Long black talons burst from his nail beds, emerging just in time to swipe across James' face. Blood splattered against the cobblestones as James reached up, pressing his hand against the ugly wound that was only an inch away from taking out his eye. Blood streamed between his fingers, running in rivulets down the back of his hand. Charlie hissed, his mouth stretching open, gums bleeding from where his metal teeth were already beginning to surface.

"I will take off your entire head," the Elder demon snarled, "if you come any closer." He turned his attention back to Henry, bloody fingers gripping the younger demon's chin as he leaned in, his lips pressed close to Henry's ear. "There now. Why are you afraid of me? I thought we had moved past all of that."

"Because you are a maniac," Henry whispered. "Let James go."

"So concerned about James? It isn't his bones I want." Charlie slid his lips over the shell of Henry's ear, tongue slipping out to flicker over the cartilage and playing with the ridges. "This is what you wanted all along, isn't it?" His hand left Henry's arm, moving down the slight indenture of his waist and crossing over to rest against his back, nails sharp enough to prick Henry through the cloth of his jacket and shirt. "Tell me, Henry. Am I what you desire?"

"So much," Henry breathed, his shoulders tensing. He might as well have had blades pressed against his back. "But you're absolutely batshit crazy…"

His words were cut off when Charlie drove his claws into Henry's back.. Henry choked, blood filling his lungs and pooling in his mouth. His lips parted, trembling as if to speak, but the only thing that spilled out was the blood, painting his chin and the entire front of his jacket red.

"Henry!" James' scream was distant. Henry felt like he was standing at the end of a tunnel, and the only thing of which he was acutely aware was the fact that Charlie's fingers were pushing deeper into his flesh, sharp knuckles bruising the torn meat as they balled up into a fist. The Elder demon shoved his arm in as far as the elbow, his hand searching the chest cavity.

Charlie considered grabbing onto one of the ribs. They always snapped so easily, and it would have given him immense satisfaction to break one and then watch Henry crumple from the inside like a paper doll. But that wasn't what he wanted, and he knew it. He started drawing his arm back, Henry's whole body shuddering. The younger demon let out an unconscious moan, and Charlie employed both of his hands for the task of grabbing onto the newly exposed part of Henry's spine.

Gripping it in both of his hands, Charlie broke it like a twig. Henry choked, more blood gurgling up his throat. The sound of his bones breaking brought flowing juices to Charlie's mouth. He stretched his mouth open wider than before, metal teeth now overlapping his already sharp, more human ones – and he sank his teeth into the back of Henry's neck. Vertebrae shattered between his teeth and he shoved the body to the ground, digging both hands into the gaping wound while fishing for succulent bones.

Something slammed into his side. Charlie fell back, blinking in confusion once before rage contorted his entire face. He snarled, jaws dripping with saliva and blood as he whipped around to confront the threat to his meal. James crashed his fist into Charlie's temple, not waiting to give him a chance to fight.

"What the fuck is wrong with you!" The younger demon wailed, his blue eyes blazing with broken spots of orange. His glasses had vanished, probably fallen onto the sidewalk somewhere. "Get away from him!"

The sound that Charlie made was not even close to human. Somewhere in between a hiss and a screech, the Elder demon swiped his claws at James again. He was all too willing to take him down for a second course. James dodged the blow narrowly, chest heaving as he could feel his whole body trying desperately to let his true form free. His skin felt tighter than a drum. If he made a wrong move, it would split open entirely and fall in ribbons at his feet. But if his true form was to break free, then there would be no stopping his downward spiral into Hell…

Moving as swiftly as a cat, Charlie leapt back onto Henry's corpse, seemingly less interested in a fight than he was in finishing what he had started. He ripped Henry's back open, splitting it down the middle so that the entirety of the chest cavity was exposed. White ribs glittered into the low streetlights, and that beautiful broken spine was just jutting free from the rest, begging to be pulled apart...

Charlie grabbed the spine, jamming his heel against the back of Henry's skull in order to break it free at the base. Henry's bones gave way with another sickly crack, and Charlie shoved the disgusting hunk of nerve-wrapped vertebrae into his mouth before getting back down on all fours. He gave James one last vile look before darting across the street and melting into the shadows.

James watched him go, his throat tight with an icy ball of agonized, unshed tears. The demon doctor collapsed by Henry's side, his hands trembling as he reached out cradle his friend's broken head, the glorious blonde hair matted with blood.

"No," James whispered. "No, please, Henry...please. Damn it, I will never forgive you for this."

His nose and throat were burning, his eyes stinging with tears that he refused to shed. It was an alien sensation. He had never cried before, and never once pictured himself being worked up to this state over *Henry*.

Somehow, he had never pictured eternity without his companion.

"You know what you have to do." Another voice, gentle and sympathetic. James squeezed his eyes shut, a surge of white-hot hatred evaporating the water in his eyes.

"Have you been here this entire time?" James growled.

Virgil hesitated. "Well, not the *entire* time."

"I don't want you near me!" James snapped, not turning around to face the angel. He didn't want to know what he might do if he was forced to abandon Henry's corpse for even a moment. On the brink of tears as he was, one sudden movement could cause everything to spill over.

"Listen to me!" Virgil dropped to his knees beside James, reaching out to grab his wrist. James let it happen, his grip tightening on Henry's head.

"His flesh form is broken." Virgil said, trying to keep his voice as imploring and soothing as possible. "You know what that means."

"He's back in Hell." James took another deep breath. It wasn't helping.

"He will be at Satan's desk in under twenty minutes. And what then?"

"Eternity in chains." James closed his eyes. "Or something like that." A hundred thoughts raced through his mind, and he could not hear Virgil's next words over the desperate clamoring in his brain. Henry was not *dead,* he was in Hell, so James had to go to Hell to get him back. It would be nearly impossible to do so without risking his own neck, but it was something he had to do. It was the *least* he could do.

James turned back towards Henry's corpse. He could see the place where the soul should have been; the chamber was empty. It had never had a soul to begin with.

Demons existed on a different plane. Their spirits were far more insubstantial. It had been easy to miss Henry's slipping away. Twenty minutes in, and James already knew he was never going to forgive himself.

"Right," James raked his hand down his face. "I have to go after him. I have made my decision — I am going Down."

"Are you?" The angel tilted his head.

"Yes, and you are coming with me." James clamped his hand down around Virgil's thin wrist, his hard words leaving no room for argument. "I am not going down there alone. And you need to get out of your fucking house."

"I am —" the angel began a stiff protest, " — not supposed to be in Hell."

"Come with me." James said again, even more insistently. "If you do, I will give you some more of my hair so you can repair Cassandra."

That gave Virgil pause as he stared at James' face.

"It is not appealing," The angel managed, "you know, the idea of sauntering aimlessly down into Hell to seek out a demon who has never been particularly nice to me." He sniffed. "This is not going to be pleasant. Not at all."

"Feelings are not pleasant." James said. "I am just starting to figure that out."

It was all over by the time she arrived. Claire nearly tripped over the body that was thrown down over the sidewalk as carelessly as a child's abandoned doll. There was another body nearby, sopped in blood and half-eaten. A chill shook her to the core as she glanced back down, nudging the one closest to her with her foot.

She could not make out many details. The largest part of the face had been entirely removed. There was still blonde hair clinging to the remnants of the skull, but the body was long beyond being identified. She bit the corner of her lip and looked around, as if there might be someone else standing in the shadows waiting for the opportunity to step forward and launch into an explanation.

But no one stepped forward. She was alone, as far as she could tell. Whatever demon she had been trailing was long gone from this place.

She would go back to her room and re-group. That was what she needed to do. She had to pull herself together and find Edmund, wherever he was.

It was being made abundantly clear; she was not going to be able to do this on her own.

Hell had a noxious, sanitized smell. It was a mixture of too much bleach with an odd undercurrent of cleaning vinegar. Henry was reminded vaguely of a dentist office as he shifted in his uncomfortable seat, a wooden chair with a flat vinyl covering that could not have passed for a cushion under even the greatest of duress.

There was no one else in the waiting room. Only he. Henry scraped his nails against the arm of the chair anxiously, looking around for some glimmer of existence other than his own. The walls were white. The front desk was white. The black leather chair at the front desk was still swaying as if someone had recently abandoned it to go refill their coffee. The computer had a dark screen, and the phone was covered in a thick layer of dusk. He was receiving all sorts of mixed signals.

Henry's eyes flitted back towards the office door which had remained ominously closed since his arrival. He knew what was on the other side and was in no hurry to encounter it. On the other hand, the waiting was driving him crazy. Perhaps if they had selected any other music to play in the background, but generic Country ballads were the bane of every universe…

He glanced at the office again, and this time the door was open. He could not see clearly inside of the room, but he knew that he had to walk inside of his own volition, or he was going to be dragged.

Henry stood up, the vinyl squeaking underneath him. He grimaced and started walking towards the office, immediately met with a cloud of thick menthol smoke.

"Well," that familiar, rumbling voice he had hoped to never hear again spoke up. Satan's eyes were like a cat's, glowing with a light of their own as he drummed his clipped fingernails invitingly on the desk. "Here you are again, Jahangir. Have a seat."

262

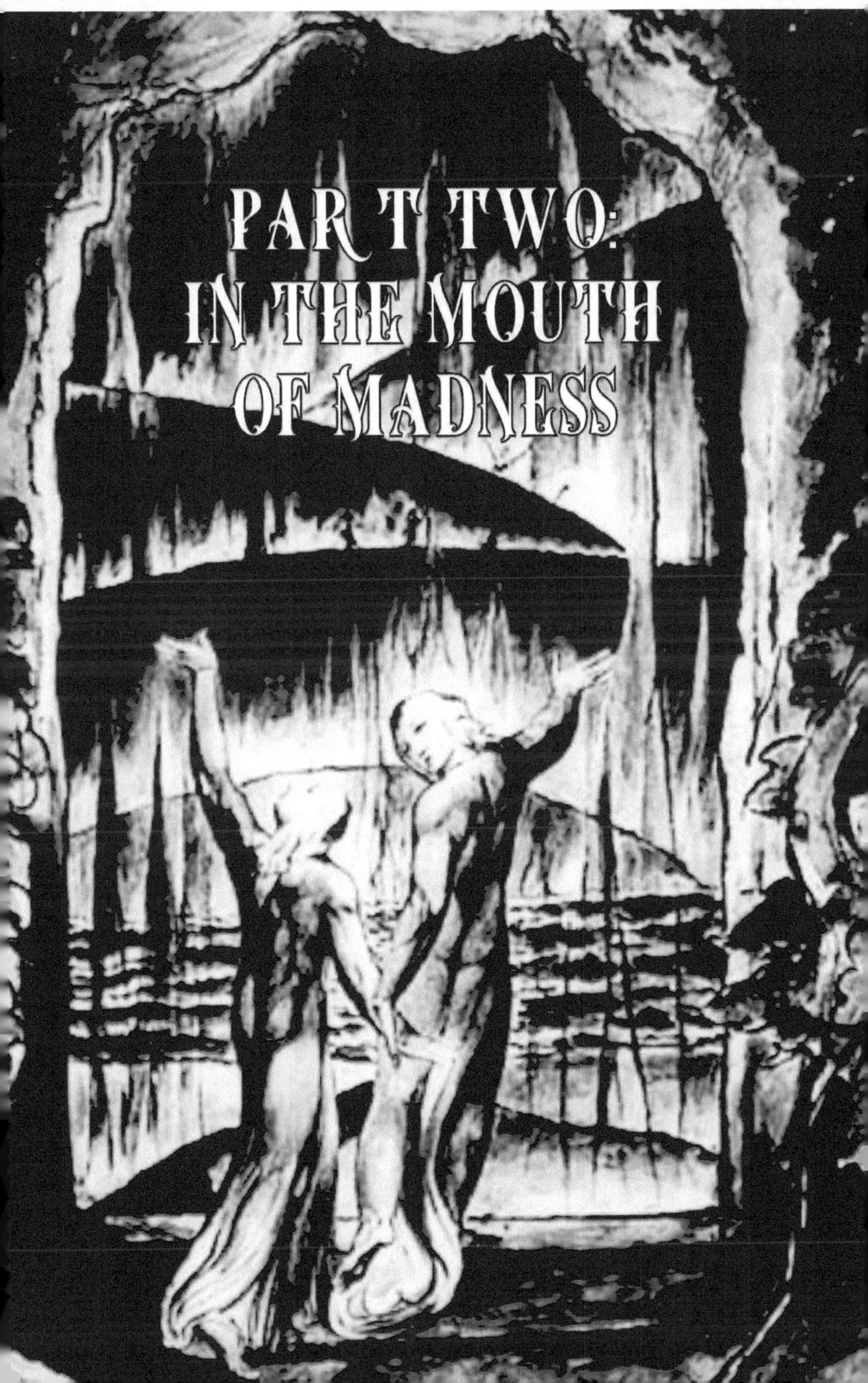
PART TWO:
IN THE MOUTH
OF MADNESS

CHAPTER XVI

He had a cellist's fingers; long and brittle as bone China, crooked from being broken again and again over the many centuries. His knuckles were permanently blue, mottled, and cold. His nails gleamed like glass, bloodless, catching the light of cream-colored votive candles as his busy hands flashed over his workspace. If he stood still long enough, he might resemble a corpse. Well-preserved and in pristine condition, despite his shabby dress: his polish-and-paint-stained shirts and his dusty, torn trousers.

As if he ever stood still. Lord Julian had not laid himself down to rest in many centuries. He did not sleep, he did not eat, but he was always moving. Sewing, painting, plucking, curling, rooting. The house was falling apart around him. Every brick that had been laid down with purpose was beginning to buckle underneath the weight of the outside world's bitter wear and tear. Even as he labored in the dim glow of his candles' dying breaths, their faint orange globes of light nearly down to the wick, he pressed two fingers against the battered side of a paint pot and moved it to catch the fast and cold rain that was drizzling through a hole in his ceiling.

Nothing splattered on the doll. That was paramount. He would have to start all over again if her paint ran, if the ugly bites of sky ruined even the hem of her dress. The silk thread was imported, brittle from age but hand-embroidered. He had stitched it all himself with his own sure hands, quick fingers and flashing needle. He'd spent hours in the candlelight paying attention to every detail. His favorites—*her* favorites—were Erica flowers, especially heather: the blossom of loneliness and wishes. He stitched it onto every curling vine, every loop and flourish. His wishes, his solitude.

If he stitched a thousand, or a hundred thousand, maybe she would come back.

Julian dragged his arm across his nose, unwilling to rub paint-stained fingers against an itch. He knew he should grab fresh candles, and possibly another pot of paint. Her face was nowhere near complete. He still had to blush the cheeks and nose, stain the lips, and add the eyelashes. The eyelashes had to be *perfect*, not so long that they curled to the browbone but not so short that they stuck out gracelessly like squashed spiders. And they had to hide the seams. That ugly slit just above where he had to tuck the eyelid into place to keep them open.

Distantly, he heard a door shut. Many doors were opening and shutting all the time in that house, so he did not even glance up from his work. If it wasn't one of the many servants his *patron* (*lover* being too generous a word to slather onto one such unprincipled libertine whose visits had become so irregular) employed, it was the wind. It bashed at the doors and windows as a relentless battering ram, and every now and again one caved to the pressure.

The candles were sputtering. The long shadows flickered over his work. Julian's lip curled in a snarl, and he furiously turned for the chest where he kept a store of his precious beeswax candles.

Another door opened, much closer this time. He heard movement behind his head. Low-heeled boots struck the stone floors, and a long leather coat swept against the rushes. Yet he paid it no mind. He just kept digging.

The footsteps came to a stop, followed by the sound of a case being set down. Lord Julian finally stood, bloodless hands full of candles as he held them close to his chest and turned back towards his workspace.

He did not even bat an eyelash at the woman who was standing near the table. He had seen her before many times, even if he could not be bothered to remember her name.

"Good afternoon, Lord Snowdon." She had a low, rich tone and her brown hands were scarred. She had such beautiful, long fingers just like his Caroline, fit for a harpsichord or something delicate.

"Is it afternoon?" His voice sounded like a pale echo of itself. He had never been one to command attention in a thunderous tone, but he knew that once he had a handsome face and a thrumming baritone to match. He had filled the halls with his music, his singing. But it had been so many years since.

Many, many years.

"The bell tower gave us fourteen chimes and the poor sun is completely shrouded behind these despot clouds." Such irrelevant talk. "Do you want your delivery stacked in the same place?"

He made a face, knotted scar tissue and a grotesquely stretched mouth contorting into a scowl. He could not even remember where his *usual place* was supposed to be. "Did Sheridan send you?"

They went through this every time. Still, she smiled. The picture of decorum. "My name is Emilie, my lord. I bring your formaldehyde to you every week." As if he might have forgotten what that was, too, she lifted a dark glass jar from within her case. She held it up to the dying light and tapped the glass with one pointed fingernail.

Lord Julian did not comment. The cogs in his head were turning, but they were always a quarter inch off their mark. Sometimes they jammed. He knew that. He set new candles down on top of the melted stubs and tried to think. *Emilie. Emilie Dalca. The witch. The devil's wife. Something of that nature. No, no. The undertaker. The undertaker, dammit. A woman; that wasn't so odd, not here.*

"Sextus' woman," he finally forced out with some certainty.

"As you like," she acquiesced.

Sextus, that blathering fool. It was starting to come back, and now he had a headache. "Leave it where you like." As long as he could find it.

Emilie nodded and started unloading the case. One, two, three—four full jars, and each one of them a good size. He would use them up by the time she returned. How clever, how good of Sheridan to make certain she came so regularly.

"Your work is coming along beautifully," she said, snapping the case shut and taking it up in her hands. The contents, now with a bit more room, clinked together. "I think she will be the prettiest one of all."

"She is not perfect," Julian said with some censure. How easy to think they were all perfect in the fervor of a low, inspired light. The new flames brought to his attention all of her flaws. The weak jawline, the imperfect shape of her chin. The uninspired blonde curls that flopped lifelessly against her temples—he would certainly have to do those over.

"She is *yours*," Emilie laughed under her breath. She did not reach out and touch the doll. "That is all that matters."

He ground his teeth. That was not all that mattered. That was not *nearly* all that mattered.

Another door slammed upstairs. Servants. Wind. *Caroline.*

He flicked his gaze upward, a fatherly sort of exasperation mingling with pain and exuberance all at once. Emilie's eyes followed his, looking up at the old bowing roof with its great wet spots and dark, gaping holes where the window whistled over ragged broken beams.

"Is your daughter well?" she asked. She set her bill down on the corner of the table.

"Lively," he muttered, already losing interest in company and turning back to his work. "Tonight."

"So I can hear." She started to move past him, grabbing the wide brim of her hat and nodding her chin in acknowledgment. "I hope the night goes well for you. Stay safe in this storm."

Julian rolled his eyes, one hazy blue and one gold. Like tops spinning in opposite directions. "Caroline likes the rain."

"I am certain she does." Emilie put her hand on the door handle. "I will be back the same time next week. Take care of yourself, my lord." And with that, she was gone. Blessed silence.

Julian huffed and reached over, picking up one of the jars she left behind. It was sealed well; good, pure stuff. He set it back down and pushed his sleeves back up over his elbow, knuckles mopping his damp brow.

Despite his general hatred for interruptions, he was glad to have a new supply. His beauty could use a little freshening, just a pump or two more in the neck. He pushed his fingers against her spongy upper arm, hard enough to bruise if there had been any blood left. If he was not careful, the delicate tissue would begin to putrefy, and then she would be useless. He would not add a mottled, decaying wreck to his beautiful displays. He had not made such a careless mistake in many years.

He must have been getting tired.

She was the Devil's wife. Or so it was whispered by lurid, gossiping mouths when they believed themselves well out of Sextus' hearing. It was also said that even the Devil had abandoned that little morgue that sat on the end of River Street, so cheekily named for the fact that it ended right where the river began. A suitable divide between the city's wealthy and its wretched poor.

She was not destitute, although no one knew where her fortune had come from. Yet she chose to reside in the slums; 'Gutterside' as it was called by those unfortunate enough to have been placed on the wrong side of the bridge. Her services, she claimed, were for the poor. And the poor had only to take one glance at her cabinets of curiosities — the glass jars of formaldehyde that hosted both animal and human abnormalities alike — before determining they were too nervous to inquire after what such *services* might be.

It was highly suspected that the only reason she chose to live in Gutterside was the direct access to corpses. Although she did not seem to favor the *easy* dead. She had no interest in the everyman who dropped dead in his own vomit after a long night of drinking, nor the old man who gave his last dying breath on the family bed. She wanted the bodies that were malformed. She wanted the gruesomely murdered. She wanted the grisly dead.

There was only one known breathing body to frequent the morgue. Lord Sextus Morgan was her only customer, though he often brought more than he left with. Tonight, he had arrived with nothing. There were no mysterious black carriages and no large, covered boxes. It was only him capering down the street in heeled black boots, his fashionable cane tapping against the ground to whatever tune he was humming at the time. He vanished through her doorway, and then the world stopped watching.

He had been wandering her house for the better part of half an hour and plucking at things on the shelves. She had not yet bothered to ask why he was here. Instead, she had spent a good portion of that time making tea, which he had no interest in. She finally sat down in a sunken chair, not taking her eyes away from him as she sipped from the chipped rim of her porcelain cup. He had given the set to her a long time ago. She doubted that he even remembered.

"Am I to assume that you are responsible for the gift that arrived on my doorstep this morning?" She finally broke the silence, blowing soft white steam off the surface of her tea.

"Not at all. The conjoined twins are new." He tapped the glass jar, larger than most of the others, on her shelf.

"I was thinking of sitting them up next to the turtle with two heads. It seems befitting." She took her first sip, the cup warming her chilly hands.

"Entirely. Do you have another admirer I should know about? Is there competition when it comes to laying curious cadavers at your feet?"

"I am going to throw this tea at you." She threatened idly, taking another sip and leaning back further in her chair to get comfortable. "And it would scar your pretty face."

"Then you could peel the skin off and turn it into a drum or the like, I am sure." He turned away from the glass. His heels were inches away from the modest fireplace and in danger of singing. But he didn't seem to notice. "Are you going to show me, or am I to wither out of curiosity?"

"I should like to see you wither." She set her teacup down, rising from the chair and crossing the room in a few short strides. "It is a fascinating process."

"I'm sure you would find me a bitter husk. Like a dried up stick of licorice." He moved to join her as she passed him by, heading into the back of her shop where no light seemed to exist. She did not keep much by way of gas lamps lying around. And the fireplace only gave off so much. He watched the darkness close around her, drawing her into its cold embrace with the familiarity of a lover. She was in love with this cool, artificial night that could be created any time she closed her doors.

A single spot of yellow light was permitted to interrupt the blackness surrounding them as she lit one of her gas lamps. He fluttered around it like a moth. She lifted it reasonably high and beckoned for the lord to follow her, moving a few paces further still. He followed silently, busy fingers twisting the heavy family ring.

She approached a long table covered with a stained white sheet. She grasped the edge, pulling it back carefully as if she was in danger of damaging what was underneath. Lord Morgan pursed his lips, setting his fingers against the body's papery cheek.

"He isn't in very wondrous condition. Oh!" his fingers slid down, touching the incision that began right at the throat. "You started without me. How inconsiderate of you."

"If I had waited on you, my lord, I might have waited all day." She rolled her eyes, brushing him aside so she could finish rolling down the sheet. "Besides, you always complain about how long the process takes. I thought you might enjoy being able to start on the most interesting part first."

"You are far too considerate." He pressed his gloved fingers against the incision, parting the dead flesh and peering at the cold layers of fat and the split muscle underneath like a precocious child. "What is special about this one, then? He seems perfectly formed. Well, for what he is."

"I wondered that myself." She swatted at his hands again. "And I will say that he has no particularly fascinating physical deformities."

"Shame." The lord shrugged. "But his parts will still sell. I'll be sure of that. Harvest everything and we will see what we can move."

"You are not listening to me." She chastised him, her amusement betrayed by the curve of her lips and the hidden tremor of laughter in her voice. "Do you want to see what I found?"

He nodded and she turned away from him, reaching out for another one of her precious jars that was resting on the edge of the table. She held it out to him and it caught the light. Its contents were as black as pitch and stuck to the sides like tar. He grimaced as he took hold of the container and turned it around in his hands.

"Emilie…this cannot be."

"It is his soul." She confirmed. "What a villain he must have been. I am sure I will take far too much pleasure in dissecting his brain."

"I have never seen a soul as disgusting as this. Villainous or otherwise. But then, I have never met a grim reaper quite like you, either." He set the jar down as if touching it was enough to contaminate his expensive garments. "I am more interested in the one who decided it was a good idea to drop this off on your doorstep. It would seem there are eyes on us."

"We have always attracted gazes." She picked up her scalpel, turning it around in her fingers so that the blade flashed when it caught the light. "You have said as much yourself."

"I was referring to the envious gaze then, not the watchful one."

"Well, it is hardly my fault that you are never more specific." She waved the scalpel in his direction. "Stay for dinner."

"Are we having villainous brains?"

"No, we are having kidney pie." She flashed him a teasing grin. "But only if you step a little closer."

"Darling, you do not wish to taste these overworked bastards." He moved out of the way all the same. "I will gladly stay and dine but only if you set down your grisly work for the time being. And by that, I mean set down your blade. Gutting two men in one afternoon is extravagant."

"You know very well that I could not slit you open." She set the scalpel down, moving to pull the sheet back up over her prize. "You are too entertaining."

"I hear that often. Shall we go back?" He extended his hand, all too eager to return the light.

She picked up her lamp and placed it in his hand, his fingers quickly scrambling to properly grasp the handle. "Do not work yourself up," she told him. "I've never seen you so turned off by a soul."

"They turn my stomach when they are sticky like that," he confessed, following her back towards the yellow and orange glow of the main room. "They are rotten and sweet."

"Sounds like someone else I know."

"Mm. Do you have anything to drink other than tea?"

"Mulled cider," she responded, her gaze sliding over him as he dropped into his favored seat. "Your favorite. Tell me why you are really here."

He did not respond at first, sliding his index finger over his soft bottom lip, pulling on it just enough to be attractive.

His thumb came up to trace along the same line in a distracting pattern. "I felt the air ripple. You know how it moves. It gets thick, and then it ripples like water when a pebble breaks the surface…our border was breached."

Emilie was already pulling off her apron, setting the crumpled linen down on top of her open ledger as she made her way towards the corner of the room that had been carved out for foodstuffs. She grabbed the pitcher of cider and two cups, pinching their rims between her fingers as she made her way back towards the waiting demon. She already had a feeling where this was going. He did not like intruders. He did not like ripples, as he put it, being made in his little world.

Everything was so meticulously constructed. Every tick of the clock planned down to the breath. He preferred it that way.

"I imagine you did the wise thing," she said, knowing full well he likely did the opposite of whatever that would be. "And you came to me before deciding to seek out any intruders by yourself?"

His smile told her everything she needed to know. "I did not confront anyone, if that is what you are worried about."

She hadn't been. "I see. And what if they had been dangerous?"

"They were not." He waved his hand dismissively before accepting a cup of cider from her. "One of them is a demon, I shouldn't wonder—*young,* he reeks of Sulphur. The other looks a bit mangled. Like he is caught in the gears between Heaven and Hell."

"I see."

"And they are both horribly dressed."

"You would have been the one to notice."

"I am more interested in how they got here than anything." His eyes gleamed in the low firelight. "No one ever can, not purposefully, which means there is another hole somewhere."

Another. She remembered all too well what happened the first time a tear appeared in his perfect universal fabric. The scars were still there. Sheridan and Julian…they never left.

"I don't think," she began carefully, "that we can win that fight again."

"I don't think there will be fighting this time, *myn lyking.*"

"Then why not let them be?"

Something moved across his face, a turn underneath the skin. It was easy to forget his natural state. She had not seen it in so long. And as much control as he had always had with his fist closed around their world, he was more seamlessly human than most. Yet every now and then, the blood would pool in his face like a gathering storm. And then 'Sextus' would become just the skin pulled drum-tight over Kaveh's face, the demon writhing underneath.

"A splinter will infect." The sound came out in shreds through his teeth as if his jaw was locked up, unable to push out anything nearly comprehensible.

She nodded, if for no other reason than to quell him, and switched subjects almost immediately. He did not scare her anymore, but she would rather not work him up to the point where his flesh started pulling apart. She wasn't sure she where she had last set down her sewing kit.

"Are you asking me to go with you, then?"

Another pause, and then he snorted.

"Would you care to do so? I have a hard time believing that they could knock down a house of cards on a windy day. They are like puppies — lost, lonely, and clumsy."

"You always did have a weakness for dogs." Emilie pursed her lips to keep down an amused smile. "As long as you store them in your house and not mine. Unless you want them sleeping in the same pen as the goat."

"I am certain Rosen would not mind the company." He laughed startling and bright, finally setting his cup down. "I have kept you from your great work, I know. And I must try to find them again before sun-up. At least, I would like to."

"My great work can wait until morning. The dead will still be here when the sun rises." She turned away from him, already looking around for her coat.

"You are not afraid of the dark, I hope?" His voice tickled her ear. She had not even realized he had moved so close, but the sudden slip of warm breath was enough to raise chill bumps on her forearms.

"Not at all," she breathed.

He lifted his own coat, and she moved her arms back to slide into the sleeves. He trailed a finger down the shell of her ear before pulling away entirely.

"The rain is thick tonight," he said. "And the moon is covered. One can barely see."

"How fortunate for me, then, that I have your superior senses to guide me." She rolled her eyes.

"Yes," her sarcasm did not seem to land. "How fortunate for you, indeed."

CHAPTER XVII

The King's Head Tavern greeted its new guests with a weathered sign that kept slamming into its rain-drenched walls, its faint blue lettering invisible in the darkness. James took notice that Virgil's glasses had been clouded by the cold air and ruined by the rain, yet he stubbornly kept them resting on the narrow bridge of his sharp nose. Virgil pursed his lips tightly in an expression that reflected disapproval, and this silent incredulity was only furthered by him shoving his hands so deeply into his pockets that his sleeves started bunching up at the elbows.

"We are staying here?" The angel asked.

"You have somewhere better?" James stepped up to the door, reaching out with some hesitation to grab the heavy iron handle. "I have slept in worse." An unnecessarily pointed remark.

The angel pursed his lips but did not respond as he stooped to step inside. The doors seemed to be getting shorter and shorter the further back they traveled. Even once he was through, he was only able to partially straighten himself up. He still had to keep his shoulders hunched so that his head didn't drag along the roof.

James followed at his side, slipping his glasses off his nose to try and wipe water droplets off the lenses. There was a fire going, but it did not seem to produce enough heat to even knock off a chill. The room was too open, too poorly constructed to hold anything other than the tightly packed bodies that were sharing benches and occupying stools in every feasible corner.

The demon cast an uncertain glance around the room, avoiding rueful glares before swinging his gaze back to the angel. Virgil just shrugged.

"I am really tall," he said, as if that explained everything. "And we are still wearing our glasses."

"Ah," James muttered under his breath. He still placed his gold-rimmed glasses back down on his nose after he had finished wiping them down. The glass was still streaky and somehow worse than before. "I did not even think about that."

"I am going to put mine in my pocket." Virgil sniffed. "It is not as though you need them, dear."

"No, but I..." James pushed the frames up again, self-conscious about making a spectacle of himself in front of a crowd. He chose to swap subjects instead. It was easier than arguing. "Would you like something to drink?"

A few expressions went to war on Virgil's brow before he finally spoke, sounding resigned, "I will have something simple. Milk, if they have it, is fine."

James nodded vaguely, starting towards the counter where a testy, lanky boy was giving him a miles-long glower. He was already wishing that he could change into shoes with something less of a heel. He had not changed once since he and Virgil left the realm that Charlie occupied, and he had been so hot on their trail since that they could not even find time to obtain new garments.

James stopped at the counter, settling his hand down on the surface as if the dips and rough knots in the wood could ground him.

"What do you have on the menu tonight?" His voice sounded rough, despite clearing his throat before speaking. The boy behind the counter did not deign to budge just yet, swiping the same dirty rag back and forth over the wood.

"Ninepence will get you a porkpie and ale," he said, his voice garbled by a severe lack of orthodonture (James had read plenty on the practice but had never given in to exercise. Although now, he was considering a response to the calling). "A penny will get you whelks. Two, three, four, six, or eight."

"Porkpie, then." He had no idea what whelks were, and he was certain he didn't want to know. "Two of them, if you will. And ale, I suppose."

"Will bring 'em right to you, if you wanna have a seat." The boy waved his rag in the direction of the dining area and James took the hint. He nodded his thanks and pulled away from the counter, moving as quickly as possible to re-join the angel. Virgil had managed to grab hold of the one table that was shoved into a deep corner, half-obscured by shadow but close enough to the fireplace that it was warm, at the very least.

"Do you want my opinion?" the angel asked as James took his seat.

"No." James never did.

"I don't think you are going to find him down there." Virgil settled his hands primly on the surface of the table, long white fingers resting on top of a jumble of knuckles. "I think he is gone for good. I think Charlie made sure of that when he tore him apart."

James ground his teeth. It had come up before, and it wasn't like he never considered that he was chasing a dead end. "You might be right."

Virgil shrugged. "Just a thought." He turned his head away, sweeping a numb glance across the room. "If he isn't there, what are you going to do?"

"I don't know." Find something to eat, probably. He was starving. He had not dared to stop for a real meal in…well, he had not bothered to measure the time. His only gauge was his stomach's intermittent growling. And how it went from a sharp, heated ache to something dull and uncomfortably deep.

"Did I not tell you?" A ringing note of triumph chimed louder than a bell right next to his ear, startling James out of his rambling thoughts. He turned in his chair, clutching the arm, and felt a brush of air that flung water droplets against his cheek as the stranger standing next to him swept off his coat and threw it over the back of the seat next to him.

"Yes," another new voice joined the first, "you are very clever."

"Not to be dreadfully rude…" Virgil began.

"May we ask who you…?" James started at the same time.

"Forgive me, I have fallen out of the habit of formal introductions." The one who had shed his coat settled into his chair and crossed his legs with quick movements that boasted too much confidence. His pinstripe trousers made his legs look ten miles long. His dirty-blonde hair was a halo around a face that was too angular to be beautiful, too fleshy to be stern. "I am Lord Sextus Morgan. And the jewel at my side is…" He gestured to the beautiful brown woman next to him. James had hardly noticed her at first; now he found himself wondering how he could have possibly overlooked her. She was a stark contrast to the creature who accompanied her. Her dark brown hair was pulled back into a braid and her eyes were the color of stained Cherrywood, missing nothing. She was sharp and he was vague. Her appearance next to him was like a bolt of lightning against a clouded sky.

"Emilie Dalca," she said. She had a warm, throaty voice. Another contrast.

"My name is James." It felt stupid to drop his name. But it was not his Biblical name, which was the only one that counted. "And this is Virgil."

"I am no such gem," the angel added unnecessarily.

"We are delighted to meet you," Sextus reassured them.

There was something about him that James could not pin down and it was starting to needle.

"What he means is that you look a little lost." A thin smile spread over Emilie's generous mouth. "And we are unaccustomed to outsiders."

"We are only passing through." James realized that he sounded defensive. He couldn't help it. Although Sextus looked comfortably settled, there was something about his posture that suggested an edge. He was ready to spring at any moment.

"You called yourself *lord*," Virgil wormed his way into the conversation. "Is this your territory?"

"Down to the cobblestones," Sextus said. "And I feel every stir."

James ran his tongue along the inside of his teeth. "If you want us out, that can be arranged. We will get up now and leave." He wished for Henry now more than ever. Henry was disarming. James was clunky and unsure of himself at best.

Henry would have swept them off their feet.

James just wanted to leave.

He did not like the look of the blonde. The woman wasn't settling on him much better. She smelled like formaldehyde; and it was barely enough to cover up the stench of rot.

"It is not so simple." Emilie's lashes drifted down just enough to wreath her cherrywood eyes. "Sextus is very fond of how things are. He has gone through great pains to preserve everything you see here. The getting in is difficult but the getting out is impossible."

James shook his head. "I do not understand."

"You must have felt it," Sextus said, frustration making his voice tight. "Did the air not get colder, thicker? Did you not feel it in your fingers like pins and needles?"

"Perhaps it did." James was painfully aware of his own impatience. "But I am not usually one to notice." It was not like he made a regular habit of breathing. He did not have to, when he was not masquerading. And ever since Henry…

It had become hard to care about whether or not he was noticed. He knew his own tells and still did little to remedy them. He had combed through enough texts to recognize that any psychiatrist might ascribe to him the word *depressed*, but that did not settle with him. Depression existed as a result of faulty neurotransmitters and crippled reward processing—mechanics, gears, things an unholy creature should not have to be concerned over. It was as if the flesh bound tightly around his snarling demonic form was trying to choke him out, and its method was by shutting down the grey organ in his skull.

Virgil's fingertips brushed against his. The contact was enough to jolt James back into the present. For the span of a few seconds, the world was dove grey and ink black as his second eyelids slipped down, shutting out the blazing colors of mortal earth. A few blinks and a swipe of his knuckles dragged them back up, the world once again oversaturated with garish color.

"This may not be the place," Virgil suggested in his featherdown voice. "Not to suggest any insult of your timing, my..." the pause suggested he had already forgotten the proper term, "lord."

"Of course." Sextus sat up straighter in his chair, his frame filling up the small seat. "I had intended to invite you into my home for the night, regardless. Undoubtedly you are going to need somewhere to sleep. You still sleep, do you not?"

James shifted his jaw. "I try not to."

"Sometimes, it cannot be helped. The young ones just drift, nodding off in chairs or rubbing their eyes and pushing their faces into blankets. The world is so loud, so colorful...have you ever seen a demon freshly born? They can barely keep their heads up. Hell is so warm and they will wrap their wings around their bodies and sleep for days. It is all very pathetic and adorable."

Demon. Now that it was obvious, James wondered how he could not have noticed it straightaway. The illusion was almost too perfect. Sextus was just a little *too* human. His tics were all perfectly timed. Every drum of his fingers, every blink. His motions were very deliberate, his smile too empty, his eyes…

His eyes were so cold, like stained glass. Check, check, *check*. James was a fool.

Virgil had to *know*. James shot a dark look at his companion, whose only response was to lift one snowy eyebrow and shrug. Fucking angels.

James shifted his jaw again so severely he heard his own teeth squealing. He tasted blood, tangy like copper.

"I do not find myself motivated to follow you," James finally spoke. "For all we know, you could be leading us directly into the mouth of Hell."

"Does Hell know you are here?" Such a sharp, violent response. Sextus did not move, but the words made James flinch.

"No," the younger demon said. "And I would rather keep it that way…if it is all the same. I have judge and jury of Hell to face if I am found before I can make my way back."

"Indeed?" Sextus' eyes narrowed. "And if I were a less scrupulous man, I am certain I would take advantage of that."

"Happy for me, then, that you are a man of morals." James spoke around the pain of his own stomach clenching.

"Gallantry incarnate," Sextus muttered, turning once again to face Emilie. "Well then. Shall we, *myn lyking?*"

294

CHAPTER XVIII

"And what did you say your name was?" The man behind the counter had been there all day, if the sweat stains underneath his armpits were anything to judge by. His lunch was resting on the desk in front of him, an open bag of chips and a half-finished generic brand soda. The buttons on his keyboard were smeared with grease, and still enough remained on his fingers that tendrils of long, loose black hair looked wet from where he kept rubbing.

"L. Hayward." Lady did not want to lean any closer than he had to in order to be heard. "Lady Hayward."

The man dug his hand into his chip bag, pulling out another fragment and popping it into his mouth. A deliberate crunch, and then back to typing. Lady wondered if this greaseball knew that it would only take a fraction of a second to carve out his eyes.

"All right then, ma'am." The man finally picked up a clipboard and set it on the counter in front of him, nudging it towards Lady and tossing up a pen. "If you could just sign right there…"

"No," Lady held up a hand, cutting him off right there. "I am not *a lady.*"

The man's expression didn't change. But he leaned back in his chair, a hiss of air as the plastic spring adjusted, and he grabbed the soda off his desk. As he unscrewed the cap, he took a moment to cut his eyes up and down, taking in the Unchaste's fitted suit, its jacket with the fashionably flared bottom over a dark purple blouse that sported a ruffled v-neck. Lady drummed his manicured fingernails against his sensible leather briefcase, hoping his impatience could at least be read if the cutting glare from behind his glasses was missed.

"Not any type of *man* I've ever seen, either," the greaseball muttered.

Lady noticed Francis tense up and brace himself against his cane.

The Unchaste had been rearing for a fight all morning but had kept himself in check this long. This man had absolutely no idea what he was asking for.

"How astute." Lady visibly scoffed. "Now return my damn identification." He did not make a move to touch the disgusting clipboard.

"Hold on, hold on." The man sat up straight again, disgruntled by the notion of having to do *extra* work. His chair rattled sadly, and he set his soda back down on the desk with a thump that was heavier than necessary. "What do I put down, then? Is it 'Mr.' or 'Mrs.'?"

"It is 'Mx,'" Lady said shortly.

"*Mix* of what? Just make a goddamn…"

"*Look,* you imbecilic inbred!" Lady swept his glasses up into his auburn hair with such ferocity that he nearly snapped the frame. "I have not been forced to choose in a good eon or so, and I will have some *very nasty* words for your superior…"

The man shot a look at Francis and rolled his eyes, as if expecting some form of commiseration or sympathy. Francis' face remained as blank as a slate. Well-trained, Lady observed.

"Here." The man behind the counter gave up. He set down a stack of stapled papers with an identification card paper-clipped onto the top layer. "You are all set up now. Is there anything else I can help you with today?" His voice suggested something. Like an inconvenience or a burp.

"Not hardly." Lady slid his sunglasses back down. "Frank, be a dear and pick those up. My manicure is too fresh for his grime to be under my nails."

Francis leaned forward without question, scooping up the papers with the card. He folded the stack over and slipped it all into the pocket in the lining of his jacket.

Lady turned on his heel and led the way out, the professional-grade hinges on the door not allowing it to slam shut behind them.

"I need a bath," the Unchaste said.

"I do not think he knew what he was getting into." Francis walked ahead, grabbing hold of the car door and pulling it open for his husband. Lady slid into the leather passenger seat, grabbing hold of his seatbelt and pulling it down across his chest.

"Frank, dear, when are you going to stop using the cane?"

"When it no longer gains us accessible parking," the demon said dryly, shutting Lady's door before moving around to the other side of the car and getting into the driver's seat.

"I suppose you think it makes you look distinguished."

"I think nothing of the sort." Francis said.

"You coordinated your outfit around it beautifully." Lady told him, even though he knew very well that Francis had not coordinated anything. He had pulled on a white blouse that morning that was not even buttoned all the way to the collar and pulled on a heavyweight jacket with brown patches on the elbows. Lady believed that it made him look geriatric and he had told him as much.

"That was a lot of trouble to go through just to book a hotel." Lady switched topics, glancing down at the brochure he had picked up before. It had been stuffed down into the side of the car door and forgotten for weeks. The corners were still bent, and the top had been bleached by the sun, but the information proved to be at least somewhat accurate. Someone had answered when they phoned. "We are going to have to find you a bathing suit."

"Me?" Francis asked. "And what about you?" He tried to sound coy, but his fear was that he only sounded accusatory.

"The beach has not earned the privilege..." Lady's words were cut off when Francis slammed his foot down on the brake, bringing them to a sudden enough halt that Lady nearly launched face-first into the dashboard.

"Break my nose, and you will need that cane forever!" Lady snarled. Francis fell back into his seat, his trembling hands still gripping the steering wheel.

"Sorry, boss—" that was all he could manage.

"What in the name of Hell were you trying to do?"

"I thought I saw—" Francis managed to pry his hands away from the steering wheel, sweeping one through his dark hair and trying to focus. "Your—my boss. *Our* boss."

"What are you—?" Lady narrowed his eyes. "You are going to have to be more specific, Frank. *Which* boss?"

Francis' fingers swiped at the corners of his mouth. "*The* boss." He said with as much gravitas as he could muster. "The one who ran our circle. Really, I—you know how I am with names. But they had the blue hair. They always smelled like cotton candy."

"Sloth." Lady visibly paled, turning his head away and looking out onto the street. "You always said the smell made you feel nauseous."

"It really did."

Any further retorts died in Lady's throat. As far as bosses went, Sloth was not the worst. They always neglected paperwork. They never left the office. They never bitched when Lady was more than an hour late for whatever obliquitous reason. Too many grievances had been sent to the shredder along with all of the other rubbish because Lady could not be bothered to take them up and Sloth could not be bothered to come down. Their relationship, on that level, was ideal.

Of course, on the list of matters egregiously neglected were things such as vacation time, leave of absences, and a dozen other policies. They never answered their email, they never picked up the phone, and they only came to the door about 30% of the time (and usually only if Lady himself came knocking).

The only thing they ever did without hesitation was follow an order straight from the top. It was well-known that Pestilence, the board director responsible for their branch, and Satan Himself were the only two capable of lighting a fire underneath Sloth's lazy ass.

So if Sloth had gone through all of the trouble of making an ascent, it could almost be guaranteed that they were not leaving without what they came for in hand.

Lady leaned forward, popping open the glovebox and pulling out the case for his glasses. He lifted them out and slipped them on just as something slammed against the window, sending his heart smacking into his voice box.

A hand, small like a child's with pointed six-inch long pink acrylic nails slid down the length of the car window from the point of impact. A sharp nose pressed against the glass , bright orange eyes wide and gleaming as a candy pink tongue snaked out, dragging itself up and leaving a trail through the fog that hot breath left behind. Lady's jaw shifted, grinding his teeth so fiercely he felt pain shoot up to his nose.

"Do you think," he began slowly, "that if we just start driving—?"

"We will wreck harder next time." Francis had already considered it. He unlocked the car and rolled down the window, unwilling to face the wrath of Hell when he had already been in the path of Lady's ire.

Those pink claws scrabbled their way into the car, arms as limp as taffy sliding in and drooping over the edge. They hung there until the window had rolled all the way down, and then Sloth gripped the door handle, popping it open so that they could ooze their way in.

Lady could not move out of the way fast enough. He all but jumped out of his seat, slipping into the back of the car and hopping on top of the mound of fabric that formed an almost-seat in the back of their small two-door. Francis remained frozen with one hand on the wheel and the other resting on the door panel, as if there was something he could press there that would eject the Sin at a moment's notice.

Sloth's glossy pink lips parted, their mouth stretching with an impossibly wide yawn that strained the corners of their lips and brought tears to their eyes. They wiped at their eyes with the sides of their fingers, artfully managing to avoid stabbing themselves in the eyeball.

"Good morning." Sloth punctuated the greeting with the tail-end of their initial yawn. "Hayward. Hislop. Or is it just one or the other now?"

"It is three in the afternoon," Lady let out in a scornful hiss.

"We never discussed it," Francis added at the same time. "What can we do for you?"

"Well…" Sloth stretched, their feet jamming up underneath the dashboard and their hands flopping back, inching dangerously into Lady's coveted space. "I actually consider myself damn lucky to have found you so quickly — *damn* lucky. Hell has an APB out for the both of you. Knowing myself, I didn't think I had a snowball's chance of finding you first."

Lady cut Francis a look, wishing, for once, that he could glimpse at his thoughts to see if they were both thinking the same thing.

"It's a good thing too, like I said. I've got a room for you and everything." Sloth licked their lips.

Well, Lady knew what *he* was going to do. It was just a matter of whether Francis could sprint as quickly as he could.

"There is a problem, here," Lady said, pulling himself up just a quarter-inch closer. "I have no intention of returning to Hell. I believe I made that *abundantly* clear. And while I do hate to be the one to tell you that you have wasted your precious time…"

The look that Sloth gave him was cold. Orange eyes froze him on the spot, cotton candy blue hair falling in dizzying spirals around steeply sloped shoulders. It was a hypnotic sight. Lady thought he would have been used to it by now, but any notion of immunity vanished when he started to feel pins and needles in his fingertips.

Everything was falling asleep.

"There, now," Sloth cooed. "What time did you say it was?"

"Three." Three, what? In the afternoon? In the morning? Was it truly so late? It couldn't be. Lady couldn't remember. His sinking lashes were blotting out the sky and the world was starting to look dark and hazy outside of the car windows.

"You look like you could use a little sleep. Look at those poor little eyes, just…drooping." Sloth set a fingernail gently against the corner of Lady's eye, dragging down his lid until it was pulled halfway over one brown sugar iris. Their touch was as good as morphine. The entire left side of Lady's face felt like it had been struck with paralysis.

Darkness was encroaching on his vision, but his mind was still racing and his heart couldn't even bring itself to pick up pace.

"Deeper, deeper. There you go. Nice and relaxed, aren't we? You too, sugar." Sloth had already extended their other hand and rested it against Francis' face in a similar manner, thumb stroking one hollow cheek. "We don't do anything in the fast lane here, do we? But it works out well. It works out well. Road trips are always better when you get to sleep the longest part of the way." They batted a glittery eyelash, and then Lady's vision went entirely black.

Even without his sight, it was still several minutes before he lost consciousness. Meanwhile, he was all too aware of the way he had been left slumped against the seat, his body contorted into an uncomfortable position so that his shoulder and neck muscles burned.

The car started up underneath them. Beach music blared over the radio, cranked up as far as the volume controls would allow.

If he was lucky, his eardrums would burst, and he would bleed out before they ever reached Hell's gates.

CHAPTER XIX

It was early—far too early. But then, Satan considered just about any hour to be too early for a board meeting. He had already managed to burn through half a pack of cigarettes in anticipation alone, and he had a brand-new box tucked into his jacket pocket.

The conference room door was already unlocked and slightly ajar. It was not unusual that someone should arrive before him, so he did not even act fazed as he used the toe of his shoe to nudge the door open.

He was greeted by the stench of rotting carrion, a unique blend of expired meat and department store perfume. Good manners were the only thing strong enough to prevent him from gagging on the initial inhale, and all that kept him from throwing an arm across his nose as he made his way towards his seat. He tried to focus on anything else—the expensive cologne he had dabbed behind his own ears, the fresh dry-clean scent on his warm jacket collar…

Death was waiting for his arrival having remained true to form and arrived tragically early. He had chosen the seat closest to the projector which *also* stuck him at Satan's right hand. That sort of move always rubbed Satan the wrong way, partially because he *knew* that Death had to be aware of how much his boss hated sitting next to him. Satan did not even have a good reason. It was impossible to pinpoint one fault to hold above all others and present as the ultimate reason why he found Death to be the most repulsive being ever to exist in Hell. Death as a being was just an agglomeration of various foul traits that came together to form the divine equivalent of a piece of gum stuck to the bottom of a day laborer's shoe.

The Horseman either did not hear his boss walk in or did not think to acknowledge it. Either way, his briefcase was open on the table as knobby fingers dug deep into the contents and thumbed through what looked like full water-stained reams of paper. Death always kept such careful records and never missed a beat at any meeting. His handwriting was impossible to read because he always used leaky fountain pens which littered the pages with ink blots. One could tell that he never kept the notes for other people, only for himself, and he had answers for every question, even the ones brought up in reference to meetings that Satan did not even remember attending.

Satan grabbed the back of his seat and pulled it away from the table, rollers clattering on the hard plastic mat that protected only a fourth of the conference room's carpet. He looked over at Death and gave the barest of nods. Death smiled back at him, flashing a mouthful of crooked grey and blackened teeth. Satan forced himself to look away and tossed a thick file down onto the table, immediately pulling out his nearly-empty pack of cigarettes and flipping open the cardboard top. Smoke-free conference rooms are afflictions only of angels.

Death watched the motion with eyes that were like two pinpricks of light in the dark, sunken caverns of his sockets. Bags that read his years like the rings of a tree trunk swooped down towards his cheekbones, dragging his bottom eyelids down with them until the red waterline was grotesquely exposed. He took a deep breath, the sound rattling past his lips as if each one had the potential of being his last.

"I love the smell of smoke." Death's voice was a dry wheeze. "Good tobacco will make your lungs ache."

"I'm not really that kind of masochist," Satan replied, tapping the sides of his cigarette pack with his fingertips. "I just have anxiety."

The Horseman lifted a hand to close his briefcase and Satan caught sight of dreadful, thick yellow fingernails with so much dirt piled underneath that it looked as though he had been digging graves by hand.

Feet crossing the threshold into the conference room spared Satan further forced conversation. The heavy door swung open so quickly that it bounced off the rubber stopper on the wall, springing back with unusual velocity and nearly colliding with the personal walking through. Pestilence deflected the door with a blow, his wet palm batting it away like a bothersome fly.

"Am I late?" Pestilence sucked in a breath that sounded like a truck downshifting on the highway. He was perpetually in the stages of 'getting over' a cold and his appearance was unfailingly, inexplicably *moist*.

Satan shook his head, popping the unfiltered end of his cigarette into his mouth and holding up a lighter to the other. "You are early. We haven't even started."

"Oh, good." Pestilence dragged his feet towards the table, grabbing a seat at the far end. He hit the back of the padded chair so that it spun a few times before he forced it to stop and let himself sink into the middle. It was his favorite chair, proven by the fact that the seat was always damp and smelled like gasoline.

"War is still MIA. He did say he could make it, didn't he?" Satan tried to remember if he had received an email back from his busiest director, or whether he had hallucinated an entire correspondence. Not one of these meetings had ever gotten off the ground without a hitch. "Famine is still out. He and Gluttony continue to make regular reports. Things seem to be going well."

"I don't know where War is." Pestilence said, dragging his arm across his nose and leaving a trail of slime up to his elbow. "Has he said anything to you?" He tilted is head towards Death and gave him a look. Death and War were usually joined at the hip. They even had each other's personal numbers.

Death pursed his lips, a sour and pious expression.

"He did not say anything this morning," was the oldest Horseman's cryptic response.

A wide shadow fell over the conference room table, immediately shutting the entire conversation down. War, with the body of a berserker and the expression of a tired dictator, was a tighter fit in the doorframe than the door itself.

"Five minutes," his voice rumbled impatiently. He held up his hand and spread all his fingers as if none of them could count. "I am not even five minutes late."

"I did not say you were late." Satan gestured to several of the empty seats. "Take your pick."

War grunted in response, taking heavy strides towards the unoccupied side of Death's seat and pulling out a chair.

He sat down and the chair's plastic coils strained underneath his weight. Death smiled at his friend, reaching over and setting a withered hand on top of the wider, meatier one.

"Glad you could make it, dear." Death chortled.

"I got caught up in a conflict. They're harder to keep tabs on when everything is nuclear and everyone is wearing the same colors." War tilted his head, craning his beastly neck to get a better look at Satan. "So what is this about? Your email was vague as fuck."

"I thought I was pretty clear." Satan flicked ash off the end of his cigarette irately.

"You said something about a demon," Pestilence chimed in helpfully, resting his yellowed sneaker on the edge of the table. "One that you had been looking for."

"Yes." Satan paused to take another drag. "Jahangir. Henry Wickes. Whatever is on his file these days. We have him in our custody. Our manner of obtaining him was not in any way I would have preferred, being free of his flesh form makes him more difficult to control. However, I believe we have him properly confined. *For the moment.* He has insisted on a trial."

"So?" War scoffed. "Baby wants a fair trial? He should have behaved better."

"Hang the bastard," Death cooed in an unsettlingly dulcet tone. "Give him another flesh form and break his neck in every place."

Satan held up a hand. "I already granted him the trial, so that much is not up for debate. I find it only fair to give everyone involved in this…*"clusterfuck"* situation at least that much. I have sent Sloth out with every confidence that they will bring back Meriwether Hayward. Mojgan and Rahman-Reza are beyond our sights, but Famine remains in pursuit. And he has the demon hunters with him."

A shared dissatisfied mutter rippled throughout the three Horsemen.

"What is the good of a trial?" Pestilence finally piped up. "We all know how it is going to end."

"I try to be just," Satan said. "Particularly in areas where God has failed or would not consider lenience. He smites indiscriminately. I am better than that."

"Sometimes." War smirked, kicking back in his seat. "I respect your ideals, boss, you know that. I don't mind playing jury if I also get to play executioner in the end."

"You are better suited as a bailiff." Death shot War a snide look, gliding his thick tongue over his bottom lip. "But a fine executioner you would be as well."

"We will work through the nitty-gritty once we have all of the demons in custody." Satan did not want to think about what horrors War might be conjuring. Torture was not the Lord of Hell's bailiwick. And he could already feel himself gaining ground with a headache. "I have added you all to the email ring so you will be consistently updated. Be sure to check your emails and actually look at your phones once a while." He shot a pointed look at Pestilence. "I want no excuses. Do I need to clarify that further?"

Pestilence lifted his hands defensively. "You will get no excuses from me, boss." He crinkled his nose like he was about to sneeze. Satan dearly hoped it was a false alarm.

"If the demons are sentenced to execution, what will become of their remains?" Death leaned forward, lacing his fingers together while the wet corners of his lips pulled into a grin.

Satan fought back a visible grimace. "Again, something that is yet to be determined."

"I should like a new ring." Death held up one of his hands, waggling his skinny bare fingers. "Perhaps a demon eye preserved in amber? They keep so well that way."

CHAPTER XX

Outside of the manor walls, the rain was picking up. Within, some of it was managing to dribble down the grey stone, seeping through where the lattice wooden pane had cracked at the sill. James was glad to be out of the bad weather. The thought was enough to bring him a little closer to the fire. Lord Morgan—*Sextus*—had breezed in long enough to set him and Virgil up by a burning hearth. He had flagged down a servant, asked for wine, and then vanished one again with Emilie. There was no telling whether they would see him again that night, a prospect which frustrated James, considering he had more questions now than before.

Virgil shed his coat, letting it fall to the floor with a heavy wet thud. The fallen angel sighed happily, rolling his shoulders and kicking aside the bundle of wet cloth with censure. He set a hand against the back of his neck, popping out some of the kinks before looking around for a chair to settle down in. James' cold blue eyes flickered down at the coat disapprovingly. Yet he made no motion to pick it up.

"You look comfortable." The demon said dryly.

"Mm," Virgil caught the look, sliding out one long leg cheekily and toeing the coat before kicking it underneath his destination chair. "And if you step any closer to that fire, you are going to be *in* it."

James looked down. He could see the reflection of individual flames on the toes of his shoes. He took a half step back, rubbing his arms.

"Damn cold." He muttered. "I know this era is bad for heating, but…"

"They are *all* bad for heating. Humanity is *terrible* at keeping warm," Virgil groused, adjusting himself to try and get comfortable in a chair that was just a bit too small for his long, lean frame. "One would be inclined to think they seek out the fires of Hell just to have something to knock off the chill."

James rolled his eyes, adjusting his glasses prudishly. "Contrary to the popular fables, Hell does not have pits of flame."

"Oh, yes? Did some recent remodeling, did you?" Virgil smirked. "Were the flaming pits over-budget? I hear microwaving their heads is more cost-efficient."

"Devilishly hard to roast flesh that way." Sextus swept back in, bearing two gas lamps with brass bases heavy enough to be used as bludgeons. "But maybe that practice has fallen out of favor? I admit to not actually recalling the last time I made my way down to Hell."

His sudden presence caused James to bite back the sharp retort that had been meant for the angel. "Is there any reason?" he asked instead. "Or did you just wander up once and never go back?"

"Closer to the latter. Although it was a touch more complicated than that, as these things always are." Sextus seemed a little wistful as he pulled up another chair, offering it to James with a little wave. James shook his head to turn down the offer and Sextus took the seat instead. The lord crossed his legs, leaning forward and lacing his fingers together underneath his chin.

"I am far more interested in what would bring *you* up *here*," Sextus said. He seemed so sincere with his large grey eyes fixed on James with intense interest. Sextus had the sort of face that men just *spoke* to and an easy demeanor which made him all the more approachable. James considered, for a split second, telling him everything.

Everything about that had been pushed down deep into the pit of his stomach. Every now and then it scratched at his ribs, attempting to claw its way back up his throat. He did not want to give in. He did not want to spew the details that were not even discussed in private. He and Virgil rarely spoke about it. And having grown so used to Henry's constant chatter, James spent a lot of time resenting the silences that cultivated so naturally between him and the fallen angel.

"You do not see many people often, I take it," James said.

Sextus shook his head. "Sheridan was the first to ever walk through. He was, *is* an immortal. I still do not know how…" His face clouded and he sank his teeth into the corner of his lip. "Even still, he remains. And that wretched creature he dragged with him as well. A bedraggled cellist with only half a face and one mad eye. You can hear him plucking at his strings well into the night, an infernal sound that Hell might benefit from utilizing. He does it no justice, his cello. It mewls like a frightened barnyard cat."

James quirked an eyebrow, his lips twitching with amusement he did not dare reveal. "I see."

"This place attracts tragedy." Sextus sounded annoyed at the very suggestion, even though it was his own. "And there is nothing more tragic than a broken man who was once beautiful."

"Or a musician who cannot play." Virgil added. "Imagine dedicating your soul to an art that did not love you back."

"Many of Julian's dedications refused to love him back." Sextus twirled a blonde curl around his finger. "He has lost everything save for what he holds hostage. I suppose if that was my fate, I would pluck out dirges on an abused string instrument as well." Sextus put his hands against the arms of his chair, pushing himself to his feet.

"You are to bed?" James asked, his eyes following the elder demon's movements.

"Rest yourselves," was Sextus' answer. "I will see you in the morning."

"You have servants, I assume?" Virgil asked. "Or are we to sleep anywhere?"

"There is an abundance of empty rooms," Sextus said, nonchalantly. "Make yourselves at home."

It felt like someone had lifted a piece of his skull and slammed a brick into the back of his eyes. Of course, in Hell, the likelihood of that being the case increased exponentially.

Lady could *feel* the chair's sticky seat before anything else. His vision began returning in increments, the blackness fading away like curtains inching back from the opening scene of an embarrassing theatre production. Faux leather squealed underneath him every time he moved. It wasn't bad enough that the material was cheap. It was also covered in a gross film that felt like someone had poured maple syrup all over the arms and the seat.

His insides quivered with a shiver of revulsion. Lady's hand jerked and he pulled it back to his side, reluctant to touch his leg or any part of his clothing that might otherwise be ruined by the unidentifiable scunge.

"Don't touch the chair," Francis warned belatedly.

"Thank you for that," Lady shot back. He looked down (another mistake). The chair was bubblegum pink and shaped like a hollowed-out bubble. He was pushed so far back into the seat that he could already tell it was going to be a struggle to climb out.

"Are you all right?" Francis' face appeared and Lady crinkled his nose. Having to deal with the chair put him in even less of a mood to be touched than usual. Even a foot away, Francis was too close for him to be comfortable.

Catching the unspoken message, Francis backed up a few steps. Lady allowed himself a deep breath, using his legs to pull himself forward so he could get out of the chair as quickly as possible.

"I am fine," Lady snipped in a belated response to Francis' question. "I am just sticky, because there is *Hell-knows-what* on this chair. My polish is chipped as gel polish should *not*. You are not using your cane. We have been abducted by my boss and dragged, *undoubtedly*, into the bowels of Hell itself. But I'm absolutely…oh!" He let out an exasperated growl as Francis picked up his cane from where it had been propped up against a wall. "There we are everything has suddenly improved!"

Francis gripped the head of his cane, swallowing a sigh that would have set off another round of verbal barbs. "Sloth won't be gone much longer," he said. "We should be ready for them when they return."

"Yes, well, this chair has already made a poor attempt to lubricate my nether regions." Lady twisted his hips and craned his neck to try and catch a glimpse of the seat of his pants. "But I do not intend to present myself for the forceful brutalization of Hell's bureaucracy. In fact, with Heaven's recent…outreach, Hell may no longer be able to claim me. I can wrap red tape around their necks until they choke."

"That is all well and good," Francis said, glossing over a good third of that statement, "But at the rate paperwork moves around here, we could be dead long before Heaven hears about it."

"Well, if they are going to kill us, I don't know why they have not done so already." Lady sniffed. "I won't last under torture, not enough to make it worthwhile. And you are barely more than an accessory to me. They will probably just stick you in chains for all eternity and make you rake coals."

"I might climb my way back out yet, raking coals." Francis said reflectively.

"Yes, but your existence would be rather meaningless at that stage, wouldn't it?" Lady set his teeth. "So if you are not too busy making happy speculation about how you might best be rid of me, perhaps you could turn your attention to the matter at hand. Seeing as how I am still alive, and I would like to get out of here."

Francis' expression flipped from confusion to remorse. He looked like he wanted to say something more, but the opportunity was lost when an obnoxious, blaring ringer butted its way into the conversation. Lady jumped, spinning around and narrowing his eyes as he glared at the desk where the office phone was sitting. He covered the distance in just a few angry steps before reaching out and snatching the phone by its neck, cutting it off mid-ring.

Who even had corded phones anymore?

"Hello?" he asked, annoyed at the instinctive rise of his own office-friendly voice. He twisted the coiled black cord around his fingers, waiting for what seemed like an eternity for a response.

"You're awake," Sloth's sleepy voice drifted from the other end. "Awesome."

"Did you just dial into your own office?" Lady glanced around, cradling the phone between his shoulder and his ear. "I have a cell, you know. You could have texted. Preferably before nearly wrecking my car and dragging me past the earth's crust."

"Are you comfortable?" Sloth's voice was a bit garbled, either from bad connection or just an awful phone.

"No. Are you going to drag yourself down here, or am I expected to sustain myself off the half-empty bottles of Schnapps in your mini fridge?"

Sloth clucked their tongue. "Hot-headed as always, Mx. Hayward. No one is in a hurry here but you."

"I disagree. If Hell itself wasn't in a hurry, this would have been handled very differently." Lady glanced over at Francis. "So, spill. What is going on?"

A dramatic pause went on for so long that Lady started to wonder if his boss had fallen asleep on the other end. He banged his receiver against the edge of desk.

"Excuse me!" the Unchaste shouted down the line. "We are not through, here!"

"They are putting you through a trial." Sloth sounded groggy and only vaguely present on the other end. "You as well as…a few others."

"Ha!" Lady sneered. "That will be a fine waste of company resources. There is a lawyer around every corner in this place! Is that why we are not in a cell? Because by the time we were booked you would have had to let us out again?"

"You are not in a cell because you don't need to be," Sloth said. "You no longer possess the ability to leave Hell at will. That is something you will not have back for a while. It's so much easier to do when you are still bound to flesh."

Lady swallowed hard, feeling an icy fist of fear close around his heart. "I see. Well, are we at least able to leave this room?"

"You can go wherever you like." Sloth yawned. "We will find you when it is time."

The phone clicked and a deadline buzzed in his ear. Lady slammed the phone back down onto the cradle, his hand tingling from the force.

"Do you know any lawyers?" Francis asked.

"Do I look like I speak to people, Frank?" Lady folded his arms. "Do *you*?"

"I know one." Francis' expression changed and he leaned onto his cane, looking down at the floor as if there was something very interesting about the flat grey carpet. "I don't think he will be of much help."

"Even a bad lawyer is better than representing ourselves. I have never been capable of thrusting myself into a good light." Lady glanced down at his hands. "I am going to wash this off. Then I'm going to see if there is a bottle of anything they haven't left half-empty in that fridge. And *then* we are going to meet up with your guy. Call him, if you have to, or whatever you think is best."

Francis chewed on his bottom lip and did not respond. He remained rooted to his spot while Lady made a beeline for the bathroom.

326

CHAPTER XXI

*V*iolet Clifton was swallowed whole.

Such large black flies. Claire could barely hear the words over their hideous buzzing.

A demon dug the silver right out of her.

She couldn't breathe. If she opened her mouth, she knew the flies would fill up her throat, her lungs…

But left the parts. The tasty parts…

The buzzing was getting louder.

Brains and bladders and lungs and guts…!

Claire drove her fingers so far down into her ears that her nails jabbed up against her eardrums. She screamed at the sharp pain, her knees trembling as she felt blood start to run down the sides of her face. It trickled down the back of her neck, hot and fast, and still that infernal buzzing…

Brains and bladders and lungs and guts. Violet Clifton was swallowed whole!

Her hands were coated in blood, hot and thick. It was streaming even faster down her neck and soaking the front of her dress, turning the green fabric as black as ink. Demon blood is bitter blood…

Claire's head smacked against the floor, her grip on the sheets not enough to save her from toppling over the side.

Her feet were tangled up as well and had pulled the rest of the blankets down to the floor. Her nightshift was soaked with sweat, clinging to her like a filmy second skin. She moaned, rubbing her face and kicking herself free, sitting up just enough to untangle the more stubborn sheet.

Edward was snoring above her head. Briefly, she considered stabbing him in the throat with one of her heels. That might be enough to make him stop.

Claire reached up and grabbed the edge of the bed, using it as leverage to pull herself back up onto her feet. She scrunched the blankets up into a ball and threw them down onto the bed, disappointed that they did not all land on top of Edward's face. She sat back down, the stiff mattress hardly giving at all as she leaned over and rubbed her face, pinching the bridge of her nose and trying to take a few deep breaths to bring herself back down to earth.

It had been a long time since she had experienced a nightmare like this. Oftentimes she did not even dream at all. Her insomnia had worked for most of her life to keep all of that at bay.

Maybe the nightmare was just one more tactic employed by Famine to keep her under his control.

She knew she was lucky to still be alive, lucky that Heaven and Hell had different methods of coping with failure. Famine had said almost nothing when she returned empty-handed the night she had gone out on her own. Of course, she could still see it; the quiet fury that made his eyes cold as granite. The way he pressed his lips together until they nearly vanished into a thin red line.

Two nights later, they were on the move again. He never brought it up, but now he expected to be obeyed.

Edward's snoring was getting louder. The longer he went on, the more he started to sound like the buzzing swarm of Claire's nightmares. She wasn't going to be able to get back to sleep. She was just going to end up lying there and waiting for morning.

Claire pulled off her nightshift, wrapping the fabric into a tight wad around her fist and pitching the sweaty bundle into a corner. She rolled across the surface of her bed and put her feet back down on the other side, sweeping her hand across the back of her neck to gather the damp hair up and twist it into a low bun. The still night air was heavy and hot even against her bare skin.

"Trouble sleeping?" Gluttony's voice, which sounded like it came from the end of a baby doll's pull-cord, came from nowhere. Claire had not even noticed she was in the room.

How long had she been there?

Claire did not turn around. She pressed her lips together and twisted her head to jerk the kinks out of her neck. Something popped, and she felt the escaping tension radiate all the way down to her shoulder.

"Do Sins have nightmares?" she asked. It was a rhetorical question and a deliberate avoidance of Gluttony's question. "Or are they a human affliction?"

"Dreams are complicated," Gluttony said. "Everyone has them. Even Sins. Even Horsemen. We just have them differently."

"I never would have thought." Claire sounded sarcastic, but she was being honest. She finally turned, bringing up one of her knees to rest on the edge of the bed as she looked over her shoulder at the Sin. "What determines when you have them? Do they ever have a meaning?"

"I don't really know if they ever have a meaning. The realm of dreams is so…" Gluttony wiggled her plump fingers above her head. "Dizzy. Interpretation is usually a wasted effort. I can tell you this, however: many dreams turn sour when you get too hot."

Claire huffed. "Maybe," she said, then changed the subject. "How long have you been over there?"

"I put your brother to bed, babycakes. I stuck around because Famine isn't too keen on leaving you alone."

"In case we run?" Claire couldn't help her smirk at that one, shaking her head at the thought of how much of a failure that particular course of action would be.

"In case Rahman-Reza creeps in through your window, steals the bottom of your jaw so you can't say a word, and then slips back out." Gluttony grinned, wide pink mouth stretching like taffy across her face. "He is my reckless wayward child. He will steal far more than your bones if you let him."

"I would bet," Claire said. She paused, plucking at the threadbare cover that was a twisted mess on top of her rigid bed. "You call him your child. I can only assume that you do not mean that literally."

"I heard the sound that made him." Gluttony moved closer, going around the bed until she was standing right next to Claire, reaching out to touch the back of her head. "It ripped through me — ferine, excruciating. Imagine how it must feel to have every bone in your body being broken at once. To have your skin being scourged with a wire brush. The moment he crawled towards me, too weak to stand, with monstrous wings as soft and trembling as a newborn bat's dragging the ground, he was mine. He had blood in his hair and on his face. He was staring but his eyes were empty. His jaw was slack, slavering. You have never seen a new demon. They are pathetic, ugly creatures with horns too heavy to let them lift their heads and claws that are too tender to even spear a strawberry."

Claire swallowed. "Are they all different? When they are not wearing human skin?"

"In some ways," Gluttony said. "And not so much in others." She pulled Claire's hair free of its knot, running her fingers through it like a comb. "They all have horns, they all have claws. They all have those nasty metal teeth that I hate. Some demons have tails, some have wings. Rahman-Reza had wings, yet Jahangir did not."

Claire felt like it was getting warmer. Maybe it was just because Gluttony was standing so close. She kept her eyes transfixed on the dark wall across from her, doing her best not to snarl whenever Gluttony's careless, sticky fingers tugged on her scalp. "You knew Jahangir that well?"

Gluttony shrugged. "Less well. I don't remember who loved him, or what circle he ended up in. Maybe he was Envy's child. It was the same with Mojgan." She started in on a braid. Once she reached the bottom, she swept her fingers through it again, the entire process beginning and ending only for her to start re-braiding a second later. "No one else has a Rahman-Reza. I hope we do not have to kill him. I think detaining him will be enough."

"It wasn't enough the first time," Claire muttered.

Gluttony growled, her gentle touch turning into a vicious grip as she pulled on the hair in her hands. Claire let out a pained yelp, ripping her hair away from the Sin's hold. She could feel a few strands snap in the process. She probably left Gluttony with a fistful.

"I know my husband keeps you hungry," Gluttony said, "but that is no reason to be a bitch."

"You keep my brother sluggish!" Claire shot back. "What is the bottom line, there?"

"Marriage," Gluttony folded her arms, "and compromise."

"I do not believe in compromise," Claire hissed. "Neither will the person I marry."

"If you ever marry. Matrimony was unprecedented for my kind and seems highly unlikely for yours," Gluttony sneered.

Claire turned her face away. Gluttony's words struck a chord and she wondered if it was written all over her expression.

It was hardly likely she would ever marry. Fair. It was difficult enough tolerating Edward. She did not want to picture her life as shadowed by another person. She was well aware of the combination of surrounding circumstances and personal flaws that made her impossible to love. But Gluttony did not have to rub it in.

She considered ramming her fist into the Sin's face and elected to save it for later. Claire was sure that she was only going to get one pass, and she wanted to make certain it counted.

Wisps of platinum hair were escaping from their practical bun, getting caught in Drucilla's long white eyelashes and pricking the corners of her maroon eyes. She reached up to rub them, belatedly remembering the black eyeliner smeared across her waterline and flinching when it transferred to her pale fingers.

The office door behind her swung open. Drucilla's shoulders straightened as she braced herself for the inevitable onslaught of verbal abuse. Since she had been plucked out of the mortal realm, it had been nothing but one thing after another. As of yet, no one could tell her exactly who had been responsible for botching her arrival to the mortal coil and scrambling her head. The script that had been authorized became a false set of memories that had then taken over completely, overriding any instructions she had also been given. For a long while, she had truly believed herself to be the unwanted daughter of an obscure nobleman.

Once the damage control team had recovered her, there was not much they could do for anyone else. And of course the demons had already fled.

All things considered, of course, Drucilla did not believe that she should be blamed for the fact that she had dropped the ball entirely with Elliot Dosett. That bastard did not deserve an ounce of salvation anyway. He was better off with his soul devoured and out of the running for reincarnation.

Smart square-toed shoes hit the plastic mat underneath the desk and Michael settled a hand against the back of his leather chair to pull it out. He took his seat across from her, and Drucilla heard the seat hiss as it sank down a full inch and put them at eye-level with one another.

Nevertheless, she gave as much of a smile as she could muster. It felt small and trembling on her lips.

"Drucilla Kerslake, am I right?" Michael cracked his knuckles, barely acknowledging her at first. He moved his wireless mouse so that his computer woke up and then started clicking through his folders.

She nodded. "Biblical name is…"

"I am not interested. One name is more than enough for me to keep up with." He finally looked at her. He had eyes like a falcon and a firm, disapproving mouth. The lines at the corners of his mouth suggested that he smiled often, but the lack thereof by his eyes said he rarely meant it when he did.

Drucilla nodded and cleared her throat, pushing her hands down into her pencil skirt and smoothing it over her chubby knees anxiously.

"I called you in here because I need help." Michael was never one for beating around the bush. "Which is not necessarily something I wish to advertise, either. I hear you have connections with Sheridan le Maurier."

"Yes." Drucilla nodded.

"He is one of the only known immortals who cannot draw his ties to the undead or the occult." He made a face at the word 'occult', as if he disliked even wrapping his tongue around it. "In fact, my sources inform me that all of his ties run right back to you."

She raised her eyebrows, trying to look surprised at this information. She could already see he wasn't buying it. "Sheridan has been around for thousands of years on the mortal coil. Much longer than I ever…"

"You were assigned a case in that area, weren't you? Back when you were still the Pilot Angel."

For the first time, Drucilla could feel blood bring a shameful color to her cheeks. She looked down and nodded.

"One..." He made a face at his computer screen and clicked a few more spots. "Lord Julian Snowdon. His wife died and you were sent down for a simple collection."

"Suicide," Drucilla said softly. "Heaven takes it very seriously."

"I am aware." He shot her another look. "What I have for you only states that he received his immortality from you, it does not state what he did to get it."

She felt a shiver run down her spine, rattling the joints of her wings and making them ache.

"He pinned my wings," she said. She had not thought about it in so long that it did not even feel real coming from her mouth.

It was Michael's turn to look surprised , although his was genuine. "He pinned your wings?"

She closed her eyes and nodded again, rubbing her face with one white hand. "He somehow knew I was coming. Or, well... I do not think he had it out for me specifically. But Lord Snowdon's wife was dying. He knew something would be there. And he meant to catch an angel. He was not after any demon. There were squares drawn on the floor, several overlapping, all done in white chalk and these symbols…" She took a deep breath. "He pushed golden pins through my wings. The floor was wood and rotted through in some parts, but there were so many pins that I could not gain enough leverage to pull my wings up and they hurt, they burned. The sigils kept me trapped in those squares. Even if I had been able to move, at that point, it was like being trapped under a jar." She cringed at her own comparison. "I know that sounds crazy."

"So, he had you trapped." Michael kept moving them forward. "And the price of your freedom was the secret to immortality?"

She nodded. It sounded so lame when he said it like that.

Michael sat back in his seat, pressing his fingertips together in that orderly way of his. "You should have let him destroy you."

She shrugged.

"Who was in charge of your case when you returned?"

"Haniel," Drucilla said.

"Well, that explains a lot." Michael made a few more clacking sounds on his keyboard, but it seemed more a method of venting than anything productive. "Did she even look twice before clearing you for light duty?"

"No." Drucilla smiled fondly.

"So, you were allowed to recover from your traumatic encounter on your own time."

She ignored his sarcasm. "I tended a lot of gardens during that time."

"And then you returned back to work. But we already had a new Pilot Angel."

"Virgil," Drucilla confirmed.

"Yes. We recently lost him, as well." Michael's brow twitched. It was getting more and more difficult for him to conceal his disgust. And, as good as he was at making Drucilla hate herself, she was enjoying watching his careful expression crumble.

"That position has always had a high turnover rate," she supplied.

"Unfortunately." He said. "So, that was why they put you out in the field."

"That is my understanding." She wondered where he was going with this. Did he call her into his office just to drag her through the most painful, humiliating experience of her existence on excruciating detail at a time?

"And then you hit your head."

"I did not..." She pursed her lips, close to a pout. Unprofessional, she couldn't help it. "I did not hit my head.

Well, I did. But, honestly, sir? I believe I was meddled with. Someone got into my head and switched enough around to make certain I would not end up coming back."

"Mm," Michael picked up a sleek black pen, tapping it against the edge of his desk thoughtfully. "Interesting. More interesting, still, that there is always a convenient reason why you cannot take responsibility for your own failures."

Drucilla just stared at him. Heat rose up to her neck, a well-suppressed temper fighting to rise. It would not be seemly to physically fight Michael in the office. Especially under the consideration that she might win.

Michael did not wait for a response as he continued, "Do you remember anything about Violet and Henry Clifton? He may have also gone by William in public for a short time, masquerading as her dead husband before abandoning that ruse faster than he picked it up."

"Very little," Drucilla admitted. She had vague sketches of Henry. Blonde hair, cavalier, and a bit dim, even for most demons. She remembered him mostly in the context of Violet. He was the shadow by her side, his hand always touching her in some way. A possessive gesture, a hungry one.

Violet was easier to recall. Divine dark eyes as brown as leaves in autumn. Wintry skin and long dark hair that looked like it would be as soft as silk to the touch. Drucilla's throat convulsed with a hard swallow.

"I remember Violet more than anyone," she added aloud. "I suppose, aside from Elliot, I spoke to her the most."

"Then you must recall she had children," Michael said. "There were a number, from what I understand. But two managed to survive." He purposefully withheld the circumstances of that survival. "Claire and Edward Clifton. They are in the hands of Famine and Gluttony as we speak."

Drucilla sat up a little straighter. "What does Hell want with them?" she asked.

"What does Hell ever want? A wider reach." Michael tapped his pen a little more deliberately. "Both children — well, they are older now — are half-demon. You can imagine that Hell doesn't get its hands on such an anomaly very often. They cannot travel dimensions very well on their own as their own ability is quite limited, so they rely upon the divine."

Drucilla tilted her chin down thoughtfully. "Forgive me, sir," she said, "but what ability do you think I might possess that any other angel does not?"

"Expendability," Michael said shortly. "Besides that, you were the Pilot Angel. Your entire job used to be wresting souls from demons and bearing them to Heaven. Flesh should be even easier for you."

"I see." Drucilla's voice softened, some of her nerves creeping back up. "Horsemen and Sins are hardly demons."

Michael shrugged. "Right now, they are right outside of the realm where Sheridan le Maurier is kept." *Trapped*, really. "If you can give them enough of a push, I can create a small opening for you to squeeze through. It would be difficult. The demon in control of this pocket dimension keeps everything sealed rather well. But Sheridan put a hole in it once. And with enough prodding, I can poke it open again. Famine and Gluttony will not be able to get through, and the Cambion will be safe there until I can fetch them, myself."

Drucilla nodded. She understood, now. "Is that all I am to do? Deliver the Cambion, then return to Heaven?"

He let out a long breath that made his nostrils flare. "If you complete this assignment—with no mistakes—I will recommend that you be reinstated as the Pilot Angel."

There it was. Drucilla gripped her skirt so tightly her hand started to go numb. "What if I make a mistake?"

"Then you won't have anything to worry about," said Michael. "You will be dead."

CHAPTER XXII

The mournful cello could be heard even from the bottom levels of the austere residence. Sheridan had only made it as far as the front door, but he could already pinpoint almost exactly where he would be mostly likely to find Julian. His lover was almost certainly holed up in the attic, pushed into a dusty corner away from every window and crack. Sunlight would not impede his artistic frenzy. And the stale air would certainly not be allowed to circulate and clear his head in any way.

Sheridan started up the steps of the grand staircase. It was wide-mouthed and branched off at the landing into two separate spirals, each like curls of ribbon flying up towards the ceiling. Julian always stayed in the left wing, these days. There were multiple floors and countless rooms, but he confined himself to the same three rooms in the same hall. He was a whole man, an immortal, but he acted less than a ghost.

He found Julian exactly where he thought he might. The attic was cold with thick white blankets of dust draped over every surface like burial shrouds. Sheridan picked his way through. The cello was impossible to follow now, its vibrato filling the small space. His high heels made imprints in the dust covering the floor, scattering crumpled leaves and the bones of small animals who had gotten trapped and died.

"Julian." He did not even know why he bothered to speak. As resonant as his voice was, it could not be heard over the man's playing. Julian was seated on a box—a luxury, it seemed, that he allowed himself a box. He usually sat on the floor, his knees draw up high and the instrument wedged awkwardly between his legs. His billowing shirt had been white at some point, but now it was closer to grey. The once-starched ruffles now drooped in limp defeat, framing his marble chest like a wreathe of dead flowers. His calloused fingertips caressed the scarred neck of his instrument, the taut strings one bad turn away from snapping – so debilitated and old, they would need replacing soon.

Julian raised his head to look at his lover, one handsome gold eye fixing on him while the other mad, clouded one remained more aimless.

Sheridan motioned, hoping the gesture might convey his desire for silence. Julian brought his piece to an abrupt halt, his bow skidding across the strings with a sharp, violent sound. The bow dropped its tip towards to the ground and he rested it there, his good eye never wavering as he waited to hear whatever Sheridan had to say.

"It is good to see you," Sheridan began, "I have missed you."

Julian did not say anything. He did not even shift. He dragged his tongue across his cheek, the movement barely visible behind his lips.

Sheridan was running out of ideas. He stepped closer, extending his hand towards his lover. Julian looked at it for a long moment and then moved his own hand back, propping his bow up against the wall and doing the same with the old cello, securing both before sliding his fingers over Sheridan's refined, pale ones.

Sheridan wrapped his hand around Julian's and pulled it to his mouth, brushing his lips over the cellist's knuckles. "You look as though you have not slept."

"What would be the point in sleeping?" Julian asked roughly, squeezing Sheridan's hand in return. His grip was strong enough to crack bone. Sheridan wasn't bothered. He brought his other hand around to pet Julian's gently, encouraging him to loosen his grip.

"You have awful bags under your eyes, my beloved."

"Whenever I close my eyes, I see *her*." Julian's voice sounded like it was wrenched from within his chest.

"One would think that should be incentive," Sheridan supplied.

"She is always crying. She doesn't like to be alone, and I…"

"But when you are awake, she does not cry?"

"She plays." Julian swallowed. "She can play when I am awake."

"I see." Sheridan transferred his free hand to Julian's hair. It used to be so thick and luxurious to touch. Now it was so oily he could barely stand to have it brush against his skin. He grazed Julian's scalp lightly, wanting to avoid both scraping up too much dirt underneath his fingernails and aggravating the angry abrasions from Julian's own ragged, anxious scratching.

"You don't know what it is like." Julian's voice was angry. Short.

"I do not." Sheridan did know what it was like, to a degree. He had stayed in bed with Julian those first few long nights when Caroline first returned. A sopping wet ghost with weepy eyes and a ghoulish scream. She left claw marks on the bedposts and wet stains on the bedspread. She hid things, plucked the strings of his cello, and cried pathetically at odd hours. The crying was what drove Julian to the brink. His inability to wrap his arms around his daughter and soothe her tears broke him more than the sight of her dead body had.

"What do you want?" Julian sounded tired. He leaned his head against Sheridan's hip.

"I told you that I missed you," Sheridan reiterated. "Is that so difficult to believe you?"

"Yes." Julian still had not moved.

"I am going to take it upon myself to make certain that you sleep." Sheridan slipped two fingers underneath Julian's chin, tilting his face up. It was such a tragedy, that face. Julian Snowdon had been the most handsome man Sheridan had ever seen. Now at least half of that gorgeous face had been reduced to nothing but a mass of white and red scars. Julian had wanted to take his own life so badly, but fire simply could not consume him. "And perhaps something to eat."

"I am not hungry." Julian had not been hungry in ages.

"We will see." Sheridan gave Julian's hair a gentle, insistent tug. Julian lingered a moment, one more deep breath with his forehead pressed against Sheridan's hip before pulling himself to his feet. Sheridan held out an arm for him, and Julian leaned heavily against his side.

"It won't work." Julian muttered even as Sheridan led him towards the stairs. "It isn't going to work."

The rain was finally staving off. It had been reduced to a light drizzle, and the wind was only a doleful hum that drummed its fingers against the exterior walls like a bored toddler. Emilie had been watching the rain from her place by the window, but Sextus' constant moving about and pacing was distracting to her thoughts.

"You are fidgety tonight," Emilie said. Her long brown hair was down and tossed over one shoulder, cascading down her chest as she worked his silver comb through the worst of the tangles.

"I am always fidgety," he said. "Less so than you, yet you are the one sitting still."

"I've had a task." She waved the comb as if to prove a point. "You can go downstairs, you know, and make further conversation if you are so curious. He is young, but I still don't think he sleeps."

"He doesn't sleep. I've never slept. We are all awake in the small hours of the morning and lurking on opposite ends of the castle. If this were a penny dreadful, there would be a monster involved."

"There has not been a monster in your little world for a very long time," Emilie reminded him, keeping her gaze steady. "And there will not be, if that is what you are afraid of."

"I am not afraid of anything," he declared. "Especially not the spindly, wispy little shadows in the night. They may crawl around and knock over lamps and make other pitiful bids for attention at their leisure."

She shook her head, a smile creeping up onto her lips. "You are going to end up greatly offending a ghost one day."

"Or greatly offending *you*." He turned to face her.

"Well," she said imperiously, "you manage to do *that* at least once a day."

Sextus laughed. It was a hollow sound, trickling off until it was as faint as the vanishing rain. He moved towards his bed, running his hand over the thick fur cover before gripping the side of pulling himself up, patting his leg for her to join.

Emily raised one eyebrow and pressed her lips together. "Did you think that would work?"

"Only somewhat." He extended his hand. "You know you are a difficult woman to beguile."

"Hardly." She stood, closing the distance between them and sliding her hand into his. "Maybe it is not so much that I am difficult as you are artless."

"You devastate me." He pulled her closer, pressing his lips against the back of her fingers.

He moved back a little on the bed and she lifted the skirt of her nightgown to give herself room to slide onto his lap. A sultry purr rolled up and down her throat as she cupped his face in her hands, pressing her soft lips against his forehead.

He twisted her skirt around in his fingers, dragging his hand up the length of her leg and pulling the fabric with him. He squeezed her thigh and her back arched as the sensation pulled a gasp from between her lips. She moved further up his lap, arranging herself more comfortably, bringing herself to rest right on the round bulge of his contained erection. Sextus pressed his hand between her jutting shoulder blades, his free hand coming around to rest against the small of her back as he pushed his face into her chest before inhaling deeply. Her breasts were impossibly soft and ample. He opened his mouth and dragged his tongue over her nipple through the fabric, pausing to draw it into his mouth, swirling his tongue around it and creating a damp little spot before releasing. He brought his mouth back up to press against her throat.

The hand that was resting against the small of her back moved down, traveling over the curve of her ass and resting against the back of her thigh. His hips rolled, pushing up against her, inviting. Emilie pushed her face into his neck, latching onto his throat, her hand coming up to bury her fingers in his thick blonde hair as she gripped it tight and sucked on his salty skin. Whatever bruise she left behind would not stay long, but she loved feeling his pulse against her tongue. Loved how his soft skin felt against her mouth.

"Sextus!" She finally gasped when she unlatched, pulling back just enough to look up at him. Her chestnut locks tumbled down to frame her face, and he rocked his hips against her again, setting the rhythm. Emilie's hands traveled down his chest, palms pressing firmly enough against him to knock him back onto the pillows. Sextus used the position of his hands against her thighs to pull her up onto him further, her legs now splayed around him.

Emilie reached down, her eyes never leaving him as her fingers pulled at the laces of his trousers. She created enough space that she could slide her hand down the front, cupping the very base, stroking it with her thumb.

He moaned, and she gave it a playful little squeeze. Her hands worked to pull him through the front of his trousers, not even undressing him properly. He was erect—his curved cock throbbing in her hands. She trailed the side of her thumb along the underside, skating over his prominent blue vein, stroking the ridge of his purple, needy head before guiding him towards her own warm, wet entrance. She rested against his head, pushing herself down slowly, feeling him stretch her open as he slid inside.

Emilie moaned softly, rocking back and forth with her body pressed against his, his cock buried deep inside of her while she squeezed her thighs around his hips. His hands came up to rest against the backs of her thighs again, pulling them a little wider, holding her close to him and teasing her second entrance with his fingers while she rubbed against him. Emilie gripped Sextus' shoulders tightly, kissing and nipping his throat as the pressure between her legs started build, the promise of an orgasm tightening in her abdomen.

Given her position, Emilie heard the door creak several seconds before he did. She didn't look up once. Yet as soon as Sextus heard the hinges creak, he pressed his hand against her chest, stilling his hips while he was still inside of her as if they were gangly youths caught during rebellious, virginal dry-humping.

"Sextus," Emilie's voice was coated thick with need and threaded with annoyance. "I am not doing this with her tonight."

"She should not be awake." He sounded more placating than irate, though she could hear the weariness edging his words. He pushed against her chest again, gently, and she slid off his length, falling down against his side and allowing him a moment to tuck his still-erect cock back into his trousers.

"A nightmare, I shouldn't wonder," Emilie said, grabbing a blanket and pulling it up over her hips. Suddenly, it was as if the room had dropped ten degrees.

"More than likely." Sextus sounded distracted. "It could be one of her ghosts." He reached out and rested a hand on Emilie's shoulder, giving it an affectionate, reassuring squeeze as he stood. He turned towards the door, then, finally facing his wife.

Lady Blanche Morgan liked to claim that she saw ghosts — shadow men with large red eyes and grim, tall hats that loomed in her doorway and never let her out. Emilie, well-acquainted with many spirits, never noticed any such things oozing from even the blackest corners of the antiquated manor.

In fact, Emilie would have dared to venture that the only thing haunting the old place was Blanche herself. A relic of the past, a nostalgic treasure that Sextus refused to let go. She was a wraith with the fragility of a cobweb and weepy grey eyes that looked as if they were covered by a layer of dust. Even with her grimy brass hair, she still resembled Sextus so closely that his love for her was near incestuous.

"Sextus…" Blanche always sounded like she had swallowed too many pills. "I couldn't…"

"Sleep?" He reached out, placing his hands on her shoulders and giving her as gentle a smile as he could muster. "Neither can I, love."

"…Escape." Her voice sharpened as she corrected him. "They were at my door."

"I'm sorry," he said. "How did you get out?"

"I had to wait for them to leave," she said. "They kept staring and their eyes made it so I couldn't move."

"That sounds terrifying." He wrapped his arms around her in a hug, pulling her thin body close to his chest. "I wish I had known."

"There is nothing you could have done," she said flatly, slightly muffled.

"All the same, I wish I had known."

She did not pull away, but Emilie could almost feel the heat of the woman's glower as it seared straight through Sextus' body. Blanche's fury was quiet, and blacker than her husband's. He burned and she simmered. Yet pitted against one another there was no safe bet as to who would win.

Sextus finally released his hold on his wife, and she looked up at him, hazy blue eyes half-lidded.

"Take me back to bed." It was a demand, and not plaintive in the least. Sextus sighed softly, pushing his fingers through her fine hair.

"All right," he said, looking from his to his companion as he addressed Emilie in turn. "I will be right back," he promised. Emilie nodded, pulling her blanket up a little higher. Blanche's harrowing glare felt like it was still crawling over every inch of her barely covered skin.

Jealous bitch, Emilie's lip curled at the thought. Some women just seemed incapable of gaining perspective from their immortality.

356

CHAPTER XXIII

"**I** knew it wouldn't be long before you reached out to me again. You can't seem to help yourself."

Francis was having a hard time coping with the voice on the other end of the phone. It sounded just like it had when he walked away from that dark, smoky office on the end of one of Hell's busiest streets so long ago. He remembered how the plaque had fallen off the door when he slammed it shut, and how it had been only a vaguely satisfying sound. The voice brought back those memories, along with the faint scent of cheap wine-flavored cigars.

"I need your help." Such a ready reveal of his desperation was probably not his best move. "Well, *we* need it…"

"*We?* I heard that you were shacking up with your boss, but I didn't quite believe it. Then again, it isn't entirely out of character for you, is it?"

Francis squeezed the phone anxiously in his hands. "Archibald."

"Archie, please."

"*Archibald.* It's not personal. Trust me when I say that this is already not easy. We need a lawyer and you just so happen to be the best."

"I know," the voice on the other end drawled. "You have all of my best success stories memorized. A guy like me doesn't end up in a place like this unless he is *really good* at what he does. I probably could have convinced the Almighty to let Cain off with credit for time served and some light community service."

There was a pause. Francis didn't have anything to say to that.

"Hey, should I get my timer going?" Archibald teased. "Is this an official consultation I should bill you for?"

Another pause. They weren't getting anywhere fast.

"All right…" Archibald sounded a bit irritated that his usual jabs at humor were not charming his disillusioned former partner. "You know where my office is. Come find me and we will get you set up with an official consultation. You know my rates. They haven't changed."

Nothing about him had changed. "I know." Francis' world was starting to tilt a little with how fast his head was spinning. "We will get down there as fast as we can. And, um—" he felt like he was going to throw up. "Lady? He's my husband, and he doesn't…know you exist."

"With a name like 'Lady' I can already tell you that we don't run in the same circles. So, what's the deal there then? Is he a bona-fide demon like you?"

"No. It is more difficult than that. He is an Unchaste, and he…"

"An Unchaste?" Archibald cut him off again. "He probably saw my papers go by at some point."

"He's not really in the soul processing department, but with my luck, he already knows what sort of skeezeball you are." Francis sighed. "I'm hanging up now. Is there anything else you need from me before we meet up?"

"You know last time you left, you forgot to say, 'I love you'."

Francis slammed the phone back down, missing its cradle but nicking the tab enough to end the call. He let the phone dangle, hovering an inch from the floor and spinning leisurely on its springy cord.

"Hey," he lifted his voice enough to be heard across the room, "are you almost ready?"

"Frank, you know I detest personal questions." Lady stepped out of the bedroom, pulling small black gloves over his hands. "Are you all right? I don't ever hear that much inflection in your voice."

Francis looked up at the ceiling, fighting the overwhelming desire to sink into the floor and vanish. He hadn't thought that Lady could hear a single word of his conversation. Or at the very least, he hadn't considered his husband might be paying attention.

"I'm fine," he said, swallowing a much more complex response that he was sure would not have interested his husband. "It's really that I...don't like lawyers. You know? They always answer the phone like they already know why you called."

"Mm," Lady agreed. "No one likes them. I find this whole situation absurd, and I think the fact that we even *need* a lawyer is bullshit." Lady folded his arms. "So, what's the price?"

Francis shrugged. "He's a spirit. They all want the same thing."

"Well, I don't have many shiny baubles on my person at the moment." Lady narrowed his eyes, lifting one arm to inspect his cufflinks. "These might do. These and your earrings."

"As long as it sparkles, it could be a jar full of brass buttons. I'm sure we will pick some things up along the way, as well. But we should go." Francis was already looking around for the exit.

"Oh, in a hurry, is he? I hope you told him exactly how much I hate to be rushed." Lady breezed past him, creating a haughty little wind.

"I did not think to mention." Francis grabbed his cane and made quick strides to catch up, grabbing the office door first and pulling it open for his husband.

Sunlight dripped through the lattice covered windows, casting sweeping gold patterns onto the wooden floor. James was glad to see it. After so much dreary grey rain, even a sliver of light did wonders for his mood. Sextus kept lamps, but they were scattered throughout the house, dim and poorly cared for. Nothing like the glittering halls of the Clifton estate. Not even like the grim radiance of the Dosett one. Elliot had acted more like a born demon than Sextus.

James brushed that thought away. It was a dangerous pattern. If he dwelled too much on Elliot, he was going to think about Henry. If he started thinking about Henry, he was going to walk himself around in circles until he drove himself mad.

The sunroom had books. They had been left on the center table stacked in a haphazard pile on one of the corners. James picked up the one resting on the very top and turned it around to glance at the cover. There was nothing written, but on the spine in faint lettering he could see *History of the*

Stars. He flipped it open and heard the spine crack a little as he started to turn the thinning pages. Block text, strict black lettering marching across the page in neat twin rows...

"Lawrie?"

It was the voice that startled him. James brought his head up, one thumb coming down to pinch the middle of the book's tender spine so as not to lose his place. It was more habitual than anything else. Ice blue eyes, medical and cold, homed in on the source. It wasn't difficult to find. The woman in the entrance looked like a ghost, but only in the palest sense. James had met ghosts before and felt like most made considerable efforts to appear as alive as possible. She looked like she had been found in an attic trunk. Her pale blonde hair and dim, dead eyes carried hints that she had been regionally attractive. Her torn fingernails, split bottom lip, and the bruises on her forehead suggested she spent a great deal of time slamming herself into the walls. The bruises on her head matched the ones on her wrist which were somehow more vivid blue and purple with rings of green and yellow blooming halfway up her forearm. There were healing claw marks on her chest and neck and a splatter pattern of old blood on her white nightgown. She had had some kind of fit, *recently.* The only thing to really suggest she was still alive was the rapid pulse fluttering in the heavy vein wrapped around her frail throat.

"Lawrie?" she repeated. She had a nice voice, even if she did sound like she was talking in her sleep.

"No." He sounded a little colder than was necessary. "James. I apologize, if I disturbed you."

She descended the three shallow steps that dipped into the sunroom. Her bare feet were in far worse condition than the rest of her. "You used to follow me as a child." She sounded like she was chiding him. "You don't think that I remember. You were a shadow too. You've got color in your skin now."

James shut the book and set it down carefully on the stack. "Ah." Nothing she said made sense.

"I remember the horns." She reached with one shaking hand as if she was going to grab his hair. "I guess…antlers, aren't they? Nana said the difference between antlers and horns is that antlers are soft like velvet and stand up straight for the sky."

"Well," James took half a step backwards. "That is not necessarily true." Could she see his horns? That was impossible. His flesh form should have kept everything concealed. No part of him should be failing. It could have just been a coincidence—she was clearly out of her mind.

"Are they made of velvet?" she asked insistently, getting up on her toes and reaching a little higher. James snatched her wrist before she could touch him. She was so thin that he regretted his own haste, afraid that he was going to snap a bone.

"No," he said. "They are not made of velvet. They are not bone, they are horns." He took a deep breath, releasing his hold but watching to make certain her hand descended all the same. "And it is not polite to touch them."

"Oh." She started chewing on her lip. It was already shredded and dark from having been torn apart and healed over so many times. He could not figure out exactly what she had left to gnaw on. "You don't remember me."

"I am not the person you think I am." Shadow people were often mistaken for demons, so it was a genuine mistake. The thought calmed him a little. Rational explanations.

"You smell."

"I try not to."

"You are scared."

"I am not!" James huffed and pushed his glasses up the bridge of his nose. "I am not, and neither are you. Although you should be, if you can see my horns."

"Sextus has horns too." Her voice sharpened a little. Flinty. "He does not like to let me see them because he likes to pretend he is human, even when he does not have to."

"I cannot think why." James allowed himself to step a little closer, more confident that she would not try to touch him again.

"He feels," she said. "And if he wears a human face, he is allowed to feel."

James took a deep, deliberate breath. His chest ached so oddly when it expanded. "Demons do not feel," he reminded himself out loud.

A little smile touched the dry corners of her lips. "Demons feel more." Her fingers twitched as her gaze wandered up again. "May I touch them, please?"

No. "Why do you want to?" He needed to remove himself from this situation.

"I still don't believe that you are not Lawrie," she admitted. "They are the same shape."

"Ah," he said with some defeat.

"So, may I?"

Without really knowing why, James descended to one knee. He held his head upright, keeping his gaze level with hers. Her eyes looked almost *dirty*. A doll left unattended to let dust and dirt accumulate.

"Lightly," he warned. "They are sensitive."

Her face lit up. She still could not push her smile into a full grin, but she reached out and rested her trembling fingers right against the curve of one of his horns. Her touch sent a jolt down his spine, startling him. Up until that moment, he still had not believed she could really see them. His head jerked, but her hand followed, resting gently against the ridges. She sighed, gliding her hand gently over the swells, down the dips, moving all the way up to the very tip. She swirled her fingertip over the point and he felt it *everywhere.* It tightened his abdomen and shot all the way down to his groin. James fell back on his heels; revulsion, confusion, and something close to fear crashing into him all at once.

"I am sorry," the woman said. Her hand still hovered mid-air but she did not make another attempt to touch him. "Did I hurt you?"

"No!" he gasped, clenching his teeth and trying to force everything down, knowing how much it showed on his face and hating it. "No, no. They are sensitive. I told you."

"Very." Her gaze slid over him again, indolent. "Thank you for allowing me."

"Of course." He pushed his fingers against his temple and used his free hand as leverage to stand. His glasses were fogged with his own breath.

"Do you eat?" she asked, flipping the subject so quickly that his head spun.

James closed his eyes to try and collect himself a little better. "Sometimes. Recreationally. As with everything else."

"Have tea with me." She turned, lifting one foot to rest against the first step and then looking over her should at him. "Please. Sextus is busy. I won't eat if I'm alone."

Needy. James nodded. Another deep breath. It was easy, perhaps too easy, to fall back into this role. The role he fulfilled with Elliot. Caretaker. Doctor. She wouldn't eat if she did not have someone there across from her, encouraging and participating. She did not want to be alone. He could indulge it. She would not touch him again.

"All right," he said, his eyes snapping open as he pulled his glasses down and lifted a borrowed handkerchief from his pocket. "Lead the way, madame."

CHAPTER XXIV

Francis knew that Archibald Bray felt that his hatred for demons was entirely justified. Their cases rarely slid across his desk, but on the occasion that they did; the defendants were always at the end of their rope, claiming he was impossible to work with. Their papers were famously easy to overlook and had a habit of vanishing once they made their way into his office. Email queries and phone calls went unanswered. Threatening letters went unopened. Office hours changed with both his mood and his ability to work with people that day, so even a walk-in appointment was unattainable.

All unrelated, of course, to the instance where a demon had broken his incorporeal heart. That was how the rumors went—although Francis remembered things a bit differently than Archibald liked to say. He had to wonder if his former lover regretted picking up the phone at all. But that was a conversation for another time.

After all, Archibald had told him—on no certain terms— that they were never going to speak again. He genuinely hoped that his former lover was doing better.

Francis pushed open the door and that little bell at the top he always hated signaled his arrival with a pitiful clang.

Archibald was sitting at his desk, looking smart as always—with his elbows on his desk and his fingers laced together and pressed up against the bottom part of his chin.

"So, Mr. Hislop," were the first words he said, "That little jaunt down the street took you longer than expected."

A little joke, all right—was it too early for them to have jokes? The day Francis left, he told Archibald that he needed fresh air and a can of lemonade. Of course, the specter would not have let that go—but if he was making light of it, perhaps he had decided it was time to put all that behind him? Francis felt his apprehension as an increasing pressur against his ribs.

Francis suddenly realized that there was too much silence in between the greeting and the response.

"I do apologize, Mr. Bray," Francis said at last. "I took the long way back."

"That will be fifteen minutes deducted from your next paycheck, I'm afraid."

"Sixty cents! Don't do it to me, sir. I have three children."

The corners of Archibald's mouth stretched. "Even now, you are so attached to lying to me."

Francis fought against a sharper response to keep the peace. He was still fairly in the habit of indulging his ex-boyfriend's manic episodes, but it was unclear—even to him—how far he was willing to let it go. Francis changed the subject by gesturing to his side. "Archibald, I need you to meet Meriwether Hayward—Lady—my husband."

Archibald sneered, not wasting a second as he sucked on his overly white, vicious teeth. "Husband? I didn't take you for the marrying type. Of course, what is a word like marriage to us down here? It only means something to those still walking on the surface. But then, I guess that's why you've come to me, isn't it? You've spent a great deal of time on the surface recently. Maybe a little too much time."

Francis raised his chin. He could tell, from Lady's expression, that his husband already hated the specter.

"Imagine my surprise," Lady interrupted coolly, "when Frank told me that he had a lawyer for an ex. But then, he never really mentioned you before today."

Archibald's smirk shriveled and all that it left behind was a withered grimace. "Convenient," he sputtered. "My middle name."

"We have been running for a while," Francis said, desperate to re-direct the conversation. "Hell finally caught up to us. Now we are getting dragged through a trial."

"Hell rarely grants them," Archibald pointed out. *'You are lucky to have one'* hung unspoken in the air.

Francis nodded. "I knew that if anyone could help, it would be you."

"I might." Archibald leaned back in his chair.

"You are one of the best." Francis punctuated.

"Maybe. Maybe not *the* best. But I was good enough for you. Once." Archibald shifted in his chair, spitting out the bitter words. "How are you going to pay?"

"While I am open to the idea of selling Frank into indenture servitude, I know how materialistic you specters can be." Lady pushed his glasses up, looking down his nose at the seated lawyer. "There are plenty of useless baubles in the deal for you. But before that even happens, I need signed paperwork on both sides and terms laid out very clearly. I did not come all the way here just to be double-crossed by a fuzzy scuzzball in a cheap suit."

"Cheap is one thing," Archibald spat back, "poorly tailored is another. Did you come with the suit when Francis pulled it off the sales rack?"

Lady's mouth fell open. Francis fell into a chair and sank down as far as he could into the seat, pinching the bridge of his nose. This had been a bad idea. Possibly his worst ever.

"Poorly tailored?" Lady seethed. "I don't know what you think you're hiding beneath that boxy blazer, but it is *not* a waistline!"

"Pithy *and* bitchy. I'm starting to think you have a type, Francis."

"Paperwork," Francis snapped. He was close to losing his control in front of them both. "Please."

"Ask and ye shall receive." Archibald dropped his hand below the desk, not taking his eyes off Lady as he pulled out the drawer closest to his gut. "There isn't any call for a rush, of course. Hell is never in a hurry and the Devil always gets his due. But 'keep the client happy', that's my motto. And speaking of keeping people happy…" The tip of Archibald's tongue flickered licentiously between his teeth. "Has Francis shown you how many he can fit at once?"

Lady froze, appalled. *"Excuse me?"*

Archibald feigned innocence. "The man has only one talent, and he does not immediately share it with his to-have-and-to-hold?"

Archibald pulled a stapled stack of papers out of the drawer and set them down on the desk, slamming the drawer shut in the same motion.

"Only one?" Francis clasped his hands behind his head miserably.

"Possibly more. Only one instance was ever memorable enough to recall. Look…" Archibald set a pen down on top of the papers. "I don't want a lot for this. You're in a bind and I'm going to help you out. Don't overthink it. But I do want one thing from you." He held up his hand and wiggled his ring finger. "I didn't think you would still have it, but I want it back."

Francis glanced down at his hand. Honestly, he had become so accustomed to putting on the ring every morning that he barely thought about it at all. It was just a simple silver band. It had meant something before.

Spirits never gave away their precious shiny things. At least, almost never. He looked back up at Archibald and shrugged.

"All right," he said, "you got it." He twisted the ring to work it loose and then slipped it easily off his finger, settling it down on the surface of the desk.

Lady's glare was burning holes in the back of his head. He knew he was never, *never* going to hear the end of this.

"Thank you." Archibald snapped the ring up. "Now if you could go over that paperwork and sign where I have marked, then we can move forward."

Francis reached out for the pen, but Lady snatched it up before he could. He glanced over at his husband. Lady was no longer looking at him, but his anger was still so blatant that he practically had steam rising off his skin.

Francis settled back down into his seat, lifting his hands in resignation and glanced at Archibald.

He wanted to wipe the smug expression off that bastard's face with his fist.

Long black talons that Henry had not dealt with in a very long time dragged across the surface of the desk, peeling up the protective seal. The chimera's tail that had not been a part of his form in so long swished back and forth impatiently underneath the desk, curling flirtatiously around the lawyer's ankle with the intention of sending unholy shivers rocketing up his spine.

Clinton looked visibly uncomfortable, and Henry could not help but smile.

"We need to go over the facts again." Clinton shook his foot pointedly, and Henry allowed his tail to slither away. "You are being charged with insubordination, contract violation, undocumented soul harvesting, reckless slaughter, endangerment of non-contract individuals, reckless endangerment of a coworker, bodily harm of a superior, careless and undocumented dimension-stepping, and also siring mortal or informally 'cambion' children. All of these are in direction violation of Section 6.6 Article 3, Sub-Article 3.

"Sure," Henry slumped onto the desk, bored.

"Do you contest any of that?"

"Well…" Henry stopped dragging his nails in favor of drumming them on the desk. "The superior in question started it."

Clinton pinched the bridge of his nose. "That will not hold up in court."

"Neither will I. Why are we going through these motions?"

"Jahangir…" Clinton began.

"Henry," the demon said shortly. "If you will. I prefer it."

"*Henry*." Clinton let out a breath. "Satan sent me down here not because he thinks you have a chance, but because he is trying to fulfill the terms of your employment, which state that you are entitled to a lawyer in the case of…" he gestured over the long list spread out in front of him, "…any of these. Let me help you. I'm just doing my job."

"What if you are bad at your job?" Henry's tail slipped under the desk again, the time curling around the leg of Clinton's chair. The lawyer gripped the desk like he was expecting the seat to be ripped out from underneath him.

"I suppose it doesn't matter," Clinton said dryly. "You don't stand a chance regardless."

"All I want is my flesh form back." Henry groaned. "I am starving. My mouth hurts. It is unethical to starve me when I haven't even been sentenced yet."

"I will see what I can do for you." Clinton sighed. "But I'm not making any promises. They think hunger makes demons more compliant."

"That has been proven false. I think it is just sadism."

"Sadism or not, there is nothing I can do about it right this second." Clinton stuffed a stack of papers back into the file he had pulled them out from and dropped them into a briefcase.

"Did they say what they were waiting on?" Henry's eyes trailed over the lawyer as he snapped the briefcase shut and stood up.

Clinton shook his head. "More questions than answers."

"You are supposed to have the answers."

Clinton grunted noncommittally in response before making his way towards the door.

378

CHAPTER XXV

He could smell rain in the air, but it was faint on the breeze from the night before. The earth underneath his bare feet was wet. Soaked through, dark, clinging to his pale toes. The surrounding trees were grey with fog. It pooled around his ankles like a shallow ocean tide. Chill bumps rose on Virgil's skin; but he could not pinpoint whether it was from cold or foreboding.

It was good to be away from the manor. He could not help feeling like the walls had started to close in, like the house itself was so austere, hugged its pride so close, that it just kept drawing its arms tighter and tighter with the intent of smother Virgil in its bosom. He hated houses, hated *walls*. His own little shop had been different. He had built it for Cassandra.

Cassandra. *Almighty above.* He missed her. In all of the time since *Archangel-fuckwit-Michael* had broken her into so many pieces, he had barely been able to assemble them again. But he kept her close, always. She was bundled up in a little leather pouch that rested against his hip, against his skin, underneath his clothes. It rubbed, chaffed—he didn't care. He would endure anything for her. He never took it off, not even when he slept.

He thought of her again. Her creamy legs, so delicately shaped. Her small white hands and how they spread over the tips of his fingers. Her gentle palms, smooth and without a single crease. Her lips—he had painted them himself. They glistened at the corners and puckered in the middle, a dark little seductive line running into the corners to create a genuine smile. Her smile was *always* genuine.

Her dark, curly hair. He loved to tug on the curls playfully and watch them spring back into place. He had not deserved her. That was why he lost her.

He would get her back again. His beautiful beloved.

His own thoughts were upsetting him. He was walking in circles, perhaps, or maybe not. He had not arrived back at the manor, but he felt like his feet were sinking into the earth where they had trod before. Looking behind and ahead, he could not see footprints. Maybe the ground was just getting softer. The trees were getting thicker, for certain. Maybe he really wasn't going in circles.

He could hear cello music. Virgil looked up as if the sound was somehow resonating across the sky, pouring from the heavens. It wouldn't be the first time one of the Heavenly Host had wandered too close to the veil and blown a horn too loud. He could not recall the last time a single member had picked up a string instrument, however, besides the Almighty-endorsed harp. God loved a harp. He hated a cello. He said they were too melancholy, and he did not want his praising chorus to sound like a cacophony of mourners.

Cacophony. The Almighty used words like that without really knowing what they meant. Yet he still boasted responsibility for creating all language in its entirety. (He wasn't. Sandalphon was responsible for every linguistic nightmare).

He was getting closer to the source. The trees were trembling down to their roots. Invisible to the naked eye, he could still feel every pulse of the music beneath their rough hides. His own bones were rattling. It was deep. Affecting. Mournful. The musician at the bow hosted an ache so deep within his heart that not even the strings could draw it out.

The ground was getting soupier. When Virgil looked down, he could see water forming over the tops of his feet with every step. It sucked at his heels, squelched beneath the balls of his feet, slick and smooth. He made a face and looked up, once more towards Heaven and then straight ahead.

A manor was coming into view, but it was not the one he left behind. Vines of ivy had taken over as the dominant resident, curling around every space in every stone and choking welts into the warped wood of every balcony railing. Delicate leaves shivered in the breeze and shook the intertwined mass, making the entire house appear to be trembling.

Maybe it was. The foundation was sinking. If time passed at all in this place, it would only take another decade for the entire structure to fall apart. Virgil wasn't sure what led him to walk up towards the door, one hand reaching out for the battered brass knob. The elegantly engraved oval had dips in the side as if it had been gripped too tight by a hand stronger than the metal it was against.

The knob was loose and turned too easily. The door, likewise, offered no resistance as it swung open. Rotted wood skittered across the ground, scattering leaves and rodents that had gathered by the bottom crevice. The wooden floors had been allowed to sink so low that mud and ivy were breaking through the spaces, expanding and warping the boards until there were holes big enough for a man to slide through. Parts of the roof had fallen in. Broken tiles and scraps of splintered beams rested against the floor, illuminated by whatever sunlight could poke its way through the holes left behind.

Virgil suddenly wished he had worn shoes. He was not going to walk out of here with anything less than twenty splinters. He picked his way carefully across the floor, brushing aside more offensive pieces with his toes.

The cello music had stopped.

Virgil was suddenly aware of a lot of things. He was made aware of the way the house groaned when the wind buffeted against its sides — wind that had not been so strong before he stepped past the threshold. He was aware of the branches shaking above his head, shedding leaves that made long, lazy spirals towards the floor through the holes in the roof.

He was aware that he could see his breath. It made clouds in front of his face, and his fingertips were numb.

Heavy footsteps thundered above his head. The first set came down with the force of a jump. Virgil nearly leapt out of his skin, spinning on the ball of his foot to try and catch sight of every corner at once. He just needed to spot the danger so he could figure out which direction to run. He was not interested in confrontation, not of any kind.

The footsteps continued, loud enough that he could trace their path. Whoever was storming his way was coming from the East Wing. The wide staircase lolled like a dead, bloated tongue and split off at the top landing like so many others, except the West Wing steps had been decimated. There was enough structure remaining that it would have been technically possible to ascend them, but it would have been difficult.

Virgil took several steps back. Morbid curiosity convinced him to linger long enough to catch sight of whatever creature had taken residence in this place, but one look was going to be good enough for him. He was ready to sprint. If he was nothing else in this mortal coil, he was fast.

The door was still accessible, despite the wind slamming it shut and then prying it back open intermittently. He took note of that. He looked at the staircase again. Fear made him jumpy. Impulsive. He was an angel, fallen or not. Any earthly creature, any *damned* creature, he could shred to pieces.

He had not come here looking for a fight. He was not going to stay long enough to bruise his fists.

Whatever image he had conjured in his head was wrong. Standing on the staircase was, what he considered worse. Virgil towered over everyone. He was no Hadraniel, but he was *tall*. This man, if he stood up straight, could have easily made eye contact. He was a giant. His shoulders were burly, and he was muscular for someone who looked like they haunted a chimney. His shirt was in tatters, which was a shame, because it was a nice shirt. He had claw marks on his chest, some healed over, some fresh. They were either from his own ragged nails or someone else's. They slashed across his throat and up towards his face as well.

It was a face Virgil would have considered clawing off, if it was his. Almost all the handsome features had been marked by a fire -and some of them had melted away completely. A sculpted doll that had been left too close to a hearth. One eye was hawkish gold and the other was cloudy blue. They did not seem to agree on which direction they were supposed to focus.

"Who are you?" He spat when he growled. His body language suggested an uncharacteristic burst of aggression that had propelled him down the stairs.

Cellists, in Virgil's limited experience, were not usually so volatile.

"Virgil Abney." He barely recognized his own threadbare voice when he spoke. "Please forgive the intrusion. I was wandering this way…"

"You got lost?" The man sneered, his upper lip drawing back to bare vicious, decaying incisors. "You are not among the first."

"Well," Virgil swallowed, "perhaps you should consider some signs."

The man huffed, a rush of air like a bull. Virgil felt a great deal like Theseus staring down the minotaur.

"Papa." A lighter voice joined the conversation. A bubbly, babbling voice like water skipping over river stones in a brook.

Virgil's head came up and he saw the man's attention immediately drawn to the crumbling West Wing staircase. Tiny white hands wrapped around the rotting balusters; the wood so weak that it offered as much resistance as pudding underneath the pressure of delicate fingertips. A little face peered out from between them, ghostly pale with the bluest eyes that Virgil had ever seen. Their vibrance harkened back to the purity of the sky in its earliest days of creation.

Mortal colors or not, he knew a spirit when he saw one.

"What is it, Caroline?" The man's voice had taken on a paternal quality with bolts of panic that struck him like hailstones.

"Who is that?" She pointed through the balusters with one accusatory finger. Almighty save this poor ragged spirit. Her hands were bloated with water.

The man did not even spare Virgil a second glance. "We do not know him, precious…"

"Are you going to kill him?"

A beat. "I don't know."

He did not like *that* part of the exchange one bit. Virgil took another step back. He jammed his bare heel against a fat splinter and cringed visibly at the flash of pain that dragged along the back of his calf.

"He would not make a very pretty doll." Caroline drew her hand back.

The gears in Virgil's head started spinning. He fixed his gaze on Lord Julian and forced a breath to make a full circulation through his system to steady himself.

This might be something he could work his way out of.

"Doll?" he asked softly. "Do you have many dolls, sir?"

There was such contempt in the man's dead, hazy eyes. "Caroline has a great many."

"Do you make them for her?" Virgil noticed his fingers were trembling as they descended to the soft leather pack strapped around his hip and thigh. He did not know why he was shaking. Even as he pulled up the hem of his shirt he could only think, *'it has been so long…'*

"Yes." Contempt was giving curiosity a little bit of room.

"I…" The moment his hand dipped into pack and touched Cassandra's smooth arm he nearly crumpled. Virgil forced himself to remain steady and scooped his hand underneath her little body, pulling her free – what work he had managed to do and all that he had left incomplete. He cupped his hands and held her broken pieces nestled between his palms. The bigger, more complete parts of her body stuck out further and the crook of his thumb wrapped around her waist to keep her in place.

The man's gold eye assessed the situation, and the severe corner softened. "You lost her."

"Pain deeper than anyone could imagine," Virgil said, as gently as he could. "I think you understand how it feels."

The man did not even have to think about it. He nodded and extended his hands. A heavy signet ring rested closely to a mourning ring that clung stubbornly to a cluster of pearls in the shape of a flower.

"Allow me." It sounded more of a command than a request. For one furious moment, Virgil did not budge. He did not want to put Cassandra into a stranger's hands. This man was unpredictable and brutish. Who knew what further damage he could inflict? But then, if he could help in any way...

Virgil squeezed Cassandra in his hands before setting her, gently, into the man's. He closed his hands around her carefully and pulled her closer to his chest, cradling the pieces and inspecting them with the calloused edges of his thumbs.

"Come with me." He turned and started walking back up the stairs. Powerless, at this point, to rebel, Virgil had no choice. The little girl's spirit had disappeared. But he could still feel her following them, and he could have sworn he felt a small, wet hand closing around his fingers.

CHAPTER XXVI

Dozens of waxy papers with saltwater taffy still stuck in the creases littered the bed. Each one had been a soft pastel color; mint green, petal pink, and lemon drop yellow. According to Edward, the color did not matter. They all tasted the same regardless.

"If you keep eating them like that, you are going to throw up." Claire had one pillow balled up underneath her head and the rest were thrown wantonly towards the edges of the bed.

"I hope so," Edward responded dryly. He unwrapped another and tugged the paper free. The taffy stuck to his fingers and he sucked it off. "It doesn't taste like I want it to."

She knew what he wanted it to taste like. "I don't think you are ever going to discover *that* taste again."

He made a sound in his throat like a high-pitched whine. "You don't know what it's like." He was almost shoving the paper into his mouth, growling around his own fingers. "You never knew…"

"Shut up." She snapped at him. "You promised."

He made a face and spat up the papers, balling them up and tossing them down sullenly onto the bed. "Do you ever wonder if you're less than half?"

"There will be less than half of you left if you keep saying things like that," she snarled.

He kept his sharp eyes on her. "I'm not the only one who doubts it." He was already peeling the paper away from another taffy and tugging it free. "I hear you at night, when you moan and toss and turn. You sat up the other night, do you remember that? You were still dead asleep when you did it."

"No," Claire said, "I don't remember."

"You sat up and you told me that she loved us."

"Who loved us?"

"Mother." He crumpled the sticky wax paper in his hand.

"Do you believe that?"

"I don't know. I don't think so. I don't think that our mother ever loved us."

Claire considered it, then nodded. "I don't think she did, either."

"Father did." Edward's voice was muffled around the candy.

Claire snorted softly. "Demons do not love."

Edward swallowed. "Neither did mother." He dragged his hand over the back of his mouth. "Not anyone. Not even him."

"Or maybe he was the only one she ever actually loved." Claire shrugged. "It would not surprise me in the least. They were made for one another. To be together."

"Do you think that is why he ate her soul?" Edward asked lazily.

Claire stiffened. "If that is so then it was…selfish. Greedy." She could not imagine being so overcome by a single person that your only desire was to devour them, to take them away from everyone else.

Edward scoffed. "I think he was just hungry." He poked at the little pile of still-wrapped taffies by his foot. "I'm hungry."

"You are always hungry," she countered.

"I can't help it." His teeth tugged on his bottom lip. "She makes me this way."

Claire pulled herself closer, leaning over so that their noses were nearly touching, and she could keep her voice hardly above a whisper while still being heard by her brother. "It is going to be like this forever," she said, "if we don't leave."

He snorted. "Yeah?" he whispered in return, although his was a whole degree louder. "You've gone completely batty."

"We did it once. We escaped a divine."

"Gluttony and Famine are not *divine*, they are…" He waved his hand like he could not quite grasp the word. Eventually, he gave up. "Besides, after all of this time, what makes you think that Michael is not going to try to pull us back?"

"Call it a hunch."

"Or unfounded hope."

"Call it what you will, then, but we need to get out of here."

"And go *where?*" Edward picked up a taffy piece and pitched it at her. It missed and jumped over the side of the bed. "How far do you think we could get on our own? We need *some* degree of protection, Claire, and whether or not you agree, we have that now."

"You call this protection?" Claire's face was becoming flushed, as hard as she was trying not to let her mounting frustration show. "You are out of your mind. What does she do to you? Does she slide into your bed at night and whisper into your ear what a good boy you are?"

He kicked her, hard — but not enough to knock her off the bed. Claire grabbed his ankle, pulling hard enough that her brother fell back. He knocked his head against the bed frame and groaned, scrambling to sit up and wrest free from her grip. He twisted his body upwards, hands going for her hair, but she took hold of his arm and grabbed his shoulders, flipping him over the side of the bed. He hit the ground hard, his hand coming up to take hold of anything that he could drag down with him. He grabbed the bedcovers and the edge of her jacket. The hard pull from such an odd angle was enough to knock her over, and Claire tumbled as well, landing right on top of her brother.

"Unf!" Edward brought his knee up and shoved it into her gut. Claire growled, not even thinking as her hand balled up into a fist and she crashed it against his cheek. Edward was barely fazed by the fact that she hit him and more upset by the way his jaw cracked when her knuckles made contact. He tried to roll over, but her arm came down like a bar across his shoulders and pinned him down to the floor.

"Are you done?" she snarled.

"I still think you are crazy." He spat at her face.

"And you can't fight. So it comes out even." She bore down harder on his shoulders. "You went down like a rag doll."

"You had the advantage!"

"Yeah. You're winded from shoving taffy into your face."

Edward huffed. "All right, all right! All right. You win."

"I need you to listen to me."

"I'm listening!" He insisted.

"We are going to find a way out of this."

"Sure, sure."

"We did not escape one divine contract to be imprisoned by another."

Edward coughed. Claire finally let him up, sitting back on her heels and pushing back a strand of black hair that he had managed to knock loose.

"We are going to die," he said, sitting upright and drawing his knees towards his chest so that he could wrap his arms around his legs. "You know that?"

"We have not died yet." Claire lifted her chin. "I'm starting to think it's harder than you realize."

"I still don't see why that would make you angry." It did not matter what Francis said. Every word out of his mouth seemed to only fuel his husband's rage.

"Of course not!" Lady said. "Why would it upset me that you would *keep* and *wear* your old lover's ring? Are you going to tell me, now, that it has no significance?"

"It doesn't," Francis replied gently. Lady rolled his eyes so far back into his head that they strained.

"I did not even realize that you had anyone before me," Lady said in a way that suggested this was the real heart of the issue.

"Should I have put it on my résumé?" Francis asked dryly. "He is letting us stay with him until this whole trial is over. I don't have a desire to speak ill of him in his own house—"

"Like he isn't aware you are a trifling bitch," Lady spat, glaring at the bed that filled the space between them. "I am not sleeping on that."

"Why not?"

"Since when have we ever shared a bed?"

Of course. "I will take the floor, then," Francis said wearily. He was ready for the argument to be over so he could get some rest. He just needed to close his eyes for a few minutes. Maybe then the headache would go away.

"Absolutely not. I refuse to trip over you in the middle of the night and break something on account of your inability to keep it in your pants."

Francis let that one go. It was too absurd to even argue.

"I do not know what grotesque atrocities you have committed in this bed," Lady continued. "I am going to sleep on the couch."

"I have committed far more grotesque atrocities in there than in here." Francis grabbed the edge of the bed cover, pulling it back. "I'm sure he has at least washed the sheets since then."

"I don't think he has washed his *hair* since you left. Let alone the sheets." Lady scoffed, grabbing hold of a pillow and tugging it towards him. Francis grabbed another pillow and pulled it off the bed, shaking his head.

"Please take the bed," Francis said. "I am not going to be able to sleep in here if I know that you are on the couch."

Lady didn't say anything. He didn't move.

Francis gave him a small smile and picked up a folded blanket from a chair behind him. He flung it over his shoulder and looked around to see if there was anything more he should take. "I will make you some coffee in a bit, all right?"

Lady did not say anything in return. He just nodded. Francis turned his eyes back onto his husband, but Lady was already turning around to disappear into the bathroom, sweeping his short red hair up from his neck into a mini ponytail. Presumably he was setting up to wash his face.

Francis held back a sigh. He didn't know how much harder he had to try to be good at this.

"**E**xiled?"

"It isn't exile," Francis said moodily, grasping the corners of his blanket and shaking it out over the couch. "We don't ever sleep together."

"Sounds rough. I didn't realize the mark of a happy marriage was being treated like you live in a prison camp." Archibald settled on the arm of the couch, crossing one leg over the other. His dress slacks pulled tightly over his knee, coming up a little too short over his bony ankle.

Francis snorted. "Hardly a prison camp. It isn't like he beats me."

"Much to your dismay?" Archibald smirked. He slid off his perch, landing on the couch and sprawling out on top of the blanket. He put his arms behind his head and stretched.

He had already pulled his dress shirt out from the waistband of his pants and unfastened the top three buttons. The slackened collar parted for a deep-set collarbone, the opening diving low enough to start in on curly black hair that spread across his broad chest. His dress slacks sagged around his hips, threatening to slip off with the next movement.

Thinking back on it, Francis could not recall a time when his ex-boyfriend did *not* look like he was posing for the centerfold of a cheap skin mag.

"That isn't funny," Francis said sternly. He had to keep his mouth set in a firm line to stop a smile from betraying him. "Do you know how long it has been since I've been part of a scene?"

"I couldn't guess. Was there anyone between me and the mini tyrant?"

"No." Francis sighed, raking a hand through his hair and tugging on the corner of the blanket which he was still clutching irately. "Get up. I'm tired."

"There is plenty of room for two."

"No, there isn't."

"There is if you get on top."

"I'm going to kick you in the balls."

"I thought that was one of your hard limits?" Archibald sat up anyway, tousled brown hair hitting the bridge of his nose. He pushed it back, and rather than staying in place, it decided to stick straight up.

"My husband is going to eviscerate you. And me." Francis made a shooing motion. Archibald finally obliged by bumping his seat down to the floor.

"I don't see why he should be upset by us talking." Clearly, Archibald wasn't going to let it go. "Considering you don't even sleep in the same bed."

"I don't make the rules, Archie. I just follow them." Francis sat down on the couch. It sank a little bit lower than he remembered. He didn't even want to think about what parts of it might have broken, and how.

"Clearly. We had our differences in the end, but believe it or not, I'm having a great deal of difficulty seeing you so unhappy."

"I am not unhappy." Francis was quick to correct him, folding his pillow in half underneath his head and pulling his blanket up over his shoulder. "I'm stressed."

Archibald did not seem to have a response. He let the pause linger long enough that any response would have been awkward and jarring, and eventually Francis' reciprocated silence was enough for him to believe that the demon had fallen asleep.

CHAPTER XXVII

James obliged Blanche Morgan's request to escort her to bed for her midday nap as soon as she was finished with her tea.

He tucked her in and asked her if she required any medication to help her sleep. She told him no, because the shadows only came at night. She slept so much better during the day.

James left her alone in her room after that, shutting the door softly behind him and turning the handle each way before releasing it completely. He wanted to make certain he could get back in, if he needed to.

He turned his back towards the door and rested his shoulders against it. James took off his glasses and slid his hand over his face, leaning his head back and taking a moment to stare up at the roof. Vaguely, he wondered where Virgil had gone. He was not too worried.

There were lights suspended from the roof. Too many lights, even for James. He did not remember seeing them on his way up, but then, he had been fairly focused on making certain Blanche did not topple down the stairs. That woman was so frail. Elliot had been all shoulders and masculine bulk. James had grown accustomed to manhandling him when the need arose. With Blanche, he was almost afraid to touch her. He had kept his hand hovering just inches away from the small of her back their entire way to the bedroom.

James rubbed at the corners of his eyes before slipping his glasses back on and straightening up. He did not want to wander too far, in case he was needed, but he also could not stand there for the better part of an hour or longer. He did not even know why he was so intent on staying close to Lady Morgan.

She had just clearly never had a proper caretaker before. Maybe her husband had filled that role, once, but he had since abandoned his purpose.

He knew it was all a distraction. He knew he had to find a way to get to Henry. But it had been so long since he felt even this close to steady ground. Like he could pause and take a breath. Ground himself in a familiar duty. A familiar purpose.

If Henry had been there, he wouldn't have been surprised.

James started walking down the narrow hallway with no destination in mind. Every footstep seemed to echo off the empty, patterned walls. With every step he remembered the Clifton household. All the memories were coming back to him in pieces. He remembered odd details, like the tables with curiously colored lamps squeezed onto every inch of available surface. He remembered the dark wood floors reflecting splashes of light, and the intricate rug that seemed to run down the entire length of an endless hallway. Its plush fibers always absorbed every sound.

Sextus' house was disappearing around him. Things were becoming more and more familiar. The pattern on the walls darkened—that plum and silver combination that Violet regarded so fondly. The air smelled like tobacco smoke. James would have been coming up on the study where Henry liked to smoke a pipe and swallow a finger or two of whiskey with any guests he might be entertaining. James could hear a pipe tapping against the wide mouth of a vase. Ashes carelessly emptied into priceless Ming.

A door creaked on its hinges. James kept his eyes ahead, not breaking his stride. It was partially a trance. Partially stubbornness. If this was all a vision, he did not want to turn and see what was sidling up beside him.

The air was getting heavier, warmer and perfumed. Something else on top of that. Something sickly.

James forced a deep breath and choked on it. His eyes watered and he rested a hand on his chest. A hand fluttered out, reaching for him, and his instinct was to grab it. He stopped himself short, finally catching sight of what he had been avoiding this whole time.

Violet Clifton had been pale enough in life to pass as a corpse on her own. Death wanted to paint her every hue of sickly grey. Her mottled skin made her look like a speckled fish wrapped in desiccated velvet. There were holes in her skirt, moth-eaten, as if the dress had been left in an attic trunk. Her bodice was ripped open down the middle, displaying even more discolored skin and a sunken clavicle that would have had a bone-eating demon salivating.

Her eyes were two dark pits, and there was not much left of those full 'thorn pricked' lips that Henry often lauded. Her bottom jaw was hanging loose on its hinges, her desecrated tongue lolling behind black teeth. Still, the weak corners of her mouth were pulled up into a smile. James could not remember a moment when she had ever smiled at him in life.

It wasn't a spirit. She was just a fragment. Not even a real memory, and absolutely not a real woman.

James had to get out of that hallway. He kept walking and Violet's fragment continued to drift beside him, as indolent as ashes carried on a breeze. The hallway was getting darker, the lamps vanishing behind his head. Now the main source of light was becoming candles resting in tall brass sticks. The colors around him were changing, the scene becoming awash with timid greys and shimmering blue; like being underwater.

James went for the nearest door. It was already partially opened, and he had no idea where it led, but he was not going to linger in that hall for a minute longer than he had to. He did not even look behind him to see if Violet had disappeared. James grabbed the door handle and pushed his way in, shutting the door perhaps too firmly.

He instantly regretted not sticking his head in to investigate before making an entrance. He had hoped for a nondescript bedroom, something of Sextus' that would snap him back into his right mind. But it was just an extension of the delusion. A path he would have given anything not to travel down.

The bedroom was easy to recognize. He had spent far too many years in this place. The tall bedposts were splitting and rotted on the inside with bugs crawling through deep runs in the splintered wood. The ragged bedcovers had been pulled off the side of the bed and were crumpled on the ground in a moldy, foul-smelling heap. The sheets were stained with blood — or what looked like blood from where he was standing.

James felt deafened by the sudden fall of silence, having gone from a creaking door and the buzz of a thousand burning lamps to absolutely nothing. His ears were ringing. James lifted one hand to grind his fingers into the most offensive ear and try to alleviate the pressure.

He needed to keep moving. He knew that. James stepped further into the room, hoping it would trigger something — a shift, maybe. Or something that would jar him back into the present. His foot jammed against something metal.

James glanced down. A wheel. Metal spokes. The silence was so absolute that when it was broken, even by the soft *sscchh* of an air machine, the sound was like a pin dragging across his eardrum.

His hand came down only to be immediately seized by a set of icy fingers. At first, he could not even think. He jerked his hand violently in an attempt to pull it away. The icy grip kept its hold, squeezing his fingers until he started to feel the tips go numb. James still didn't pull his eyes away from the wheel, even though the chair and the steady puffs of the air machine gave away the hand gripping his immediately.

Maybe he had hated Henry's wife. But James had always hated Elliot more.

Only an illusion. He had to remind himself of that. A memory; not even a ghost. James tried to jerk his hand away again, but Elliot was not letting go. James finally lifted his eyes to look the dead lord in the face. He had forgotten so many of the details. Or maybe it was that death's sallow coloring highlighted every flaw so well. Such as the notch in Elliot's right brow where he had fallen out of bed and bounced his skull off the corner of a dress. The ripped bottom lip that was the direct result of a slipped razor. The slightly crooked nose that had been broken once before. The raw places beside his nail beds where he had picked away too much skin.

Elliot parted his cracked lips and a shallow breath rattled past his teeth. The tubes wrapping around his rotted face had long gone yellow.

There had been a time when that yearning, desperate look was rooted in a far more attractive face. James hadn't wanted to kiss him then. He couldn't imagine anyone wanting to kiss the boy *now*.

He tugged his hand away one last time and Elliot finally loosened his grip. The body went slack in the chair, arm falling lifelessly to the side, hand banging against the wheel spokes. James had to suppress a shiver of revulsion as he moved around the chair, not stopping until he was standing directly behind it. He wrapped his fingers around the handles, disgusted with how easily his fingers slid into the grooves; as if the device was made for him to push.

He leaned over until he could smell the decay in Elliot's dusty hair.

"Not even now," he whispered. "There was never hope for us." He shoved the chair away. Floorboards broke apart in its wake. The walls were already starting to sink – *melting*.

He just had to keep going. If he kept walking straight, maybe it would end. Maybe he would hit a wall and there would be something to snap him out of this.

"You should be kinder to your charges."

James' heart leapt into his throat. The walls were still sinking. The color was still running to the floor. Paper was peeling up. Mirrors were growing dark with tarnish.

Henry was lounging on the bed. Rumpled blue velvet pushed against the contours of his long, lean body. James had never seen him naked before. He had barely even dared to picture it. His light brown skin was impeccable. Smooth, with sparsely freckled shoulders and moles placed strategically against every kissable crease. There was blonde hair on his arm and around his one visible dark nipple. There was blonde hair between his legs also, spirals of gold that vanished into the dark crease where the blankets obscured everything else.

James was not even aware that he had been breathing until it stopped.

"Henry." It was so hard to say. And he knew it wasn't real. He knew not an inch of that sublime form was even close to being real. That did not stop him from moving closer, or from reaching out to touch.

"James." He remembered Henry's voice so well. Including that flippant tone, the way he always flicked his tongue playfully over James' name.

James could not swallow past the iron lump forming in his throat. "You are dead."

"Does it matter?" Henry lifted his hand and his fingers curled inward towards his palm, beckoning James closer. "What does a dream lack, besides consequence?"

Consequence. Was that what he was afraid of?

He remembered what it had felt like when Blanche touched him. When her gentle fingertips had landed on his horns—the revulsion that sank down into his marrow.

Hallucination or not…James was not certain he could live with that feeling if it came from Henry's hands.

"You do not have to do anything that you do not want to do." Henry rolled back a little further, baring the rest of his thigh. His cock was still soft but getting firmer by the moment. James could see the sensitive foreskin already pulling tighter across the thick shaft.

James licked his lips, wishing he could pull his gaze away. He hoped his face was impassive as he was trying to make it appear.

"I have never—" James did not even need to finish his sentence. Henry knew it. Even if he didn't know, he could have guessed.

"You think about it often, don't you? You wonder what it would have been like, if he had not ripped me apart." Dream Henry flashed a smile, wicked and insincere. "I would have given it to him, you know. If he had been interested in me. I would have let him fuck me."

James did not want to hear this. He did not want to think about Henry with Charlie.

"What sort of state am I in, that a vision of your taunts is my greatest comfort?" James muttered. He stepped closer to the bed, still. He was close enough now that he could have reached out and touched Henry's golden-brown shoulder.

"A desperate one." Henry's hand came up. His fingers brushed across James' knuckles. James held in a breath, waiting. His fingers twitched at the touch. It was not like Henry had never touched him before, but this was different.

He wanted for the disgust. He waited for his stomach to turn, for his heart to feel like it was being squeezed.

Instead, he felt warm. James turned his hand over and Henry's slid in to fit perfectly against his. Their fingers intertwined together, and Henry tugged him gently towards the bed.

The bed felt broken. The mattress sank down too far when James applied even the pressure of his knee. He almost fell into Henry's arms, nearly bumping his face against his bare chest. Henry laughed—a bright sound. He wrapped his arms around James and pulled him close for a kiss, pushing fingers through his tight back curls and gripping them tight at the base of his skull.

James' head was spinning. Henry's hot tongue played against his lips, prodding for entry, and James parted them only slightly. Henry's tongue found its way inside, gliding, filling James' mouth and prolonging the kiss. James moaned around the heated slip of silk, a soft sound thrumming in the depths of his throat. Henry finally pulled back, just a little, and kissed James' cheeks—his forehead—with gentle, damp kisses.

He suddenly felt a sharp pain between his legs. James did not even realize he was hard until he tried to shift, and the inseam of his trousers pulled the wrong way. He hissed and reached down to adjust. He had never felt himself hard before. It was a bizarre sensation. He was so sensitive that a brush from his own hand was electrifying. He was stiff and it was painful. James had no idea what to do about it, although he had read *plenty* on the subject in medical textbooks.

Henry's hand found him between his legs. Light brown fingers squeezed and sent another jolt of pain shooting up James' throbbing shaft. The pain sank into a sweeter ache. He gasped—he didn't mean to—and leaned into Henry's hand.

Henry brought his free hand up to rest against James' chest, pushing him back towards the bed and grinning – planting lush kisses against his cheek, his throat, and moving further down with each one. He unbuttoned James' shirt as he went, sliding his tongue down the last couple of inches along the dip of James' sternum.

"Please." James' throat was tight. He did not even know what he wanted. He took his glasses off his face and set them down against a pillow. He stared up at the moth-eaten canopy over his head, trying hard to focus on the elaborate embellished plaster peeking through the tattered holes.

"Shh," Henry's hands brushed aside the panels of his vest and shirt, baring his chest. They slipped down to cup

James' ass, squeezing it firmly, and then cradling his hips. Henry pinched the fabric of James' trousers and tugged them down, exposing first his hips and then his toned thighs. He only had to undo one button to get them that far and stopped mid-way. The material was constricting, and James could hardly part his thighs the width of two spread fingers. There was something thrilling in the illusion of being bound. His heart was racing in a way that he was not even conscious of. It was just the way his mortal form was responding to the stimulation. His blood was roaring, and he could hear it racing in his ears.

James was embarrassed by how his cock sprang up the moment Henry freed it from his drawers. It was so heavy and needy, quivering and dripping beads of clear pre-cum that slipped down the head and vanished down the veiny length. The head was dark purple with blood. When Henry touched the very tip, James' cock jumped, excited. Henry placed his fingertips against the slit, gathering up some of that slick pre-cum and sliding it around the head of James' cock. James' breath quickened. The muscles in his thighs were tightening, but he could not do much. He felt frozen, save for his hands, which were gripping the covers underneath him. They were unpleasantly damp and rotted through. They felt thin enough that his fingers could tear them apart. But he did not care. He needed something to ground him.

Nothing felt real. Nothing *was* real. If this was the house, as Blanche had tried to warn him, then why…then why would it…?

Why would it choose *Henry?*

"Do you love me?" What an odd question. Henry would never ask it.

James did not know how to respond. He just took another deep breath. "Please," he said again. His voice was so soft, so weak, he could barely recognize it coming from his own mouth.

A smirk touched the corner of Henry's mouth and he lowered himself down. He touched the head of James' cock, giving it a kiss. James moaned, clamping a hand down over his mouth to stifle the sound. Henry smiled and kissed James' cock again, this time sliding his tongue over the rounded head, licking up all the pre-cum and prodding the slit. It yielded even more for him.

Henry opened his mouth and slid down further. His lips enveloped the head of James' cock and James had to stifle another whimper. He was shoving his own fingers into his mouth now, trying to quell every moan, every weak, simpering sound that Henry was pulling free from his throat. His nostrils flared with every hard, fast breath. Henry's mouth sank down onto his cock, taking in the entire thing. He could feel that heated tongue stroking the sides of his cock, the thick vein that throbbed on the underside. It moved all the way down until Henry's mouth closed around the base. He sucked, then, pulling back his head only a little.

This was what it had to feel like, to have your soul swallowed.

Stars were bursting across James' vision. The flaking pastel paint on the roof above his head was starting to flutter down. It was like snow swirling above his head. Everything smelled like plaster and rot. But Henry's mouth was all that mattered. When he finally released his suction, he dragged his lips all the way up the length of James' shaft, kissed the head, and then went back down. James gave up on trying to withhold his moans. He threw his hands above his head—grasping for anything—and found part of the canopy. He grasped it, not caring if he brought down the whole damn thing on top of their heads. His hips were rolling. He did not have control of their movements any longer. He thrust—afraid of hurting Henry, of pushing his cock too far down the other demon's throat. But Henry—

this version of him, at least—did not seem to have a gag reflex.

Henry moaned. The deep vibrations made James' cock ache all the way down to his balls. He could not hold himself back much longer. He was honestly surprised he had lasted this long. Henry's mouth was just so warm and so wet.

"Henry," he breathed shakily. "Henry, Henry, I think...I might..." He did not even know what was going to happen. He could feel the pressure building at the base of his cock. He did not know if the result would be desirable or repulsive, if Henry knew when to stop but *oh*, if he would not stop. James did not want him to stop, ever.

He wanted to push his palms against Henry's face and force him away. But he wanted it to keep going. He wanted Henry to push him over the brink until he shattered.

It was so tight in his abdomen. His very core was as taut as a wire. His thighs quivered again, hips jerking, and James felt himself very close to tears. The hot pricking at the corners of his eyes annoyed him to no end. It would be stupid to cry.

Henry's tongue slid up the side of his throbbing cock one last time and James could not hold back any longer. He cried out and released at the same time. Henry sucked down every last bit of his will, licking it off the top and finally pulling off James' cock entirely with a wet pop.

James sat up. Tears were slipping down his cheeks, traitorous and hot after his body had been ruined by what was arguably the most beautiful thing to ever begin as a quiver in his stomach and shake him down to the foundations. Something indescribable, divine, a gift. He should have been grateful. He *was* grateful. Maybe that was why he was crying.

He reached out for Henry's hand. He wanted to capture him, pull him close. Have those arms wrapped around his chest until the illusion faded away. He needed to feel steady. He needed his breath to stop shaking. He needed something to alleviate the way his chest felt constricted, and his throat felt like he could not swallow.

Instead of flesh, he grasped a handful of velvet bedcovers. They had gone from murky to royal blue and were only slightly rumpled from what he could assume had been his own fits.

The illusion was gone. James gripped the bedcovers tight and looked around. The room was filled with what little light was allowed to stream between the modest split between thick curtain panels. The walls were elegantly papered and the paint on the ceiling was not flaking.

One of Lord Sextus' guest rooms, after all.

Who knew how long he had been here, how long had Blanche Morgan been awake? He would have to go find her. At the very least, that was all his spinning brain could even think to do.

James stood. His knees were trembling. The slightest amount of pressure would no doubt cause them to buckle.

He held on to one of the bed's thick posts as he tried to compose himself.

The button of his trousers was still very much undone.

It had all been so horribly vivid. Yet the meaning of it was still lost to him. Was it all a manifestation of his own guilt? Was he motivated, terribly, selfishly — by the hope of a reunion that would lead to something carnal? Or was his spirit simply longing in a way that his flesh could not measure? Was physical pleasure the only expression of affection and *need* so deep and inviting that it consumed every part of his consciousness?

He had never understood the things he saw in Henry. He envied the fine characteristics, but he had always dismissed them as feckless, faulty — everything down to those flirtatious little glimpses and the cheeky little flicks of his tongue. Henry did not fit the mold of Hell. He was too good for it. And he carried James along with him, dragging him down the maddening path that granted them both absolute freedom. Freedom of choice, freedom of affection — liberations that were unknown to most demons.

He owed Henry everything. He knew that, now. And his gratitude was fighting to spill out from every pore. Gratitude, yes, and maybe something else. Something he could not name, something he desperately wanted to understand. But it was only in finding, and freeing, Henry that he would ever be able to gain answers.

After all, he could not help but think — Henry would do the same for him.

CHAPTER XXVIII

"It is the best we could do."

"It is seamless." Henry held up one of his hands, admiring the way the light reflected off his light brown skin. He liked the way his nails gleamed like glass, how colorless and human they managed to be. "I do not think I could have asked for better."

"It is as close to your original flesh form as we could get. There are a few marked differences." Clinton folded his arms, stuffing a crinkled file underneath one armpit.

"Well, I have not noticed any so far." Henry said. "Unless that is a hint I should check below."

Clinton snorted. "Are you pleased?"

"Yes." Henry wished he had a mirror. Clinton was making him paranoid.

The lawyer shook his head. "You know flesh makes it easier to bind you here, right? You're only making everyone's jobs easier."

"I don't care." He didn't. He was stuck here anyway. "You don't know how much I missed this."

"Mm. You will still have to wear clothes for the trial."

"I think it will go a lot better if I don't." Henry winked. His flesh form made him giddy. Even in the bowels of Hell there were a hundred more sensations than his demon form could even comprehend.

Clinton pulled the file back out from under his arm. "If you are happy with it, maybe we can move on? We have a lot to go through, here."

"Ah, of course." Henry sighed and turned back towards the desk, staring forlornly at the worn-down chair. "You know, for working pro bono, you're a lot...more than I expected."

Clinton sucked on his teeth. "You can tip me generously when we've won our case."

"Isn't *tipping* a lawyer just a form of bribery?"

"That all depends on how you look at it."

"What is the fare, then? You are not out hunting for souls, so it has to be something else. Brains? Hearts?"

"Livers. Can we move on?"

"Brined, or un-brined?" Henry flashed a grin.

"Focus." Clinton dropped the file onto his desk. It smacked heavily against the wood.

"I am focused on how to pay you back for your generosity." Henry ran a tongue over his lips.

Damn. He had missed that feeling.

"I want you to—*look at me*—I want you to focus on keeping your head low. And I know it's hard with those big damn horns of yours, even with a flesh form to mask them." Clinton set his teeth. "But trust me, you don't want to shake anything up that might turn the tides against you at this stage. We are on thin, thin ice…"

"Do you think they will execute me?" Henry sounded bored.

Clinton bristled. "They will do far, far worse. And you will wish your bones weren't welded to that skin suit."

"You suck all of the fun out of everything." Henry pitched a crumpled piece of paper at him. "Has anyone ever told you that?"

The pastry folded in half with barely a touch, the jelly center buckling as soon as Gluttony used her fingers to lift the browned edges. She pushed the entire thing into her mouth at once—an impressive feat to most. But Famine had seen her take more.

"You are upset." It wasn't a question so much as an observation as he sipped his ginger and lemon tea.

"I don't know what you mean." She sounded more than a little sarcastic as she grabbed another pastry. This one had an even softer center. Gluttony adored cream cheese. She folded it in half and then in half again, then she opened her mouth even wider than before to make sure she took it all in one bite. The corners of her mouth were like rubber. They did not even squeak with the strain.

"Just a hunch." He made a face at her grotesque display. "If you eat them slower, you will not eat as many."

"I will eat as many as I like."

"We will find him."

That gave her pause. She had moved on to tea cakes. It was so soft in its nature that it was crumbling in her fingertips. Gluttony looked at her husband, bottom lip quivering, her eyes wide and sad.

"You don't believe that," she said.

He didn't. "If he doesn't want to be found, he likely won't be."

"The hunters have proven useless." She sniffed.

"You could make an appeal to Hell," he suggested.

Gluttony shook her head. "Hell wants him dead."

"Hell wants him to stop being a problem."

"Like I said." The tea cake vanished into her mouth.

"If we have to kill him ourselves to spare him what is worse, we will," Famine vowed.

That much he could promise her, at least.

"I have never loved a child as I have loved him. And I will never love another." She sighed, eyeing another tea cake. "You do not understand because you are not maternal."

"Mm." As if gender meant anything.

"He is voracious and terrible. He is only doing as his nature demands. He is what I groomed him to be…" She started gnawing at her bottom lip. Famine leaned over and swatted at her hand to get her to stop. If she started going down that path, she would chew right through. Auto-cannibalism was her default, and he would rather not encourage it.

"You are stressing yourself out." He took another sip of his tea, sitting back once he was satisfied she had not tasted blood. He prodded at the plate of teacakes with his fingertips and bumped it her way. She snatched up another and glanced at him suspiciously, narrowing her eyes before taking a bite out of the corner. The whole thing nearly fell apart.

"Cambion are useless." She repeated herself banefully, crumbs flying off her lips and landing on the tablecloth.

"I know." He sounded just as disgruntled as she. "We will be rid of them, soon."

"Never soon enough." She dropped the rest of the tea cake into her mouth and finally went for the half-filled wine glass she kept at her ready. She drained it down to the dregs and clutched it in one hand while sucking icing off the fingers of her other.

Famine nodded. Something was not settling well with him, all of a sudden. It was a feeling that started as a prick at the back of his neck and traveled all the way down to his stomach. Of his entire body, his stomach was the least sensitive. *Gut feelings* did not really apply to him. So if something stopped to percolate there, he was not inclined to ignore it.

Yet, he did not feel like moving and leaving his wife to her own devices. There was only a single tier of desserts left and he did not want her to start chewing on her hands.

He brushed the feeling off, dismissing it as an effect of the ginger and lemon tea. Bullshit, and he knew it.

If the Cambion were up to anything, he would discover it soon enough regardless.

It had been a long time, but Drucilla had done this before. Or, at the very least, something like it. Wrestling any given soul from the hands of a starving demon was no small feat. Demons fought dirty. It was the reason she had chosen so many broader, heavier forms in flesh. Because if nothing else, she was not above a body-slam.

Sins were different. *Horsemen* were different. To compare a demon to a Horseman was to liken a cocker spaniel to a rottweiler.

The other difference here was that her marks were still alive (or would be, until Michael got his hands on them).

Oh, no. She could not think about it in those terms. *Lambs to the slaughter* was an idea that left a lump in her throat. And she had no reason to believe that at all. For all she knew, Michael just wanted to tame them, utilize them. He never said anything about wrenching off their heads and shoving them down the throat of a Bosch-worthy giant.

Although that *was* something that she could see him doing. In her defense, it was.

She knew that Famine and Gluttony were nearby. She could smell them in the air. Horsemen did not have much of a scent, or any real kind of trace. But Sins always reeked. Less like Sulphur and more like rotten peaches.

And they could cover the distance in less than a minute. Drucilla had to perform the entire operation as if she was working within a timeframe of less than that.

Drucilla started to move towards the door, then thought better of it. She glanced up, scaling the building with her eyes. It was not very tall. Buildings of this era never were.

Wings. Angel of the lord. Impressive display. No room for arguments.

Drucilla closed her maroon eyes and tugged on her lavender-colored blazer. She slipped it off her shoulders and threw it into the crook of her elbow. Her wings could materialize through anything. But she was not a fan of how the material was pulling on her shoulders.

Her wings, heavy and dappled grey, had a six-foot span and liked to take up every inch of that space if they had not been out in a while. It felt good to stretch them, to shake out the feathers a little bit. They desperately needed to be brushed. She would figure that out later.

She fell into a crouch. Palm flat against the ground, feeling the hum of the earth through the cobblestones, knees bent. And then one powerful jump.

Claire had just moved away from the window when it shattered. She reeled back even further, throwing aside the pair of boots she had been clutching in her hand and diving for her gun. Edward was already on his feet, his own weapon in hand. He had only managed to get one arm through his shirt before the intrusion, and it hung off his shoulder like a white flag.

An angel. God dammit. God fucking dammit.

Almighty be damned.

"What do you want?" Claire shouted, gripping her gun with trained expertise. She was absolutely ready to fire, even if there was nothing in that gun that would take down a divine. Demons, maybe. Not a fucking angel.

"There is no time." The angel was entirely white. White hair, white skin. The only spot of color on its entire being was a set of maroon-colored eyes that shimmered like fresh cuts of belly meat. "Come with me. This is your only chance."

"Did Michael send you?" Claire's hands were shaking. She gripped her gun tighter to try and mask it.

"I am here to save you." The angel looked from Claire to Edward, appearing slightly exasperated that one did not have shoes and the other was only half-dressed. "Grab what clothing you need and come with me."

"*Why* are you here?" Claire spat, grinding her heel into the floorboard to plant herself stubbornly until she had an answer.

"Consider it a mercy for your souls."

"Why are we better off with you than with them?" Edward found his voice at last.

The angel was losing a bit of steam. "I think that should be obvious."

Claire was getting bolder. "You did not have to break the window."

The angel set its teeth. It leaned forward, dark eyes smoldering with what could only be described as divine pique.

"I will tell you once more: I am here to save you. And we have no time. Grab what you can or what you will. And then take my hands." The angel extended its white hands and held them both up for offer. "To trust is holy."

Claire still hesitated. "We are not holy creatures."

"But the holy will have you, or the wicked will tear you apart." The angel's voice was weighted with certainty. "What you choose to do with your lives, Cambion, comes down to this moment. They won't last much longer, once I leave this building."

Brother and sister exchanged looks. Edward did not say anything to Claire. He just slipped his other arm through the flapping hole in his shirt.

Claire grabbed her shoes and slipped them on. She would lace them up later.

For some reason, she could not shake the feeling that this creature looked *familiar*. But then, maybe all angels looked the same to a degree.

"Where are we going?" Claire asked. She grabbed her gun, her holster, her extra bullets.

No more time. They had to go. "Come and see."

CHAPTER XXIX

Francis' neck hurt when he woke up. The couch was not nearly as comfortable as he remembered it. And he had not been expecting very much to begin with.

"Good morning." Archibald glanced him over. "Stiff?"

Francis coughed. "You need a new couch."

Archibald shrugged. "That one has memories." He was sitting cross-legged on the floor, feet bare and a mug of steaming coffee tucked between his thighs. He lifted the mug and shifted his legs to stand up. "Are you hungry? I can find something for you. Or I can just make you some coffee."

Francis shook his head. He wasn't much of anything at the moment. "I'll be okay. Thank you. Is Lady awake…?"

"Oh, yes." Archibald settled back down and sipped his coffee before continuing. "He came out an hour ago, took one look at you, and walked back into his room. He slammed that door shut so hard I thought he was going to wake you up. I'm glad he didn't. You were out cold and needed the rest."

"Sure." Francis pinched the bridge of his nose, pushing his fingers into the corner of his eyes. He could already feel exhaustion settling back in. Maybe he could forgive the couch if it meant a little more sleep. "I should go talk to him."

"I wouldn't." Archibald warned. Francis was already standing.

"Best not to let it fester." He stepped over the low coffee table and glanced over at the spirit, making a somewhat disgruntled face. "Shouldn't you be going over case files, or doing anything that is even remotely helpful?"

"Breakfast is important." Archibald held up his coffee mug for illustration.

"That isn't breakfast." Francis shot back even as he grabbed the bedroom doorknob. "Consume something solid."

"You going to give me something solid?" Archibald called after him, but the bedroom door was shut in his face.

Francis realized, immediately, he should have knocked. Lady was in the process of dressing; pulling a starched white blouse up over his freckled shoulders and buttoning it up the ruffled front. Luckily, he was turned away so all Francis caught sight of was the slip of bare skin. That didn't stop his face from turning bright red. The most skin he had ever seen at once on his husband was Lady's face and ungloved hands.

He waited until Lady had grabbed his blazer, pulling it on as well and moving to fix his hair before reaching behind and rapping his knuckles against the door. Lady stiffened and turned around, eyeing Francis with suspicion but relative impassivity.

Francis cleared his throat before attempting to talk, although he felt like his voice still squeaked. "Did you sleep pretty well?"

"Surprisingly, I slept." Lady folded his arms across his chest. "He stayed in there with you all night. Did you know that?"

Francis shook his head. "I was out cold, after a while."

"Does he not have his own bed?"

"Probably. Or maybe he broke it. Spirits don't really sleep; they sort of just…sit."

"Mm."

"It was weird when we first started dating. I got used to it."

Lady uncrossed his arms and turned, moving to sit down on the side of the bed and pull on his shoes. Candy apple red boots with black toes and heels and a double string of buttons that stopped just above his ankle.

"I think that he is still in love with you." Lady's words were like sparks flying from his mouth.

Francis was entirely taken aback. "I don't think so."

"You wouldn't." Lady lowered one shod foot with decided force and then pulled up the other to slip on his second boot. "But then, you are not incredibly clever one hundred percent of the time."

Francis chewed on the inside of his cheek. "What makes you think he is still in love with me?"

"He sat in the same room as you all night, presumably watching you as you slept. He asked to take back the ring he gave you. Which is less for his own petty satisfaction and more of a clear device being used to drag you back into an emotional slog." He finally set down his second foot, standing again and brushing off his slacks. "And I do not appreciate it."

Francis nodded. "I understand your concerns. What are we supposed to do? He is going to represent us."

"I will represent myself if it keeps you from him," Lady said. "And do not mistake this for petty jealousy. I saw him without his shirt this morning, and I *know* you have made a clear upgrade."

Francis couldn't help but smile. "I am out of my league with you, sir."

"Clearly." Lady sniffed.

"I will talk to him." Francis took a few steps closer. He felt safe doing so because Lady was already pulling out his neat black gloves. "I don't think it is necessary to storm out of his practice yet. Better here than wherever Sloth may try to hold us. But I will let him know that he is acting…"

"Dastardly," Lady supplied.

"…Inappropriately," Francis finished with a broader smile.

"If you don't, I will. You know I will."

"I absolutely know that."

"My husband will not be harassed by some third-rate lawyer whose takes tender in the form of button jars."

"So a higher-rate lawyer can harass me all he likes?" Francis teased.

"Mm." Lady spared him a smile in return. A small one. "If it gets us decent representation."

Sheridan le Maurier had been an occultist before he became immortal. Now, he supposed he could still be considered an occultist. But the mystical beyond had lost a great deal of its mystery. These days he just considered himself a maker of immortals.

He had made three, excluding himself. He could have made more, but he was limited within this realm. He had underestimated the power that a demon could hold over such a stringently contained pocket universe. That had been his error and it had cost him.

It cost both of them. Caroline had not been able to take it. They had been happy together for years before it all got to be too much. Julian wanted her to be immortal, but he wanted her to be a woman before he allowed Sheridan to perform the ritual. They had no way of knowing that Sextus' hellscape would slow her aging to a halt.

A crone trapped in the body of a twelve-year-old girl. What was she supposed to do?

Too little, too late on both their parts. Julian blamed himself. Sheridan blamed him, too.

Caroline had found the secret before either of them. And, ironically, it was a path neither of them could follow.

They both had their ways of coping. Julian did it badly. He had his dolls, his music, her ghost. Oh, how he clung to that ragged spirit. How many times had he gripped Sheridan's arms and professed that he saw their dead daughter standing at the foot of his bed, crying until she gurgled and drowned on her own salty tears?

Sheridan, for his part, had his own collection. Angel wings were his passion, as much as moths or butterflies for any other enthusiast.

He had accumulated a few over the decades. They slipped through a hole every now and again. Small, frightened. Trapped like bugs underneath glass. He always found them batting their wings against the shimmering walls where the world behind them cast warped reflections. He had a few methods of getting them down. He found shooting them through the throat was effective, and that a crossbow was the preferred weapon of choice. He could pull them down that way on a line—struggling, thrashing. It was always more difficult than it was worth. Besides, he did not want to risk damaging their wings.

His more recent methods were more sophisticated. There were wires strung through the treetops made of purest gold and razor sharp. It would not harm the bone or feathers, but it would slice through ligaments like a blade through ham. They would descend in pieces, but he only needed the biggest piece.

Black wings. White wings. Speckled wings, in particular, were his favorite.

And if that heavy thrum in the air was at all telling, as it had been so reliably in the past…then he was about to add a new set to his display.

Michael told her that he could get her through. He also warned her to walk.

Drucilla put away her wings before even attempting to enter the bubble. She had come in blazing with them once before. She did not need Michael's warnings to remember the gold pins and blazing, tormenting pain.

Claire looked just like her mother. That was the first thing she realized when their feet were finally on solid ground. Edward looked like the lesser version of Henry. The smaller, unrefined likeness.

It really was not fair to uphold a human to the standards of a demon's crafted flesh. It was just an unfortunate hand that Edward had been dealt.

"What is this place?" Claire had not torn her hand away from the hilt of her pistol yet. It was holstered at her side and ready to be drawn at the slightest hint of treachery.

Drucilla looked from the gun to the woman standing in front of her. Claire cut an imposing profile with her cinched waist jacket and heeled boots. Her hair was pulled up in a way that very much suited the time she had been born into. Every pin was well in place, no doubt held by her iron will alone.

"A dimension held in place by a demon known as Kaveh." She was sure that was not his proper name, but she had not done extensive homework. "You will be safe here."

"We are not safe where any demon is concerned," Claire said, narrowing her eyes. "We hunt them down. Are you delivering us into the hands of hell-being with a grudge?" She was one beat away from whipping out her pistol and shooting this angel between the eyes. More for satisfaction than effect. She wished she had some gold bullets.

Drucilla pursed her lips. "Do I look as though I am interested in the affairs of demons?"

"We don't know anything about you," Edward said. "And have just as little reason to trust angels."

That did not make her feel better about delivering them to Michael. She decided to leave that part out.

As far as the terms of her assignment were concerned, her part of the arrangement had been fulfilled. The Cambion had been delivered safely. As far as she could tell, they had not been followed by Famine and Gluttony.

She could leave. She could absolutely abandon them at this moment and wash her hands of the entire situation.

Would she really be re-instated as pilot angel?

Drucilla looked at Claire again.

Almighty have mercy. She looked so much like Violet.

"You can trust me." She did not sound reassuring even to her own ears. "I pulled you free from the hands of a Sin and a Horseman. That was no small beer, I will have you know."

For maybe the first time, she saw Claire's shoulders relax. The hint of a smile crinkled the corners of the woman's eyes, but it did not even brush across her lips.

"We could have done it," Claire said, "eventually."

"Few brush with a Sin and live," Drucilla said. "Once they were done using you, they would have left your bodies floating in a river."

"Oh?" Claire shot back. "And what do you care?"

Drucilla was growing exasperated. Or flustered. She wasn't sure which.

"You don't have to trust me, then," she said. "But you do have to follow me if you want a place to stay."

"We can find our own inn." Claire's hand finally left her pistol, and she flexed her fingers.

ΉΉΉ

"Sure." Drucilla's eyes scanned the distance. She caught sight of elegant turrets and had to suppress a full-body shiver. "But I already know where we can stay."

XXX

The door frame was crooked. It slouched at such an angle that Virgil had to stoop more than usual to enter. His shoulders almost got wedged in the corners. He had no idea how the lord of this place stepped in and out on a usual basis.

As soon as they were through the door, the man passed Cassandra back to him.

Virgil bit the corner of his lip.

"I do not believe I introduced myself properly," he said. "My name is Virgil Abney…"

"Julian." No title. No surname. Nothing more than the absolute barest offering. The big man picked up some things as he went. Papers and ribbons and scraps of cloth that he dropped back on the floor only a few feet away. Virgil could relate to that method of 'tidying up'.

"This is where you work?" Virgil was just trying to keep the conversation flowing. This place made his skin crawl. As a heavenly being, he knew death when he smelled it. And it was *strong* within this room.

There was evidence of carnage everywhere. On a table large enough to support two bodies there were deep gouges in the wood, pieces of ripped nails wedged into the creases and dark bloodstains spotting the surface. He was able to take in all of that. But there was something about this place that was bothering him.

All of that death, all of that blood and not a trace of a soul anywhere? Not a flicker of light as angels saw them, or even a bead of jelly as demons did? Nothing to suggest that any living thing had ever existed or died within these walls. And that was rare. Usually, an unclaimed soul would be absorbed by its surroundings. The walls would hold it in, trapping it in the corners, eating away at its light until there was nothing left but a shade.

Any fitful poltergeist would eventually lose wind. It would eventually fade into nothing, only a fragment, then a flicker. One day the house would be quiet, the imprint of a tortured spirit left behind like a smoke stain on the wallpaper.

He should have been able to feel them. He should have been able to feel *something*. But Virgil could not catch sight or scent of anything.

What did that mean? Was he *feeding* these souls to that…demon?

It seemed unlikely. It seemed highly unlikely but, Virgil supposed, it was not improbable.

"You can set her on the table." Julian pinched at his nose a few times, inhaling deeply and trying to assess the tools at his disposal. He still had not turned around to face Virgil again.

He wasn't getting used to the smell. It was just settling in even heavier. Uncomfortably.

Virgil obeyed, walking up to the table and finding the cleanest spot he could, he set Cassandra down gently. He moved his hands out from underneath her with some reluctance, cradling her head until the very last moment.

"What is your medium, then?" he asked. "Porcelain, resin? Paste, paint? What beauties do you conjure behind closed doors?" A chill ran up his spine. He rubbed at his own forearms, trying to generate heat before realizing he could warm his own palms for the purpose.

Divine energy was so difficult to control. Virgil always feared that even poking the great golden beast would rouse it altogether and erupt it within his chest. He didn't feel like being torn apart at the joints by his own being.

However, he considered this an emergency. He allowed just a trickle of energy to flow through to his palms. The heels of his hands began to glow faintly, and he rubbed his arms again.

Much, much better. Divine power felt warm and tasted sweet on the back of his tongue when it came in small flows. He knew any more of it would be scalding, and the sweetness would make all his teeth ache.

"Caroline cannot feel it." Julian finally turned back around, setting a heavy box on the table that looked like it had not been opened in *well* over a decade. The thick layer of dust did not even stir when he brushed his hand across the top. The locks had rusted shut but were simultaneously so eaten through that all it took was one judicious pry from his big hands to spring open the lid. "Believe me when I say that I tried it all—wood, paste, porcelain, and cloth. I tried to fashion dolls of any material. Nothing would last. She could not grasp any of it in her hands and…" He closed his eyes, as if the memories caused him physical pain. "She screamed. She screamed, and she wanted to throw them in her frustration but she could not. She could not hold them. She could not play with them. So she just screamed. I did not sleep until…" He set his hand down on the table. "I discovered, finally, what she *could* hold."

Virgil already knew the answer, but he could not get past the lump in his throat to beg the question.

Julian's one golden eye glanced up, and Virgil followed his gaze.

His heart plummeted. If there was anything on his stomach, it would have been out of his mouth in a second. Virgil leaned, grasping the edge of the table, unable to tear his eyes away from what was bolted to the ceiling.

Bodies. Dozens. He could not count how many. Their strings were screwed into the rafters. The beams, reinforced by steel, were still beginning to buckle from the weight. Each joint was disconnected and then joined back together, swinging on a rudimentary hinge. He could not see high enough to get a good look at their faces, but they were all blonde. Endless rows of fake, springy blonde spirals that curled around their shoulders and framed their petite jaws.

Their clothes were made with care. Pink satin and stiff white lace. Costly material. Each skirt, bodice, and pair of hose were tailored to exact measure. Their feet were bare. The bottom of their hose stained black. It looked deliberate, and not as though they had simply been dragged across the dirty floor before being hoisted up.

His stomach turned again. He knew now why their souls were not staining the walls or crawling over the table.

Their souls were still bound inside of them. Sewn in. It was unlikely that they would ever be set free, not unless each one was cut down, ripped open, and it was forcibly torn from behind their heart.

"She can touch dead flesh." Julian shrugged. He did not know why. "That is why I made her so many dolls."

"You indulge her," Virgil said dryly. It was a stupid thing to say, but he could not think of anything better. "A child should not have so many…toys."

Fury made Julian's brow twitch, the raged expression dissipating almost as quickly as it appeared when he turned his focus back towards Cassandra. "She is an only child."

Well. That made sense.

Virgil tried to pull his focus back to Cassandra, as well. Her beautiful eyes soothed him a little. He reached out and stroked her black curls, a tender and skittish touch. "I do not want her made from flesh. She is perfect as she is."

"Of course, she is," Julian agreed. "Stay by her side while I work."

Virgil nodded. He had no intention of leaving his beloved in this cold necropolis alone.

"How did she die?" He knew he shouldn't ask. Something in his gut told him that. But he could not keep it off his tongue and it sprang free before he could choke it back down.

Julian inhaled again. Watching that big chest expand and then decompress was hypnotizing.

The silence that fell between them was deafening. Virgil's ears began to ring, and for what felt like hours, he could not even hear the rattle of tools.

"It was by her own choice," Julian finally said. "Caroline is headstrong."

The angel licked his lips. "Her own choice?"

The look in Julian's hawkish gold eye was damning. "You must have noticed something about this place."

"Yes. I hate it."

"You cannot leave it." The lord set his teeth. "Unless the demon lets you loose or you find another rip in the walls. I begged Sheridan to help me keep searching for a way, but he did not want to leave. He did not know everything, I don't think…"

"We stopped looking, eventually." Julian's gaze fell back to Cassandra. "When we came here, he had already discovered life everlasting. I don't know what he thought he was going to do with it. We both drank from it. He told me…" Julian snorted. "Well. Nevermind what he told me."

The hairs on the back of Virgil's neck were standing up. Life everlasting. He knew Julian was immortal, but he had not dared to guess *how.*

'We both drank from it.' Had Julian tasted angel blood?

Virgil was absolutely going to be sick.

"He wanted to make Caroline immortal too," Julian said. "But we decided to wait until she was…older. No longer in the body of a child. Well. Her mind aged. Her body stayed…the same." It was clearly becoming more difficult for him to continue. "She was still a child after her mind had already advanced in years. She eventually became too…" He sought for the right word and gave up. "Tired. She wanted to be a child again. She hugged me that morning and told me she loved me more than anything." Tears were stinging his eyes. He turned his head to the side to shove his face into his shoulder and keep the drops from hitting poor Cassandra's mending body. "She went to play. She was out on the jetty and she—fell." He gripped the edges of the table, abandoning his work to try and steady himself. "She *jumped*." He ground his teeth so hard that the calcium squealed. Blood started to fill his mouth and trickled down the corner of his bruised lip. "She drowned. It was the only way. We are immortal. We cannot follow her. But she *left*."

"Except she didn't leave," Virgil prompted gently. He wanted to leave. He was going to bolt as soon as he saw an open opportunity, but he could not leave Cassandra here. He would grab her from this insane man's hands if he had to. "She is still here. Her soul is trapped in the bubble, still."

"There truly is no way out!" Julian's grin looked more like a grimace. He kept grinding his teeth, shifting his jaw from side to side. He was gripping the table so hard that the skin drawn tight over his knuckles looked to be on the verge of splitting. "The demon could release her. Or devour her. Anything. End her misery. But he won't. He won't, he won't, he *won't*…and I don't want him to. By the Everfather I *don't want him to.*"

"What do you have left, with Caroline gone?" Virgil's fingers crawled across the table, and he took hold of Cassandra's hand. He started pulling her closer to him, carefully, keeping an eye on the man across from him. One blow from Julian could upend all of his work. The table was steady. Big. But the work, the precious work was so delicate…

"Only as much as you, without *her.*" Julian snapped, blood and spittle flying from his lips as he shot an accusing glare at the angel. "Get her out. *Get out.* Leave me. Leave us…" he finally pried his hands free from the table edge. They were trembling visibly.

Virgil did not need to be told twice. He grabbed Cassandra and pulled her close to his chest. She was still a little loose in some places, but the work Julian had performed on her broken limbs was superior. Even without being entirely whole, he did not fear that pieces of her would drop as he ran…

Virgil hunched his shoulders and ducked his head to bolt through the door. He turned immediately once he stepped outside of it, racing for the stairs, not caring if he had to leap over chasms to get back downstairs.

Once he was free of the room, Julian screamed. It was an unearthly, feral sound. Like a dog being tortured. Like someone was pounding an iron stake through his heart.

Virgil picked up the pace. He could let out his wings, but that would only hinder him in this confined space. Besides, it had been so long…

He had to find James. He *absolutely* had to find James.

There was only one thing they were going to be able to do to escape this.

CHAPTER XXXI

Emilie knew the angel for what it was. But she could smell Sulphur on the other two. That confused her because it was not a very strong smell. They were not new demons by any stretch. In fact, the longer she looked, the less she was convinced that they were demonic at all.

Emilie finished locking her door behind her and started moving towards the group that was walking boldly down the streets, headed right into the city. This side of town, they fit right in. Slightly dazed. A little rag-tag. Shoes probably not on the right feet and a small arsenal dangling from belts and in under-arm holsters. The angel was unarmed, as far as Emilie could tell.

If Sextus saw them here, he was going to pitch a royal fit. It was going to be big enough to shake the handful of heavens he had trapped in here along with everything else.

Emilie sidled up to them, adjusting her strides to match their own so she did not outpace them nor fall behind. The boy saw her first. His hands went to the holsters underneath his arms and gripped the chipped pearl handles of two very respectable guns. Emilie held her hands up to show that she was unarmed, giving them an easy smile as she continued her approach.

The boy nudged the girl in front of him with his elbow, but she did not even need the signal. She was already turning, pistol in hand, and the angel had an arm out as if that could stop either of them.

"Don't shoot," Emilie said, raising her voice to make sure she could be heard over the short distance. "You don't look like you are in any position to turn down friends."

"We don't have friends," the girl said.

"That's true. We don't even like each other," the boy retorted. That got him an elbow in the ribs.

"I am a mortician." She held up her case as proof. "I live just down that way. I could not help my curiosity…"

"Move along, then," the girl said flatly. "We are not interested in satiating your curiosity."

Emilie had to bite back a sharper retort. "How long have you been in this realm?"

"Three minutes," the boy answered, shooting a glance at the angel as if to confirm. "Give or take."

"You must know, then, the lord of all of this is very temperamental," Emilie said dryly. "He does not take kindly to strangers, and he will be *especially* displeased to learn there is another tear."

The angel narrowed her eyes. "How much do you know of the lord of this realm?" she asked.

"Enough." Emilie's smile became caustic. "You could say we are on first name terms."

"So, lucky you found us before he did?" the girl asked sarcastically. She had not put her gun away and did not look as though she intended to do so. "I have heard that enough times to know how little it usually means."

"The last thing I want to do is turn you over to him," Emilie promised. "It would end as badly for you as it would for me." She looked them up and down again, trying to assess exactly what she could offer that might lure them away from Sextus' direction. "May we try this again? You look tired. And I have shelter."

The boy looked towards the girl, and she reluctantly turned to face the angel. The angel's blood-colored eyes had never once left Emilie.

"Stop and rest," Emilie continued to urge. "I can be more aid to you than he."

Which was true. Sextus was in a poor mood.

"I would fear more for you than us," the angel said. "And for no reason related to the demon."

Emilie lifted one eyebrow and shrugged. She did not know what that meant. She was certain it would be made clear. "I have business I can attend to, if you are discontent with my offer..."

"We will rest with you." The angel sounded weary. She still had one hand out in front of the two accompanying her, but it was wavering. She was clearly resting on the verge of exhaustion, herself. "Not for long. We cannot afford to linger. But if you have a place where we might collect ourselves…"

Emilie's smile reappeared. It looked more genuine, this time. "Come with me. Luckily, we did not leave it far behind."

When Virgil found James, he was seated in the solar room on a padded chaise lounge. A thin woman was stretched out on the rest of the chair next to him, her little feet tucked up and her head resting on his lap. He was not touching her, otherwise. One arm rested on the back of the chair and the other hand rested on the padded arm of the seat itself.

Virgil paused, trying to drink in this drastic shift in energy since his departure. It only took him a few moments to recalibrate, then he collected himself enough to approach the chaise lounge and kneel beside it, his fingers brushing over James'.

The demon startled. He turned his face towards Virgil, and the angel could see a set of milky lids peeling back away from those cold blue eyes.

Had James been *asleep?*

"We have to talk," Virgil whispered, trying to stay respectful. Even with the angel kneeling, they were still at eye-level.

"What about?" James asked, his voice also low.

"First of all." Virgil gestured towards the sleeping woman and raised his brows in question.

James glanced down at the woman and then shrugged. Clearly, no good explanation existed. "What else did you want to talk about?"

Virgil leaned in. "I met someone. And he is trapped here, like us. How much do you know about pocket dimensions?"

"Enough, now, that I know I never want to see one again."

"There is only one way out." Virgil paused, aware of the gravity of what he was about to say. "We have to release our flesh forms."

James regarded him in disbelief. "You mean we have to die."

"Yes."

"We have to kill ourselves, no less."

"Yes."

"That will send us straight to hell."

"I know."

"That is the exact *opposite* of how we wanted to get there."

"I know."

James shifted his weight. The woman in his lap muttered something and turned to face the back of the chair. James didn't seem to care.

"There has to be another way," the demon insisted.

"Not a one." The angel squashed that. "She would have surely found it. The only thing she could do was throw herself into an ocean and choke on the brine. Caroline was a smart girl. If there had been any other way…she would never have left her father like that."

"Caroline? No, don't tell me." James shook his head. "There is no guarantee our souls would leave, either."

"You are right. Except I used to be the Pilot Angel," Virgil said. "And I can squeeze our souls through *any* spot."

James drummed his fingers on the arm of the chair. "I hate this idea."

"I knew you would," Virgil said.

"I don't think I trust you anymore."

"You have to," Virgil pressed, leaning in more insistently. "It is this or nothing. And while I am happy to stay here and waste away my days, I know you want to find Henry. You are not going to reach him any other way."

Henry. James thought about the vivid hallucination.

Henry's skin had felt so real.

"I will do whatever it takes to get him out of Hell," James finally said. "It just seems counter-intuitive to ruin my own chances of survival before I even get to him."

Virgil nodded. "If there was any other way."

James sucked in a deliberate breath, ruminating on it for a moment longer before nodding.

"Well. We don't have a choice, do we?" He shifted his weight again, sliding his hand underneath the woman's head and moving his leg out from underneath her. He lowered her head gently back down to the cushion and stood.

"You've got to be cramping," Virgil said.

"I am." James looked down at the woman one last time. "She needs someone to care for her."

"That person is not you," Virgil said, maybe too sharply. "She can summon her own demon."

"She has one." James glanced up, as if Sextus could hear them in the floors above. "He's just not very good at his job."

"Pity." Virgil grabbed James' hand. "Let's not waste time."

Claire was grateful that the woman—Emilie, she had said her name was—kept a dark house. At least for now. All of her lamps were doused, as if she kept them for company but never desired to light many of them herself.

Claire had not seen that many lamps in one place since her own childhood home.

Maybe Emilie was not lying about the nature of her relationship to the reigning demon.

Edward collapsed into a chair by the fireplace almost immediately upon arrival. He seemed dazzled, enchanted by this woman. To a degree, Claire could hardly blame him. Emilie was beautiful. Her energy was gentle, exuberant. She knelt down beside Edward's feet with a bowl of hot water and a cloth. She slipped off his shoes and his stockings, rolling up his breeches to the knee and then sliding her hand back down his calf. Claire would never have exposed herself like that for a stranger. But Edward had his own guns. He could take care of himself.

"How are you holding up?" Claire turned her attention towards the angel. "You never told me your name you know…"

"Hadn't I?" The angel leaned against a wall, grimacing as she did so. She seemed reluctant to sit down, but the obvious weight on her shoulders from her wings was causing her discomfort. "It is Drucilla."

"Mmm," Claire said, looking her up and down. "Your other name?"

Drucilla shifted. "'Izevel."

"I am Claire. You probably knew that."

"I did."

"Angels know everything, do they?"

"Not everything." Drucilla finally straightened up.

"You should sit." Claire gestured to one of the chairs arranged by the hearth. Drucilla shook her head.

"That will make it worse," she said. "But thank you," she tacked on.

"What is wrong?" Claire took a step closer. Drucilla could not help but flinch a little.

"My wings," Drucilla responded grouchily. "I unfurled them and now they're a wreck. I don't really know what to do. Well I *know* what to do."

"Which is…?"

"They need to be brushed." Drucilla grabbed hold of one shoulder both from discomfort and embarrassment.

"And you can't do it yourself?" Claire guessed.

"It is very difficult to do. They are always at their worst right at the joints." She rolled her shoulders again. Just speaking about it made the ache feel like an unbearable itch.

Claire hesitated. "I could do it for you," she offered. At that, Drucilla's hands came up, making her seem almost defensive.

"Oh, no." If she could have backed up further, she would. "I would not ask you. It is a tedious task. And you need to rest, yourself." Her flushed face was not convincing Claire that the monotony of the task was the reason she was protesting.

"I do not need to rest. I am well." Claire cocked her head. "And you can't walk around like that. If we need your wings again, it's going to hurt, isn't it?"

Drucilla nodded reluctantly. "It is a task," she said again. It was half a plea.

"I am up to it." Claire turned towards Emilie. "Excuse me…is there a brush I can borrow?"

"A soft one," Drucilla added.

"I have a set on my vanity in the room down the hall," Emilie said, not looking up from her work of massaging Edward's feet with the hot cloth. "Grab what you need. You can use that room, if you prefer privacy."

"Yes," Drucilla gasped. "Yes, please."

"Come on, then." Claire started walking down the hall. Emilie's door was closed but unlocked. Claire opened it up by pulling on the handle and ushering Drucilla in first. The angel immediately took her jacket off again, rolling her shoulders and hissing at the burning ache that tore across her muscles. She threw the lavender jacket down, not caring where it landed, and started to unbutton her blouse. Claire made her way to the vanity to investigate.

A neat set was arranged on the vanity's table. It was doubtless the most expensive thing this woman owned. The set was silver and the bristles on the brush were horsehair. The comb's teeth were ivory, and the mirror had been polished to a shine, resting face-down. Claire picked up the brush, it was heavy in her hands, and turned to face Drucilla.

Drucilla was naked from the waist-up and had allowed her wings to materialize, keeping them folded up behind her back as carefully as she could manage so as not to knock anything over. Claire nearly dropped the brush at the stunning sight.

She never thought the angel would be so *beautiful*. The wings were massive, a soft brown with dazzling white speckles like a wren. They were the only color against her pale, nearly transparent skin. Drucilla held her arms, and the motion across her chest only served to accentuate how heavy it was. Her full, sumptuous breasts were pushed up from the constriction. Claire got a glance at the rims of pale nipples, still so close to being white that the faint traces of pink were nearly indistinguishable.

Creamy flesh formed perfect rolls down her sides, creasing her back towards the dip of her spine. They slid down into the clear indent of a waist, then swelled into round, full hips. Further view was restricted by an unforgiving, sudden strip of black fabric.

Drucilla scowled when she noticed Claire was staring.

Claire tried to swing her focus back around to the task. She gestured towards the bed with the brush. "Will it help if you stretch out on your stomach?"

Drucilla nodded. "I think the floor will be more supportive."

"The floor works for me."

Drucilla got down on her knees and then lowered herself onto her hands. Claire knelt down beside her, leaning over and trying to assess how best to begin. With no clear instructions, and having never done this before, she decided she would start where she felt it was most logical and then work her way out from there. If Drucilla was uncomfortable, she trusted the angel would correct her.

She started at the base. The joint looked a little swollen and like it ached. Claire pushed her fingers into the muscle — they were so tense and tight. No wonder they hurt. She set the brush down beside her knee and started with the massage instead. She applied as much pressure as she could, making her fingers into small, tight circles as she worked her way around the joints.

"Does that help?" she asked.

"Yes..." The gesture elicited a small moan from Drucilla's throat. "You really do not have to..."

Claire ignored her half-hearted protests. She kept applying pressure into the ache, eventually working her way down towards Drucilla's lower back. She switched to using her knuckles at that point, pushing them in, working her entire hand into the tense area. Once she had finished, Drucilla's shoulders were a little more relaxed, and the joints around her wings looked less swollen than before.

Claire picked the brush back up and started with short, gentle strokes at the base. Drucilla moaned again, her toes and fingers curling when the horsehair brushed touched her feathery wings. Claire smiled, she couldn't help herself, and kept working. She continued following the grain down the length of Drucilla's wings, watching them spread out further the more the angel was able to relax. They were *just* going to manage avoiding the walls. How great they were in length and *size*…Claire's own arm was starting to ache the further down she worked. She graduated from short brushes to long, luxurious strokes. The angel pushed her face into her hands and purred, a contented throaty sound.

The second wing went much easier than the first. Claire had it down to a science by that point. She did not know how long she had been at it, she only knew that she was starting to enjoy every one of Drucilla's reactions. She wanted to see how many sounds she could possibly pull from the angel before she finished her task.

Drucilla finally pulled her head up, taking in a deep breath and moving her hand to swipe a few sticky thread-like strands of hair away from her brow. "Are you close?" She breathed.

"Almost." Claire just had a few more inches to go. "How are you feeling?"

"Much better." Drucilla groaned and closed her eyes, dropping her head back down to her arms. "That feels so good."

"I am glad to be of service." Claire finally smoothed out the last few feathers. Her hands were cramping, but it was well worth it. Drucilla's wings were gorgeous and glossy now that they had been set aright. And the angel herself was practically glowing.

Claire set the brush down and sat back on her heels. Drucilla started to sit up as well, pulling her wings up with ease and shaking them out a little before folding them back. They vanished from sight as they did so, although for a few seconds longer Claire could still hear the primary feathers dragging across the floor.

"Thank you," Drucilla said, turning her maroon eyes towards Claire and giving her a soft look. "It has been eons since anyone has…thank you. It means a lot to me."

"You are welcome." Claire tried to be dismissive, but her heart was fluttering behind her ribs. She felt it all the way down in her gut, but she could not even tell what *it* was supposed to be.

She did not want Drucilla to put her clothes back on, but she said nothing as the angel picked up her brassiere and started pulling the straps up her arms.

"I should probably check on my brother," Claire said hastily, her eyes still lingering on Drucilla's white stomach; how soft and round it was.

"Wait." Drucilla, still on her knees, reached out and took Claire's hand—dragging her thumb over the back of the woman's knuckles. "Is there anything I can do for you?"

Claire swallowed hard and shook her head. "I have to check on Edward." She said again, aware of the weakness in her own voice. She scrambled to her feet and kicked the brush towards the angel. "You can put that back." She said. With that, she turned and bolted from the room.

Waves crashed against the rocks, turning the darkest grey black. James could barely hear his own thoughts over the roaring of the water. There was no sand on the beach—only pebbles. They left marks on Virgil's bare toes and lodged into the heels of James' boots.

"There is no going back, after this," James said, as if he could still convince himself or the angel that there was somehow another way. The saltwater stung his nose and lungs. But he wanted to take the moment in and value it for what it was. His last few breaths on the mortal coil. Vivid in color and steeped in the smell of the briny sea and an oncoming storm.

Virgil took a deep breath. "I've never drowned before," the angel finally said. "Will it hurt?"

"Only if you allow yourself to feel the pain," James said dryly.

Virgil nodded. "I have a feeling that I will," he said. "And I will allow myself to feel every burning, struggling final breath. He held out his hand to James. "Now, or never."

The demon looked at the offered hand, but he did not accept it. He met Virgil's eyes once and then turned his face back towards the sea.

It wasn't even really *that* deep.

He was not usually one to linger on the sentiments on the mortal coil, so he was not certain why he had already spent so much time delaying the inevitable. The ocean spray had already ruined his clothes.

Like Virgil had said—now, or never.

James took one step towards the ocean and felt the water close around his ankles.

A few more steps and it would be over his head.

CHAPTER XXXII

The same thing waits for everyone at the end of the line. That knowledge had been ingrained into James since his creation.

Hell's gates stood tall and proud: a behemoth wrought in iron that stretched on forever, vanishing behind curtains of white mist on either side. The posts were thick and buried deep in the ground, spiked tips jutting up towards Heaven like raised spears. Above the gate there was ancient lettering carved out and filled with beaten gold. It gleamed orange in the dull light, a gradient of hellfire.

A massive desk was sitting out in front of gates, easily twice the size of the person seated behind it. It had a broad surface, tilted down like a preacher's podium, and there was a single book resting on top. It was a log, nothing more, but it looked far more impressive than that. It should have been a holy text. Or at least there should have been a nasty spell wedged into the middle of the spine. Instead, it was full of names (and possibly obscene sketches), if everything that James had heard about Baalberith turned out to be true.

Baalberith, who had unofficially been dubbed 'Hell's Secretary' by far too many, was the one seated behind the desk on a tall stool that left his legs dangling, feet swinging a good inch or two above the ground. His short, feather black hair was sticking up in places, oily from where he could not stop running his hands through. Of his bi-colored eyes, one brown and one blue, the blue one was starting to shrivel. It looked like a shrunken grape, rolling around in his socket with nausea-inducing ease. His other eye was in better condition, rotating in the opposite direction of its more embarrassing fraternal twin to glance at James and Virgil as they approached.

He was already reaching for his pen, although it seemed more like something to fidget with than for any purpose.

"A demon coming in the back way?" Baalberith tapped his pen impatiently against the edge of his desk. That was going to get on James' nerves. Fast. "Trying to sneak your angel in?"

James glanced at Virgil. "He isn't *mine.*"

"Likely." Baalberith sneered with thin, pale lips curling back over viciously crooked teeth. He was among the oldest documented Unchaste; angels with their names still floating around in Heaven's registration were easy targets on his shit list. "You know how it is. No angels."

He had been an archangel, or something similarly underwhelming. He was supposed to be good with people. *Right.*

"Well, he is supposed to have Fallen, or something like that. His paperwork got muddy." James shrugged, searching for pockets on the clothes Sextus had given him until he remembered that he was no longer wearing them. The water had freed him from his mortal form, throwing him back into demonic territory. His demon form did not wear any garments, and all he managed to do was nick himself on his own wicked talons. "I've got a warrant out for my apprehension, and I want to settle things on my own terms, so I came in the back way. I've got this thing clinging to me like a burr."

If Virgil was insulted, he never said so. He kept his eyes fixed steadily on Baalberith, staying as still as a waxwork figure. It was both preferable that he didn't speak and unsettling that he could stop like that on a dime.

Several long seconds were allowed to slink by as Baalberith chewed on the idea. James kept feeling his insides run cold as specters passed through him—blind to anything standing in their way, focused only on their wandering. He didn't take it personally.

"You have nice eyes," Baalberith said to Virgil. James could already see where this was going. He didn't like it.

"I might let you through," the Unchaste said, withering blue eyes staying dead center in its socket while the other, yellowing brown one wandered around of its own accord, "for one of them."

Virgil's jaw clenched. James was already shaking his head.

"Not even on the table," James hissed. "You are out of your mind — but nice try."

"Is that how it looks to you? Because it looks to me like you aren't getting through *this* way without my say-so." Baalberith was back to tapping his pen on the side of his desk. "Just one of them. Either one, really. I will let you choose." A smile oozed across his face. "I will even let you be the one to pluck it out."

Virgil's expression still hadn't budged. If this was all a charade, then James would find himself acquiring at least a small level of admiration for the fallen angel. Virgil finally moved, breaking the stillness as if he had been in a trance the entire time, and clutched his shoulder. He gripped his own flesh as if the feeling was all that was keeping him grounded.

"I don't think I can do it myself." His gentle words dropped an icy ball into the pit of James' stomach.

Baalberith grabbed the edge of his desk, pulling himself up and stretching himself across the surface. He slithered down the side, putting him just a few steps away from

Virgil. The former pilot angel was the taller by far. And here in Hell, there was nothing to keep his wings from flaunting their dusky heron-like beauty. He looked like he could engulf Hell's secretary without any trouble.

Next to him, Baalberith—with his docked wings and short stature—looked like a child.

Baalberith lifted one bony hand, finger curling curiously in the air as his serpent tongue flickered over his cracked bottom lip.

"A human could never force himself to endure that much pain," he said. "An angel, however—we do as we are told. If you are commanded, you will do it."

Virgil sucked in a breath. "It has to come from a higher being," he said. "And because I have not been processed as Unchaste, you rank lower than I. You do not have the strength to make that command."

Baalberith's lip curled back again, both his hands lashing out without a single warning. He grabbed Virgil's shirt, using the leverage to pull him down so that the angel was forced to bend over nearly double. Virgil's long, white hair was falling swiftly in thick sections from its ponytail. Baalberith continued dragging him down until their faces were nearly level.

Baalberith's wicked fingers latched onto Virgil's face, crawling over his socket like a spider before long nails pierced through the corners. Fleshy pink parts gave immediately underneath the pressure. Virgil screamed, reaching up to grab Baalberith's wrist, but he could not pull the Unchaste's hand away. Blood was starting to race down his cheek, but Baalberith's fingers were still taking too much space. The Unchaste took hold of the eye, hooking a finger around it and popping it out as easily as a grape. The pain dragged an agonized moan from Virgil's slender throat. His whole body was trembling so violently that James was afraid it would drop.

Baalberith pulled his hand away, releasing his hold on the angel at the same time. Everything about the scene felt surreal as it moved. At first, there was barely a trickle of blood—then it was gushing from the gaping black hole in Virgil's face, pouring down his cheek and neck, ruining the collar of his garment. He couldn't seem to stop shaking, but he managed to at least keep himself upright. Blood was streaming from between his fingers as he managed to keep his shaking hand clamped down over the empty socket.

Baalberith looked at James, his expression alone daring the demon to make a move. James reached out, touching Virgil on the shoulder, but that just ripped another scream clean from the angel's lips. Virgil turned away, trying to pull in a few deep, ragged breaths and calm himself down. There was no time to waste, and they had to keep pressing forward. For the same token…time was not real, although the angel looked like he was in agony.

"We don't usually bleed like that," Baalberith said. He opened his mouth, popping the eye onto his tongue and swirling it around his cheeks, sucking off the blood before spitting it back out. He turned the eye around in his fingers like a jewel, studying as if making certain that he was satisfied with his take. He must have determined that he was. He reached up to his own, withered eye and popped it out like it was nothing. Not even a hint of pain flickered across his face. The eye, like a sagging grape, dropped despondently to the ground and stayed there. It stared up at James with hollow apathy.

Baalberith touched the top part of his cheek, dragging it down until the skin had pulled back from the bottom of his eye socket. He slipped the new eye into place, blinking a few times and rubbing his eyelid to make sure everything was in place. The eye made a horrible squelching sound as it settled into its new home, rolling around freely in the socket before the iris finally looked forward. One stark, nearly colorless eyeball stared James down from its place next to a dark brown companion.

Baalberith seemed to notice that James was watching and tapped the corner of his brown eye intently. "Don't worry. This one is going too. Maybe next time, I'll take one of yours. Then it will be almost like a matching set. I haven't had one of those in a while."

"And maybe," James said smoothly, "I will see the marrow sucked from your bird bones first."

It wasn't entirely an empty threat. He had ways of making it happen. It was enough to deter Baalberith for the time being. He stepped back towards his desk, grabbing hold of the edge and pulling himself up onto his stool. James made sure he was sitting before turning back to Virgil.

The angel was standing straight, now. Blood soaked the entire front of his shirt and his collar was sticking to this throat. Blood webbed across his prominent Adam's apple. He had cleaned up as much as he could from his face, and the wound had finally managed to stop bleeding. It was already starting to heal, and even if the eye would not come back, at least he would not be walking around with an open wound the *entire* time.

The gate behind Baalberith was starting to open on its own. The hinges hissed, the bars grinding against one another as the rails slid back. Baalberith did not look up again. He just picked up his pen and started making some notes—or some doodles—in his book.

"You know, it is funny," he said, still not looking up. "I was told to *keep an eye out* for the likes of you two."

James' throat went dry. He did not like where this seemed to be going.

"They can read you like a book, ya'know? They know exactly what moves you are going to make and why. They just do not know the day, nor the hour. I guess that is where we all find ourselves coming up short."

"What are you talking about, Baalberith?" James snipped.

Baalberith finally looked up and grinned. "Come on, Mojgan. I know you aren't that young. Did you really think you could outsmart the Lord of Hell?"

As soon as he spoke, James' vision went black.

When James opened his eyes, the first thing he noticed was that he could not move his hands.

It was until the second attempt he made at lifting his arms that he realized his arms were strapped down to a chair. *Bolted down*, more realistically. The straps had been welded into the side of the chair that held him. He knew he would not rip his thick skin if he tried to pull free, but he also knew it would be pointless. These things were designed to be inescapable, even by a demon.

"Do you find yourself pondering over your wrongs?" a voice, unfamiliar to him, asked. James could not see where the voice was coming from, but he still shook his head.

"I have committed no wrongs," he said. Pain shot up his spine even as the words left his mouth. It was like someone had tried to run him through with a large bore needle. Yet to his knowledge, no one had touched him.

"Hell is not in the habit of punishing the Unworthy," the voice continued. "Reach inside of yourself, Mojgan, and think about why you are here."

Another jab. This one he felt deep in his stomach. James lurched forward, gasping. He almost threw up everything that was churning around his insides.

He ground his teeth. He could already taste blood.

"There was a contract violation." He spat. "Some — many eras back. Is that what you are referring to?"

'Contract violation' was a very mild way of phrasing it, he knew.

Another, harder, jab. He felt it in the back of his skull. Pain covered his brain and pressed against the walls of his head, making his ears pop. James screamed—the scene in front of him moving out of focus again.

"That is not the confession that you were brought here to make," the voice carried on. "You are not looking deep enough. Would a contract violation warrant all this? Come on, then. Out with it. Confess it all and you can have a fair trial. And it will all be over so quickly."

"You want me to give you something you can use in court?" James let out a disbelieving gasp. "I have nothing to tell you! You know everything. What could I have to tell you that you cannot scrape from the inside of my skull?"

He could hear footsteps. Whoever was doing this to him was closer than he realized. Their voice carried as if from several feet away, and they had chosen to mask themselves from him. But they were near. Too near for comfort.

"Perhaps you would like for me to be more direct," the voice said. "We know what you did to Jahangir."

James froze. "What do you mean?"

"We know that you tore his bones from his flesh and sent him straight to hell."

"What?" James' fury overtook his disbelief. He tugged on his bonds again wishing he could do anything at all to break them. "I am not—I never—it was Rahman-Reza! You *know* that…!" All of Hell knew. It had to. "I do not—bones are not my—Henry is—!"

"Henry is your *brother*," the voice growled. "You were born from the same sound. You were barely decades apart. How rare it is, for the same sound to produce twice. It must have been maddening. You could not stand him for jealousy of having been born first."

James' head was spinning. "That isn't true." His voice, even to him, sounded like a whisper. Jealousy—a cardinal sin—often rewarded, but only when executed properly. His thoughts were in even more turmoil than before, crashing against each other within the confines of his pounding head. "We were born from the same sound—and yet we are so entirely different. The things that I have felt towards Henry—" He could not bring himself to finish the sentence. *Felt.* Was he allowed to use such words, here?

"You cannot even properly deny it." The voice got so close to his ear. He could feel breathing on his cheek and skating down his neck. But he still could not *see* anything. "You pin it all on another demon. Why are we to believe you?"

"Because Rahman-Reza eats *bones,* and I do not!" James' fist clenched. "If we are from the same sound, as you claim, you must know that! And you must know that no demon deviates from what they eat."

"You could have dismantled him in such a way that another demon would be forced to take the blame." The voice scoffed. "It would not be the first time that I have seen such a thing done."

James was panicking. He could feel his chest getting tighter but there was no way to alleviate the pressure. "Is Henry here?" He knew he sounded desperate. "I want to see him."

"To what end?"

"He can identify me! He can attest to my innocence!" It all sounded so hollow. Innocence could not be found where Hell did not want to see it. James was doomed, and if he was going to be sent into oblivion, then he did not want his last memory of Henry to be how he was lying on the ground, a pile of meat floating on a deep pool of blood.

"If there is a shred of innocence about you, only a lawyer would be able to find it." A finger trailed down his cheek. James' forehead broke out into a sweat. "You have one, don't you?"

"No," James gasped. "I do not. And I will not speak further until I can speak to someone — *anyone* — outside of this room."

"Then you are going to be in here a long time." The voice said, still uncomfortably close. "And until you confess, I see no reason to even let you out of this chair."

"I have nothing to confess." James almost let out a whimper.

"We will find out, won't we?" The voice started to slip farther away as the pain appeared again, like needles being jammed underneath his nails. James lurched forward again, curling his fingers and biting back a scream—but that just made the pain even worse.

There was no more breath on his neck. Loneliness sank down into his bones with a magnitude he had never felt before. He was truly, terribly alone in this place. No one was coming to his aid. He was a fool to have ever thought that he could make it through, unscathed, sweep up Henry like some hero from a myth.

If anything, James deserved the pain he was in. He had spent far too long placing the blame for his feelings on other factors. He would not take the fall for a murder he did not commit. He would not let himself go down for Rahman-Reza's crime, but he could not avoid the responsibility any longer. Hell was holding him accountable, but he had not held *himself* accountable for anything. His list of sins was much wider and longer than Satan himself could ever record. And he could not help but think, in the depths of his despair, that if he had done more sooner — if he had taken more action, if he had sought to warn Henry rather than run away from all the things he felt — the jealousies, the anger, the resentment, and the uncertainty — then Rahman-Reza would have never gotten so close. They took down a Sin together, but it was the demon who had wriggled his way between them. Apart, they were weak. James had *allowed* them to become weak.

It was the first rule of the hunt. *Separation*. That is why demons never let their prey form attachments with one another. Humans had a funny way of clumping together. The bonds they formed made them stronger willed, which made their contracts fragile.

James took another ragged breath. The silence, the darkness, and the stillness were too much. A breath, however forced and unnecessary, was at least something he could *feel*. Something outside of the pain.

He had failed Henry too many times, but he would not sink into despair and fail him again. Even if it meant that James gave up everything. Even if it meant turning his mortal form over to the demon he loved.

Loved. He loved Henry. He adored him. It was a damning, filthy, human emotion that filled him with as much of a sense of overwhelming ruin as it did the relief of admitting the word to himself, even in private.

It would destroy them both, but not anymore than the denial had already driven them apart.

'Here, I reconcile with myself,' James could not quite bring himself to force the thought into voice, even though there was (assumedly) no one around to hear it. *'I love Henry Wickes. I love Jahangir, with every fiber of my being both spiritual and natural. And I will live to see him again.'*

CHAPTER XXXIII

Virgil opened his eyes; but it did not make a difference. There was a blindfold pulled across his eyes. His light eyelashes rustled against the rough fabric.

He swallowed. The motion itself was difficult because there was a band across his throat. It was thick — or so it felt. And it burned whenever he leaned too close and pressed his skin into the edge.

It was gold. It had to be.

Virgil settled back against the seat, trying to avoid touching the band as much as possible. The back of the chair was thin. He could feel it resting right along the line of his spine. The cuffs around his hand were gold, as well. His wrists already felt raw. Or maybe it was just that they ached so much he could not tell the difference. He could have sworn he was bleeding, but he tried not to think too hard on it.

Virgil wet his lips with the tip of his tongue and strained to hear something, anything, that might give him a clue as to what was about to happen.

So far, nothing.

He wanted to call out, but he was afraid of what would answer.

His wings were bound somehow behind the chair, doubtlessly with gold thread. He wondered if there was any part of him that he could move without risking burning through a limb.

Finally, Virgil could not take the silence anymore. "Hello?" he asked. But nothing responded. He didn't know if that was worse. The silence swallowed him, sitting heavy — oppressive. He wiggled his fingers and tried to test his cuffs again but the pain that shot up his arms reminded him that struggling was not worth it.

Of course, why would they bother torturing him? A frightened angel bound in gold would do all of the hard work for them.

There was nothing he could do but wait. And in a place where time did not exist, who knew how long they could let him do that?

Archibald threw his feet up on his desk. The rubber soles thudded had barely hit the surface before he answered his phone, swinging the cord up over his legs with some dramatic flair.

"Archibald Bray, top lawyer in — oh, yes. Ah. Of course. Yes. Yes, I understand, I…yes, Mx. Yes I do. I do." He kept going on, twirling the black cord around his fingertips and watching it curl. Francis watched every gesture nervously from the other side of the desk.

Finally, Archie hung up the phone. He looked over at Francis first, then Lady in turn, and shook his head. "That was direct from Sloth," he said. "Did you know Mojgan has been found?"

Francis felt his stomach turn to ice. "No. Is he being held, now?"

"He and some angel he apparently had in tow." Archibald reclined in his chair again for a moment, fidgeting with one diamond earring before sitting up, setting his feet down on the floor. "They're moving the trial up."

"What?" Lady stood at the same time, snatching Francis' sleeve in his gloved hand and hauling his husband up with him. "We have next to nothing prepared. And surely, they don't mean to do it all at once? The crimes are different. Allegedly."

"I don't know what their plan is. I just know I was told to get down there and bring you two with me." Archibald was already searching for his blazer. It took him nearly three minutes to realize he had left it slung over the back of his chair. "If we are late, they will come grab us. We don't want it to get to that point."

"No," Francis agreed. He turned towards Lady. Instinctively, he wanted to reach out and touch his shoulder. But he knew that reassuring gesture would be received about as well as a nail file through the eye. "Whatever the plan is, we have to trust it."

"This isn't Heaven, and I have faith in nothing," Lady said.

"Trust in the process, if nothing else. And Archibald. He is the best, remember?"

"The best in pulling a defense out of his ass, I should hope. Because that is what we are going to have to do." Lady was already walking towards the door, buttoning the two smart little buttons on his feminine blazer and messing with the ruffles on his shirt. "Have they assigned anyone to James?"

"I asked if they wanted me to recommend someone. But he has elected to represent himself. And the angel has no rights to an attorney." Archibald shrugged, flicking off the lights to his office as they left. "Who knows what will happen to him, honestly?"

"Is your problem with angels, then?" Lady snipped.

"I have no problem with the ones that pay me," Archie said.

"Do we know about Henry?" Francis changed the subject. "Will he be there?"

"We will find out, won't we?" Archibald ushered them inside the elevator and then punched the number for the lobby. "I really hope I'm not forgetting anything."

The problem with Hell was that it was different for everyone.

In Henry's case, he was alone.

Once they had opened the courtroom doors, not even Clinton was allowed to walk in with him. They let him in alone, and it was dark. A chill hit his skin — ice cold, and it bit him down to the bone. He had not really considered the consequences of walking into his trial while wearing mortal flesh. He was already shivering.

Henry walked until he hit a single spot of light on the floor, indicating, doubtlessly, where he was supposed to stand. He tried to cast a look around, but everything was pitch black. He could not make out a single face. Maybe it was all a farce. Maybe they would just strike him down here.

Maybe it would not be so bad if everything wasn't so damned *silent*.

The beam of light widened until it was more of a spotlight, and it was centered right on Henry. It was not any warmer. If anything, the white light made him feel more chilled.

A stream of smoke curled, reaching out towards the light from the surrounding darkness. A dark hand followed it, and then an entire arm. Henry looked down, the tips of Satan's shiny shoes making their way into focus. Within that moment, all of Satan's form materialized, the Lord of Hell standing barely inches away from him with a cigarette clenched between his fingers and grey smoke pouring from his lips.

Everything smelled like menthol.

Henry had only been in Satan's presence a handful of times. And during those instances he had been under great duress, so he did not really count them in his head. Now, every single one of them seemed to count as he could not imagine what he had missed before about his lord's *presence.* Satan was tall, of course, and broad-shouldered. But that was not the entire thing in a nutshell. Satan made the act of smoking a cigarette look imposing. It was something about his eyes, Henry determined. How deep and dark they were. How absolutely fathomless, like staring down the throat of a well.

"Do you know why you are here?" Satan's voice was oppressively dark.

Henry's knees were trembling. "I have been told enough times since my arrival."

"Your crimes are fairly egregious. Destroying a Sin in any capacity, even if only their flesh form, is considered nearly unforgivable."

"Yes, I…" Henry had to pause to clear his throat. "I have been made aware."

"Do you regret any of the actions that brought you here?" Another puff of grey smoke.

"Very nearly not a single one," Henry said. "The only thing I regret is allowing the person who sent me here to get too close."

And even that was not entirely true. He would have done it all again.

"Reportedly you mentioned that Greed 'had it coming'."

"Yes, well. I did not have a very good lawyer."

Satan smiled. Somehow, that made Henry's knees even weaker. He felt the tremble running throughout his entire body.

"You are a cocky young demon."

"You act surprised." Henry tried to avert his gaze. He couldn't bring himself to keep staring in those fathomless eyes. But something about the way Satan held it made it impossible to drop.

"I expected some level of acrimony from you. Yet I will admit…" Satan paused to take another drag from his cigarette, the tip glowing orange and belching more pungent smoke. "I would be kneeling, if I were you."

Henry dropped to his knees. A puppet with its strings cut. He was finally able to avert his eyes, lowering his head towards the floor. He covered his face with his hands, trying to rub the ache from his eyes with his fingers. "What will happen to me?" he finally mustered up the courage to ask.

"Nothing you were not prepared for," Satan said. "I am going to banish you. You knew that I would."

"I had an inkling." He had been more worried about being hurled into the belly of Hell. This, in retrospect, was a nice surprise. "Banish me where?"

There were a thousand options. Hell had multiple layers. Then there was purgatory to be considered. Henry dearly hoped that it would not be purgatory.

"Back to the mortal coil. Which I know sounds like I am giving you exactly what you want." Satan replied. "But you will be bonded with your mortal flesh. Do you know what that means?"

Henry shook his head. He could have guessed, but he would rather be told outright.

"It means that when you die again on the mortal coil, that will be it for you. Your spirit will be put into circulation just like any human soul. You will be eligible for reincarnation, and after you go through the cycle once, you might as well be mortal. Your soul will be as edible as any other."

Henry sucked in a breath through his teeth. "Until then…?"

"You maintain some of your nature."

"So, just be careful not to die."

"It isn't as easy as they make it look." There was something pointed in the words. "Is it?"

"No." Henry's head sank back towards his hand. He would have to become accustomed to a whole myriad of things, with mortal flesh. He would have to remember to breathe. Or would he do that regardless? A thousand questions were pecking at his brain, such that he nearly forgot where he was and the gravity of his situation.

Still, he dared to ask one more question. He looked up at his lord.

"What about James?" he asked.

Satan paused again; his feathers slightly ruffled by the question. "What do you care?"

"He has been my companion," Henry said softly.

"I must admit that I find it distasteful how close the two of you have become," Satan said in return.

For a being who had been cast from Heaven for loving, he was being surprisingly callous.

Or maybe that was just a rumor, after all. Henry supposed he would never find out.

"Is our bond so heinous?" Henry asked. "Or is it simply that you do not understand it?"

"Whether or not I choose to understand it, it hardly matters now," Satan said dismissively.

"Will he be banished as well?" Henry chose the established word 'banished' over something like 'set free', which was what nearly slipped out of his mouth.

Satan allowed for another effective pause before he answered Henry's question. "They pressed him for more. They could not get him to confess to anything. He would do nothing to break his unshakeable bond with you. He never crumpled or admitted to anything he did not commit. He could have spared himself a lot of pain, had he just told us that he was the one responsible for your death. He did not. He would have suffered for an eternity rather than have anyone believe he would ever hurt you."

Henry's heart skipped.

"And that is what I do not understand," Satan said. "How when you give him so little, he still holds so fast. In my opinion, as Jahangir or as Henry Wickes, you have never done anything to make James Highmore love you." He sighed. A big, heavy sound. "He will be banished to the mortal coil as well. We will send you together, but he is under no obligation to stay with you once you are past the gate. Expect him to leave you behind, Henry, once he realizes what he has sacrificed for you. That is what I would expect."

Henry heaved a sigh. "You expect a great deal from me."

"Actually, I expect nothing at all." Satan finally put out his cigarette, casting the entire room back into complete darkness. "Not anymore."

ady's version of Hell was very crowded. Much like the middle of a busy street where everyone was a pedestrian, and no one watched where the hell they were going.

He had stepped into the room with Francis and that bag-of-bile Archibald, but they had both vanished before he could even acknowledge either. Francis disappearing sent a wave of nausea rolling over him. Panic, or something like it.

"Francis' personal hell was easy." That familiar, corporate voice met him over the noise of the crowd. But Lady couldn't quite tell exactly where Satan was. "All I had to do was stick him in a room with you and bolt the door."

"I am certain you find yourself hilarious." Lady spun on his heel, trying to place the face of his superior in the crowd. "But you are probably closer to the truth than you realize."

"Do you know why I bothered to give you a fair trial, when my entire board was against the idea to begin with?"

"Not a clue." Tired of spinning, Lady planted his heel firmly against the ground and waited. "You wanted to play fair?"

"Something like that." Satan finally did materialize, grabbing hold of Lady's hand to keep from knocking him over. The Unchaste rocked back anyway, a shiver rocketing up his spine from the touch. He could feel Satan's skin, even through his gloves.

"Let go," Lady said. His voice came out faltering.

Satan did not. He brought his other hand up and pinched the tips of Lady's gloves, jiggling them a little bit until he pulled the entire thing off. The glove fell to the ground, and Satan wrapped his hand around the Unchaste's again.

Satan's skin was hot. Lady tried to recoil, but his grip was held fast.

"What do you want from me?" the Unchaste snipped. He was trying to maintain his fighting composure and kept failing. Satan made it hard. Skin contact made it even harder.

"I want you to ruminate upon your crimes," Satan said. "Turn them over in your brain. Do you regret any of them?"

"No," Lady said flatly. "I don't regret any part."

"Not one?"

"Maybe the part where I pulled Francis in it with me." He couldn't believe the words even as they came out. Lady clamped his mouth shut and turned his head away, pressing his lips together defiantly. "You can't get me to say more than that."

"It is all part of the process. You got a lawyer to defend you, but that turned out to be useless. So really, what was he for?"

"I beg your pardon?" Lady whipped his head back around.

"Archibald Bray," Satan said. "He played a role outside of your useless defense. He made you realize that there was something Francis was missing. And it gives you a nice excuse to feel hurt about it, doesn't it?"

"I would rather go back to talking about my crimes."

"I am going to send you to the mortal coil," Satan said. "I am going to bond your soul to your flesh—you know what that process is like, you have seen the paperwork. But the paperwork is nothing in comparison to what it is really like. The true agony of being made mortal. I could put Francis through it all with you, or I could pardon him altogether. He is only as guilty as you made him, after all. He is in the waiting room now, sitting next to that greasy spirit with all the chest hair and that weak mouth you hate him for. He could return to his duties, maybe even return to the one he used to love. Or he could suffer, and die, mortal with you. So I ask you, Meriweather Hayward. Do you have regrets for your crimes?"

Lady shut his eyes again. He wanted the words to stop. He did not want to think about Francis being sealed up like that, trapped inside of a mortal flesh where he could not tear himself free. "If I say I have regrets, what will that do?"

"Give Francis a choice," Satan said. "A choice he never had."

Lady's eyes snapped open. "So this was never about me."

"This part is. You are banished. That is your punishment. Now it is about him. You see? Not everything comes down to you."

Lady wanted to spit at the lord of hell through his teeth.

"Your repentance will assure him a choice. He can choose whether or not to ascend to the mortal coil with you. On the other hand, if you refuse to repent or express any chagrin, he will go with you. Your pride is the greatest cost. And your own selfish desires. Can you live on your own, without Francis Hislop attending to your every need?"

Lady was trembling, visibly now. He wanted to pull his hand from Satan's grip. He felt like he had been burned. But he could not struggle free, short of kicking his superior, which seemed more demeaning than effective.

What was it worth? Would Francis choose to stay? He was always a man who hated change. But if Lady were in his shoes…

A choice he never had. Fuck you!

Francis had always had a choice.

Hadn't he?

Lady went limp against Satan's grip.

"I will repent it all," he said, defeated. "I will express regret, if that is what you want. There is no reason for Frank to…" His throat threatened to close up over the words, "suffer any longer for what I have done."

Satan released his grip on the Unchaste's hand. Lady crumpled to the ground. Clutching his hand to his chest as if wounded, his free hand searched the ground for his glove. It was dirty, like it had been stepped on, and he plucked it up quickly, pulling it back down over his fingers.

"You realize that you may be alone." Satan tilted his head. "For the rest of eternity. It is a possibility."

"If he doesn't want me, then I don't need him." Lady did not want to look at Satan again. He did not want to risk being grabbed a second time. He did not want the gathering tears in his eyes to betray him.

Satan sighed heavily. "And still, you miss the point, Mx. Hayward. You miss the point entirely."

CHAPTER XXXIV

The radio blared all the way up until the car pulled into its designated parking space. For a moment, even Famine did not care that they were returning with their tails tucked between their legs. Gluttony swung her door open before he even had time to park and squealed happily.

"It's so good to see home again!" She declared.

"We have to give our report back to the board before we can get any further," Famine reminded her, reaching into the backseat to grab his leather portfolio before stepping out and swinging his own door shut.

"Yes, yes." Gluttony spun around on the ball of chubby foot. "But we are *home*, Famine. Can you not take a step back and be *glad* about something for once in your existence?"

Famine huffed.

Disgraced or not, he was glad to be back. He hated every era. He hated the mortal coil. He was glad to be back and would be happy to return his nose to the grindstone. The field was not his area of specialty, although it was more his than anyone else who sat at that table.

They were still no closer to finding Rahman-Reza, either. He knew that settled heavily on his wife. He was determined to sniff out their wayward child no matter what the cost, but maybe the cost was something that could actually be bought. Hellhounds, rather than some grubby Cambion.

They would discuss it all over a whiteboard. Satan was not going to be too terribly displeased. They were coming in during a good time. Famine had heard about the victory achieved over the collective demons and the stray Unchaste who had been causing so much trouble on the service.

He only wished he could have been part of *that* meeting. He was sure Death had a thing or two to say about the results. War would have worked himself up into a self-righteous fit.

Famine extended his hand, and Gluttony slipped hers right across his palm to grip his fingers. Hand-in-hand, they returned to the office building.

They had lost the Cambion — and to an angel, no less. But that was not the top concern at the moment.

They still had to find Charlie Banks.

Sheridan le Maurier was exactly what could be expected from an artificial immortal. Cold, condescending. Michael hated him and everything he represented.

What he hated more was having his orders disobeyed. *Consistently.*

"I wish I could help you." The immortal's eyes slid over him like he was a moth in a tent, being keenly observed for a proper chance to harvest his wings. He kept them tucked close to his sides. As snow and white as an egret. No words in any translation of the holy texts had been able to describe them with accuracy. "I have not seen the pilot angel since I drank her blood."

The urge to declare that Drucilla Kerslake was no longer the pilot angel was strong. But it was beside the point, and it was petty. Michael considered himself above pettiness in any form.

"I did not think she would stop to see you. But I also cannot think she would have anywhere else to go." Michael pinched the bridge of his nose. He could feel something like a sinus headache settling in nicely. "Kaveh would not take her in."

"No, Sextus has been in a foul mood. You can tell by the way the trees wither. They are so bright when he is well."

"And their leaves are brown when he's in distemper. Yes, that sounds like one right out of the book. Where the universe feeds off the one who holds the reins." He finally released his nose. He wanted to shake out his wings, but he felt like flashing them in front of the immortal was tempting, something he did not want to stir. "Any idea of who might take a wandering angel and two grimy street urchins in for even an hour?"

"I have not made a point of acquainting myself with the locals." Sheridan was reaching the end of his patience with the archangel as much as Michael was reaching his. "I am afraid I cannot be of much help to you at all. Yet think of it this way." The immortal spread his hands. "If they managed to slip through as you believe, then it is, as they say, like shooting fish in a barrel. You will stumble upon them eventually."

"Yes." Michael had no time for this. "Thank you for the insight."

He did not dare put his back to Sheridan as he made his exit. He had seen the wires in the treetops, and he would have to take it on foot from here.

He would find them *eventually*. They could not hide forever. Sheridan was right about that.

But Michael was growing tired of chasing them. And when he did find them, maybe he would shoot them down after all.

The mortal coil was heavier than James remembered it. Or maybe that was just the feeling of his mortal flesh, feeling pavement for the first time.

Not cobblestone, not earth. Real asphalt. His whole body ached like he had been hit over the head with a cinderblock.

The road was dark. A row of streetlamps lit the way, but barely. Little circles of yellow light that did nothing for the very center of the street. The houses behind them were sparse and pushed so far back that James knew he had gone unseen. It was a quaint little suburb, and each house was resting on top of a mound surrounded by a thick wall of neatly trimmed shrubs and azaleas. If anyone did happen to pull away their lacy curtains and glance down into the road, he would have looked entirely normal. At least, that was his hope.

He wasn't certain how accustomed these people were to strangers just showing up in the middle of the night.

A sound came from behind him. James turned, still on his knees, and his heart leapt into his throat.

His heart. He could feel it beating in his chest. He was painfully aware that it was happening, but he could also do nothing to stop it. His breathing — he *was* breathing — was pushing itself out through its nostrils in very deliberate huffs. Yet still, a subconscious act. He wasn't sure how he felt about that at all.

Henry was sprawled out on the pavement behind him, slowly coming around and trying to pull himself together. James crawled towards him, reaching out to grasp his hand and squeeze it in his own.

Flesh. Real flesh. He had felt Henry in his hands before, but it was somehow different this time.

"Are you all right?" Those were the first words out of his mouth. To him, they sounded stupid. The most basic question that one creature could ask another.

Henry nodded, a groan accompanying his words. "I am fine." he said, lifting his head a little and looking up at James. "I don't know why I feel like I have been gutted with a shovel."

James smiled, unable to stop a soft hiss that became a gentle laugh. The air was warm, and so was Henry's hand. Hot, soft flesh. Blood coursing beneath the surface. But he could *feel* it all and he knew that Henry wasn't doing it on purpose. It was no longer a façade; it was all genuine. Genuinely *human*.

But the demon was still there, as well. He knew as much just from looking into Henry's brilliant blue eyes and watching the clear eyelids slip up and down a little hazily.

"We are going to be fine," James said, resting his hand against his stomach in a sympathizing gesture. "I feel it too. But we are going to be fine."

Henry huffed, although he smiled at James and adjusted himself, trying to bunch up his shoulder muscles and push himself up off the pavement. James' hand against his chest kept him in place. Henry stayed pressed against it for only a moment before falling dramatically against the street in resignation and wiggling his fingers.

"You need to move your hand," Henry said, "if I am going to sit up."

"I know." James leaned over him, brushing away all the tangled blond hair that was getting in the way of Henry's handsome face. Even with such a small gesture, his breath caught in his chest—and the holding of it, for the first time, made his lungs start to ache. He could feel it all—more brilliantly than before—he could feel it. *Really* feel it.

Henry's lips were only inches away from his. That sharp tip of his nose was nearly touching James'.

"I was starting to think I would never see you again," Henry said softly.

"I never doubted it," James said. "I knew I would find you."

"Hell swallowed us up and spit us back out again."

"As Hell tends to do," James sighed.

Henry waited for the span of another heartbeat, and then he closed the gap between them. His firm mouth pressed against James' lips and, in that moment of collision, James' entire body tensed. He hesitated only a moment before he allowed his body to relax, pushing his hand into Heny's hair to rest against the nape of his neck. He pulled Henry closer, his mouth searching desperately. Those soft, kissable pink lips that he had dreamt of, desired, and fought for. The leagues of pain, measured in eons, that had kept them separated closed within an instant. Henry's arms wrapped around him and James allowed himself to be pulled close until they were pressed together in a tender embrace.

Lady stood by the lamppost. He thought about interrupting the reunion but was glad he decided against it as soon as he saw Henry and James lock lips. On one hand, it was about time. Those two had been simmering in sexual tension for so long that Lady would have been surprised if this was the first time they had explored each other's mouths so thoroughly.

On the other hand, it was irritating—borderline repulsive, even. He did not want to watch the two of them start dry-rubbing against each other in the middle of the street. He would absolutely interrupt before it got to *that* point.

A hand landed on top of his. He was wearing gloves, but the contact was still like static electricity. Lady yanked his hand away, pulling it close to his chest defensively and using the other one to guard it.

The memory of Satan's hand, of his intrusive hold, was still very fresh. He wasn't sure that would ever leave him.

Francis' shy smile was bathed in the gold of the dim lamplight. It reflected off his lenses and made it clear exactly how spotty they were. "I was afraid you weren't going to wake up." His voice was so hushed it was almost a whisper.

Lady felt frozen. He wanted to force out everything he had to say at once, but all that came out was, "Frank?"

"In the flesh." His husband spread his arms and took a took a step or two back to show off. "Is that too terrible a pun?"

"It is horrible." Real tears were in Lady's eyes, now. Tears like he had never felt them before. Hot and bountiful in his nose and his mouth and…very, very felt. "You are fired."

He ran towards Francis. He did not even think about what he was doing. The Unchaste leapt into the air, their bodies colliding as he wrapped his arms around his husband and squeezed him so tightly that Francis almost lost his entire fresh supply of mortal air.

Francis froze, not moving for a moment as if waiting to see if Lady would change his mind. The Unchaste did not budge. Francis wrapped his arms around Lady in turn, hands resting gently against his back, and pulled him close, daring to land a kiss on the top of his husband's ginger hair.

"They gave you a choice," Lady muttered into Francis' suit jacket, "and you came back to me anyway."

"Given the choice, I will always come back to you. Even when I'm not." Another gentle kiss. "I will fight my way back."

"That was stupid of you," Lady sniffled. "We are going to die together, here."

"Maybe sooner rather than later, with this bad knee." Francis reached down to pat it, opening his arms up enough that Lady could back away without feeling pressured to hang on longer. The Unchaste did take a step back, but still lingered closer than he ever had before.

"Yes." Lady tried to regain his composure. "We are certainly prey for the apex predators, now."

"You may have to go on without me," Francis said. "You know, leave the weak behind."

Lady scowled and considered swatting him, but he didn't. "Francis Hislop." He sucked in a deep breath. "You should know by now that I will never leave you behind."